AN ACT
OF FOUL
PLAY

An Act of Foul Play

A Lady Hardcastle Mystery

T E KINSEY

THOMAS & MERCER

Text copyright © 2022 by T E Kinsey
All rights reserved.

Published by Thomas & Mercer, Seattle

www.apub.com

Amazon, the Amazon logo, and Thomas & Mercer are trademarks of Amazon.com, Inc., or its affiliates.

ISBN-13: 9781542031486
ISBN-10: 1542031486

Cover design by Tom Sanderson

Cover illustration by Jelly London

Printed in the United States of America

An Act of Foul Play

Chapter One

I've never been entirely sure of the reason for the interval at the theatre. Is it that the actors desperately need a rest after all that standing about and talking? Do all the audience members really need to visit the insufficiently provisioned toilets? Can no one survive an extra hour without a glass of disappointing wine?

It was Lady Hardcastle's birthday and she had invited her Bristol friends to join her for a celebratory meal at Le Quai, a French restaurant which had opened in the city at the end of the summer and had instantly become *the* place to eat. Among the invitees was our suffragette friend, Lady Bickle, who had further suggested that we begin the evening with a trip to see her friend's play, which was being performed to enthusiastic reviews at the Duke's Theatre.

And so it was that our party had descended upon Frogmore Street in our finery to join Bristol's theatregoers in an evening of 'riotously mirthful entertainment', as the *Bristol News*'s critic had put it.

He wasn't wrong. By the interval I found that I'd been laughing so much that my cheeks were hurting, and I was glad of the rest. Perhaps that's what intervals are for after all, though it wouldn't explain the need for them during a melodrama or a morality tale.

Whatever the justification for the break, as the curtain fell on the first act, the laughter and applause died down and almost everyone rose to leave. I found myself alone in the box as my companions joined the crush to exit the auditorium to meet their own intermissionary needs.

Lady Bickle and her husband, Sir Benjamin, set off for the bar. Inspector Sunderland and his wife, Dolly, didn't announce their intentions, which I took to mean that they were bound for the lavatories. Local journalist Dinah Caudle and her fiancé, Dr Gosling, the police surgeon, mulled their options for a short while before they, too, decided on the bar.

Lady Hardcastle, of course, wanted both.

'Are you coming, Flo?' she said.

'I'm fine, thank you,' I said with a smile. 'I might get up and stretch my legs in a bit.'

'As you wish, dear.'

She joined the others.

I swapped seats for a better view and leaned forwards on the padded rail to look about the auditorium. The Duke's Theatre was a decent size but it somehow still managed to have a pleasing intimacy. It was a wonderful building and I had always loved going there, most especially when the show was a good one. And this one had been utterly joyous so far. Lady Bickle's friend, Hugo Bartlett, was a splendidly funny writer, and the cast brought his words to life with such wonderful skill that I hadn't wanted the first act to end.

The safety curtain was down, concealing the source of the bangs and clatters coming from the stage and making them all the more intriguing. In truth I knew they were just evidence of the hard work of the unseen, under-appreciated stagehands, but I liked to imagine something a little more mysterious.

The Sunderlands were the first to return.

'That was quick,' I said.

'There was a queue,' said Mrs Sunderland.

I nodded. There was always a queue.

There were more clatters and rumbles from behind the safety curtain.

'I've always wondered what goes on back there,' said Inspector Sunderland as he took his seat. 'You must have an idea, Miss Armstrong. Circuses and theatres can't be as different as all that.'

'I don't suppose they are,' I said. 'In which case I imagine that horny-handed sons of toil are hefting furniture and scenery about, then holding it all down with twenty-eight-pound cast-iron weights. Which they probably drop—' There was another massive bang. 'Like that.'

'What an exciting life you've led,' said Mrs Sunderland. 'I do envy you sometimes, you know.'

'It's had its moments,' I said.

'It most certainly has,' she agreed. 'You've done so many wonderful things and travelled to so many wonderful places. I've never been further from home than Brighton.'

'We went there for our honeymoon,' explained the inspector.

Mrs Sunderland touched his hand.

'And what a lovely time we had,' she said. 'But I'd still love to visit some of the places you and Emily talk about.'

'I've been very lucky,' I said. 'The only disadvantage is that I have to do it all in the company of you-know-who.'

Mrs Sunderland laughed.

'You are dreadful,' she said. 'I've never met two better friends.'

There was movement behind us. I turned to see who had returned.

'Speak of the devil,' I said.

'Should my ears be burning?' said Lady Hardcastle.

'I was just saying what a terrible old bag you are,' I said.

'Quite right, too,' she said. 'Though there was a time when servants would be more discreet about their employers' failings.'

'Surely you wouldn't want me to lie,' I said.

'You make a good point. Budge up now, though, there's a poppet. Let the old bag rest her weary pins.'

I shuffled back into my own seat.

'You weren't gone nearly as long as I expected,' I said.

'Queues, dear. As far as the eye could see. Serried ranks of cheerful theatregoers waiting patiently to either empty themselves or fill themselves according to their needs or desires. I weighed it all up and decided that the interval would be more entertainingly spent in the company of my friends than among strangers. By the time I'd made my way to the front of the second queue, I'd have no time to drink my brandy anyway because the play would be over.'

'It's a very funny play, don't you think?' said Mrs Sunderland. 'Georgie's friend is so clever.'

'The mysterious Hugo Bartlett,' said Lady Hardcastle. 'Has anyone met him?'

The Sunderlands shook their heads.

'Lady Bickle said she'd introduce us after the show,' I said. 'We can all compliment him on his brilliance then.'

'Georgie has led a fascinating life, too,' said Mrs Sunderland, wistfully. 'Why have I not led a fascinating life, Ollie?'

'Because you were foolish enough to marry an ambitious young policeman,' said the inspector. 'He held you back and condemned you to a life of mundanity and ordinariness.'

She touched his hand again, this time adding an affectionate squeeze.

'I wouldn't change it for the world,' she said.

We settled into companionable silence and leafed through our programmes as we waited for the second act to begin.

We waited.

Time hangs heavy when you're waiting for a performance, but this interval really did seem to be taking for ever. People who had returned in good time, possibly before they had fulfilled whatever need had driven them out of the auditorium in the first place, were chattering irritably. I heard the phrases 'bloody long time' and 'I wish they'd get on with it' floating up from the stalls. One or two of them got up and went out again.

Eventually we heard the sound of the interval bell, and the auditorium rapidly refilled.

The grumbling was replaced by an excited murmuring, which gradually grew as people took their seats and chattered animatedly to their companions, in appreciation of the entertainment so far experienced and in anticipation of the entertainment yet to come.

There was a subdued, almost ironic cheer as the safety curtain rose to reveal the still-closed, red-velvet tableau curtains. There was a loud noise from behind them as a piece of furniture was shoved into position on the stage at the last minute.

After a few moments more, the house lights dimmed and we all, for reasons I still can't explain, applauded enthusiastically. The door opened behind us, letting in light from the corridor and eliciting tuts of disapproval from several people in the stalls, who, quite by chance, had managed to take their places only a few moments earlier. People, I firmly believed, who would never have noticed if they'd been looking at the stage instead of gawping at the boxes. The door closed and the four missing members of our party shuffled to their places in the darkness. They clumsily resumed their seats and a man in the fifth row of the stalls looked up.

'Will you be quiet!' he said, sternly.

The curtains swept apart to reveal a new set. Act Two, we now saw, was to take place around a large round table in the corner of the ballroom, in the aftermath of the party the four characters had been preparing for throughout Act One. On the table there were champagne bottles upended in ice buckets, empty glasses, and several plates containing the half-eaten remains of a buffet supper. The chairs were askew, as though the four friends had all jumped up for one last dance.

Or three of them, at least. One of the group was lying on his back, downstage left, with a stage dagger protruding from his chest and a very convincing bloodstain spreading across his evening shirt. The play had taken a darker turn than I was expecting.

Few others had been expecting it, either, and there were one or two gasps from the audience, and a rushing whisper like wind in a wheat field as people expressed their surprise at this new development.

The three remaining friends – one man and two women – entered stage left, chattering and laughing as though returning from the dance floor.

'I say, Bertie,' said the man, 'you missed a sight there. Didn't he, girls? Old Biffy Blenkinsop was trying to kiss—'

He was cut short by a scream from one of the women as she noticed the body on the stage.

I've never been terribly convinced by women in books and plays who scream when they see a dead body. I know my life as a lady's maid, part-time spy and full-time nosy parker has brought me into contact with more dead bodies than the average woman will see in . . . well, ever . . . so I might very well have become inured to it, but I've never once screamed. I'm more likely to say, *Oh no, not again.*

It was a testament to the actress's skills, though, that her shock seemed entirely real. I had turned to Lady Hardcastle to comment on her convincing portrayal of a horrified woman when I noticed the other actress making frantic gestures towards the wings. As the curtains swished closed, the actor strode towards his colleague and we heard, 'Good lord,' before they closed completely.

There was a moment's shocked silence from the audience, but then the hubbub started as the house lights came up.

Once the audience could see their companions, the speculation began. What was going on? Was it a real dead body? Had someone been murdered? Several people tried to push their way out, but their progress was halted by the mass of the curious who wanted to stay and find out what was going on.

Inspector Sunderland was already out of his seat.

'That looked . . . well, it looked real,' he said. 'I'd better go and have a—'

He stopped talking as the curtains ruffled and a man in evening dress fought his way through the gap to appear on the stage. He held up his hands for silence and the audience quickly quietened.

'Ladies and gentlemen,' he began. 'I'm afraid this evening's performance of *The Hedonists* will not be continuing. We apologize for spoiling your evening. Your tickets can be refunded at the box office, or exchanged for tickets for a later performance. Once again, we apologize for the disappointment.'

The disappointment manifested itself in the form of a loud groan from the audience, with one or two shouted questions about what was going on – but, strangely, no one moved.

The inspector was still on his feet. He approached the balustrade of our box and leaned forwards.

'Excuse me, sir,' he said in a loud, clear voice. 'Inspector Sunderland of Bristol CID. Would you mind telling us what has happened?'

'Inspector?' said the man, shielding his eyes against the spotlight that was now shining on him. 'Would you mind awfully joining us on stage, please? Your colleagues from the police station are on the way.'

His comment elicited a fresh hubbub, this time tinged with alarm.

The man on the stage held up his hands again for silence, but the commotion just grew louder. Inspector Sunderland also needed silence.

'Ladies and gentlemen,' said the inspector. 'May I have your attention, please.'

He was ignored.

'Ladies and—'

I tapped his arm and indicated that I would deal with it. I put my fingers in my mouth and let out an ear-piercing whistle.

In the shocked silence that ensued, the inspector continued. 'Ladies and gentlemen. It seems that this has become a police matter, so I would ask that you all remain in your seats for a while longer. Mr . . . ?'

The man on the stage realized he was being addressed.

'Adlam,' he said. 'Edwin Adlam. I'm the theatre manager.'

'Mr Adlam, would you be so kind as to instruct your staff to man the doors until my colleagues arrive. No one should leave the theatre.'

The hubbub was replaced by angry shouting.

The inspector waited for it to die down.

'If this is as serious as it appears,' he continued, 'it is essential that we speak to each of you.'

'I've got to get home,' called the man from the stalls who had told us to be quiet. Several people agreed with him that they, too, needed to get away.

'And I i'n't stayin' 'ere if there's a murderer on the loose,' said another.

This set off another round of panicked conversations and renewed efforts to leave the theatre.

'And you shall,' said the inspector. 'My colleagues will be here in just a few moments, and you'll be free to go long before the scheduled end of the play.'

The hubbub grew again, but curiosity and instinctive obedience to the instructions of authority overcame fear, and even those who had been most keen to leave resumed their seats. The inspector turned to us.

'I'd better get backstage,' he said. 'Gosling? I think you might be needed.'

'Right you are,' said Dr Gosling. 'Excuse us, all. We'll be back as soon as we can.'

The two men made their way out of the box to where a member of staff was already waiting to take them backstage.

For a while, people were sullenly compliant and remained seated. There were occasional expressions of fear and concern, and a good deal of irritation that they were being prevented from leaving the theatre, but from the one or two conversations I could overhear clearly it seemed that there was a grudging acceptance of the inspector's logic: if the play had gone ahead they'd be sitting in their seats for another hour anyway, so they weren't actually being delayed at all.

What the inspector had neglected to consider, though, was that had they been watching the play they'd have been pleasantly distracted by the on-stage hilarity and the hour would have flown by. As it was, they were left with nothing to entertain them and the mood gradually shifted from disturbed disquiet and resentful resignation, through impatient irritation, and on to aggrieved agitation.

People had begun standing and looking around, with many engaging their neighbours in conversation about how dreadful it was that we were all being kept there. Standing led to moving, and one or two of the more belligerent patrons approached the auditorium doors, where they were politely but firmly invited by the theatre staff to return to their seats.

Mrs Sunderland, though, was troubled.

'Who could have done such a thing?' she said.

'If anyone can find out,' said Lady Hardcastle, 'it'll be your Oliver.' She smiled. 'Do you know, in all the years I've known him I've never called him that to his face? He's always Inspector Sunderland to me.'

'He laughs about you trying to get him to call you Emily, too,' said Mrs Sunderland. 'I told him not to be so silly, but he won't have it. I think you'll always be Lady Hardcastle and Inspector Sunderland, dear.'

'I expect we shall.'

'I say, you don't think we're in danger, do you? With a murderer on the loose in the theatre, I mean.'

'No, we're safe as can be. Ollie and Simeon are backstage and we have Flo in here to protect us.'

'I suppose you're right,' said Mrs Sunderland. 'And about the other thing, too – Ollie *will* catch whoever did it. The sooner the better – that poor actor deserves justice. He seemed like such a nice young man, too. I mean, I know he was playing a part, but you can tell, can't you? Such a tragedy to have his life stolen from him like that.'

'I don't even know his name,' said Miss Caudle, scanning her programme. 'Isn't that awful?'

'He was Paul Singleton,' said Lady Bickle, sadly. 'And he really was a lovely man. A bit of a rogue, but a twinkly-eyed one, not a wicked one.'

'I'm sorry, dear,' said Lady Hardcastle. 'I'd forgotten you knew him.'

'I know them all.' She looked towards Mrs Sunderland. 'The writer is a friend of mine. Well, his sister is – we attended finishing school together in Switzerland. We were absolutely inseparable while we were there, but I've not seen her for years. One day, though, this chap appeared at the door and introduced himself as her brother. Ordinarily I'd have been suspicious of someone turning up at the house unannounced like that, but I could see the family resemblance at once. He said his sister had suggested he drop in since he was working in Bristol, and I'm jolly glad she did. We invited him to dinner, didn't we, Ben?'

'We did indeed. Splendid chap. Not quite as funny in real life as in his plays, but good company nonetheless.'

'Very pleasant,' agreed Lady Bickle. 'I expressed an interest in his work so he asked if we'd like to meet the company who were putting on his play at the Duke's. They're wonderful people. They'll be devastated.'

'They will,' said Lady Hardcastle. 'It's terrible to lose a friend like that.'

Miss Caudle turned to me.

'Will you be helping Ollie again?' she asked. 'I'm going to have to file a story as soon as I can get to the office – it would be lovely to have a source inside the investigation.'

'We should probably leave it to the police, don't you think?' I said. 'Just this once.'

'She's right, dear,' said Lady Hardcastle. 'It's one thing to try to solve mysteries in our own back garden, but it's much more like interfering when we start trying to get involved in crimes in the city.'

The truth was that we had plenty of experience of interfering in investigations away from home, but I was glad she was taking my side. I was always happy to help, but I often felt we'd be better off keeping out of it and just reading Miss Caudle's accounts in the newspaper.

'You're probably right,' said Miss Caudle. 'And Ollie will have no trouble catching the killer, anyway. It's not like there's a huge pool of suspects.'

'Exactly,' I said. 'We're better off out of it.'

The mood in the auditorium had largely calmed, but civilization is fragile and relies on the consent of the civilized. It doesn't take much to erode that consent, and being cooped up in a theatre – no matter how luxuriously appointed it might be – was more or less all it took.

After thirty minutes there was still no sign of Inspector Sunderland or Dr Gosling, and the assembled throng was growing increasingly restive. Visits to the exit doors were becoming more frequent and the resulting interactions with the staff more confrontational.

'This is going to get ugly sooner rather than later,' I said quietly to Lady Hardcastle. 'They're frightened and frustrated. I'd quite like to get you and our friends to safety if I can.'

She smiled and gestured around the box.

'I think we'll be fine in here,' she said. 'The door is quite secure and no one will be fool enough to scale the walls to get to us from the other side. And besides all that, where would we go?'

'I'd find a way,' I said. 'I just don't want to be in here when the fighting starts.'

'I'm sure it won't come to that. We should wait with our fellow theatre-goers. Everyone here thinks they have a special reason for leaving, and they're all perfectly correct – we all do. But none of us has any more right to leave than that fellow down there.'

As she spoke, a young man grabbed his lady friend by the hand and made a run for it down the aisle at the side of the auditorium. Nearing the exit, his run became a charge as he turned his body slightly and aimed his shoulder at the doors. The two ushers who stood in his way decided that their job most definitely did not include roughhousing with the patrons, and they stepped hurriedly aside to allow him to pass.

The audience quickly became aware that something was afoot and turned as one to watch the couple's progress.

They seemed about to make it to freedom when the double doors opened and the young man careered into a police sergeant. The policeman stood over six feet tall and must have weighed at least sixteen stone, most of which was muscle. The man simply bounced off and fell backwards, dragging his lady friend with him into an untidy tangle of limbs, dislodged hats, and disarranged clothing.

Smiling, the sergeant reached down and helped the young couple to their feet.

'Ups-a-daisy,' he said. 'Not a rugby player, I take it, sir?' With another friendly smile he patted the younger man on the shoulder. 'Never try to tackle a bigger man standing upright – you'll always end up on your backside. Got to keep your body low, you see?'

The sergeant mimed crouching low with his arms out wide as though to tackle someone. The man mumbled something we couldn't hear.

'No need for that kind of language, sir,' said the sergeant, standing up. 'Just take your seat and we'll have you out in a jiffy.'

Grasping the lady's hand once more, the young man attempted to dart around the sergeant to freedom. The audience, who had been watching in silence up to this point, erupted into delighted laughter as the sergeant grabbed the man by the collar of his overcoat and lifted him a good six inches off the floor. The man ran in mid-air for a second or two, his arms and legs flailing uselessly. Once he had come to rest, the sergeant placed him gently back on the ground.

'As I said, sir, I really would appreciate it if you would take your seat.'

Spreading his arms once again, the sergeant shooed the couple back into the stalls and watched as they skulked back to their row.

'Now, then,' he said in a voice that carried as clearly as that of any of the actors who had been on the stage earlier. 'I have spoken to Inspector Sunderland and he says you'll all be free to go in a very short while. All he wishes is that we have your names and addresses so that if he needs to contact you to make a statement as a witness of this evening's terrible events, he knows where to find you.'

There was more disgruntled muttering at this, and at least one 'Bloody cheek!' from the Grand Circle, but with someone now clearly back in charge it seemed that they were once more inclined to consent to civilization.

'Those of you with coats in the cloakroom,' he continued once the grumbling had subsided, 'should form an orderly line through the doors at the rear, where my men will quickly note your details. The rest of you should leave by the side doors, making sure to speak to the policemen posted there as you go. Keep it calm, keep it civil, and keep it moving. We'll have you home in time for cocoa.'

He gestured towards the opening doors and people began to gather themselves to leave.

There was some shuffling but no actual movement in our box.

'You go on, dears,' said Dolly Sunderland with a weary sigh that spoke of a lifetime of taking second place to her husband's job. 'I'll wait for Ollie.'

'Nonsense,' said Lady Hardcastle. 'We'll wait together. I'm sure they won't be long.'

'Don't be silly,' said Miss Caudle. 'It's your birthday outing. You shouldn't be sitting here waiting for our chaps. I'll stay with Dolly and we'll join you as soon as we're able. Well, almost as soon. There'll be a short delay while I give them a dressing-down for abandoning you on your birthday, but once they've been suitably chastised we shall hasten to Le Quai and rejoin the celebrations.'

'No, honestly—' began Lady Hardcastle, but she was cut short by the arrival of the men in question.

'Still here?' said Dr Gosling, blithely. 'We thought you'd be on your way by now . . .' His voice trailed off when he caught sight of Miss Caudle's expression. 'Well . . . I . . . that is to say . . .'

'I'm sorry, my lady,' said Inspector Sunderland with a shake of his head, 'but we're going to be detained for a while longer. Please go on without us.'

'Are you sure, dear?' said Mrs Sunderland.

'Quite sure. We'll be as quick as we can, but there's no point in you all sitting here. Enjoy your dinner. We'll try to be there in time to toast the birthday girl.'

Sir Benjamin had said very little since the body had been revealed on the stage, but he looked up at his old friend Dr Gosling now and said, 'Anything I can do, dear boy? I feel a little useless sitting up here.'

'It's all under control, old thing,' said Dr Gosling. 'There are no marks on the body other than the stab wound. It's only professional fastidiousness that's preventing me from declaring cause of death here and now. I'll wait until after the post-mortem, of course, but I'm certain I'll not find anything else. Your considerable talents would be wasted, I'm afraid. I'm only staying to keep Sunderland company. Poor lamb gets out of sorts if he's left on his own.'

The inspector rolled his eyes and Sir Benjamin laughed.

'Right you are,' he said. 'I'll take care of the ladies, don't you worry. We'll save you some champagne.'

'We ladies can take care of ourselves, thank you very much,' said Lady Bickle. 'We shall be the ones taking care of *you*.'

Sir Benjamin smiled and bowed his head.

'Quite right,' he said. 'Quite right.'

'Good luck, old thing,' said Dr Gosling. 'We'll be as quick as we can.'

'Come with us,' said the inspector. 'We'll show you out through the stage door to save you queuing up. I have your names and addresses, after all.'

We followed him through a locked door – he had been given a key by the theatre manager – to the backstage corridors, and eventually made our way out into the cool November air.

◆ ◆ ◆

It was a short walk down to the Tramways Centre and Magpie Park and then along Clare Street and Corn Street. Le Quai was hidden away in a back street near St Nicholas Market, and even on a Tuesday evening the area was alive with diners and pleasure seekers. A cheerful little man with an adorably friendly dog stood on a street corner roasting chestnuts on a brazier, and if we hadn't been on our way to stuff ourselves at a fashionable restaurant I would definitely have stopped to buy a bag.

We were greeted at the door of the restaurant by the maître d'hôtel, a charmingly gracious and graceful man who went by the name Jean-Pierre Dubois and spoke perfect English with an exotically Parisian accent.

On our last visit, Lady Hardcastle had attempted to engage Jean-Pierre in conversation in his own language, which was when he revealed with a winning smile and a cheeky wink that he was actually Wally Dudden from Totterdown and the closest he had ever been to France was a holiday on the Isle of Wight with his Aunt Hilda when he was six. We loved him all the more for it and vowed to keep his secret.

'*Bonsoir, madame,*' he gushed, clicking his fingers for someone to take our coats. 'And Miss Armstrong, also. How wonderful to see you. And Miss Caudle – thank you so much for the wonderful piece in the *Bristol News*. Chef, how do you say it, jumped over the moon with his joy?'

'My pleasure, Jean-Pierre,' said Miss Caudle with a smile.

'And Sir Benjamin and Lady Bickle. You grace us again so soon.'

'We just can't keep away,' said Lady Bickle.

'And there is Mrs Sunderland hiding at the back,' said Jean-Pierre. 'You look so beautiful as always, *madame*, so *élégante*.' He looked in the open diary on the lectern by the door and ran a long finger down the list of bookings. 'We have a table prepared for eight this evening. Have we made a mistake?'

'No, Jean-Pierre, dear,' said Lady Hardcastle. 'Inspector Sunderland and Dr Gosling will be joining us later. They've been detained on a work matter.'

He looked once more at the group. 'Ah, but of course, I should have realized who was missing. It must be important to keep them away from such beautiful ladies.'

'You're a shameless charmer, dear,' said Lady Hardcastle, 'but you're right. It is rather important and we really are rather beautiful.'

'We shall see you to your table at once. Is it a special occasion that brings such a distinguished party to Le Quai? You are like old friends, but we have not seen you all together like this.'

There was a pause. Lady Hardcastle liked to be made a fuss of, but was surprisingly shy of soliciting it. I didn't want to be the one to embarrass her, but Lady Bickle had no such qualms.

'It's Emily's birthday,' she said, gleefully.

'Oh, my dear Lady Hardcastle, you should have said something.'

'Well,' she said sheepishly, 'one doesn't like a fuss.'

I resisted the temptation to snort.

'I shall not ask how old you are, but I suspect no more than *vingt-cinq ans, non*?'

I was waiting for Dr Gosling to say, 'Hah! And the rest,' but then I remembered he wasn't there. I smiled at the thought.

'I don't know what you're smirking at, Flo,' said Lady Hardcastle. 'I could pass for twenty-five.'

'Of course you could,' I said. 'From a distance. In the dark.'

Jean-Pierre wagged an admonishing finger at me and led us, smiling, to our table.

Le Quai had opened at the beginning of September but we had eaten there at least four times since then, and it already felt comfortably familiar. The outside was plain and anonymous, with only the Parisian lettering above the door giving any hint as to the wonders within. The interior, though, was another matter entirely. It was larger than you might imagine and had been decorated in the Art Nouveau style favoured by the most fashionable restaurants in Paris. '*Très chic et très moderne,*' as Jean-Pierre might haltingly say.

We were seated by Jean-Pierre himself, who introduced us to Gaston, our waiter. Menus appeared as though from nowhere, as did ice buckets and champagne.

Sir Benjamin rose to his feet.

'Before we're too stuffed—' he began.

'Or too squiffy,' interrupted Lady Bickle.

'Or that,' he conceded. 'Before we're too stuffed or too squiffy to remember why we're here, let us raise our glasses in a toast to the birthday girl. To Emily. Happy birthday.'

We repeated the toast enthusiastically and sipped our fizz.

Lady Hardcastle stood.

'Unaccustomed as I am to public speaking—'

'Oh do shut up, darling, there's a poppet,' said Miss Caudle.

'Right you are, dear.' She sat. 'I was just going to thank you all very much for coming out. It's been a wonderful birthday.'

'Aside from the part where one of the actors was murdered,' I said.

'Aside from that, dear, yes.'

'I've been trying to be stoic about it,' said Lady Bickle. 'You know, stiff upper whatnot and all that – didn't want to spoil the evening. But I confess I'm rather shaken by the whole thing.'

'I am, too, dear,' said Mrs Sunderland. 'I don't know how Ollie copes with it week in, week out, I really don't. One look at that poor man lying there on the stage and I nearly passed out, I don't mind telling you.'

'I was sick when I saw my first proper murder victim, wasn't I, Flo?' said Miss Caudle.

'In the rhododendrons,' I agreed.

'Hydrangeas,' said Miss Caudle and Lady Hardcastle together.

I shrugged. Everyone laughed.

'I think we can all agree it was a terrible thing,' said Sir Benjamin. 'But please let us not dwell on it any longer – it's Emily's birthday, after all. I propose a happy, murder-free night, and we can mourn poor Singleton tomorrow.'

'Hear, hear,' said Miss Caudle. 'Now, who's having the bean soup? It's delicious. You really must try it.'

Despite the tragedy, we really did have a splendid evening. Inspector Sunderland and Dr Gosling managed to join us in time for the *fromages et desserts* and managed not to talk about the case.

Lady Bickle had already very kindly offered to put Lady Hardcastle and me up at their lovely house on Berkeley Crescent, and that turned out to be a very good thing indeed because Sir Benjamin's prediction came true. By the end of the night we were all too stuffed and too squiffy to do anything but summon the local blue-painted motor cabs and make our way to our various homes.

Chapter Two

I woke dismayingly early the next morning. I was briefly befuddled to find myself in an unfamiliar room with an unfamiliar clock ticking on an unfamiliar bedside table. I reached for the candle and matches but instead my hand collided with an unfamiliar vase. As I struggled to consciousness I remembered that I was in a room in the Bickles' house on Berkeley Crescent and that the vase had been repurposed as an electric lamp. I eventually found the switch and had the briefest view of the room before I hurriedly shut my eyes again to keep out the sudden burning glare of the bulb.

I opened them tentatively and squinted in the direction of the ticking. It was seven o'clock. I groaned. We'd been out until gone three and I'd expected – or at the very least hoped – that with no work to get up for, my brain would let me sleep in. But it wanted me up and awake, no matter what.

I turned off the light and tried to doze, but it was too late. I was properly awake now.

I'd packed a book in my overnight bag in anticipation of just such ridiculous behaviour, so I slipped out of bed with a sigh and retrieved it. I switched the light on again and settled back in bed to read.

A little over an hour later, at about ten past eight, I heard a knock at the door.

'Yes?' I said, lowering my book.

The door opened a crack and Lady Hardcastle's head appeared, her face beaming mischievously.

'Good morning, tiny servant,' she said.

'And good morning to you,' I said. 'Did you sleep well?'

'As well as any forty-four-year-old has a right to expect,' she said. 'It's not often that I'm up before you, though.'

'It's almost unheard of. I've been awake for more than an hour, mind you, so I'm not sure it counts.'

'Ah, but I'm dressed,' she said, opening the door with a flourish to show me her elegant day dress. 'So I win.'

I looked her up and down. She was, indeed, dressed, but . . .

'I'd accept defeat if you'd remembered to brush your hair,' I said.

'I did brush it.'

'Only the front.'

'Oh, there's no point brushing the back – nobody can see it. By the time they get even so much as a glimpse I've already sailed by, and then who cares what they think?'

'I care,' I said. 'We need to sort it out before you appear in public.'

She sighed.

'Very well,' she said, resignedly. 'Can it be soon, though, please?'

'Of course. Are we in a rush?'

'Not a rush as such . . . but I would like to see if there's any breakfast. I'm absolutely starving.'

I laughed.

'Give me a few minutes to get myself ready,' I said, 'and I'll come and do your hair. You're next door, aren't you?'

'Don't be long,' she said, and closed the door.

◆ ◆ ◆

We arrived in the dining room to find Lady Bickle reading the *Daily Telegraph* with her feet up on the chair next to her.

'Morning, ladies,' she said without putting down her newspaper. 'Plenty of food on the sideboard – help yourselves.'

'Thank you, dear,' said Lady Hardcastle. 'Have we missed Ben?'

'I'm afraid so. He has important surgeon things to do this morning.'

'He's not operating, surely? Not after last night.'

Lady Bickle laughed.

'Have no fear,' she said, 'it's board business. He just has to sit there nursing his headache and pretending to be interested in budgets.'

'Oh, the poor chap. I could never do that. Flo tries to interest me in the household budget but my eyes just glaze over and I start wondering whether one could train a cat to play the piano, or how many sheep we could fit into the Rolls in an emergency.'

This was a lie, of course – Lady Hardcastle took a keen interest in the household budget down to the last farthing. But the habit of playing the dizzy socialite was so deeply ingrained that she sometimes couldn't help herself, even among friends who might be impressed by her accomplishments.

'I know what you mean, dear,' said Lady Bickle. 'Life is altogether too short to be troubling oneself with such tedious trivialities.'

I suspected that this, too, was a lie. Lady Bickle had proved herself an immensely capable woman when we had worked with her and her fellow suffragettes during the 1910 General Election. She was no fool but perhaps she, too, felt the need to hide her light under a bushel. Or under her bustle, perhaps.

'What about you, Flo?' she asked. 'Where do you stand?'

'I'm still trying to work out what sort of emergency would necessitate the urgent transportation of even a single sheep, my lady, let alone a small flock of them.'

As Lady Hardcastle and I took our seats with our plates of food, I noticed with a smile that we had both chosen exactly the same things: bacon, fried eggs, sausage and grilled tomato. We had even put our slices of toast on the same side of our plates.

Lady Bickle put down her copy of the *Telegraph* and sat up.

'I wanted to ask you two a favour,' she said.

'Anything, dear,' said Lady Hardcastle. 'You know that.'

'It's this business with dear Paul Singleton. I know nothing can bring him back, but I do so desperately wish to see justice done.'

'Inspector Sunderland will see to that, don't worry.'

'Oh, I know he will. But would you mind awfully . . . well . . . looking into things for me?'

'I'm not sure there's much need for that, dear. Inspector Sunderland is one of the most capable policemen I've ever met.'

'Oh, I didn't mean to disparage dear Ollie. No, indeed. I just wondered if your involvement might perhaps speed things along. At the very least you might be able to keep abreast of the investigation for me? Casually ask him how things are going, that sort of thing.'

'You know him well enough by now to be able to do that for yourself, surely.'

'Oh, we're pals, all right, but not in the way you are. I'm not sure how long he'd tolerate my inquisitiveness before he began to see it as interference. But you two have worked with him rather a lot and he respects you. If you were to take an interest he'd be flattered. And he might even ask you to help, which would address Flo's concerns about interfering uninvited.'

'I think you overestimate our standing, dear, but it would be a pleasure.'

Lady Bickle smiled.

'Thank you,' she said. 'You know, I just can't for the life of me think why anyone would want to kill him. He was a charmer. Rakish. Puckish. I can imagine him becoming a little wearing after a while, but not enough to want him dead.'

'We can't be certain yet that he was definitely the intended victim,' I said. 'Killers have been known to make mistakes.'

'We can't even know for sure that the killer had anyone specific in mind,' said Lady Hardcastle. 'He might just have wished to kill any actor. Or anyone connected with the play. Or just anyone at all.'

'Oh, but that makes it even worse. That he was killed for a reason is bad enough, but to think he might just have been in the killer's eyeline when they decided it was time for someone to die . . . that's just terrible. No, I shan't have it. Someone had a twisted reason for killing Paul Singleton, and Inspector Sunderland must find out who, and what that reason was.'

'He'll be working on it already,' I said.

'Of course he will,' said Lady Bickle. 'I'm sorry. I don't doubt him. It's just . . .'

'We understand, dear,' said Lady Hardcastle, kindly.

'There's a limited pool of suspects,' I said.

'Only everyone in the theatre,' said Lady Bickle. 'It must hold, what, a thousand people?'

'Easily,' I said. 'But we can rule out everyone in the audience.'

'Oh? How so? Anyone could have gone backstage and stabbed him.'

'Actually, no,' said Lady Hardcastle. 'Flo's right. It couldn't have been anyone from the audience. Don't you remember? When the inspector led us backstage he had to unlock the door. It's worth checking whether there are other ways of getting from front of house to backstage but I'd be willing to bet that if that one door was locked then so would any others.'

'Could they not have gone out through the main entrance, sneaked round the back and then slipped in through the stage door?'

'Have you ever been to the stage door at the Duke's?' I asked. 'We had to follow up on a little . . . "business" there a year or so ago. It started out in London but we ended up in the alley behind the Duke's and the doorman there is a formidable fellow. No one was getting past him.'

'So it's a member of the cast or one of the stagehands, then?' said Lady Bickle.

'That would be my guess,' I said with a nod.

'Mine, too,' said Lady Hardcastle. 'Though how they managed to stab a man to death on an open stage quite eludes me at the moment. How did they get him alone on the stage? How did they get close enough to attack him? How did they do it without anyone seeing? And how did they get away? It's not beyond the inspector's abilities to fathom it, but he has his work cut out.'

'Well, quite,' said Lady Bickle. 'And so would you please be kind enough to help where you can and keep me up to date with his progress? I should really appreciate it.'

'Of course, dear. Consider us your eyes and ears at the heart of the investigation.'

'Thank you. How are the sausages? Cook is trying a new butcher and I'm not certain yet whether I like them.'

'I'm not sure yet, either,' said Lady Hardcastle. 'I shall ponder as I munch. Is there anything interesting in the newspaper?'

'Not really. An article advising readers to pay more for a decent motor car. Protests against the war in Tripoli. An article on the Harrods page about "Bizarre fur motor coats, crushable fur hats, and a Parisian 'Frock and Coat' costume." Oh, and some nonsense from Birmingham about a meeting organized by the National League for Opposing Woman Suffrage. There was lots of windbaggery about how dreadful an idea it is to allow women to vote, and how it mustn't be left to Parliament but has to go to a vote by the people. Which would be fine if women were counted as people and we could vote on it. It's all so very frustrating.'

Thoughts of the murder at the Duke's Theatre were put temporarily to one side as we discussed Lady Bickle's work with the Women's Social and Political Union – the Suffragettes.

Breakfast was over all too soon and we packed our bags for our return to Littleton Cotterell. With one last promise to Lady Bickle to keep an eye on the murder investigation, we lashed the bags to the luggage rack of the Rolls and set off for home.

◆ ◆ ◆

'Do we have any buns at home, do you know?' asked Lady Hardcastle as we drove into the village. 'Will Miss Jones have bought any, do you think? You know, on the off chance that we might fancy a little something with our morning coffee?'

'I shouldn't imagine so,' I said. 'Why? Are you in the mood for buns?'

'I am, indeed. Something with icing, perhaps. Or currants. Or jam. Yes, jam. Jam doughnuts. Be a pet and stop at Holman's, would you?'

I pulled up outside the baker's and hopped out to see what he could offer us.

'Hello again, Miss Armstrong,' said Mr Holman as I entered. 'What have you forgotten?'

'I . . . er . . . Sorry, what?'

'Mum's the word,' he said with a wink. 'Wouldn't want to get you into trouble. Nuff said. What can I get you?'

'Half a dozen jam doughnuts, please,' I said, still bemused.

Mr Holman laughed.

'I'll play along,' he said with a wink.

I returned to the motor car and handed Lady Hardcastle the bag.

'Your treats, my lady,' I said.

'All for me?'

'I bought extra in case Edna and Miss Jones fancied one.'

She opened the bag and counted.

'But there are six here,' she said.

'That's so I don't have to go out again when you say, "Oh, but Flo, dear, I fancy another doughnut." This isn't the first time I've played this game, you know.'

I drove off.

My friend Daisy Spratt came out of the Dog and Duck to wash down the pavement outside the pub door, and I gave her a cheery wave as we passed by. Her own wave was more baffled than cheery and she stared at us in puzzlement.

Lady Hardcastle noticed the look.

'What have you done to upset Daisy?' she asked.

'I have no idea. She was fine when I talked to her yesterday.'

'I'm sure you'll sort it out. You always do.'

I parked neatly on our little driveway and followed Lady Hardcastle to the door with our bags. Edna was crossing the hall as Lady Hardcastle entered, carrying a broom in one hand and her 'toolbox' of cleaning cloths and polishes in the other. She greeted Lady Hardcastle and then stopped in her tracks when she saw me.

'Good morning, Miss Armstrong,' she said. 'How did you . . . ? I mean, you were just . . .'

'Is something the matter, Edna dear?' asked Lady Hardcastle.

'I think I know,' I said. 'Mr Holman was behaving oddly, too.'

'He was?'

'He was,' I said with a nod. 'And you saw Daisy. But I recognize the signs now. Pardon me for a moment, I'm going to yell uncouthly . . . Gwen!' I called. 'Gwenith! Come out here right now.'

My doppelgänger appeared at the drawing-room door wearing the cheekiest grin ever to adorn the face of a human being.

'Edna Gibson,' I said, 'I have the honour of presenting my sister, Mrs Gwenith Evans.'

'*Bore da*, Mrs Gibson,' said Gwen with a little bow. 'And Lady Hardcastle.'

'Hello, dear. How lovely to see you again.'

'You too. And I'm sorry, Mrs Gibson.'

'Call me Edna, my lover.'

'Well, Edna, I'm sorry for confusing you. It just seemed like too good an opportunity to miss. I didn't think I'd pass so easily, but the baker assumed I was little Flossie and so I thought . . .'

'"Little" Flossie?' said Edna with a chuckle. My twin sister and I were, of course, of similar stature, and she was clearly amused at the idea of either one of us referring to the other as 'little'.

'I'm twenty minutes younger,' I said with a sigh. 'So I've always been her little sister.'

'And don't you forget it,' said Gwen.

I put down the bags and stepped across the hall to hug her.

'It's been too long,' I said. 'Why didn't you tell us you were coming?'

'I didn't know myself. It was one of those spur-of-the-moment things, you know?'

'I do. Where's Dai?'

'His brigade's gone down to Shoeburyness on exercises and I thought, "Why am I sitting up here in Woolwich with nothing to do when I could jump on a train and go and see Flossie?" Before I'd had time to write to you, I was at Paddington with my bag and a packed lunch for the train. I stopped at Bath to see an old friend – her husband was a mate of Dai's in the regiment, but he was invalided out and they moved back to Bath to be near her mother, see? So I stayed there the night and came up here this morning.'

'Confusing the baker on the way. Did you meet anyone else? Outside the pub, perhaps?'

'A chirpy, dark-haired girl was on her way into the pub and asked me how the play was, yes.'

'That'll be my pal Daisy. What did you tell her?'

'Very moving, I said. Beautiful.'

'That'll confuse her – I told her it was a comedy. No wonder she gave me a funny look when we drove past her. How long are you stopping?'

'As long as you'll have me. Dai's lot are away for a few weeks. I'll not impose for that long, of course, but a week or so would be lovely if that's all right.'

'Of course it is, dear,' said Lady Hardcastle. 'It would be delightful to have some company.' She turned to Edna. 'Could you give one of the guest rooms a little spruce, please, Edna dear? Then we can get Gwenith settled.'

'I shall do it right away, m'lady,' said Edna.

She ambled off towards the stairs.

'We have doughnuts if you'd like one,' said Lady Hardcastle, waving the bag. 'We'll leave yours in the kitchen, Edna.'

'Thank you very much,' said Edna, looking over her shoulder. 'I do like Holman's doughnuts.'

'Ah,' said Gwen. 'Doughnuts. Wait there.'

She disappeared into the drawing room and returned moments later with a bag of her own.

'I bought some, as well.'

◆ ◆ ◆

Over coffee and far too many doughnuts, we caught up with Gwen's news and brought her up to date with our own recent adventures. We wrote to each other often so she already knew a little about the aeroplanes and the cider orchard, but she hadn't heard the full details and, obviously, she wasn't aware of what had happened during the previous evening at the theatre.

'That all makes the life of an artillery wife sound a bit tame,' said Gwen when we had finished.

'Tame, perhaps,' said Lady Hardcastle, 'but no less satisfying for that. Dafydd's promotion is wonderful news.'

'He's done well for himself,' agreed Gwen. 'A lad from Merthyr now a battery sergeant major in His Majesty's Royal Artillery. I'm very proud. And my life's comfortable and happy compared with many. But flying about in aeroplanes and watching secret rituals in orchards is a different world, isn't it? And it's months since I even went to the music hall, let alone a play where one of the actors got killed in the interval.'

'To be fair,' I said, 'that's the only play we've ever been to where one of the actors was killed.'

'There was that comedian who died at the Hackney Empire,' said Lady Hardcastle.

'Because you shot him. That doesn't count.'

Gwen laughed.

'See?' she said. 'Much more exciting than a sing-song down at the Crown and Cushion. Did you ever imagine we'd all end up where we are, Floss?'

'Not for a moment,' I said. 'Who could possibly have imagined all this when we were sneaking about the circus pretending to be each other?'

'So today's antics aren't a new development?' said Lady Hardcastle.

'I doubt there have ever been identical twins who haven't played that game. It never ceases to be funny. Do you remember old Mr Roberts at the butcher's in Aberdare, Gwen?'

'That poor old boy,' said Gwen. 'We used to run him ragged. He never could tell us apart.'

'I find that hard to believe,' said Lady Hardcastle. 'You look so different.'

'That's because we're sitting next to each other. If we were on our own . . .'

'No, I'd still know which of you was which. Flo's been working with me for seventeen years now, don't forget.' She very seldom said 'working *for* me'. 'I'd know instantly. Quite aside from anything else, she has a small mole beside her left ear which you do not.'

'There's people we grew up with who never spotted that,' said Gwen, obviously impressed.

The doorbell rang.

'Want to test it out?' I said. 'Let Gwen answer the door and see what happens.'

'Thruppence says they don't notice,' said Gwen.

'Go on, then,' said Lady Hardcastle. 'You're on.'

Gwen got up and straightened her dress.

'Am I presentable?' she said.

After years of living with Lady Hardcastle and mingling with people of every nation and every social class, my accent had lost a lot of its character. Gwen had a good ear, though, and was able to impersonate me perfectly.

I had a good ear, too, and her accent was even easier – it used to be mine, after all.

'You'll do,' I said.

She went out into the hall, leaving the drawing-room door open so we could hear.

The front door opened.

'Good morning,' said Gwen.

'Ah,' said Inspector Sunderland. He seemed to be slightly confused. 'Is . . . ah . . . is Lady Hardcastle at home?'

'She is, sir. Just a moment and I'll tell her you're here.'

'Thank you.' There was still doubt in his voice. 'Are you . . . are you Florence Armstrong's sister?'

'Well, you're no fun,' she said with a laugh. 'You just cost me thruppence.'

'I'm so sorry. I'm Inspector Sunderland.'

'Ah, I've heard all about you. Gwenith Evans. Armstrong as was.'

'Pleased to meet you. Are they in?'

'Oh, sorry, yes. Come in.'

The door closed and two sets of footsteps crossed the hall.

'Good morning, Inspector,' said Lady Hardcastle as he entered the drawing room. 'Do excuse our shenanigans. The Armstrong girls were sure they could fool you but I was doubtful.'

'You weren't fooled even for a moment?' asked Gwen.

'It was most disconcerting. I couldn't fathom at first why you didn't seem to know who I was. Then I remembered that Miss Armstrong had often talked about her twin sister, so I looked more carefully. You have no mole by your left ear.'

Gwen laughed.

'Well, I suppose that's your police training,' she said. 'But bakers and barmaids are more easily fooled.'

'I suppose that must be it,' he said.

'But now that's all explained, do come in and make yourself comfortable,' said Lady Hardcastle. 'There's coffee in the pot and more doughnuts than we can possibly eat.'

'Thank you, my lady. I don't wish to interrupt a family reunion, but if I can have a few moments of your time – and a doughnut – that would be splendid. I confess to being rather partial to doughnuts.'

He sat down and I poured him a cup of coffee.

'Now, then, Inspector dear, what is it that troubles you? Something to do with the theatre murder, perhaps?'

'It's the theatre murder, yes,' he said as he munched appreciatively on his jam-filled treat.

'And what can we do? I should warn you that we've talked about it a little and I'm afraid we've no insights at all as yet. But we're always happy to help with your cases – you know that.'

'I do indeed, and I'm always most grateful. But I'm afraid it's not my case – that's partly why I've called.'

'Not your case? Oh dear. What's happened?'

'Oh, nothing bad. I was initially involved because I happened to be at the theatre when the body was discovered, but one of my colleagues – Dick Wyatt – was on duty at the time and it's rightfully his case. He offered to let me have it since I'd already set the investigative wheels in motion, but the chief superintendent wants me to deal with another matter so Wyatt is taking over after all.'

'Oh, that's a shame. I was rather hoping we might be able to follow the progress on this one.'

'Ah, well . . . now, you see, that's the other reason for my dropping in. I'll be out of the office quite a lot and . . . well, I'm not one to speak ill of my colleagues as a rule – you know that – but Wyatt . . . Wyatt is . . .'

'A bit of a chump?' I suggested.

'More than a bit, I'm afraid. He's lazy, inattentive to detail, and lacks . . . intuition? Perception? Intelligence, perhaps. Let's not beat about the bush, he's a complete duffer. Without someone to keep him pointed in the right direction he'll just arrest the first person he talks to, and that'll be that. It'll go to the magistrate, who'll throw it out for lack of evidence, and the killer will slip ever further from our grasp. And worse than that, I'm worried he'll actually work to frustrate things.'

'How so?' asked Lady Hardcastle.

'He has something of a reputation as a bit of a . . . a Lothario. No, perhaps that's maligning him. He's not a bounder, but his head is easily turned by a handsome lady, and there's no shortage of those at the theatre. I fear he might allow his fancies to get in the way or, worse still, work to actively scupper the investigation in order to protect whichever actress has caught his eye.'

'Do you really think that's likely?'

'Not likely, but certainly possible. I want to get this killer. I want to catch every killer, you understand, but this one ruined my night out.'

'Fair enough, Inspector dear. And what can we do?'

'Can you find a way to get yourself in among them? The theatre people, I mean. Lady Bickle knows them – could she introduce you? If you're around them you might hear something, see something. Would you work your usual magic to progress the inquiries and keep an eye on Wyatt for me while you're at it?'

'I'm sure we could arrange something. What say you, Flo? Fancy mingling with the thespians?'

'I'd be happy to. But . . .' I looked at Gwen.

'Oh, don't mind me,' she said. 'I can amuse myself. I'm imposing on you as it is – it's not like you invited me.'

'You never know,' said Lady Hardcastle, 'we might be able to make use of you if you're game. I often think I could do with two Armstrongs, and you were saying only moments ago that you thought your life was mundane.'

'Really? Well, I'd love it. Count me in. Anything you want.'

'Are you sure about this, my lady?' asked the inspector. 'I'm more than aware that I'm imposing, too. I really don't have any justification for asking you to help me.'

'Nonsense, Inspector dear. I hope you know by now that you'll find help here whenever you need it. And it'll be a lark. Oh, does this Wyatt fellow know us?'

'Only by reputation. I don't think he's ever seen you.'

'Even better,' she said. 'I fancy we might not be Emily Hardcastle and Florence Armstrong when we meet the theatricals or Inspector Wyatt. I feel a subterfuge coming on.'

Inspector Sunderland gave one of his familiar chuckles.

'Don't go overboard, my lady,' he said. 'It's not one of your SSB missions. I just want to know how things are going.'

'Nonsense. If something's worth doing, it's worth doing to excess. We shall have fun *and* keep you apprised. Georgie Bickle will be pleased to help, too – she wants to know what's going on just as much as you do.'

'Very well, then,' said the inspector. 'Thank you. Are there any more of those doughnuts?'

Chapter Three

With Lady Hardcastle's declaration that we should 'strike while the iron's hot' because 'there's no time like the present', we had made arrangements to visit Lady Bickle the next day. I chastised her for speaking in clichés but she told me that was 'the pot calling the kettle black', and that, anyway, novelty wasn't the 'be all and end all' of compelling discourse. I bowed to her superior wisdom.

And so it was that the next morning we left Gwen at the house writing a letter to Dai and made our way to Berkeley Crescent, opposite the museum and art gallery, shortly before eleven.

Lady Hardcastle rang the bell.

A few moments later, the door was answered by Williams, the Bickles' white-haired butler.

'Ah, Lady Hardcastle,' he said. 'And Miss Armstrong. The mistress is expecting you. Do, please, follow me.'

He led us through to the drawing room, where Lady Bickle was already pouring two more cups of tea. Williams left without further folderol or fanfare and Lady Bickle greeted us warmly.

'How wonderful to see you both again so soon,' she said. 'Do sit down. You didn't say much when you telephoned. Have you news?'

'News of a sort, dear, yes,' said Lady Hardcastle.

She briefly recounted our conversation with Inspector Sunderland of the previous day.

'And so we come to you,' she concluded, 'with our caps in our hands, to beg you for a favourable introduction to your actor friends.'

Lady Bickle laughed.

'Don't be so silly,' she said. 'I asked you to keep an eye on things, after all, and they'll be delighted to meet you.'

'Ah,' I said, 'but will they be delighted to meet Violet Goodheart and Joanna Webster-Green?'

'And who are they when they're at home?'

'The two ladies who wish to start their own theatre company in Bournemouth, and who desperately need the advice only an experienced group of players such as your friends can provide.'

'And they'll be reporting back to you?' said Lady Bickle.

Lady Hardcastle laughed.

'They *are* us, dear,' she said, kindly. 'We'll be playing the roles ourselves.'

'Oh. But why?'

'Thanks to our recent exploits we have a certain . . . reputation. If we swan in as ourselves and start asking questions they'll close ranks and we'll never find out anything, so we have to be someone else.'

'Oh, my goodness, I feel such a fool. Of course you will. I forget that you do this sort of thing all the time. I say, what larks.' She grinned girlishly, but then a practical thought struck her. 'Oh, but how do I know you?'

'That's an interesting question. How does she know us, Flo?'

'We're members of the Dorset branch of the WSPU,' I said, 'and you met us at a suffragette beano. All the branches of the South West Region got together for a day of lectures followed by dinner at a hotel in Taunton, and you came over to speak to me because you were impressed by the self-defence demonstration I'd given in the afternoon. We got along famously and I introduced you to my good friend—'

'Of the two names I think I want to be Joanna Webster-Green,' said Lady Hardcastle. 'It's a good name. It has an air of dependable respectability about it. Although I think perhaps you would call me Jo.'

'Perhaps I would,' I agreed. 'It's much friendlier. But would you be happy with this chummy hypocorism?'

'Very much so,' said Lady Hardcastle. 'It has a charming informality that speaks to my friendliness and approachability.'

'It does indeed. Actually, though, shouldn't you be *Lady* Webster-Green if we're in Bristol? If someone recognizes you and calls you "my lady" you'll be stuck if you're plain old Mrs Webster-Green.'

'A very good point, dear. Joanna, Lady Webster-Green it is, then. Known to her many friends as Jo. As for our roles in the partnership . . . Violet is the business brain, I think, while I am a widow with more money than good sense—'

'It always pays to keep the fiction as close to the truth as possible,' I interrupted.

'Quiet, you. I am an artistic visionary and it is my dream to bring the magic of the dramatic arts to the fine people of Bournemouth. And perhaps Poole.'

'Do you have an artistic vision, then?' asked Lady Bickle.

'Not so you'd notice,' said Lady Hardcastle. 'But we find it doesn't pay to overcomplicate these things so it shouldn't matter too much.'

'Oh, but if there's one thing writers and actors love to talk about it's—'

'Themselves?' I suggested.

'Well, yes, they do that rather a lot. But when they're not doing that they love nothing more than talking about writing and acting. If you're going to be telling that story about yourselves, you'll have to be prepared for some questions about what sort of things you hope to produce.'

'You make a good point,' said Lady Hardcastle. 'I shall come up with something suitably pretentious before we meet them. Flo – I mean Violet – will look convincingly aghast at the awfulness of it all, and our marks will be well and truly hooked.'

'I can't wait to see you in action,' said Lady Bickle.

I smiled at her enthusiasm.

'But don't overplay it,' I warned her. 'Be wary of getting too excited and try not to over-elaborate the stories. If you decide to add detail to anything we say, make it something we can easily remember or they'll tumble us when we inevitably forget and get it wrong at a later date.'

'Ah, yes. Jolly good. I say, this is rather exciting, isn't it?'

'Actually, yes,' I said. 'I love pretending to be someone else.'

'It does have its appeal, I must say. Sometimes I long to be someone else, even if only for a short while.'

'Have you ever thought of acting, dear?' said Lady Hardcastle. 'I always fancied you might have a talent for it. And it would certainly give you the opportunity to be someone else for a couple of hours a night.'

'I did once, long ago – as a girl I harboured dreams of a life as a great Shakespearian actress. But when I finally got my chance and performed as Juliet in the school play, it wasn't a comfortable experience at all.'

'Oh, dear. Did it not go well? I know what that's like.'

'Actually, I was well enough received, but the school newspaper was scathing in its review of the play as a whole. And they hated poor Helena Bartlett as Romeo. She was a rather capable actress as it happens, but the reviewer thought her altogether too busty to convincingly portray a ruggedly handsome young man. I was enraged by the unfairness of it – judging her performance by her looks, I mean. It rather put me off, I must say. What might they have said about me if they hadn't had poor Helena to pick on?'

'Ah, yes,' said Lady Hardcastle. 'I've been on the receiving end of poor notices, but in my case the criticism was entirely fair. I played Guildenstern in a college production of *Hamlet* during my first year. I was utterly dreadful and the critics weren't afraid to tell the world about it. But I did get to say that bit about "Fortune's privates" and that always got a naughty laugh, so it evened itself out for me.'

'I think I'll stick to what I know,' I said.

'You've never acted?' said Lady Bickle.

'Gwen and I were cast as angels in the school nativity play when we moved back to Aberdare. It didn't quite work out, though.'

'Surely no one would give a school nativity play a bad notice.'

'Oh, the play was fine as far as I know, but my part was cut.'

'I've not heard this story,' said Lady Hardcastle.

'I'm not proud of it,' I said. 'Although, actually, perhaps I am. It was Arthur Jones's fault. He was playing one of the shepherds and he kept trying to trip Gwen as we crossed the stage for our big speech. She thwarted his efforts for the most part, but he finally managed to get her during the dress rehearsal. She tore her best dress as she hit the deck, and bent her cardboard wings. So I walloped him one. Or two. Actually, I had to be pulled off him by the teacher. I was sent home and invited not to take any further part in the proceedings.'

'Who's Gwen that you should protect her so fiercely?' asked Lady Bickle.

'Her twin sister, Gwenith,' said Lady Hardcastle. 'They were terrors in their youth as I understand it.'

'I choose to remember us as charmingly mischievous,' I said. 'But we always stuck up for each other.'

'But you were not would-be actresses,' said Lady Bickle.

'Not I, certainly – I can't speak for Gwen. I suppose we all have to act to some extent, though, don't we? She plays the part of the dutiful military wife no matter how else she might think of herself.'

Lady Bickle nodded.

'It's true,' she said. 'We all play our roles.'

'And if I do ever get the urge to act,' I said, 'our line of work provides me with plenty of opportunities to rummage through the dressing-up box and pretend to be someone else.'

'I suppose so. But what about the physical danger?'

'There's an element of that, perhaps, but what about those scathing reviews in the newspapers you were both talking about? If I'm going to be attacked, I much prefer a fair fight where I get a chance to hit back.'

Lady Bickle laughed.

'You make a good point,' she said. 'Even now my own humble endeavours are not free from public criticism. You should see some of the names I'm called for doing nothing more than asking politely for women to have a say in how the country is run. You'd think we were demanding the abolition of men's votes rather than the simple addition of votes for women.'

'You see? The hugger-mugger world is violent and cruel, and full of men who would do us harm, but when they try we usually have a decent chance to defend ourselves. I can only imagine the frustration and fury of being criticized in print with no right of reply.'

'And the actors will love you if you understand that. I'm sure they'd love you both anyway, but you know what I mean. When do you wish to see them?'

'Whenever's most convenient,' said Lady Hardcastle. 'But the sooner the better, I think. You and Inspector Sunderland both want us to poke our noses in and he doesn't have a high opinion of Inspector Wyatt, so I'd rather we were in there rootling about as soon as we can. Perhaps we should start with your friend the writer—'

'Hugo Bartlett,' said Lady Bickle.

'Ah, yes, that's the chap. And if he's the one among them you actually know, he's the one we should start with. He'll be our way in to the group.'

'Technically I suppose you might say his sister Helena is the one I know, but yes.'

'But he's the one who dropped in on you, isn't he? If you could introduce us to him we'll take it from there.'

'I shall telephone him at the theatre at once,' said Lady Bickle, as she rose and headed for the door. 'Do help yourselves to more tea. And the cakes, too. Cook made them specially when she heard you were coming.'

The Bickles' cook was something of a dab hand when it came to pastries, and I popped a selection on to two plates once I'd refreshed our cups. It was always a treat to visit the Bickle household.

Hugo Bartlett had been only too happy to talk to us and suggested we meet him the following morning.

And so it was that, shortly before eleven on Friday, we parked the Rolls on Park Row and made our way halfway down Christmas Steps to Crane's Coffee House. The shopfront was narrow and its windows small, and I wasn't sure what we'd find once we went through the door.

I needn't have worried. Despite the irredeemably tarnished reputation of their owner – the revolting Oswald Crane – Crane's Coffee Houses had a splendid reputation of their own for cleanliness and good service. The interior of the Christmas Steps branch was modern and well appointed, if a little gloomily lit. It defied the slightly down-at-heel appearance of its exterior and felt instead cosy and welcoming. We were approached by a smartly turned-out young waitress.

'Good morning, ladies,' she said. 'Table for two, is it?'

'For four, actually,' said Lady Hardcastle. 'We're expecting guests. Or perhaps they're expecting us. I'm not quite certain of the order of precedence.'

'Ah,' said the girl. 'Would you be Lady Webster-Green and Miss Goodheart, by any chance?'

'Why, yes, we very much would.'

'Then your companions have already arrived. They asked me to look out for you.'

'Thank you, dear,' I said. 'Lead on.'

It actually was rather fun not to be a deferential lady's maid from time to time.

The waitress led us deep into the furthest corner of the coffee shop, where we found Lady Bickle and a short, young-looking man with a well-kempt beard neatly trimmed to a subtle point in the style favoured by the King. He stood as we approached and I was struck by how stocky he was, with the solid, barrel-like body of a wrestler.

'Hello, ladies,' said Lady Bickle, eyeing our change of costume. 'How lovely to see you again. May I introduce Mr Hugo Bartlett. Hugo, these are my dear friends Lady Webster-Green and Miss Violet Goodheart.'

'How do you do, ladies?' said Mr Bartlett. He was softly spoken – not at all the brashly confident man I had been expecting. But perhaps writers were the quiet ones. The actors would be louder, I was sure.

'How do you do?' said Lady Hardcastle and I together.

Mr Bartlett smiled in acknowledgement and politely waited until we were both settled before resuming his own seat.

'It's very kind of you to agree to see us, Mr Bartlett,' said Lady Hardcastle. 'Thank you so very much.'

'It's entirely my pleasure,' he said. 'Any friend of Georgie Ingram is a friend of the Bartletts. Sorry, I mean Bickle, of course. Do forgive me, my dear – Helena talked about you so much when you were at school together, and I'm afraid I shall always think of you as Georgie Ingram.'

'That's quite all right, dear. To be truthful, I enjoy being reminded. It was all rather jolly becoming Mrs Benjamin Bickle. A badge of honour, one might say, a sign that one had grown up. But then Ben received his knighthood and I found myself changing yet again to Lady Bickle, and it dawned on me that I was just an extension of my beloved husband. Whither he goest, and all that, but I began to wonder where *I'd* gone. The old me. Whatever happened to dear Georgie Ingram? Surely she's in here somewhere.'

'I was Joanna Muffet before I married,' said Lady Hardcastle. 'Couldn't wait to be rid of it. Can you imagine going through childhood being Little Miss Muffet? Fortunately, I'm rather fond of spiders, or it would have been much worse.'

Mr Bartlett turned his dark brown eyes on me.

'What about you, Miss Goodheart?' he said. 'Are you good of heart?'

'I like to imagine so,' I said. 'At least, I try.'

He laughed politely.

'Georgie tells me you two are thinking about starting a theatre company,' he said. 'In Bournemouth?'

'We are,' said Lady Hardcastle. 'Or, at least, I am – Violet acts as the voice of reason and tries to rein in my wilder notions.'

'And is it a wild notion?'

'If we do it well and wisely,' I said, 'it needn't be wild at all. And that's rather why we wanted to meet you, to talk about your marvellous company.'

'You're very kind. I can't pretend to be an expert, but whatever advice I can give is yours for the asking.'

'Thank you. When we were making our plans for a visit to Bristol we spoke to La—' I stopped myself. We were Lady Bickle's friends – I'd call her Georgie like everyone else did. Then I wondered whether I should instead have just barrelled through it – she *was* Lady Bickle, after all. Then I decided it was too late so I probably ought simply to carry on and correct myself. Or feign a stammer. A stammer might cover it. But I'd have to keep it up, possibly for days. Weeks, even. I went with the correction. '—to *Georgie*, and she suggested she introduce us to you, what with you being such a successful impresario. But after we had finalized the arrangements yesterday, we learned that you were at the centre of the most awful incident at the theatre.'

'Awful,' said Lady Hardcastle. 'We wondered before we left our guest house this morning whether we should telephone Georgie and cancel. Out of respect, do you see? We really don't wish to intrude at such a terrible time.'

'It is a terrible time,' said Mr Bartlett, sombrely. 'Paul Singleton was a wonderful actor and a dear friend, and we are all shocked and deeply saddened by the events of Tuesday evening, but . . . well, the show must go on, as they say. We have to put our grief to one side, paste on our painted smiles and step out under the lights to entertain our public. And the awful truth is that the tragedy has generated so much interest in the play that the initial two-week run has sold out and the theatre management has asked us to extend.

We were to take a break and then move on to the Theatre Royal at Bath, but the touring production of *The Worst Woman in London* has been told the Duke's is unexpectedly unavailable and we are to run for an additional fortnight.'

'And so you don't mind our witless prattle?' I said.

'Not in the least – I'm sure it shall be anything but witless. And we shall be talking about the theatre, and there's nothing theatre folk like more than talking about the theatre.'

Lady Bickle winked at us from across the table.

'Thank you,' said Lady Hardcastle. 'And if you're happy to talk, well . . . you see, I have the opportunity to acquire property in the Bournemouth area which has marvellous potential to be converted into a theatre. The town is well served by theatres already but I wish for something a little more . . . well, one never wishes to appear too much of a snob, but I should like to be able to provide something a little more sophisticated. Comedy like yours, for instance. It brings the house down, but it's not broad knockabout stuff. It has style and wit. There are thoughtful themes in there among the laughs. I should like to create a space where intelligent comedy like yours can flourish, away from the bawdiness of the music hall.'

'You flatter me, Lady Webster-Green.'

'Please, dear, do call me Jo. But I mean it. Somewhere between High Art and Base Entertainment, there is, I feel, room for thoughtful comedy. I'm thinking of calling it the Thaliaeios after Thalia, the Greek goddess of comedy.'

This seemed like an ideal moment to roll my eyes, so I did. Lady Bickle saw me and suppressed a giggle.

'I see,' said Mr Bartlett. 'Well . . . ah . . . that would be . . . an eye-catching name, certainly, if perhaps a little difficult to say. Perhaps we can come back to that later. But your central idea is intriguing. How do you envisage running it?'

'Well, dear, that's rather why we've come to you. How do you run your company? How many of you are there? What are your roles? How are you organized? How are you paid? Tell me everything.'

She took a hefty swig of her coffee and leaned forward.

This was all the invitation Mr Bartlett needed, and for the next half an hour he spoke almost non-stop about his theatre company and their work. Lady Hardcastle flattered him with wide-eyed attention, while I, as sensible Violet Goodheart, made copious notes.

Bartlett spent quite a while describing the financial arrangements of the group, which he thought quite complex and innovative but were, in reality, little different from the partnership agreements holding firms together throughout the land. But we let him explain it to us as though he were a business genius and we but simple provincial women struggling to understand the intricacies of the commercial world. In this way we slowly gained his trust and allowed him to relax sufficiently that he might talk about what really matters in any business: the people.

'This is utterly fascinating, Mr Bartlett—' began Lady Hardcastle.

'Hugo, please.'

'Thank you, dear. It's most illuminating. I'm not certain I follow all the details, but Violet understands, I'm sure. A more . . . egalitarian arrangement like yours might suit the sort of company I hope to create. But one needs the right personnel, don't you think? The right mix not only of talent, but of temperament.'

'Indeed you do, and that's where the Bartlett Players are especially blessed.'

This was the first time I'd heard the group's name, and I smiled to myself as I inadvertently wrote *Bartlett Pears* and had to cross it out. I briefly wondered about righting wrongs and settling scores at the head of Armstrong's Avengers, but the idea of naming something after myself didn't sit well with me. I clearly lacked the egomania of the playwright.

'Are there just the five of you? Four now, sorry. Is that a sufficient number for this sort of endeavour?'

'Not quite, no. We were eight before Paul's death and that served us well for most productions. When we need more we hire them ad hoc, usually from a pool of known and trusted actors. We seldom trouble with auditions.'

'Eight? Goodness.' Lady Hardcastle was in her element as the overenthusiastic would-be impresario. 'I had no idea. However do you find things for them all to do?'

'They're all actors, but they all have other skills and there's always enough to keep them busy. For *The Hedonists*, for example . . . have you seen it?'

'Your play? Sadly not. We arrived at Bristol on the day of the tragedy, and by Wednesday morning it was, as you said, completely sold out.'

'Oh, my dear Jo, you must see it. I shall leave tickets for you at the box office – we always hold a few back for special guests. Just the two of you, is it? No husbands or men friends to accommodate?'

'Oh, that would be delightful. Thank you. And yes, it's just the two of us.'

'Don't let me forget, Georgie,' he said. 'You should come again, too – see it all the way through this time. You should have told me you were coming before, though – no friend of Helena's should have to pay to see one of my plays.'

'You're kind, dear,' said Lady Bickle, 'but we were a sizeable group. We were celebrating another friend's birthday.'

She looked at Lady Hardcastle and winked again. I contemplated kicking her under the table, but that would only draw more attention to it and there was still a chance that Bartlett was too wrapped up in himself to have noticed.

'Well, I'll add you to the party this time,' he said. 'One for Ben, too?'

'I'm not sure without asking him, dear. He's often busy in the evenings – committees and whatnot.'

'Four tickets will be no trouble. But where was I? Oh, yes. The company. Four actors on stage for *The Hedonists*. Harris Bridges is Johnny. He's a splendid fellow. Been with us since the beginning. Lots of experience before that, too. He's our stalwart. Rosalie Harding is Mona. Very skilled and quite, quite beautiful. Used to be engaged to Bridges.'

'Does that make things awkward?' asked Lady Hardcastle. 'When couples in the company break off engagements, I mean.'

'Oh, it's worse than that,' said Mr Bartlett. 'And worse for Rosalie now, too. You see, she left Bridges and took up straight away with Paul Singleton.'

'The murdered man.'

'Exactly. Well, I say "took up straight away", but everyone suspected they'd been carrying on together while she was still engaged to Bridges.'

'Oh, my word. You don't suppose . . . ?'

'Suppose what?'

'Well, that gives Bridges a strong motive for killing Singleton.'

'It does, rather, and you're not the first to think it. Inspector Wyatt is very much of the same opinion.'

'Goodness,' said Lady Hardcastle. 'How awful.'

'Well, quite.' Bartlett seemed slightly put-out to be reminded of the sordid business of real tragedies. I got the impression he would much rather retreat into the imagined tragedies of the theatre. Perhaps it was that he had more control over them – real life is messy, after all, and rarely wraps up neatly. He gazed into the distance for a moment before coming back to himself and continuing. 'Paul's role will be taken by his understudy, Patrick Cowlin. We rotate the lead roles depending on the actors' strengths, and Paul was particularly blessed as a comic actor so he took the part of Johnny, with Cowlin working as stage manager. I thought about casting Cowlin in the first instance, actually, but Paul knew exactly how to read every line to get the biggest laugh. Cowlin is more of a heroic lead, but he'll still be wonderful as Bertie. Very handsome, too.'

'Was he upset at not getting the role?'

'Oh, they're always upset. Each of them believes themselves to be the only one capable of playing any part, but they get over it soon enough. They always know that their turn will come. So he'll be playing Bertie, Rosalie Harding is Mona, and the beautiful Sarah Griffin is Peggy.'

'But who will be stage manager now that Mr Cowlin is playing Bertie?' I asked. It felt like the sort of practical problem that would trouble Violet greatly.

'Nancy Beaufort is the female understudy so she'll cover that,' said Mr Bartlett, apparently pleased that I was so interested.

Lady Hardcastle made a show of totting up the names on her fingers.

'You mentioned eight people,' she said. 'But even including you that's only seven.'

Mr Bartlett beamed. We were paying attention to the smallest details and he knew he had us completely enthralled.

'Emrys Thornell is our director,' he said. 'He's the eighth.'

'I see,' said Lady Hardcastle. 'Are you not interested in directing? Maintaining full control of your artistic vision?'

Mr Bartlett smiled through his beard.

'I'm happy to entrust my work to Emrys,' he said. 'He and I work closely together, but I don't relish the argle-bargle of directing. Actors require such careful handling, you see? Directing is a finely balanced business of buoying up their fragile egos to give them the confidence to perform, and reining in their overbearing egos to stop them taking over completely. I find it all terribly stressful. And the shouting. My God, Jo, the shouting. I couldn't do it. Couldn't do it. I'm not one of Nature's shouters – I'd much rather sit in a peaceful corner with my typewriter, crafting the words for them to say.'

'They sound like wonderfully interesting people,' I said.

'They do,' agreed Lady Hardcastle. 'I don't suppose . . .'

'You could meet them?' he said. 'Of course. We love nothing more than meeting anyone with an interest in the theatre. I'm sure they'd be delighted to hear about your plans. As would I. I know these things can be delicate so I've not wanted to ask too many questions, but if you would like to tell me more . . .'

'Would you all be free for lunch tomorrow, perhaps? My treat, of course. Georgie will know of somewhere, I'm sure. We could all discuss it together.'

'It happens that we are,' he said. 'We'd usually have a matinée performance on a Saturday – actually, we'd often do a couple of matinées in the week, as well – but the theatre is short-handed and can't run to two performances a day. We've agreed to perform on Mondays, though. That's usually our day off. It gives them one more house so they don't lose too much money. Got to keep the wolf from the door.'

'That would be splendid,' said Lady Hardcastle. 'Do you know of anywhere suitable?'

'There's Le Quai,' said Lady Bickle. 'It's a new French restaurant in town owned by a thrillingly innovative young chef. From Toulon, you know. His food is exquisite and he puts on an absolutely marvellous luncheon.'

I almost groaned out loud. Why would she try to take us somewhere where they already knew us? She was a formidably bright young woman and I greatly admired her for her work with the WSPU, but she was rapidly turning into a liability here.

Lady Hardcastle, though, was undaunted, and sought to give her an excuse to think of something else.

'That sounds lovely, dear,' she said. 'Would they be able to accommodate such a large group? I should like to meet as many of the Bartlett Players as I can.'

Lady Bickle, I could only hope, had realized her error.

'Oh,' she said, 'I hadn't thought of that. I shall make enquiries. And if not, I'm sure we can come up with something.'

'I'm sure we shall,' said Lady Hardcastle. 'Now, who's for cake? I've heard wonderful things about Crane's cream cakes. And we need a fresh pot of tea. Can you catch the waitress's eye from there?'

After a good deal of head-bobbing and tentative waving, the young waitress was eventually summoned and refills ordered.

'Are there any pitfalls we need to look out for?' asked Lady Hardcastle as she tucked eagerly into a cream-filled bun. 'You know, things you wish you'd known when you started out? Or things you've heard theatre owners talking about?'

'There are plenty of little things, but if you find experienced actors for your core troupe they should be able to guide you through the worst of them. As for the theatre itself, I should say the same thing applies: get the right staff. And make sure they're trustworthy. The Duke's is suffering a terrible run of petty thefts at the moment. One or two things have even gone missing from dressing rooms.'

'Good heavens. We shall have to take great care.'

Our conversation turned from the theatre company as Lady Bickle reminisced about Mr Bartlett's sister Helena, and Lady Hardcastle and I recklessly improvised details of our own false biographies that I could only hope we would be able to remember later.

The coffee house was becoming increasingly busy as lunchtime approached, so we used it as our excuse to leave Mr Bartlett to his work and to 'return to our guest house'.

We braced ourselves for the steep climb up Christmas Steps, and I briefly regretted the extra cake I'd eaten, thinking I could do with as little ballast as possible as we trudged back up towards Park Row.

We'd only gone a little way up the smooth, steep pavement when Lady Bickle tapped my arm.

'Look up there,' she said, pointing with her other hand.

I lifted my eyes in the direction she had pointed. Two women were coming carefully down towards us, holding on to each other and stepping as gingerly as though they were descending the north face of the Eiger rather than a flight of stone steps in the middle of a city. One of them I recognized from the play – she had been Mona, though I couldn't remember her real name – but the other, much younger, woman was unfamiliar.

They spotted Lady Bickle and waved. The distraction from the apparently complex task of walking down some steps, combined with the physical motion of the wave, caused the younger woman a momentary panic. She gripped her companion's arm even more fiercely. I honestly thought for a moment that she might topple, and that I'd find myself responsible for trying to arrest her fall.

The one who had played Mona so wonderfully gave Lady Bickle a smile and a flick of the eyebrows at her friend's awkwardness. Lady Bickle let out a delightful laugh.

'Hello, darlings,' she said. 'Can you make it?'

We waited as the two women tottered down to us.

'Jo,' said Lady Bickle, turning to Lady Hardcastle, 'Violet, allow me to introduce my new friends from the theatre, Miss Rosalie Harding and Miss Nancy Beaufort. Rosie and Nancy, this is Joanna, Lady Webster-Green, and Miss Violet Goodheart, two friends from the WSPU who are interested in opening a theatre in Bournemouth.'

There was a lengthy round of how-do-you-dos and handshaking, and I suppressed a smile to see how relieved Nancy was to be standing on more solid ground.

'Are you on your way to see Hugo?' asked Rosie. 'He said he was meeting some friends of yours.'

'We've just left,' said Lady Bickle. 'We had a lovely chat, though. It's a shame you couldn't be with us.'

'I'm not sure there's much we could have added. We're just poor players, strutting and fretting and all that. Although some of us are more fretful than others.' She nodded towards Nancy.

'The steps are steep,' said Nancy, indignantly. 'And these new boots are slippery. I didn't want to go base over apex and end up in a tangled heap of broken limbs at the bottom. You ought to be grateful for my caution – you'd be the one carrying me back to the digs.'

'Beggar that,' said Rosalie. 'I'd be the one selling tickets for the acrobatics display.'

'Well, it would have been wonderful to see you, fretful or otherwise,' said Lady Bickle. 'Jo is treating us all to lunch tomorrow. Do please come along to that, won't you? Hugo will have the details.'

'I've never been known to turn down an invitation to lunch,' said Rosalie. 'That's very kind of you, Jo. I'd be delighted.'

'Me too,' said Nancy with a smile. 'Thank you.'

'I look forward to meeting you in less precipitous circumstances,' said Lady Hardcastle. 'Good luck with the rest of your descent.'

'I'm not sure I can go much further,' said Nancy. 'These flagstones are no better than the steps. What about that coffee house, there – Crane's? What's that like?'

'It's very nice,' I said. 'That's where we met Hugo Bartlett. You might find him still there if he hasn't sneaked out while we weren't looking.'

'Ooh, lovely,' said Rosalie. 'Hugo's always good for a cup of tea and a free bun. Come on, Nance, just a few more slippery steps and we can get you into the warm.'

There was a lengthy round of goodbyes and handshakes, and we left the two actresses to totter off to Crane's.

Lady Bickle said her own goodbyes at the Rolls and I took the wheel for the drive back to Littleton Cotterell.

As I drove home, we discussed the suggestion that we dine with the actors at Le Quai.

'It's not a terribly good idea to be pretending to be someone else in a place where we're so well known,' said Lady Hardcastle. 'I don't know what Georgie was thinking.'

'She's not one of Nature's dissemblers,' I said. 'All that winking and nudging – I nearly kicked her under the table several times. But then she was suddenly so carried away with the pretence that she forgot she wasn't trying to show off Bristol's finest restaurants to two visitors and suggested Le Quai.'

'We shall have to come up with something else.'

'Unless . . .'

'Unless what, dear?'

'Well, we might be able to turn the fact that we're known at Le Quai to our advantage. With the staff on our side it becomes a place we can control, don't you think?'

'I like the way you think, young Flo. Yes, indeed. If we set things up properly we shall be safer there than anywhere. Jean-Pierre will help us, I'm sure.'

Lady Hardcastle telephoned the restaurant as soon as we arrived home, to enquire about the use of their private room. She was told that its circular dining table could comfortably accommodate a dozen covers and that seating ten would allow for a most luxurious dining experience. She booked the room for noon on Saturday in the name of Lady Webster-Green, and immediately telephoned Lady Bickle to ask her to invite the Bartlett Players to have lunch with us. Before curtain-up at the Duke's she had called us back to confirm that the entire company would be present.

Chapter Four

Saturday morning was wet and cold. Part of me felt it was the price I had to pay for having enjoyed the glorious summer so much, but if that were true then a greater part of me resented the weather for such petty point-scoring. Flo had enjoyed a few weeks of warm weather, so Flo must be cold and miserable until Easter. It didn't seem entirely reasonable.

Although we weren't due to meet the actors until noon, there was plenty to do, and so I took Lady Hardcastle her starter breakfast shortly after seven. I lit the lamp and clattered the tray. Irritable grumbling emanated from beneath the covers.

'Good morning,' I said, brightly. 'Coffee and toast.'

'It's not even light yet,' said an unseen voice that could easily have belonged to the troll who lives under the bridge in 'The Three Billy Goats Gruff'.

'You're correct. It's five past seven. Sunrise is in fourteen minutes' time – I checked the almanac because I knew you'd complain. It's already starting to get light, though, and we have to get moving because you want to be out of the house by ten.'

'I refuse to believe I would ever have suggested I be awake before dawn if we don't have to leave until ten.'

'And yet here I am, as instructed,' I said. 'I made contemporaneous notes of the conversation in shorthand if you wish to review them.'

The covers snapped down to reveal the frowning face of my employer.

'Did you really?'

'No, of course not. Don't be daft. But you did make a clear and unambiguous request to be woken before a quarter past seven because you have "a lot of things to do before we go out".'

'Hah!' she said triumphantly. 'Got you. It's only five past. I have ten more minutes. Begone, tiny servant, let poor Emily snooze a while longer.'

I picked up her wristwatch from the bedside table and made a performance of looking at it.

'Nine minutes now,' I said. 'Miss Jones has to deal with a personal matter this morning so Gwen and I are making breakfast. It'll be served at half past.'

'I'll be there,' she grumbled.

I returned to the kitchen, where Gwen was keeping an expert eye on the sausages.

'Is she all right?' she asked.

'She is,' I said. 'She's not overjoyed to be awake, but she seldom is. She'll be fine once she starts moving.'

'I envy you your life sometimes, Floss.'

'You're not the first person to say that to me this week. One of our friends said it at the theatre. What's so special about my life?'

'You always seem so happy. You've got a nice job, an employer who's also your best mate, a beautiful home. You've been all round the world—'

'Yes, she said all that, too. I refrained from pointing out that wherever I've been in the world, people have tried to kill me.'

'You're still here, though, aren't you? What are you moaning about? You've done all right for yourself, young Flossie.'

'So have you, mind,' I said. 'You've got Dafydd. You've got your mates. You've got a lovely home, too, don't forget.'

'Oh, I'm not saying I've not got nothing, but sometimes . . . I mean, you know more about politics than I do. What if there's a war like they say there might be? Dai will be—'

'Dai's a BSM now – he'll be safely behind the lines looking after his men.'

'I do hope so. These sausages are done. Got any bacon?'

'I'll get it. You put some toast on.'

We finished making the breakfast and carried it through. As the hall clock struck the half hour, Lady Hardcastle materialized at the morning-room door like a ghostly apparition in her white nightgown and a heavy woollen shawl.

'You could have put some clothes on,' I said. 'We've company.'

'There simply wasn't time, dear,' she said. 'You were very insistent that I be here for half past on the dot. I distinctly remember being warned of dire consequences were I to be late.'

'Pish,' I said, 'and fiddlesticks. You do talk bilge sometimes.'

Gwen smiled and nodded.

'See?' she said. 'Best mates.'

'Hmm,' I said. 'I'm still pretty sure my "best mate" would be properly dressed when she had guests.'

'You don't mind, do you, Gwenith dear? You're family.'

'It's your house, Lady H, you do as you please.'

'There. You see? Now what do you suppose it was that was so important I demanded to be roused from my slumbers before cockcrow?'

'You didn't say,' I said. 'Correspondence? Research?'

'Possibly. I am in the middle of a slightly odd conversation with Harry about the activities of some foreign agents in London . . .

have you met my brother, Gwenith? I'm not sure you have. He works for the government.'

'In the same way you do?' asked Gwen.

'In a manner of speaking, though he's more likely to be found behind a desk than out in the field getting his delicate hands dirty. He's notionally our guv'nor, but it'll be a chilly day in Hades before I acknowledge any such thing in public.'

'And you're talking to him about what?'

'Oh, he has a bee in his bonnet about some strange advertisements in the *Times* personal columns. Thinks they're linked to some chaps his Special Branch thugs have been keeping a clumsy eye on. I'm not sure I agree with his assessment but I'd feel a proper noodlehead if I pooh-poohed him and he turned out to be right. But I'm not sure I'd have got up early for that – he can wait.'

'Something to do with the theatre murder?' I suggested.

'No, that's why we're going out. I wouldn't have wanted . . . No, wait, I have it. The crime board. I was going to make some notes on the crime board and have a proper ponder before we went into town. Oh, I say, well done you.'

I shrugged at Gwen, who laughed.

'So, what's a "crime board" when it's at home?' she said.

'I find I think better when I can see all the threads of the case at once, so I keep my notes on a school blackboard on an easel. Drawings, maps, connections . . . slowly but surely the picture resolves itself and I can see the solution.'

'Sounds clever.'

'It's surprisingly helpful,' I said. 'And surprisingly awkward to carry about. And every time I think we've put it in the attic for good, I have to haul it back downstairs again.'

'I'll give you a hand after we've tidied up breakfast,' said Gwen.

'Oh, we can leave the tidying to Edna,' said Lady Hardcastle. 'She gets quite tetchy if we interfere too much with the tidying up. You two can fetch the crime board for me. More toast, dear?'

◆ ◆ ◆

With some sweating, a small amount of Welsh swearing, and a surprising lack of twinly coordination, Gwen and I brought the crime board down to the drawing room. We set it beside the fireplace and made a pact never to move it again. Lady Hardcastle had adopted the habit of shifting it from room to room as the whim took her, but we unilaterally declared that it would stay where it was until the case was solved.

I left Gwen to chat to Edna and sort out some more tea while I helped make Lady Hardcastle presentable, and then we reconvened in the drawing room, settled on the comfy chairs.

Lady Hardcastle made sketches of the four actors we had seen at the performance on Tuesday evening: Harris Bridges, Rosalie Harding, Sarah Griffin, and the late Paul Singleton. She added the theatre manager Edwin Adlam, the writer Hugo Bartlett, and Nancy Beaufort, the understudy we'd met outside Crane's.

We described the events to Gwen as best we could remember, and Lady Hardcastle started one of her timelines at the bottom of the board.

'Who was in the last scene before the curtain came down?' she asked.

'All of them, as far as I can recall,' I said.

'So that's the last time we all saw Paul Singleton alive,' she said, making a note. 'By the end of the interval he had been murdered, so the murder occurred sometime between the end of Act One and the beginning of Act Two. That doesn't leave much time.'

'It was a long interval, though, don't you remember?'

'It took for ever, didn't it? A good half an hour, I think. Still a bit tight, though.'

'It takes a second to stab a man through the heart.'

'True, true. What else do we know?'

Using the notes I had made during our meeting at the coffee house, we filled in as many details about the theatre company as we could, including the speculation that actor Harris Bridges had the best motive so far, having been jilted by his fiancée, Rosalie, in favour of the late Paul Singleton.

'So he did it, then?' said Gwen. She sounded slightly disappointed.

'It's possible,' said Lady Hardcastle. 'But motive on its own isn't enough. Somehow the police have to prove he had access to the knife and was in the right place at the right time to do the wicked deed.'

'That shouldn't be hard, though – they were all in the right place at the right time. And anyone can get hold of a knife.'

'You're our knife expert, Flo,' said Lady Hardcastle. 'Did you happen to notice . . . ?'

'A bollock dagger with a . . . let's call it a tight barley-twist handle,' I said.

'What sort of dagger?' asked Gwen with a delighted chuckle.

I sighed.

'They're called bollock daggers,' I said. 'Sometimes kidney daggers. They get their name from the lobes at the base of the handle forming the guard. You might expect to see quillions there – little arms that make it look like a cross – but these just have little blobs to stop your hand slipping off the handle and down the blade. And they look like—'

'I can imagine what they look like,' said Gwen, still hugely amused. 'Are they rare? The daggers, I mean, not the . . .'

'They certainly weren't in the past – they've been around for hundreds of years and they've always been popular. Without a cumbersome guard they're easy to carry and conceal, you see. Elizabethan men were particularly keen on them, so I imagine it was a theatre prop for their Shakespeare productions, or their Jacobean revenge tragedies.'

'If that's the case,' said Lady Hardcastle, 'then everyone in the theatre would have had access to it.' She tapped her chalk thoughtfully on the board. 'Could it have anything to do with the thefts?'

'There are thefts?' said Gwen.

'Some petty pilfering,' I said. 'Hugo told us about it. I doubt it's connected.'

Lady Hardcastle made a note on the board anyway, then stood back to contemplate the sparse, but growing, web of connections.

'It's not much,' she said, 'but it's a start.'

◆　◆　◆

Although our table was booked for noon, we parked on St Nicholas Street a few minutes before eleven and made our way round to Le Quai. It was a lively part of town, with the courts and banks to one side of us and the busy High Street to the other. I loved Bristol and often wondered if perhaps we should have lived in town rather than out in the middle of nowhere. But then I remembered our modern house, our wonderful friends, and the sights and sounds – and smells – of the Gloucestershire countryside, and I decided we'd probably made the right choice. But still . . .

'Do you think we should rent somewhere in town?' I said. 'A little pied-à-terre in Clifton, perhaps?'

'We do spend rather a lot of time down here,' agreed Lady Hardcastle. 'But does Clifton do "pieds-à-terre"? It's all grand houses as far as I can make out.'

'A nice town house on Royal York Crescent?'

'It's something to think about, certainly. But we're starting to spend a lot of time in London, too. Perhaps we should think about taking some small apartments there instead. I rather like those big red mansion buildings in Kensington, near the Albert Hall.'

'Or how about both?'

She chuckled.

'And have my friends accuse me of being a profligate spend-thrift? What about the staff? The rates? The bills? There are so many incidental expenses. But it would be rather jolly, wouldn't it?'

'It was just a thought,' I said.

We approached the door of Le Quai and found the blinds up, but the door locked. Lady Hardcastle rapped on the jamb with the handle of her umbrella and leaned in to peer through the glass pane in the door.

'There are people in there moving about,' she said. 'I can see them.'

She rapped again and an irritable face loomed out of the semi-darkness. It was Jean-Pierre.

'We are closed until 'alf past,' he said, crossly, in an exaggerated form of his usually pleasing French accent.

Lady Hardcastle grinned and pointed to her own face.

'Ah,' he said. 'It is my old friends. One moment.'

He unbolted the door and opened it.

'Good morning, my lady,' he said. 'I didn't realize it was you. But I am afraid we are still closed, even to our dearest friends.'

'I know, dear,' said Lady Hardcastle. 'But may we step inside for just a moment? I have a favour to ask.'

He stood aside and allowed us to enter.

'The thing is, Wally dear,' she said conspiratorially, 'we rather need your help with a little . . . subterfuge. It's actually frightfully important.'

He started a little at the use of his real name, but it seemed to have the intended effect and his face became serious.

'What can I do?' he asked in his own Bristolian burr. 'Is it one o' your cases?'

'It is indeed,' she said. 'You know of the murder at the theatre on Tuesday evening?'

'I do. One of the actors got stabbed. It's all anyone's been talkin' about.'

'I have booked your private dining room for lunch under the name of Webster-Green, and the entire theatre company shall be joining us.'

'I wondered who that was. Table for ten for lunch. Chef was delighted.'

'Happy to oblige – I'm rather looking forward to it. Even if we get nothing from the meeting, the meal will doubtless be exquisite.'

Jean-Pierre bowed humbly, as though he were responsible for the quality of the food.

'But when we arrive,' she continued, 'it is absolutely imperative that you do not acknowledge that you know us. Lady Bickle will be among our group so please greet her as you normally would, but you have no idea who Lady Webster-Green and Miss Goodheart are.' She gestured towards me and I curtseyed. 'As far as the actors know, we are visitors from Dorsetshire.'

'Leave it with me, my lady,' he said, reverting to his French persona. 'Gaston and Madeleine will be serving in the private dining room, and I shall make sure they know that you are here incognito.'

'Thank you, dear.' She slipped him an extremely generous tip. 'Don't make too much of it, but do please try to make sure there are no slip-ups, or we'll be scuppered.'

Jean-Pierre looked discreetly at the gratuity and beamed. He leaned towards us.

'Thank you . . . Lady Webster-Green,' he said as Wally Dudden once more. 'And don't you worry. Gordon and Madge knows all about pretendin' to be someone else.' He winked.

'You're a good man, Jean-Pierre,' said Lady Hardcastle. 'This won't be forgotten. We'll leave you to your work now and see you in an hour.'

'I look forward to greeting you and your glamorous party,' he said.

'Steady on, dear. They're only actors.'

With a smile and a wave, Lady Hardcastle swept out.

I followed her and we made our way back to the Rolls.

'We ought to move this,' I said when we reached it.

'Why, dear? It's perfectly safe here, isn't it?'

'Perfectly safe,' I said, 'but very distinctive. How many Rolls-Royce Silver Ghost Roadsters are there in Bristol, do you think?'

'Just this one, I hope. I do like having a unique motor car . . . Oh, I see what you mean. Rather difficult to be in disguise as Lady Webster-Green if we're tootling around in Lady Hardcastle's motor car. We'll find a suitably discreet spot and walk back.'

Shortly before twelve we returned to Le Quai, where Jean-Pierre took our coats and showed us to the private dining room on the first floor. He introduced himself warmly and was scrupulous throughout in calling Lady Hardcastle by her assumed name, even though the rest of our party had yet to arrive.

'This is enchanting, Jean-Pierre, thank you. Please show our guests in when they arrive.'

'Certainly, *madame*,' he said with a bow.

'Oh, and do you have any Krug '99?'

'The Krug, *madame*? *Non*. We have Pol Roger from that year, though.'

'Wonderful. Can you bring two bottles, please, and put another two on ice for later.'

'Of course, *madame*. Gaston will be with you presently. Enjoy your meal.'

He left us to decide on the seating arrangements.

'I though we ought to sit over there, on the far side,' said Lady Hardcastle, pointing across the table. 'If we leave a gap we can get two in between us and one each on either side. Maximize our contact, as it were.'

'Good plan,' I said.

We shuffled round the table and were just about to settle down to wait, when the door opened and Jean-Pierre entered, leading Lady Bickle and an assemblage of smartly, but not expensively, dressed actors.

'Allow me, my lady,' said Jean-Pierre, ushering them in. 'Your guests have arrived, Lady Webster-Green. Right on time.'

'We always pride ourselves on being able to make our entrances on time,' said the man at the front of the group. I recognized him from the play as Harris Bridges. He was just as handsome without his stage make-up, and carried himself with self-assured poise.

Lady Bickle eased her way through the throng at the door and took over from Bridges.

'Lady Webster-Green,' she said, 'and Miss Goodheart. Thank you so very much for inviting us all to luncheon. I think I ought to try to introduce everyone. Let me see. This is Harris Bridges.' She indicated the actor with the impeccable timing.

'Your prize for being first in line is to sit next to me,' said Lady Hardcastle, patting the seat of the chair.

Bridges needed no further persuasion and was making his way around the table before Lady Hardcastle had finished her second pat.

'Then we have Sarah Griffin.'

I recognized her from the play, too. She was the younger of the two actresses we had seen, and was even more beautiful in real life than on the stage.

'If you would sit between Violet and Mr Bridges, dear, that would be splendid.'

'Next is Emrys Thornell.'

A bespectacled man in a jacket of burgundy velvet smiled through his neatly trimmed beard.

'You sit with Violet, Mr Thornell,' said Lady Hardcastle.

'This is Patrick Cowlin.'

Another handsome man, younger than Bridges and with a slightly intense look about him.

'And you sit here with me,' said Lady Hardcastle, patting the chair to her left.

'Hugo you know, of course,' said Lady Bickle. 'And that's us all for the moment.'

She sat next to Patrick Cowlin, and Hugo Bartlett made himself comfortable next to her.

Lady Hardcastle looked around the table.

'We seem to be two short, dear,' she said. 'Where are Nancy and Rosalie? They said they'd come and I was so looking forward to meeting them in less dangerous circumstances.'

'Dangerous?' said Sarah.

'We saw them on Christmas Steps yesterday,' said Lady Bickle. 'Nancy was absolutely convinced she was about to tumble to her death.'

'Nancy can be like that. But it's not like her to miss a nosh-up.'

'I'm sure it's nothing,' said Lady Bickle. 'They're staying in the same digs so they've probably been held up together.'

'Fighting the landlady, I shouldn't wonder,' said Bridges. 'She's a . . . formidable woman.'

'She's an absolute horror,' said Sarah. 'I refuse to stay there when we visit Bristol.'

'That's probably it, then,' said Lady Bickle. 'I don't expect they'll be long, but I think we should start without them.'

'Of course, of course,' said Lady Hardcastle, genially. 'And they'll be all the more welcome when they get here.'

It took a few moments to get everyone settled, but we got there in the end.

Gaston arrived with two ice buckets on stands, each holding a bottle of champagne. He set them down in the corner of the room and then presented one of the bottles to Lady Hardcastle.

She took her reading glasses from her handbag and put them on, making an unnecessary show of inspecting the label.

'Just what the doctor ordered, dear,' she said. 'Thank you.'

Ordinarily she would have accepted the bottle with an airy wave of her hand, having discreetly glanced at the label to check it was the wine she had ordered. Lady Webster-Green, apparently, was a good deal more fastidious about these things. Unless the airy nonchalance was the act and this was the real Emily Charlotte Ariadne Hardcastle née Featherstonhaugh. I smiled to myself and wondered what Violet Goodheart's character quirks might reveal about me.

While all this was going on, Madeleine had arrived with a tray of champagne coupes, which she added to each place setting. I wondered briefly if she would remove any of the other glasses but reasoned that until we had ordered they would probably have to remain. I was right, and the table was soon glinting with a forest of glassware.

With a practised flourish, Gaston tore off the top of the foil capsule, twisted the cage free and released the cork with a soft pop. He opened the second bottle with the same smooth ease and presented Lady Hardcastle with both corks, each back in its cage. He poured everyone a glass of bubbling decadence before silently disappearing.

Lady Hardcastle picked up her glass and I thought she was about to propose a toast – or at the very least offer a welcome to our guests – but Harris Bridges beat her to it. Before she could open her mouth he was already on his feet. I spotted the momentary flash of irritation in her eyes, but I doubt anyone else saw it. She covered it immediately with her customary warm smile.

'Lady Webster-Green,' said Bridges, slightly too loudly for the small room. 'Miss Goodheart. Friends. It has been a difficult few days, and we bear our burden of grief as we try to carry on, but I think that's what Paul would have wanted. We had our disagreements—'

Stage manager Patrick Cowlin let out a derisive *pfft*, and Sarah Griffin rolled her eyes.

'—but he was a good egg, and I think I speak for us all when I say that we shall miss him dearly. But as he always said, "The show must go on." So raise your glasses, please, ladies and gentlemen. To Paul.'

Everyone solemnly returned the toast.

Still on his feet, Bridges turned to Lady Hardcastle on his left.

'I'm sorry if this is rather too sombre for the occasion, my lady,' he said, 'but this is the first time we've all been together like this—'

'We're not all together,' said Emrys Thornell, disdainfully. 'Nancy and Rosie are late. Remember?'

Bridges glanced at the two empty chairs.

'Ah . . . well . . . yes . . .' he said.

Sarah rolled her eyes again.

'Well . . . ah . . .' He had clearly not been expecting to be bar-racked for toasting their departed colleague. 'All I was going to do was to thank you, Lady Webster-Green – and you, Miss Goodheart – for inviting us for this splendid luncheon and—'

'Oh, do sit down, Bridges, there's a good chap,' said Thornell. 'You're making an ass of yourself now.'

Bridges began to puff up, but a quick glance around the table told him the room wasn't with him and he slowly subsided into his seat.

'Thank you, dear,' said Lady Hardcastle, as though completely unaware of the tension that had gripped the room. 'But I rather feel that you're the ones doing me a kindness. As Mr Bartlett might have told you—'

'Hugo, please,' said Bartlett, softly.

'As Hugo might have told you,' she continued, 'I have it in mind to try to establish my own theatre company on the south coast, and my motives for dragging you here are entirely selfish – though, I hope, benign. I wish to get to know you all a little better, to find out what makes a group like yours tick. You all seem to get along so well—'

I glanced around the table for signs of disagreement . . . and found them everywhere. Sarah Griffin rolled her eyes yet again, Patrick Cowlin let out another *pfft* which almost drowned out Hugo Bartlett's tut, Emrys Thornell let out a small 'Hah!' under his breath, and Harris Bridges looked down at his menu and shook his head. It was possible that he was dismayed by the price of the *Suprême de Barbue avec Sauce Hollandaise*, but it was more likely that he, too, completely disagreed with Lady Hardcastle's assump-tions about their group.

Lady Hardcastle herself noted all this, too, I was sure, but Jo Webster-Green was made of more oblivious stuff and continued without even the slightest pause.

'—and I just want to know what mix of personalities I should be seeking to assemble, in order to form the ideal troupe. Do you say "troupe"? Please tell me I've not got it wrong.'

'You're right enough,' said Bridges, 'though many prefer "company". You know, when I gave my Hamlet in the West End in '96, I—'

His no doubt riveting anecdote was interrupted by the arrival of Jean-Pierre, who ushered in an extremely flustered Nancy Beaufort. She had very obviously been crying.

'Good lord, Nancy,' said Bridges. 'Are you all right? Whatever's the matter?'

'It's Rosie,' she said. 'She's been arrested. The police inspector says she murdered Paul.'

Chapter Five

Everyone at the luncheon table started talking at once. Most expressed disbelief at the very idea of 'dear Rosie' being capable of such a thing, but I noted that Sarah Griffin didn't join in. Harris Bridges seemed to have appointed himself the leader of the group, and he gave them a few more moments to vent their incredulity before trying to bring them to order.

'Friends,' he said, holding up his hands for calm. 'Friends, please.'

'It's just not possible,' said Nancy. 'She and Paul were so much in love. She wouldn't have killed him. She couldn't.'

'She couldn't,' agreed Patrick Cowlin. 'Not Rosie. She's not got it in her.'

'Everyone's got it in them,' said Sarah. 'Isn't that the basis of almost every play we perform? Everyone has something terrible hidden inside them.'

'Well, of course you'd think ill of her,' said Nancy. 'She stole Paul from you.'

'She didn't steal . . . Oh, never mind. But my point stands. We don't know what anyone is capable of until they do it.'

'But Rosie could never . . .' Nancy said again. 'She just . . . I mean, she's been in a shocking state since Paul's death. She—'

'Since Paul's murder,' said Sarah. 'Let's not be coy.'

'Well, that rather amplifies my point, wouldn't you say? She was heartbroken at having the love of her life cruelly taken from her.'

'Or racked with guilt at having stabbed him to death in a fleeting moment of rage.'

'Ladies, please,' said Bridges. 'This isn't getting us anywhere. Nancy, just tell us what happened.'

'It was just as we were getting ready to leave,' she said. 'I'd gone into her room to ask if I could borrow her scarf – you know, that blue silk one with the knotted fringe? She doesn't wear it much but I thought it would go wonderfully with this dress. It's exactly the right shade for my new overcoat, too, I—'

'So you went to her room . . .' said Bridges.

'I did. And we were there chattering away. I do love sharing digs with her, especially here in Bristol. It's so wonderful to have an ally when we're staying at Mrs Rippon's. She's an absolute menace, you know. Of course you do. The rest of you won't stay there. But—'

'And then what?'

'Oh, of course. Then we heard a terribly loud rapping on the front door. Not the friendly rat-a-tat-tatting of a pal or a salesman, but the fierce, insistent hammering of someone on official business.'

I briefly worried that Sarah might make herself giddy with her renewed burst of eye-rolling.

Nancy continued, undaunted.

'There was a pause, then we heard Mrs Rippon opening it up. There were voices. Mrs Rippon's was indignant – I'm not sure she knows any other way to behave, to be honest. I don't think I've ever seen her approve of anything. The other voice belonged to a man. There was a good deal of to-ing and fro-ing but we still couldn't hear exactly what was being said. After a minute or so of that, there were boots on the stairs and Rosie's door burst open. Mrs Rippon said, "You can't just go burstin' into a young lady's room like that.

What if she's in a state of undress?" Though, to be honest, I just think she was put out that she wasn't the one doing the bursting-in. She would have loved that. But there, standing in the doorway, with Mrs Rippon hovering in the background like some sort of evil carrion crow waiting to pick at the carcass after a kill – she always looks like a crow to me. It's the black shawl . . .'

'A policeman?' offered Bridges. 'There was a policeman at Rosie's door?'

'There was,' said Nancy. 'It was Inspector Wyatt. And that enormous sergeant from the theatre. Do you remember him? I'm not sure why he had to come. They can't have been expecting Rosie to cut up rough.'

'What did he say, dear?' asked Lady Hardcastle.

There was a moment's surprised silence as everyone stared at her, as though they'd forgotten we were there. I rather hoped Bridges was irked at having the spotlight taken from him, but he hid it well if he was.

'He said, "Miss Rosalie Harding, I am arresting you for the murder of Paul Singleton on Tuesday, the seventh of November." Then there was some business about her having the right to silence, and taking things down and using them in evidence. Do you remember the play we did in '09 where Pat said "Trousers" in rehearsal when he was arrested? The Lord Chamberlain's Office would have had a fit if we'd left it in.'

'Did he say anything else?' asked Lady Hardcastle. 'Did he give any reason for the arrest?'

'Not at first. Rosie said, "But it wasn't me. I didn't kill him. I loved him." She was already starting to cry. And Wyatt said, "The murder weapon was from the theatre's props store and you had access to it. I have it on good authority that you were seen with it during the day." And he snapped the handcuffs on and led her out. I tried to follow, but the burly sergeant told me there was nothing

I could do, and then they were gone. Mrs Rippon started on at me about having a murderer in her house, but I didn't listen. I just put on my hat and coat and rushed straight here.'

'If it was in the props store,' said Sarah, 'then we all had access to the knife. If that's his only evidence it could be any of us. And actually—'

'It wasn't used in the play, though,' said Emrys Thornell. 'So one wonders why she might have had it during the day. If, indeed, she did.'

'And who this "good authority" might be,' said Patrick Cowlin. 'Perhaps the inspector ought to be talking to him to find out why he was trying to drop Rosie in it.'

'She was bringing it to me,' said Hugo Bartlett. 'I'm working on a comedy about a troupe of players putting on a Shakespeare play. I wanted to be reminded what an Elizabethan dagger looked like.'

We were interrupted by the arrival of Gaston, who had come to refresh our glasses and take our orders. I had expected that the shock of the news might have dulled their appetites, or at least made it hard for them to concentrate on the menu, but they each rattled off their order without a trace of hesitancy. Even poor, distraught Nancy managed to order a heroically large meal for herself. I'd seen the like in the circus as a child when audiences were down and times were hard – if there was free food on offer, nothing would stop performers from wolfing it down, no matter what else might be going on. Money was clearly tight in the theatrical world, too.

Lady Hardcastle opened her mouth to speak, but Bridges beat her to it.

She hid her irritation slightly less well this time, and I briefly wondered if Bridges was going to get an earful, but she quickly regained her composure and allowed him to continue. Once again

I thought no one had noticed, but Sarah gave me a conspiratorial wink. His behaviour was clearly nothing new to her.

'What happened to the knife after that?' asked Bridges.

'It was stuck in Paul's chest between the third and fourth ribs,' said Cowlin, drily.

'Patrick!' said Bridges. 'A little decorum, please.'

'I put it on that little table in the corridor,' said Bartlett. 'It wasn't quite what I wanted. And, as with the "trousers" gag, I thought the Lord Chamberlain's Office might have trouble with the amusing exchange that came to me about a "bollock dagger".'

'I can imagine any man having trouble with a bollock dagger,' said Sarah.

'Especially Paul,' said Cowlin.

Bridges glared at him.

'I'll not tell you again, Patrick,' he said.

'I'm not entirely certain you have the authority to tell anyone anything, old thing, but my apologies if anyone feels I have been insensitive.'

'So if Hugo put the knife out on the table in the corridor, anyone could have taken it,' said Nancy. 'Wyatt has even less reason to suspect Rosie.'

'Did any of you see it there later in the day?' asked Lady Hardcastle quickly, before Bridges could butt in again.

'It was there during Act One,' said Sarah. 'That's what I was about to tell you just now when I was so rudely interrupted.' She looked at Thornell. 'I had to nip to the you-know-where during Paul and Rosie's argument scene. It was still there when I came back, too.'

'So we can assume it was on the table in plain view right up to the moment it was used,' said Lady Hardcastle. 'That's interesting.'

'How is it interesting?' asked Bridges.

'Well, it prompts one to surmise that the murder wasn't planned. An organized killer wouldn't leave the acquisition of the murder weapon to chance. They'd sort it all out beforehand – they wouldn't hope they'd find something suitable when the time came, or, having found an acceptable weapon, they wouldn't leave it lying about where someone could tidy it away. It would be concealed somewhere convenient for retrieval at the fateful moment. Mr Singleton was murdered on stage during the interval, so if the dagger was out in plain sight during the first act, it's safe to assume that the killer picked it up on the spur of the moment.'

'Good heavens,' said Sarah. 'How very clever. I should never have thought of something like that.'

Lady Hardcastle responded with a demure shrug and a shy smile, as though she didn't consider herself even remotely clever and, gosh, how lovely of Sarah to say so. Her acting skills had improved markedly since her failed appearance as Guildenstern, and were now something to behold – even I was fooled for a moment.

The first course arrived and conversation briefly halted as the actors dived hungrily into their food. I looked past Bridges and Sarah, catching Lady Hardcastle's eye. She gave me a this-is-going-well smile and I nodded. We were learning a lot.

Lunch passed all too quickly and we left Le Quai with many questions still unanswered, but I was, at least, beginning to get a feel for who the Bartlett Players were. Once the initial shock of Rosalie's arrest had been thoroughly explored, they calmed down and took a polite interest in our plans for a Bournemouth-based theatre company. They had a great many interesting suggestions to make and I caught myself wondering if it might actually be a good idea. Perhaps we should abandon the Secret Service Bureau, leave the crime-ridden streets of Littleton Cotterell, and open a comedy theatre by the seaside. I smiled to myself at the thought.

With lunch finally over, we stood on the street in the chilly November air as the actors said their goodbyes. They were effusive in their thanks and I tried to remember if I'd ever previously been called 'darling' so many times, by so many people, in so few minutes. It ought to have been irritating but it was actually oddly touching.

Mr Bartlett asked if we'd like to visit the theatre one evening.

'I haven't been able to secure any tickets until late next week,' he said, 'but you'd be more than welcome to visit us backstage on Monday and see how the show is run, if that would amuse you.'

'It most certainly would,' said Lady Hardcastle. 'Thank you.'

'Come to the stage door any time after six. I'll make sure Haggarty is expecting you. He adopts a rather gruff manner when it comes to keeping people out, but he's a charming fellow underneath it.'

'Thank you, dear, that would be wonderful. We shall see you on Monday.'

Although we had collectively managed to get through half a dozen bottles of Le Quai's finest champagne, neither I nor Lady Hardcastle had drunk more than a glassful each, so I was able to look on with amusement as the players tottered off towards the theatre. I hoped either that they would sober up in time for the evening show, or that a little tipsiness might add spice to their performances.

Lady Bickle, too, had been less than abstemious. She had been giggling charmingly and flirting outrageously with Patrick Cowlin throughout the meal, and was now swaying gently in the autumn breeze as we waved goodbye to her theatrical friends.

'How are you getting home, dear?' asked Lady Hardcastle, kindly.

'I thought Stanley was going to pick me up, but I seem to have forgotten to tell him.'

The Bickles called their chauffeur Stanley even though his name was Alfred – Stanley had been their first chauffeur's name, and it had become a family joke to use that name for all of them. I'd asked Alfred about it once – or Fred, as he preferred – and he'd said he honestly didn't mind what they called him as long as they were polite about it and paid his wages on time.

'I actually quite likes it, to tell the truth,' he'd said. 'It's a way to separate work and private, too, if you knows what I mean. I can be Stanley at work, then Fred when I goes home to the missus.'

I thought it a little rude myself, but offence is in the ear of the behearer, so I let it be.

'We can't let you walk back like that,' said Lady Hardcastle. 'One of us can run you home in the Rolls and then pop back for the other.'

'Or you two go on in the car and I'll meet you at the top of the hill,' I said. 'I don't mind the walk.'

Lady Bickle's face was scrunched in puzzlement.

'Walk back like what?' she said, having finally worked out what was troubling her.

'You're squiffy, dear,' said Lady Hardcastle. 'Soaked. Spiffed. Three sheets in the wind. All mops and brooms. You are in Liquorpond Street with more than a touch of boskiness about you. You are wet-handed, what-nosed and whittled. You are, in short, as tight as a boiled owl.'

Lady Bickle stumbled slightly as a light gust plucked at her overcoat.

'I fear you may be right, dear,' she said, with another delightful giggle. 'Do you think anyone noticed?'

'Of course not,' I said. 'You were charming. You always are.'

'Oh, thank you, dear. You're so very sweet.'

Lady Hardcastle looked as though she might start teasing her, but I gave her a warning look and she satisfied herself instead with a grin and a wink.

'If you're sure you don't mind taking Shanks's pony, then,' she said to me, 'I'll get our fuddled friend home safely.'

I walked with them as far as the Rolls and then set off across the Tramways Centre on my way towards Park Street. I dodged among the trams and the motor taxis, over to the shops and the Drawbridge Hotel on the other side.

It was a long, steep walk up Park Street. The shops were busy and there was plenty of traffic on the road. I crossed just after Great George Street so as to be on the left-hand side when I finally reached the top.

On I trudged. I considered myself a reasonably active person. I still followed the exercise regime taught me by our friend in China, and I wasn't afraid of a brisk walk, but by the time I finally rounded the corner on to Queens Road I was puffing like a badly maintained hot-water geyser.

I paused by the WSPU shop at number 37. The windows, as always, were full of posters, and I smiled at the sight of the mannequin in the white dress and green, white and purple 'Votes for Women' sash behind them. For a moment I contemplated popping in to see if Lizzie Worrel was working that day. We'd kept in touch with her since the business during the General Election of 1910, though we'd not actually seen her for a few months. It would be nice to talk to her, but I didn't want to get stuck chatting when I ought to be joining Ladies Hardcastle and Bickle.

The Rolls was parked on Berkeley Square with Lady Hardcastle's customary exuberant disregard for neatness or other road users, so

I knew they'd arrived at least moderately safely. I rang the bell at number 5, Berkeley Crescent.

Williams answered the door almost immediately.

'Good afternoon, Miss Armstrong. Or should I say, "Miss Goodheart"?'

'They told you, then?'

'Lady Bickle could hardly contain her excitement at being involved in a subterfuge, miss,' he said with a smile. 'They're waiting for you in the drawing room. I shall bring tea in just a moment.'

He took my hat and coat and I found my own way to the drawing room, where I knocked and entered.

Lady Hardcastle tiptoed towards me with her finger to her lips.

'Quiet as a mouse,' she whispered. 'The poor dear's fast asleep. One minute she was chattering and giggling, the next there was a mighty yawn and she just flollopped.'

'I'll get her lady's maid to bring her a blanket,' I said.

'You're a poppet.'

'I am, it's true,' I said. 'Since we're in town with time on our hands, what say we nip down to the Bridewell to see if Inspector Sunderland is about?'

'Oh, what a good idea,' said Lady Hardcastle. 'We can swap news.'

I found Miss Gossman sewing a button on Lady Bickle's overcoat and told her what had happened. She tutted affectionately and assured me that she would take care of her mistress.

Lady Hardcastle, meanwhile, had written a note, which she left on the table beside our sleeping friend.

We retrieved our hats and coats, tiptoed out, and returned to the Rolls.

To my slight dismay, Sergeant Massive Beard was on desk duty at the Bridewell when we arrived. We'd encountered this surly guardian of police headquarters more than once before and had never been welcomed. Nor, now I came to think about it, had we ever learned his real name.

As always, he was sitting at a desk behind the counter, writing in a large daybook. The sound of ladies' boots on the tiled floor did nothing to break his moustache-sucking concentration.

Lady Hardcastle approached the counter and waited.

He carried on writing laboriously in the ledger.

She rang the bell.

He continued to ignore her.

She looked at me and raised her eyebrows.

'I say, Sergeant . . . ?' she said, looking to me to supply his name.

I shrugged. I had no idea what his name was.

The sergeant, though, finally deigned to look up.

'Lady Hardcastle, isn't it?' he said, imperiously. 'I'll be with you in a moment . . . my lady.'

He returned to his work.

Lady Hardcastle rang the bell again.

The sergeant slammed down his pen, then spent an agonizingly long while trying to blot the resulting ink spatter, which had, I fervently hoped, ruined the neatness of his ledger. He glared at Lady Hardcastle as though his petulance was entirely her fault.

He stood and approached the counter, still looking most put out at this impertinent interruption.

'Yes?' he said. 'What can I do for you?'

'Would you be an absolute poppet,' said Lady Hardcastle in her best dizzy-socialite tones, 'and tell Inspector Sunderland we're here?'

'Is the inspector expecting you?'

'No, I shouldn't think so.'

'Then I'm afraid I'm not at all sure I should disturb him. The detectives are busy men.'

'They are,' she said, smiling. 'And they work wonders keeping the streets safe for the citizens of this magnificent city. But if you would do us the kindness of picking up that new telephone by your elbow and calling him, we can find out whether he'd be delighted to see us or whether he would prefer we sling our hooks.'

I wondered why we had to go through this same rigmarole whenever we visited the Bridewell. Perhaps it was a special Bristol Police policy to weed out time-wasters. Or perhaps it was simply that Sergeant Massive Beard enjoyed tormenting us.

Either way, the sergeant seemed to realize that on this occasion the irresistible police force had met the immovable Hardcastle object, and I almost felt sorry for him as I saw the will to fight drain from him. With great reluctance, he picked up the telephone. He flicked a couple of switches and waited.

'Sorry to disturb you, sir,' he said after a few seconds, 'but there's a couple of' – he paused pointedly as he looked us up and down – 'ladies here to see you . . . Lady Hardcastle and her companion . . . Yes, sir, that's right . . . Very well, sir. Thank you.'

He replaced the earpiece.

'You know the way,' he said with a dismissive wave of the hand. He didn't wait for Lady Hardcastle's thanks before returning to his newly stained blotter.

We set off towards the stairs.

Inspector Sunderland's office was neater than the last time we'd seen it. Gone were the teetering piles of manila folders and scraps of loose paper. The teacup beside the blotter on the battered desk was alive with steaming, fresh tea and there were no dirty cups to be seen. I nodded appreciatively.

He stood to greet us.

'Welcome, ladies,' he said. 'Do, please, make yourselves at home.'

His visitor chairs were also unusually free of clutter, and I smiled as I sat.

'I can be tidy sometimes,' he said, noticing my look.

'Of course,' I said. 'But you have to admit that it's quite a difference from the last time we were here.'

'That was nearly two years ago. You can't expect me to live in a pigsty for ever.'

'Well . . .' I said, looking at Lady Hardcastle.

'You do make such a fuss, dear,' she said. 'I know exactly where everything is in my studio.'

'So do I. It's on the floor.'

'Oh, pish and fiddlesticks, you old fusspot. Good afternoon, Inspector dear, thank you for seeing us.'

'It's always a pleasure, my lady,' he said. 'And to be honest I'm delighted to have an excuse for a break. Would you care for some tea?' He gestured towards a large pot on his desk.

'Not for me, thank you, no,' said Lady Hardcastle.

'Nor for me,' I said. 'We've just come from lunch at Le Quai so I'm stuffed.'

'It's all right for some, eh? How the other half lives.'

'We were there on your behalf, Inspector dear,' said Lady Hardcastle. 'We were talking to the theatre troupe.'

'Ah, then I take it back,' he said. 'Though I'm afraid I don't think the Chief Constable would entertain an expenses claim.'

'I'm sure I can swallow the cost, if not the last of the petits fours – I confess I'm rather stuffed, too, and I had to admit defeat.'

'And how were they?'

'Delicious. The chef is a marvel. There were some little tiny almond things that looked frightfully appealing, but I couldn't eat another morsel.'

'The actors, my lady. How were the actors?'

She flashed her twinkliest smile. She knew what he'd meant.

'The actors? Most of them were fine, though one was absent.'

'Ill? Done a bunk?'

'Arrested.'

'By Wyatt?'

'Yes. He clomped in to Rosalie Harding's digs this morning in the company of a burly sergeant and hauled her off to the chokey.'

'That's quick work,' said the inspector, though he didn't seem genuinely impressed.

'Quick, yes, though I might have said "hasty", myself. It may yet turn out that she's guilty, but his sole reason for the arrest was that she had access to the murder weapon and had been seen with it earlier in the day.'

'Have you spoken to him, then?'

'No, one of the other women was in her room borrowing a scarf at the time. She saw everything. It's a lovely scarf, incidentally. They have wonderful taste, these actors. But anyway, when we spoke to them over lunch it turned out they all had access to the knife, so a decent defence brief will make mincemeat of him.'

The inspector frowned.

'This is precisely what I was afraid of when he took over,' he said.

'Can you do anything?' I asked.

'Not without contradictory evidence. There are still rules and procedures to follow. I agree with you that the arrest is probably the result of an inept officer going off at half-cock, but we have to allow the possibility that he might be right, even if for the wrong reason.'

'Then we shall make it our business to find more evidence,' said Lady Hardcastle. 'We're going to be backstage at the theatre on Monday evening, when we should be able to get a better idea of how the events of that fateful night played out.'

'Thank you,' he said. 'I do appreciate your efforts. Are you sure you won't join me in a cup of tea?'

I was poised to tut disappointedly should Lady Hardcastle tell him she wasn't certain we'd all fit in such tiny cups, but instead she said, 'Oh, go on, then, if you're having another.'

Chapter Six

Back at the house we discovered that Gwen had persuaded Miss Jones to help her prepare roast beef for dinner. Gwen herself added the finishing touches when we arrived home, and we sat down to eat as soon as Lady Hardcastle had fetched a couple of bottles of her favourite Bordeaux from the wine rack.

The meal was magnificent in its simplicity. Roast beef, roast potatoes, perfectly cooked cabbage and carrots. The gravy was a culinary triumph all on its own. I congratulated Gwen on her efforts, saying she was almost as good a cook as I was. This earned me a kick under the table, but that's what sisters are for.

Lady Hardcastle carved the beef. Ordinarily, if Miss Jones hadn't already neatly cut it into wafer-thin slices, we just hacked at it ourselves. But today we had a guest – even if she was family – and so Lady Hardcastle hacked at it alone. In fact, she was surprisingly adept with a knife and made rather a good job of it.

Despite our earlier protestations of fullness, we found ourselves inexplicably hungry and tucked in eagerly.

'Pass the horseradish, Floss,' said Gwen around a mouthful of potato.

Shaking my head, I pushed the small bowl of freshly made horseradish sauce across the table.

'So, how was lunch?' she asked as she spooned the piquant condiment on to the side of her plate. 'Did the actors behave themselves?'

'They were reasonably good company,' I said. 'Those of them that were there, at least.'

'You had no-shows? It's not like performers to miss a free lunch.'

'One of them had been arrested,' said Lady Hardcastle. 'And her pal was caught up in it all.'

'So it was one of the actresses? I can't say I'm surprised. I always thought they were a funny lot. Which one?'

'Rosalie Harding has been arrested,' I said. 'But on the flimsiest of evidence. I'm not sure she did it.'

'You'll have to keep digging, then. But the rest of them enjoyed themselves?'

'They seemed to,' said Lady Hardcastle. 'Hugo Bartlett has invited us backstage on Monday by way of thanking us for the meal. But what of you, Gwenith dear? I worry that we have abandoned our houseguest.'

'Your unexpected, uninvited houseguest,' said Gwen. 'Don't you worry about me – I've been amusing myself. The ladies took me into the village after lunch and we had a lovely time at the Pig and Bucket.'

'Dog and Duck,' I said, reflexively.

Gwen laughed.

'Oh, you too?' said Lady Hardcastle. 'How marvellous. That's one of my absolute favourite games. I can't count how many times I've pretended to get a name wrong just to hear that adorable tone of frustration and disappointment in her voice as she sets me straight.'

'She just can't stop herself,' said Gwen with a mischievous grin.

'You'll both get what's coming to you one of these days,' I said.

'I am all atremble,' said Gwen. 'But tell me about your lunch. Was it delicious?'

'It was wonderful, dear,' said Lady Hardcastle. 'We're very lucky that such a talented chef has chosen to come to Bristol instead of London. And I was most impressed by the amount of food our thespian guests managed to put away.'

'And the champagne,' I added.

'They can drink, can they?' asked Gwen.

'They'd give your Dai's army mates a run for their money, certainly.'

'Not sure actors or artillerymen could beat that lot in the Cat and Bagpipes in the village, mind you.'

I sighed but said nothing. Gwen grinned.

'Those farmhands can definitely drink,' she said.

'They're a thirsty lot,' agreed Lady Hardcastle. 'I'm glad you had a nice afternoon, though. Did your appearance cause much of a stir?'

'My resemblance to little Flossie went unnoticed. Daisy worked it out, of course – she thought it was a "right laugh" – but everyone else just assumed I was her. I was with her mates, after all.'

'I'd not say Edna and Dan were my "mates",' I said.

'No, but Blodwen Jones is one of your pals. *Duw*, but she was telling some tales.'

'I'm sure she was. Some of them are true, too – she, Daisy, Cissy Slocomb and I have had some . . . adventures.'

'You'd never think she was part of your little gang, the way she talks to you here.'

'She's at work when she's here,' I said.

'I suppose. It was fun, though – they're a grand lot in your village. Oh, and Daisy wants a word with you both.'

'Oh dear,' said Lady Hardcastle. 'What have we done now?'

Gwen laughed.

'You'd know that better than I would,' she said. 'But she wants your help with something.'

'I wonder what it could be. We'll have to ask her this evening.'

There was a lively atmosphere in the Dog and Duck by the time we arrived at about eight o'clock that evening. Saturdays were always busy, as everyone celebrated the end of another week's work.

Gwen and I left Lady Hardcastle to try to secure a table while we went to the bar.

Daisy was rushed off her feet as usual.

'Good evenin', ladies,' she said cheerfully when we finally managed to attract her attention. 'Oo-er, look, there's two of you.' She laughed. 'I could do with two of me tonight, I can tell you. What'll it be?'

'Two brandies, please, Dais,' I said. 'Got to keep out the cold. And . . . ?' I looked at Gwen.

'Glass of port, please,' she said.

Daisy cocked an eyebrow.

'I wondered who was drinkin' it on your table this afternoon,' she said.

'We're all a bit posh in our family,' I said.

'I'll have to see if we've got any,' said Daisy.

'I can't have drunk it all,' said Gwen. 'I only had two. Or three. Five at the most. Maybe I did drink it all.'

'No, it's not that. We've' – she leaned in close – 'we've 'ad some thefts. Someone's pinchin' the booze. I wanted to speak to you and Lady H about it, see if there's anythin' you could do.'

'I'll have to ask Herself,' I said. 'But I'm sure we could think of something.'

'Joe says he'll pay you. "Offer 'em the goin' rate," he said. What *is* your goin' rate?'

I frowned.

'I'm not sure we've ever been paid for our detective work,' I said. 'We just seem to do it out of a sense of duty.'

'Well, if you could find a way to see it as your duty to catch our pilferer, Joe would be eternally grateful, I'm sure. Free drinks for life at the very least, I reckon.'

'He might come to regret that,' I said. 'It's us, don't forget. But I'm sure we'll help if we can. If you get time for a break, come over and see us – you can tell us all about it.'

'Right you are. I'll get those drinks for you.'

She managed to find enough port for a decent measure for Gwen, and we took our glasses to set off to look for Lady Hardcastle.

We found her in the snug, where she had settled at the table by the window. The snug wasn't very popular with the locals and it was really only ever used by some of the village ladies. We found ourselves in the company of the vicar's housekeeper, Mrs Grove, and a farmer's wife whose name I could never remember. They nodded slightly baffled greetings and returned to their gossip.

'Ah, the Armstrong girls at last,' said Lady Hardcastle as we sat down. 'How's Daisy? Did you find out what she wanted?'

I gave Lady Hardcastle her brandy.

'There has been a spate of thefts,' I said. 'Intoxicating liquor is being removed from the premises by person or persons unknown, and Old Joe wishes, quite understandably, to put a stop to it. He wonders if we might help. He has offered gold and rubies, spices and fine silks, riches beyond the dreams of princes, even unto half his kingdom, if we can use our talents to capture the culprits.'

'Has he really?' said Lady Hardcastle.

'Well, not in so many words. He did offer to pay our going rate, though, and I estimate our current going rate to be at least that plus a quarter of mint humbugs and a ha'porth of chips. Daisy will be coming over later to give us the details and make us an offer.'

'We'll do it for nothing more than the heartfelt thanks of a grateful landlord.'

'I thought we might.'

'It's our duty.'

'I thought that, too.'

'Then it's agreed.'

'Can I help?' asked Gwen after taking a hearty sip of her port.

'Of course you can,' said Lady Hardcastle. 'The more the merrier. Do you have a plan?'

'Not yet, but leave it with me. I'm sure I'll think of something. There's just one thing, though: what's a spate?'

'Flood,' said Lady Hardcastle and I together.

'Then why not say that?'

'She makes a good point,' I said. 'A river might be in spate, but there's only ever spates of thefts and burglaries. You didn't have a spate of birthday presents.'

'That *was* a veritable spate, though. I'm a very lucky lady.'

'Oh, have I missed your birthday?' asked Gwen.

'It was on Tuesday,' I said. 'The seventh.'

'Happy belated birthday, then.' She raised her glass.

'Thank you, dear. You're most kind. But I don't know. Perhaps only undesirable things come in spates.'

'Perhaps,' I said. I looked up and saw Daisy coming towards us from the public bar. 'Talking of undesirable things . . .'

'You shut your trap, you,' she said. 'Can I join you?'

She sat down without waiting for a reply.

'What are you doing out here?' I said. 'I thought you were rushed off your feet. We weren't expecting to see you till nearly closing time.'

'Joe said I could take a break now, seein' as how I was goin' to be on official pub business.'

'Ah,' said Lady Hardcastle, 'the thefts, yes. Flo has mentioned them, but she was light on the detail. Can you tell us more?'

'We's a little light on detail ourselves, to tell the truth. Once a week – on a Thursday, usually – someone goes down into the cellar and pinches a bottle of sommat from the shelves at the bottom of the steps. We've tried keepin' an eye on the door, but it's round the back on the way to the jakes, so you can't see it from the bar. People's comin' and goin' all the time so you can't tell if they's off to use the facilities or pinch the booze. You 'as to stand outside and watch – that'd stop 'em all right – but eventually you gets called away to do somethin' else. That's when they strikes. We asked some of the more trustworthy regulars but they a'n't noticed nothin'. The thief always does it when it's busy, see, so no one sees anythin' out of the ordinary, just blokes comin' and goin' like always.'

'And they might be in on it,' said Gwen.

'They might – we thought of that – but it's hard to keep that sort of thing a secret, i'n't it. The more people who knows, the more chance someone'll let the cat out of the bag.'

'You're wise, Daisy, very wise,' said Lady Hardcastle. 'You should explain that to my brother Harry some time. His department has so many wild notions about conspiracies, about the secret plans and machinations of the country's enemies, but he never manages to convincingly explain how the sort of nincompoops who run the governments of the world could manage to concoct such elaborate schemes while still being incapable of feeding and housing their own populations. If you add your thoughts on the inherent difficulty of keeping a secret that large numbers of people know, we can shoot down the majority of his flights of fancy without having to put on our hats and trudge round the streets of Europe's great cities in search of non-existent plots.'

'I don't know about that,' said Daisy. 'Mr Featherstonhaugh always seems so brainy. He must know more than the likes of me.'

'Appearances can be deceptive, dear. I grudgingly allow that my darling brother is a very capable chap – we've trusted our lives to his abilities more than once – but don't let his bluff confidence fool you into thinking he knows it all. He was taught Bluff Confidence at school along with Latin and Greek, and the principal purpose of all three is to make him and his kind appear much cleverer than they really are.'

'Have you tried hiding in the cellar?' I asked, keen to get us back on track.

'Tried it last week,' she said. 'They waited till I had to nip to the you-know-where, and by the time I got back there was a bottle of scotch missing.'

'Surely someone must have seen them that time,' said Gwen.

'Joe was supposed to be watching, but he got distracted. Like always, no one else saw nothin' but, like always, it was busy, so people was back and forth all the time anyway. We—'

She was interrupted by Joe's toothless call from the public bar. 'Daisy!'

'Duty calls,' she said.

'Leave the problem with us,' said Lady Hardcastle. 'We shall put on our thinking caps and devise a means of catching your liquor larcenist.'

Daisy returned to her work, and we got on with the serious business of putting the world to rights.

◆　◆　◆

We returned to the house not long after ten o'clock with the problems of the world still unresolved and with no plan for catching the

Dog and Duck's phantom hooch thief. We were, though, in fine spirits and not yet ready for bed. I made cocoa and we retired to the drawing room, where Lady Hardcastle sat at the piano to play.

'Any requests?' she said, performing a series of flashy arpeggios.

'Play something cheerful,' said Gwen.

'Your wish is my command.'

While Lady Hardcastle played, Gwen and I studied the crime board.

'You're no nearer to a solution, are you?' said Gwen. 'I mean, you can fill in a few more details about this lot, but you don't know who did it.'

'Straight to the heart of it, as always,' I said. 'No, we're no nearer. Actually, that's not quite fair. We're getting an idea of who everyone is, at least. But what we need to do first is get Rosalie out of chokey. We couldn't say anything at lunch because Jo and Violet aren't amateur sleuths, but I do think it's our priority.'

'I agree, dear,' said Lady Hardcastle from the piano.

'How are you going to do that?' asked Gwen. 'Oh, you could bust her out.'

'Actually, we could,' I said. 'We've done it before—'

'Get out of it, you have not.'

'You've heard all the stories – you know we have.'

'Not in England, though.'

'Oh, I see what you mean. No, never in England – we like to keep the rozzers on our side in England. What we need is to find her an alibi.'

'How are you going to do that?'

'I don't know. What do you think, my lady? How are we going to do that?'

'We'll have to start asking people to tell us the story of the evening again,' said Lady Hardcastle without missing a beat.

'Won't they wonder why you're so curious, though?' asked Gwen. 'I mean, you're supposed to be talking about building a new theatre in Bognor—'

'Bournemouth,' I said before I could stop myself.

Lady Hardcastle laughed.

'A new theatre in *Bournemouth*,' continued Gwen with that special ha-ha-I-win-again smile that always made me want to kill her. 'So it's going to look a bit odd if you start asking lots of questions about their friend's murder.'

'You're not wrong,' I said.

Lady Hardcastle stopped playing.

'We need to take one of them into our confidence,' she said.

'This Sarah you've been talking about?' asked Gwen.

'She's my first choice,' said Lady Hardcastle. 'I think we can trust her to keep quiet. She's more than a little cynical about the rest of them.'

'She certainly is,' I said. 'Did you see her rolling her eyes every time that pompous twit Bridges opened his mouth?'

Gwen looked at the crime board.

'She has a motive for killing Singleton, though,' she said. 'Look: he jilted her for Rosalie.'

'True,' I said, 'but there was something about the way she was talking when someone brought that up at lunch. She seemed irritated by the way Nancy assumed Rosalie had stolen Paul from her, as though there was more to it. She didn't seem unduly upset by his betrayal, just annoyed by other people's reactions to it. There is another problem, though.'

'Oh?' said Lady Hardcastle.

'Yes. Don't you remember? When Nancy said Rosalie was innocent, Sarah wasn't at all convinced.'

'Only in as much as she thinks anyone is capable of murder.'

'If she could provide Rosalie with an alibi she would have spoken up then.'

'Ah, but during that spiky exchange with her, Nancy did land one good punch. She said that Sarah would obviously have it in for Rosalie. Regardless of who stole who from whom or what the exact circumstances were, Sarah could still feel a little spiteful glee at seeing her love rival banged up for a few days. I doubt she'd want to see an innocent woman hanged, though, no matter what had gone before. She might just be temporarily "forgetting" something that would exonerate Rosalie. If we allow her to tell the tale again, she might "remember".'

'Perhaps,' I said.

'We can be circumspect,' said Lady Hardcastle. 'But we have to trust someone at some point, and she's our most likely ally at the moment.'

'What about the writer?' asked Gwen. 'He invited you to the theatre – he obviously likes you. And your pal Georgie thinks the world of him.'

'I'm not sure about him,' said Lady Hardcastle. 'I can't quite put my finger on it, but there's something not quite honest about that man.'

'I have to agree,' I said. 'He's charming and pleasant, but there's more to him than meets the eye and I'm not certain I trust him, either.'

'You know best,' said Gwen. 'I've not met them.'

'It could still blow up in our faces,' said Lady Hardcastle, 'but I think we have to try with Sarah. No need to reveal our true identities yet—'

'That would almost certainly scupper everything,' I said.

'But if we say we're alarmed by Rosalie's arrest and want to help to free her, that might get her to tell us more.'

'We can but try,' I said.

'This is all very exciting,' said Gwen. 'Is there anything I can do to help? I'm a pretty good judge of character – I could come with you and size these actor people up.'

'I confess I had been wondering how to get you involved,' said Lady Hardcastle, 'but the problem was, and remains, transport – we only have a two-seater to get the three of us into town.'

'Unless . . .' I said.

'Unless what, dear?'

'Well, if you can amuse yourself for a few hours, Gwen and I could run into town without you. I could show her the sights and then perhaps we could drop in at the theatre.'

'Oh, I say, what a splendid idea. Of course you must. Would that be fun, Gwenith dear?'

'I don't know,' said Gwen, doubtfully. 'Is she a safe driver?'

'Imagine, if you will,' said Lady Hardcastle, 'a motor car driven not with the reckless exuberance of Mr Toad, but with the caution and timidity of Moley. It won't be in the least bit dangerous, but it might be quicker to walk.'

'I don't know who Mr Toad and Moley are,' said Gwen, 'but I can imagine Fussy Flossie behind the wheel, now you say it.'

'If you don't want to come, Gwen,' I said, 'you only have to say.'

'No, no, Floss *fach*, I'm sure we'll have a grand time.'

Gwen and I were up reasonably early next morning and drove uneventfully into town. It being Sunday, all the shops were shut and there was hardly anyone about, but it was good to be out with my sister. We rarely saw each other and it was comforting to be sitting with her in the burbling Rolls as I gave her a tour of the city.

Or tried to, at least. It occurred to me as I pointed out the hospital, then the Prince's Theatre, the WSPU shop, Lady Bickle's house, the museum and art gallery, that I didn't know very much about Bristol at all. I could find my way about with relative ease, but I didn't *know* it. I could tell her where to get a decent pair of shoes or a nice cream bun, but I was only dimly aware of its history and the lives of the people there.

I took her up to the Downs, and we stopped briefly on Circular Road to take in the view of the Avon Gorge. I drove along Ladies Mile, but only so I could point out that it was barely three-quarters of a mile long. We stopped at the observatory and took in the view of the Egyptian towers and elegant span of Brunel's wonderful Clifton Suspension Bridge.

'Now there's impressive, tell your mam,' said Gwen, laying on the Valleys accent and taking me instantly back to our childhood. 'He knew how to build a bridge, old Isambard. And what a name, too. No one calls their sons Isambard any more. Can you imagine it? "I've just put baby Isambard down for a nap." And there he'd be in a little top hat, sucking on a cigar and snoozing away with a contented smile on his little face.'

'But think of the things he'd make with his building bricks,' I said.

'Although if that sort of name-related thing worked, you'd be a famous nurse and I'd be a seamstress like Auntie Gwenith.'

'As it is, I'm a lady's maid and a tour guide.'

'Better at the one than the other,' said Gwen.

'I know,' I said. 'Sorry. We should have done this when everything was open.'

'Know any good tea shops? We could at least have a sit-down in the warm.'

'There's a Crane's in the village,' I said, pointing in the general direction of Clifton.

'Village?'

'Don't ask. Clifton is in the heart of the city but still refers to itself as a village. Or there's one on Christmas Steps.'

'That sounds more festive.'

'And quainter,' I said. 'It's in an older part of town. Come on, then – coffee and cake at Crane's.'

I parked, as usual, on Park Row and we made our way down to the coffee shop. We were shown to a table for two, where Gwen, unaware of my usual preference, took the seat facing the door. When out with Lady Hardcastle I almost never sat with my back to the exit, and it felt decidedly odd to be looking at the dim interior of the café instead of looking out for danger coming in from outside. But there really was no danger here and I let it pass.

A pot of Crane's excellent coffee arrived, accompanied by a selection of cakes. It felt as though I'd done nothing over the past few days but eat cake. There were worse ways to pass the time, though, I decided, and tucked in.

If chattering were a competitive sport, Gwen would have been British Champion (Ladies). We had always talked easily and I loved her company. We were deep in a discussion about the pleasures of an electrified home – hers and Dai's house in Woolwich was 'on the electric' – when I heard familiar voices behind me. It took me a few seconds to recognize them as belonging to some of the actors from the theatre.

'. . . won't get suspicious?' said Nancy Beaufort.

'Of what?' said Harris Bridges. 'We're three colleagues meeting for a Sunday-morning coffee. Nothing suspicious about that.'

'You both have a point,' said Patrick Cowlin. 'But it only becomes something we need to think about if anyone sees us all together. And, let's be honest, it's eleven o'clock on a Sunday – everyone else is still in bed.'

'Still with us, Floss?' said Gwen, who had been waiting quite a few seconds for a response to her most recent observation about the longevity of electric light bulbs.

'Sorry,' I said. I leaned forward and spoke more quietly. 'Those people behind us are some of the actors.'

Before I could tell her not to, she craned round me for a better look.

'Oh,' said Cowlin. 'Good morning, Miss Goodheart. Fancy seeing you here. Thank you so much for lunch yesterday, it was marvellous. Wasn't it marvellous?'

The other two agreed enthusiastically.

I worried briefly what Gwen might do, but I should have known better than to underestimate her. She was an Armstrong, after all.

'I can see how you might be confused,' she said with a smile and her uncanny impersonation of my accent. 'I'm afraid I'm not Violet. I'm her sister, Mrs Iris Foster.'

There wasn't even a hint of hesitation before she trotted out the false name. I wondered why she'd bothered since they didn't know her anyway, but it was still impressive to behold. I backed her up by turning round to greet them with a smile of my own.

'Good heavens,' said Cowlin. 'How . . .' I imagined he was trying to think of something other than 'marvellous'. He eventually settled on '. . . extraordinary,' but that made him wince. 'Oh, but I didn't mean . . .' he said, quickly. 'It's not that beautiful twins are curiosities . . . I just—'

'Do stop blathering, Patrick,' said Bridges. 'Good morning, Miss Goodheart, Mrs Foster. Would you care to join us? I'm sure they wouldn't mind if we pushed the two tables together.'

'We wouldn't want to interrupt you,' I said.

'Nonsense. Our business can wait. It would be far more enjoyable to share our morning with new friends.'

'In that case, let's see what we can do.'

After a good deal of scraping and shuffling, and having endured the disapproving looks of the waitresses, we managed to push the two tables together and arrange ourselves around them. Harris Bridges, as I had expected he would, took charge.

'We met Miss Goodheart yesterday,' he began.

'Violet, please,' I said with what I hoped was a winning smile.

'Violet,' he said. 'A pretty name. But your sister—'

'Iris,' said Gwen.

'Iris, yes. What a fragrantly floral pair. Iris hasn't met us, so allow me to make the introductions. I am Harris Bridges, a humble player. This enchanting young lady is Nancy Beaufort, soon to be a star. And finally, our handsome companion is another of our company, the formidable talent that is Patrick Cowlin.'

As we how-do-you-do'd, I tried to get a second first impression of the actors. Harris Bridges was exactly as we'd seen him at lunch the day before: self-assured to the point of boorishness and only half as clever and interesting as he thought he was. I had thought Nancy a twittering ninny, but a day on from the trauma of seeing her friend arrested she looked calmer and more thoughtful. Cowlin had seemed a touch cold at lunch, making a joke about the stabbing and endlessly expressing his impatience with Bridges's pomposity, but in this smaller group he, too, came across – at first glance, at least – as being a little more like the sort of person you might be prepared to spend some time with. My life had depended in the past on these snap judgements and I hadn't always been completely correct, but I was usually there or thereabouts.

'Violet has been telling me about her lunch yesterday and how exciting it was to meet real actors in the flesh,' said Gwen. 'Are you all in the current production?'

'I am now,' said Cowlin. 'I've taken over from Paul since . . . you know . . . but I was originally just the stage manager.'

'That's still a vital role, though—' I said.

'Oh, very much so,' interrupted Bridges. 'Can't carry on without our stage manager or our understudies. Nancy here is our female understudy.'

Nancy, it seemed, was being saved from the burden of having to answer for herself.

'Ah, yes,' said Cowlin. 'Understudies. Vital work.'

His tone was ironic. This was not a man who was impressed by the idea of having to herd the other actors about backstage and learn their lines while they got all the adulation and applause.

'But if I understood our conversation with Hugo Bartlett correctly,' I said, 'then you'd have had your chance at leading roles in other productions. Is that not right?'

'It's perfectly correct,' said Cowlin. 'But "chance" is the operative word. One always has a "chance". It's just that some get more chances than others.'

'Now, now, Patrick,' said Bridges. 'Let's not air our private grievances in front of our new friends. We can save that for later.'

Nancy looked at Gwen and smiled.

'Do you live in Bristol, Mrs Foster?' she said.

'No,' said Gwen, 'I live in London now. My husband is a military man.'

'Oh, the army. Now *that's* glamorous. And it's a proper job, too. I do feel sometimes that what we do is more than a little frivolous. We're not what you might call "useful", are we?'

'Do you really think so?' I asked. 'A game I like to play is to imagine the world without a particular sort of person and see what difference their absence would make. It's easy with doctors, nurses and teachers – things would become rather grim rather quickly. Road sweepers, dustmen, servants, tram drivers – we'd all live much less pleasant lives without them. Builders? Plumbers? Carpenters? A terrible loss. What about stockbrokers? Might we miss them?

Businesses might find it a little more difficult to get investment capital, but they'd find a way. Most of us wouldn't notice their absence at all. Now take away entertainment. What would life be like with no actors, no singers, no writers, no musicians? There'd be no books, no plays, no songs. No music hall. No dance. No symphonies or concertos. No jokes. No poems. Do you still think you're not useful?'

Nancy was smiling, and nodding enthusiastically, but she didn't get a chance to answer.

'I say,' said Bridges. 'You're quite the advocate for our craft. We should have you around when we're negotiating a pay rise. I'd like to talk to you and your business partner in a few days. I think we might share some common ground.'

Nancy sighed. Cowlin shook his head. He was clearly used to Bridges but still irritated by him.

'Have you been to see our play?' asked Bridges.

'Hugo is trying to get us tickets for later in the week,' I said, 'but he invited us backstage tomorrow evening.'

'I shall have to keep an eye out for you,' he said. 'Perhaps I could show you round.'

'That would be lovely, if we'd not be in the way.'

'Not at all,' he said. 'Always nice to have new people about the place.'

Two waitresses arrived with our orders, and made a point of serving us with exaggerated courtesy while simultaneously making it plain that we had transgressed all manner of rules and conventions by daring to make our own seating arrangements. Ordinarily I would have been mortified at breaking the rules, but Violet Goodheart was a great deal less concerned than Flossie Armstrong about such things, and I found myself rather delighted to have set a cat so entertainingly among the pigeons. Even though the infraction itself was utterly trivial, their obvious irritation was a joy to behold.

By the time they had gone, the mood at the table had lightened and conversation turned to more mundane matters. We discussed everything from the quality of the coffee to the strengths and weaknesses of Mr Asquith's government, calling at the delights offered to the visitor by the City of Bristol and the growing tensions between the Great Powers.

An hour had passed by the time I paid both bills and Gwen and I said our goodbyes.

After a brief discussion on the way back up to Park Row, we decided that we had wrung out all the excitement that the city had to offer on a Sunday, and set off on the drive back to the village.

We arrived home to find Lady Hardcastle in the drawing room, her face, hair, and engineer's overalls covered in what appeared to be plaster dust.

'You've been busy,' I said.

'There was an incident with a bag of plaster of Paris,' she said. 'I've managed to clean up the mess in the orangery, but . . .' She indicated her own whitened state.

'It suits you,' I said. 'Do you need a hand?'

'Would you mind, dear? I'm rather afraid of missing bits and finding myself set in a grim plaster mask.'

While we were upstairs, Gwen busied herself in the kitchen, and by the time Lady Hardcastle was once more clean and presentable there was a light lunch waiting for us in the dining room.

'Thank you, Gwenith dear,' said Lady Hardcastle. 'Although you really don't need to keep doing this. I shall get a terrible reputation if people find out I make my house guests prepare my meals.'

'It's the least I can do,' said Gwen. 'Putting a few bits and bobs on plates is hardly slave labour. And Blodwen had done all the hard work before she left.'

'Dear Miss Jones,' said Lady Hardcastle. 'We're so lucky to have found her. She could be running her own kitchen in a grand hotel in London, you know. She could certainly give Monsieur Whatshisface down at Le Quai a run for his money if she would only believe in herself and take the leap. I've offered to back her financially but she won't hear of it.'

'She has her mother to look after,' I said.

'Her mother doesn't need looking after any more than I do – she just likes having Blodwen around.'

'Is that why I'm stuck here?'

'Because I like having you around? Of course it is, dear.'

'I did wonder. But you're deluding yourself if you think you can look after yourself. It would be an act of cruelty and neglect to leave you to your own devices.'

'I fear you're right, actually. Who else would wash plaster out of my hair on a Sunday afternoon, after all?'

'Who indeed?'

'Nevertheless, thank you, Gwenith. This looks delicious.'

'My pleasure,' said Gwen.

'And how was your adventure this morning? Did you see much of the city?'

'It was lovely,' said Gwen. 'I'm rather taken with Bristol.'

'It's a shame you were there when all the shops were shut, though. We'll have to take you again later in the week.'

'As often as you like. And we can go to Crane's again as well. That was great fun.'

'Ah, yes, I wondered if you might stop for a coffee.'

'We ran into a few of the actors while we were there,' I said.

'Oh? Who?'

I briefly recounted our meeting as we helped ourselves to beef pie and boiled potatoes.

'That's intriguing,' said Lady Hardcastle. 'I wonder what they're up to.'

'Something they didn't want the others to hear about, certainly,' I said.

'Any motive for murder there?'

'It's possible, I suppose, though I can't see it at the moment.'

'Patrick Cowlin isn't happy about being the understudy,' said Gwen. 'I definitely think that might have made him want Singleton dead.'

'We've seen people killed for less, certainly,' said Lady Hardcastle.

'I'll put it on the crime board as soon as we've finished lunch,' said Gwen with a proud grin.

'If she carries on like this, I might not need you at all, Flo dear.'

'That's perfectly fine,' I said. 'I'm opening a theatre in Bournemouth.'

Chapter Seven

Lady Hardcastle, Gwen and I went for a long walk on Monday morning to explore the village. During our wandering conversation, Lady Hardcastle and I tried to work out if there was a way of transporting Gwen into town with us to visit the theatre but, to our surprise, she turned us down.

'I'd love to, honestly I would,' she said, 'but I've promised Daisy and Blodwen that I'll go to the pub with them this evening.'

'They won't mind,' I said. 'I often let them down if I'm called away.'

'And don't think they haven't noticed,' she chided. 'One of the Armstrong girls has to be true to her word, and it's going to be me. I'm sure there'll be other chances to see the theatre.'

'Oh,' I said, mortified that I might have offended my friends. 'Have they said anything?'

'Of course not, you ninny. They're too proud of you and your exploits to take umbrage, but I really would like to be the one member of the family who doesn't let them down.'

And so it was that Lady Hardcastle and I set out in the early afternoon on our own to take advantage of our invitation to hobnob backstage with the cast and crew of *The Hedonists*.

We parked the Rolls outside the Bridewell and strolled towards the High Street. Even in the chill of a November afternoon there was plenty of hustle and bustle, with shoppers young and old thronging the streets in search of both life's essentials and the joys of inessential frippery.

We passed a pleasing while in the bookseller's, where we stocked up on writing paper, notebooks, ink and pencils. From there we spent a few jolly minutes amusing ourselves by making up stories about the possible future owners of the shirts and blouses on display in the tailor's window. None of the blouses were to my taste, but a short while later I was tempted by a pair of elegant 'wet weather boots' in George Hunt's on Clare Street. After some amount of umm-ing and ahh-ing I decided that sixteen shillings and ninepence was an unnecessary expense. My boots were fine.

By six o'clock we had exhausted the possibilities of the High Street and its surrounds and picked our way back across the Tramways Centre and thence to Frogmore Street. We found the alleyway leading to the stage door and presented ourselves to Haggarty, the stage-door manager.

He looked up from his book as we approached his booth.

'Good evenin', m'dears,' he said, affably.

This was slightly surprising. When we'd seen him the year before he had been a good deal less welcoming, and I'd been expecting cold suspicion at the very least, if not outright hostility. My relief at not having another tiresome encounter with an overzealous gatekeeper was replaced almost immediately by a feeling of dismay and panic. Perhaps he recognized us from our previous visit and our cover would be blown. It was hardly a matter of life and death, but it would make our nose-pokery a tad more difficult if our deceit were to be discovered this early in the game. The ruse hadn't been essential, but I agreed that it might make the troupe lower their guard if they thought they were dealing with a pair of wealthy idiots from Bournemouth rather than two amateur sleuths from Littleton Cotterell. That would be undone if Haggarty remembered an armed scuffle outside his stage door a year before, and the two delightful women who had subdued the Austrian agent without a shot being fired.

My worries were unfounded.

'You must be Lady Webster-Green and Miss Goodheart,' said Haggarty. 'Mr Bartlett said you was comin'. I'll let him know you's here.'

He spoke briefly on the house telephone and a minute later we were joined by Hugo Bartlett himself.

'Good evening, ladies,' he said with a smile in his soft voice. 'How kind of you to come.'

'How kind of you to invite us, dear,' said Lady Hardcastle. 'We shall do our utmost not to get in the way, but we're frightfully keen to see absolutely everything we can.'

'You shan't be in the way at all – wander at will, dear lady. I'm afraid I have urgent matters to attend to elsewhere, but I've cleared your visit with Adlam – he's one of the world's more relaxed theatre managers. He's letting it be known that you're to have the run of the place. He's rather taken with the idea of someone starting a theatre from scratch.'

'Oh, that's very kind of him. Thank you for arranging it.'

'Think nothing of it.'

Lady Hardcastle inclined her head in acknowledgement.

'How is everyone?' she asked.

Bartlett looked puzzled.

'How do you mean?' he said.

'After the murder, Rosalie's arrest. How is everyone coping?'

'Oh. Oh, I see. Well, you know . . .'

'No, dear, I'm not entirely sure I do. You must all be terribly upset.'

'We are, of course,' said Bartlett. 'But then . . . well, the show must go on.'

'I suppose it must. But we mustn't keep you from your urgent business. You're quite certain we shan't be in anyone's way?'

'Quite certain, dear lady. Just explore. But do please try to see at least some of the play – I'm inordinately proud of it.'

'We wouldn't miss it for the world,' I said.

'Indeed, no,' said Lady Hardcastle. 'I'm sure your pride is entirely justified.'

'Thank you, thank you,' he said. 'Now, how about I show you how to get to the stage, then I shall leave you to your own devices? This way.'

He set off at a brisk pace along the corridor.

The walls were lined with old playbills advertising more than thirty years of theatre and music hall. I was sorry to have missed Professor Fitzherbert's Marvellous Trained Dogs, and I was sure the Flying Forzini Brothers had spent a season with the circus in the seventies. The Unrivalled Andertons might have been worth a tuppenny ticket, too, but I was not at all saddened never to have seen a performance of 'Mr Adolphus Bedlington's highly acclaimed melodrama, *The Disappointing Wife*'.

We passed many, many dressing rooms, the green room, and the 'little table in the corridor' where the dagger had been left on that fateful day. Eventually, he led us up three wooden steps and through a door marked *STAGE*. My childhood in the circus should probably have disabused me of any notions I might have formed concerning the glamour of the entertainment world, and we had been backstage at more than one theatre in the course of our work. Nevertheless, I still felt a tingle of excitement as we stood in the wings and looked out at the stage itself.

It was set for the first act of *The Hedonists* and I was briefly transported back to the joy of Tuesday evening. The lights, the energetic young cast, the costumes, the laughter. Maybe if it hadn't been for stupid Arthur Jones I could have been an actress. It could have been me stepping out in front of an audience, holding them spellbound with my portrayal of . . . But who would I play? I didn't see myself as the love interest. The chirpy best friend, perhaps? The evil villainess? Oh, but what if Gwen had joined me? We could have made our fortune as acting twins. Playwrights would be falling over themselves to exploit the comic potential of two actresses who looked exactly like each other. At the very least we could have made that Shakespeare play with the twins a little more convincing.

Lady Hardcastle tapped me on the shoulder.

'Are you still with us, Violet dear?' she said.

'Sorry . . . Jo,' I said. 'I was daydreaming.'

'It gets people like that,' said Bartlett. 'I can't tell you how many civilians I've seen standing by the side of a stage, lost in their own private fantasies of stardom.'

I was a little embarrassed to have been so transparent, but I gave him an apologetic smile.

He looked indulgently at me for a moment and then said, 'Well, ladies, I ought to be getting about my business, and I'm sure you'll have more fun on your own. This is a reasonably typical example of theatres all over the country so you should be able to get some ideas for the redesign of your own building. You have the run of the place, and if anyone says otherwise, send them to me.'

'Thank you, Hugo dear,' said Lady Hardcastle. 'Are the actors out of bounds? Do they like to be left alone before a performance?'

Bartlett laughed.

'It's not Ibsen,' he said. 'They're putting on evening clothes to play energetic young folk off to a party, not mentally preparing themselves for an emotionally draining evening of intense drama. There's barely any acting involved for a couple of them.'

'I'm sure you're just being modest,' said Lady Hardcastle. 'And a little unkind to the cast. I'd wager there's a level of emotional sophistication to your work that requires a great deal of skill.'

'You flatter me, Jo, but I just write jokes. Really I do.'

With a cheery wave, he slipped gracefully away.

'What do you think, then?' asked Lady Hardcastle once the door had shut behind him and we were alone. 'Explore the building or talk to the actors?'

'I'd like to start by trying to get a feel for what actually happened that night,' I said. 'Let's walk it through and see if we can see how events might have played out.'

'An excellent notion. How shall we proceed?'

'Work outwards from the discovery of the murder,' I said. I stepped on to the stage and pointed to the approximate spot downstage where the body had been lying as the curtain came up for Act Two. 'Singleton was there, I think.'

Lady Hardcastle took off her overcoat and laid it out on the indicated spot.

'Can you see it from the wings?' she asked.

I moved back behind one of the black curtains that shielded waiting actors from the audience.

'No,' I said. 'I can only see straight across the stage. That would account for the surprise as Rosie, Sarah and Bridges entered.'

'We're assuming Singleton was due to make his entrance later?'

I rejoined her on stage.

'No,' I said, 'don't you remember? Bridges's character enters with the two ladies and he addresses a comment to Singleton's character as though he's at the table waiting for them to return from their dancing. I imagine Singleton usually made his own way on stage before the others and they just assumed he'd be there as usual. It's odd that Cowlin didn't check he was ready before he opened the curtains, but perhaps he was hoping to catch him out one night. If Act Two opened without Singleton, maybe Cowlin thought Singleton might get the sack and he'd get the part after all.'

'It's a possibility, certainly,' she said. 'So how did Singleton get there? He left the stage with the others at the end of Act One and they . . . they what? Returned to their dressing rooms? The green room?'

'We shall have to find out,' I said, making a note in Violet's notebook.

'Stagehands set the stage for Act Two. Furniture was moved, flats were flown' – she pointed up to the extraordinarily high ceiling, where the scenery flats hung from ropes – 'and the set was dressed with props from . . . ?'

I looked around.

'Over here,' I said, pointing. 'The props table is against that wall.'

'Splendid. So they prepared everything for Act Two and then, their work done, they retired for a well-earned cup of tea, leaving the stage empty.'

'They took about ten minutes,' I said. 'Fifteen at the most.'

'How can you be sure?'

'I'm not sure, as such, but the bangs and thuds stopped after about that time.'

'They're a noisy lot, then?'

'Unusually so. There was a lot of very audible activity while you were all out being dismayed by the queues. The Sunderlands returned. There was one final bang – I told them it was probably a stage weight being dropped – and then everything was peaceful.'

'Which leaves the stage empty for a good quarter of an hour.'

'It does. Plenty of time to . . . what do you think? Lure him on to the stage and kill him?'

'I'm not sure,' she said, thoughtfully. 'I can't get away from the idea that it was unplanned. Sarah said she saw the dagger on the table in the corridor during Act One, and I stand by my assertion that a murderer with a plan wouldn't leave the weapon to chance.'

'Unless they had half a plan, and the easy availability of the dagger made it possible to carry it out there and then.'

'Planned but impromptu, you mean? I suppose that's possible. A ready-made scheme just waiting for an opportunity.'

'The killer could have grabbed the dagger at the beginning of the interval and then put their plan into action,' I said. 'That would work. They invite Singleton to the stage on some pretext, stab him, and then disappear before the curtain goes up.'

'That's certainly how I imagine it at the moment, yes. It's feasible, isn't it?'

'Risky, though,' I said. 'It's a very open place. The crew might have gone, but Cowlin was stage manager – he could have come back to check that things were ready.'

'Which makes Cowlin a rather nice suspect, wouldn't you say? He'd draw no attention if he were milling about up here, and he could position himself in the wings in just the right place so he could claim not to have seen the body before the actors walked on stage.'

'If he knew Singleton was dead and lying on the stage, it would also account for him not checking where he was. It was a risky oversight if anyone thought to ask him about it, but I'll put him on the list,' I said, making a note.

There was a sudden flurry of movement from the auditorium, as one of the side doors opened and a figure rushed up the aisle to the exits at the rear of the stalls. The stage was lit by work lights but the auditorium was all shadows and gloom, so I could just make out that it was probably a woman. She moved fast and was gone before I could discern any details.

'Did you see that?' I asked.

'The ghostly woman in the aisle?' said Lady Hardcastle. 'I did. I wonder where she came from.'

'The toilets?' I suggested.

'She'd been stuck there since Saturday night, you think?'

'All right, then, clever-drawers. Backstage?'

'Possibly,' she said. 'But who on earth could it be?'

'She wasn't moving like one of the youngsters. Sarah?'

'Possibly, but where was she going in such a hurry?'

Before I could come up with a suggestion, we heard the door on to the stage opening behind us. We both turned to see Sarah Griffin with a surprised look on her face.

'Hello, you two,' she said. 'Are you on your tour?'

'Hello, dear, how lovely to see you,' said Lady Hardcastle, with a look to me that said *It wasn't her, then*. 'In a manner of speaking, yes. Hugo let us in, showed us the way here, then said, "I'm sure you'll have more fun on your own," and left us to it.'

Sarah laughed. 'That sounds like Hugo. Brain the size of Birmingham but somewhat lacking in the social graces. How are you getting on?'

'We were just taking a look at the stage,' I said, 'and then we thought we might explore the rest of the building. You know, to try to get an idea for how these places are laid out. The property we have in mind is more of a hall than a theatre, but as we said at lunch, we have an opportunity to make some alterations. We could make it more like a purpose-built theatre if we had a clearer idea of what actors expect. Facilities and what have you.'

'To be honest we just hope for somewhere clean to get changed and a toilet that works. Would you like a guide?'

'Do you have the time, dear?' said Lady Hardcastle.

Sarah indicated her clothes.

'I'm already dressed for Act One,' she said. 'Make-up on and everything. I like to be ready early.'

'Then a tour would be splendid. Thank you.'

Sarah pointed to Lady Hardcastle's coat.

'Is that yours?' she said.

'Oh, yes,' said Lady Hardcastle. 'I wanted to feel like I was on the stage rather than just visiting. Silly, I know.'

'Not at all. It's where we found Paul, though, that's all. It looked so strange lying there. Brought it all back.'

'Oh, my dear,' said Lady Hardcastle. 'I'm so terribly sorry. I had no idea. Here, let me pick it up. I meant no disrespect.'

'Of course not, don't be silly. How could you possibly have known?'

Lady Hardcastle retrieved her overcoat.

'Nevertheless,' she said, 'I am desperately sorry.'

'Not another word,' said Sarah. 'Come on, let me show you round before curtain-up.'

Sarah had tried to give us a more detailed backstage tour, but time got away from us and she was called to a pre-curtain meeting in the green room before she could show us 'the storerooms and so on downstairs'.

We had watched the play from the wings and the second act proved to be every bit as funny as the first. The tragedy of Paul Singleton's death and the shock of Rosie Harding's arrest did nothing to dampen the exuberance of the performances, and the comedic twist at the end brought the house down.

We were saying our goodbyes when an ashen-faced stagehand barged into us.

'I say, old chap,' said Bridges, 'steady on there. You'll have someone over.'

'Sorry, Mr Bridges,' said the young man, 'but I gots to get to Mr Adlam's telephone. It's urgent, like.'

'Oh, dear. What's the matter?'

'It's Davey Browning. He's been killed.'

All conversation around us abruptly ceased.

'Killed?' said Sarah. 'Definitely killed?'

'How do you mean, Miss Griffin? He's definitely dead. I knows a dead man when I sees one.'

'No, I mean he didn't have a heart attack or something? It wasn't an accident?'

'Not unless he stabbed hisself in the back with a chisel by accident,' said the young man, his original distress giving way to irritation that his assessment of the situation was being brought into question.

'Where did you find him?' asked Lady Hardcastle.

The young man looked at her in puzzlement. He obviously had no idea who she was, but the clothes, the accent, and the fact that she was backstage with the actors clearly meant that she had every right to ask him whatever questions she wanted.

'He's in the workshop, ma'am,' he said. 'In the corner. I was just switchin' off the lights and gettin' ready to lock up when I saw him lyin' there. 'Orrible, it was.'

'Had he been there long?'

'No idea, ma'am. To tell the truth, I a'n't seen him all evenin'. We's overmanned tonight for a change so I thought he'd taken an opportunity for a skive. He sometimes did that, Davey. Skulked off to avoid the heavy work, like.'

'Who else has access to the workshop?'

'Everyone, ma'am. Anyone can get in there any time.'

'But no one else saw him?'

'I reckon they'd-a said, don't you?'

'I reckon they would at that,' she said, kindly.

'But he was tucked away in the corner by the shelves where we keeps all the screws and that. I only saw him because I was goin' round checkin' the place was empty afore I locked up.'

Lady Hardcastle smiled.

'Thank you, dear,' she said. 'You'd better get to the telephone and call the police. Inspector Wyatt is dealing with the other murder – I should think he'll want to be informed.'

The young stagehand knuckled his forehead and hurried off. Pandemonium erupted in the corridor as anxious voices competed with each other in their demand for answers and reassurance.

Lady Hardcastle tapped the back of my hand with our private 'follow me' code, and we slipped discreetly away from the group. In their panic and distress they had turned to each other, unconsciously shutting out the incomers, so our departure went unnoticed as we made our way quietly through the corridors to the workshop.

The door was unlocked so we slipped in and took a look around. It was a large, airy space. The windows high on the outside wall, and the skylights in the roof, would have provided ample working light during the day, supplemented by six electric lamps hanging from the ceiling. Boards, planks and battens of various sizes were stacked neatly in racks along the walls. The floor was swept clean. The workbenches were tidy. Those tools we could see were well maintained.

And in the corner, concealed by more racking, was the body of one of the stagehands.

He was lying face down, with a fine chisel, or possibly a screwdriver, driven to its handle between his upper ribs on the left-hand side. There was also a messy wound on the back of his head.

'I don't think Simeon will have trouble determining the cause of death,' said Lady Hardcastle. 'If that . . . are we agreeing with the young lad and assuming it's a chisel?'

'I wondered if it might be a screwdriver,' I said.

'Possibly. Either way, if it tore the thoracic aorta, or is long enough to reach the heart, he'd have bled to death in minutes.'

'It takes a lot of strength to drive something that deeply into a fully grown man,' I said.

Lady Hardcastle pointed to something lying on the floor not far from the body.

'Or a blood-stained mallet,' she said. 'To judge from the amount of bleeding from that head wound, I'm going to go out on a limb and suggest that the killer clouted him round the head with the mallet and then finished him off by hammering the chisel into his heart.'

'They definitely wanted him dead.'

'They definitely did. Can you see anything else of interest?'

I quickly scanned our surroundings again. The fastidiousness with which the workshop was maintained worked both for and against us. The well-swept floor revealed no footprints, but the tidiness meant that it would be child's play to spot anything that was out of place. Nothing was. All the materials were neatly stacked in their racks. All the drawers were closed, all the boxes neatly arranged.

'Not a thing,' I said. 'No signs of a struggle, no evidence of any other motive than to kill the poor chap.'

'I agree,' she said. 'Just to be on the safe side, though . . .'

Lady Hardcastle knelt and quickly went through the dead man's pockets, careful not to disturb things too much.

'Tobacco, a pipe, matches,' she said, enumerating the objects as she found them. 'A length of string, a pocket knife, a bus ticket . . . There's nothing here, but . . .'

'But what?'

'But I'm not the first to rifle the man's pockets. The way he was lying on his jacket . . . I'd say someone has already done what I've just done and then put him back. I'll leave him exactly as I found him on the off chance that Wyatt knows what he's doing and spots it himself.'

'Good thinking,' I said. 'And speaking of Wyatt . . .'

'Indeed. We ought to get out before he turns up. I'm not in the mood to answer his inane questions about what we were doing in here.'

'Nor to spend an evening in the cells on suspicion of having committed the murder ourselves,' I agreed.

'Quite. Let's get back to the others.'

Wyatt's questioning was as inane and perfunctory as we had feared. There had been much wailing and gnashing of teeth from the actors, but we learned nothing from their responses other than that no one knew anything about the murder and everyone was very, very upset. Everyone was questioned except Hugo Bartlett, but no one commented on his absence, and in the kerfuffle I neglected to mention it.

Neither Wyatt nor the uniformed sergeant accompanying him had asked for our addresses when we gave our own brief account of having seen nothing, though they did ask us to tell them if anything occurred to us later.

We said our goodbyes once more and stepped out into the decidedly chilly night air for the brief walk towards the Bridewell, where we had parked the Rolls that afternoon. It had been an overcast day and the temperature had been tolerable if not balmy, but it had fallen fast and we would definitely have a frost at home. I was wondering if my overcoat and muffler would suffice on the journey back, even with the motor car's folding roof fixed firmly in place.

The theatre crowds had cleared, and though there were still diners abroad, the streets were quiet. The chestnut seller was just beginning to pack up and I persuaded Lady Hardcastle to stop so I could buy two bags before he put everything away.

While the man scooped two generous helpings of freshly roasted chestnuts into brown paper bags, I made a fuss of his adorable dog. I told the man to keep the change and he wished us both well.

'I saw you eyeing these the other night,' said Lady Hardcastle as she nursed the scorching-hot bag in her gloved hand. 'If nothing else, they've brought life back to my frozen fingers.'

'You know how much I enjoy roasted chestnuts. Do you remember that lovely little chap on Shaftesbury Avenue?'

'The one with the harmonica?'

'That's him,' I said. 'He had quite the pash on you.'

'And who could blame him? If nothing else, my efforts to satisfy your chestnut cravings kept him in beer and baccy, with plenty left over for the rent and a daily helping of pie and mash. Of course he was infatuated, but I fear it was my money he lusted after.'

I was too busy munching carefully on my first, far-too-hot chestnut to make any further comment.

We arrived at the Rolls.

'I'd better drive home,' she said. 'Then you can finish those.'

'You're very kind,' I said as we clambered inside and settled into our seats.

She pressed the starter button and the engine turned over for a brief moment before coughing and giving up. She tried again. This time just the cough.

'Bother,' said Lady Hardcastle. 'It's either Fishy's starter motor or something Rolls-Roycey. Would you be an absolute pet and try to start it with the crank for me, please?'

I handed her my bag of chestnuts and hopped out.

The Rolls had been built to Lady Hardcastle's specifications and fitted with an electric starter motor designed by her motor-racing friend, Lord Riddlethorpe – 'Fishy' to his friends. We had briefly driven a prototype car of his own creation but it had blown up spectacularly on the Gloucester Road, and he gave her a starter motor for the Rolls she had bought as a replacement, by way of apology.

I had thought my days of hand-cranking were behind me, but here I was outside the police station in the freezing cold, trying to coax a precision-engineered marvel of the modern age into life.

Nothing.

'Oh dear,' said Lady Hardcastle from inside. 'It doesn't seem very well, does it?'

'It's probably something we could fix if it wasn't dark and cold.'

'And if we had some tools,' she agreed. 'This really is most disagreeable. What time is it?'

'You're the one with the watch,' I said, climbing back in beside her.

She checked it.

'Oh, splendid,' she said, 'it's only half past eleven.'

'Why is that splendid?'

'Georgie should still be awake. She can put us up for the night.'

'That's a tad presumptuous.'

'Nonsense – she'll be delighted.'

'Perhaps so. We could get a taxi home instead, though.'

'It's worth a try, I suppose, but I still think Georgie is our best bet.'

'Shouldn't we telephone her first?'

'At this time of night? Who answers the telephone at half past eleven expecting anything other than the grimmest of grim news? No, far better to arrive at the door like two waifs, desperate for a bed. And, anyway, where would we find a telephone?'

I nodded towards the front door of the Bridewell, the central police station.

'Good heavens,' she laughed. 'Can you imagine even trying? We're not exactly their favourite people.'

I was forced to concede this one.

'There'll be taxis outside the Grand or at the Tramways Centre,' I said.

'Best foot forward, then,' she said. 'And if they won't take us home, they can at least carry us up the hill to Georgie's.'

To a man, every taxi driver we met from the Grand Hotel to the Carriage Company's office at the Tramways Centre refused to take us all the way to Littleton Cotterell at that time of night. The best we could do was to get one of them to take us up the hill to the Bickles' house.

◆　◆　◆

The taxi dropped us off at the bottom of the steps leading to Berkeley Crescent, and we waited for it to leave before we approached the door to number 5. Lady Hardcastle winced apologetically as she rang the doorbell. I thought it was a nice touch to look so sheepish, even though no one could see it.

It took a while but eventually we heard footsteps in the hall, then the sounds of bolts being drawn and a key being turned in the lock. The door finally opened and a frowning Sir Benjamin looked down on us.

His frown turned to a smile when he realized who had called so late.

'Emily,' he said with a laugh. 'I should have known it would be you. Come in, do.' He stepped aside to allow us to enter. 'What on earth . . . ?'

'Good evening, Ben dear,' said Lady Hardcastle. 'We find ourselves somewhat stranded. The Rolls simply refused to start and none of the motor taxis in town would take us home.'

'We offered them double the fare to cover the journey back, but they were adamant,' I said.

Lady Bickle arrived in the hall, somehow managing to look even more beautiful than ever. It must have been the result of good breeding. Or that exquisite evening dress.

'Emily,' she said. 'Flo. I thought I heard your voices. What on earth . . . ?'

'Car trouble,' said Sir Benjamin. 'The poor dears are stranded.'

'Then you must come in and get warm,' said Lady Bickle.

'Thank you, dear,' said Lady Hardcastle.

Lady Bickle looked at her husband.

'Come along, Ben,' she said, 'don't just stand there. Take their hats and coats.'

'Ah, yes,' said Sir Benjamin. 'Of course.'

Freed of outerwear, we were led into the drawing room, where a fire was crackling welcomingly in the grate.

'Make yourselves comfortable,' said Lady Bickle. 'Have you eaten?'

'Not since lunchtime,' said Lady Hardcastle.

'I do have some chestnuts,' I said, holding out the bag.

'Oh, I say, they look rather tempting,' said Lady Bickle. 'Do you mind?'

'Help yourself,' I said.

'I don't mind if I do. Thank you. Ben, dear, pop down to the kitchen and see if you can cobble something together. A light supper for our guests seems to be in order.'

With a smile and a mock bow, Sir Benjamin departed.

'Now, then,' said Lady Bickle. 'Obviously you shall be staying the night and we can deal with your motor car in the morning. The servants have gone to bed but I'm sure we can muster the knowhow between us to get fires lit and beds turned down in the guest rooms.'

'You're very kind, dear,' said Lady Hardcastle. 'Thank you.'

'Yes,' I said. 'Thank you.'

Assumptions and prejudice are terrible things, but I confess that Lady Bickle's beauty and bubbly manner always made me underestimate just how sharp she was. She came across as just another flighty society lady but she was as bright and capable as anyone I'd met.

Lady Hardcastle was interested in more prosaic matters for the moment.

'How was your head on Saturday, dear?' she asked.

'My head?' said Lady Bickle. 'What about my . . . ? Oh, I see. Of course.' She laughed. 'Champagne never gives me a headache. It makes me giggly and sleepy, but I awake fresh as a daisy and ready for anything.'

'You lucky thing.'

'I am fortunate in so many ways, but I confess that one is an especial joy. But enough of me and champagne, what of you? How did you get on at the theatre?'

Between us, Lady Hardcastle and I recounted the events of our evening backstage with the Bartlett Players, starting with our tour with Sarah Griffin and ending with the discovery of the body of the stagehand.

'Another murder?' said Lady Bickle once we'd finished. 'How utterly dreadful. Are you quite all right? Of course you are – you're used to such things. But the others must be beside themselves.'

'They were convincingly distraught,' I said.

'"Convincingly"? You think they were trying to convince? You think they were pretending?'

'I'd wager at least one of them was – one of them killed him.'

'It's all so terrible. And so very hard to believe. I've not known them long, but I struggle with the idea that one of them is a killer.'

'It's the most reasonable of all the possibilities now,' said Lady Hardcastle. 'Someone in that theatre has killed two members of the cast and crew of *The Hedonists*.'

'It's awful. You must catch them. Catch them and bring them to justice.'

'Give us time, dear,' said Lady Hardcastle. 'We're still getting the lie of the land.'

'And we do have a friend on the inside now,' I added.

'It seems as though you do,' said Lady Bickle. 'I like Sarah Griffin. She's disinclined to take nonsense from anyone.'

Sir Benjamin entered bearing a large tray on to which he had crammed a large plate of unevenly cut sandwiches, four wonky slices of cake, a jug of water and a brandy decanter. I would have expected one of England's most renowned surgeons to be more adept with a knife, but it seemed that cake and sandwiches were a greater challenge than human flesh.

'Who's disinclined to take nonsense?' he asked as he set his burden down on a low table. 'One of your WSPU pals? I don't imagine them taking any nonsense at all.'

'Sarah Griffin,' said Lady Bickle.

Sir Benjamin shrugged blankly.

'Oh, Ben, you could at least pretend to pay attention. She's one of the actresses in Hugo's play.'

'The plain-looking young one? Dark hair?'

'No, she's the blonde one. About my age. Very beautiful.'

'Not as beautiful as you, my angel.'

'Well, obviously not. Do you have her now?'

'I do indeed. And no, she'd not take any nonsense.'

'Quite so.'

Sir Benjamin made to leave again.

'Plates, cutlery and glasses on the way,' he said. 'And would you ladies prefer tea or coffee?'

'Coffee, please,' we all said together.

'I shall be but a moment.'

He disappeared again.

'It's good to have someone on our side,' said Lady Hardcastle, as though none of that had happened. 'Your pal Hugo is a decent enough fellow but he's always so businesslike. We need a proper ally and I think we might have found one.'

'It should make things a good deal easier,' I agreed. 'I'd definitely like the rest of her backstage tour. I think she's more likely to show us what we need to see than Bartlett. He'd just want to show us the glamorous bits and tell us stories about the history of the building and the great actors who worked there.'

Lady Bickle laughed.

'That does sound like the sort of thing Hugo would do, yes,' she said.

'He didn't stay with us long,' I said. 'He had "urgent matters" to attend to so he left us to our own devices.'

'That sounds like him. It was probably an excuse. I always get the feeling there's a limit to how much time he's prepared to spend in the company of others. He's friendly and charming enough for a while, but then he hits the buffers and has suddenly to be elsewhere.'

'We can all be a bit like that sometimes,' I said.

'We can,' she agreed. 'His sister is such fun, though. Wild and impetuous. Always up to mischief. And so funny with it. There was an American girl at the school in Switzerland who called her Helena Handbasket – apparently that's where she was going. It's odd that her brother should be so . . . so . . .'

'I struggle to find an adjective, too,' said Lady Hardcastle. 'Difficult chap to pin down, your Hugo.'

'Isn't he, though?' said Lady Bickle. 'He's charming and pleasant but I just can't seem to get even a glimpse of the inner Hugo. He gives nothing away.'

'That's Englishmen for you,' I said. 'But we're hardly ones to talk. We've made a career out of giving nothing away.'

'True, true,' said Lady Bickle. 'Will you tell Sarah your real purpose?'

'I did wonder about that,' said Lady Hardcastle.

'She might be even more help if she knows, especially now there's been another murder.'

'She might. What do you think, Flo? Should we?'

'It crossed my mind,' I said. 'But it's a huge risk. Even if she didn't immediately shut up because she was annoyed we'd deceived her, we couldn't be sure she wouldn't tell the others.'

'I have to say I agree,' said Lady Hardcastle. 'I think there's still something to be gained from being Jo and Violet for a little while longer.'

'That sounds reasonable,' said Lady Bickle. 'What do you make of the others?'

'Harris Bridges is simply awful,' said Lady Hardcastle without having to pause for thought.

Lady Bickle laughed.

'Oh, my word, but isn't he, though?' she said. 'He'd be a shocking bully if they let him get away with it. I think Nancy is afraid of him.'

'She's a sweet little thing, isn't she? I confess I had to stifle more than one laugh while she was telling the story of Rosalie's arrest the other day. So earnest, so easily distracted. She's a hoot.'

'It can't be her, then,' said Lady Bickle.

'Why not?' I asked. 'Sweet little things have been known to murder. And this lot are all skilled actors, too, so she might not be so sweet underneath.'

'It's more likely to be someone outwardly dreadful like Bridges, though, don't you think?'

'It is,' I conceded. 'But don't be so quick to dismiss someone for being a sweet little thing. I'm enchanting, but I could kill you with a flick of my dainty wrist.'

'She could,' said Lady Hardcastle. 'I've seen her do it. But we'll put Nancy to one side for now, nevertheless. I'm inclined to disregard Rosalie for the moment, too. It's entirely childish on my part, but I refuse to believe that this Wyatt fellow could possibly be right.'

'He certainly has no reason to arrest her at this stage,' I agreed. 'But we can't rule her out just because you've taken against him.'

'True. But we ought to find a way to get her released until there's some proper evidence against her.'

'Who else?' asked Lady Bickle, who seemed to be caught up in it all slightly more than we were. 'What about Sarah?'

'She's blunt but rather fun,' said Lady Hardcastle. 'I think she's the sort of person you'd want with you if you were planning a mischievous night out.'

'I agree,' said Lady Bickle. 'Patrick Cowlin?'

'Remind me?'

'The stage manager and understudy,' I said. 'He was playing Bertie tonight.'

'Intense,' said Lady Hardcastle. 'Another good-looking boy, though. Played his part well. Definitely benefited from Singleton's death – it got him a lead role in the play.'

'They're all rather good-looking,' said Lady Bickle. 'Apart from sweet little Nancy. She's quite plain. Oh, but listen to me being awful. It was only the other day that I was railing against the school paper for reviewing Helena Bartlett's looks rather than her performance. Three out of ten, Georgina – must try harder.'

Lady Hardcastle and I laughed.

'I doubt there are many among us who haven't judged a book by its binding,' said Lady Hardcastle. 'And Nancy is rather plain, after all, though oddly attractive with it. She has . . . a quality. Who's left? The director chappie?'

'Emrys Thornell,' I said.

'Didn't see much of him this evening, though at lunch I found him rather supercilious.'

'He does have a condescending air about him,' agreed Lady Bickle. 'But perhaps that's what one needs to be a theatre director.'

'Perhaps it is, dear,' said Lady Hardcastle. 'Perhaps it is.'

'And what do you make of this new murder, this stagehand?'

'I've been trying to fathom how it fits in with everything else. Paul Singleton was stabbed to death almost publicly. The killer wanted his body found quickly. His death had to be seen. But the poor stagehand—'

'Davey Browning,' I said.

'Yes, poor Davey Browning is killed in secret, his body hidden away, the killer possibly hoping no one will find him till morning. It doesn't immediately feel like the work of the same person.'

'Unless,' I said, 'the first murder was the one with the grand motive – jealousy, passion, revenge, something like that. That was the one the killer intended as a bold statement. "This person deserved to die because of the great wrong they did me." But perhaps the second was just housekeeping. If Davey Browning had seen something he shouldn't, he might have been a threat to the killer, so his murder was just a way of keeping him quiet. The longer it took to find him, the fainter the trail would become. We've established before that there are only three motives for murder: passion, money, and to cover up another crime. It seems perfectly possible for the same person to kill for two of those. They killed Paul out of passion, they killed Davey to cover it up.'

'You're right, of course,' said Lady Hardcastle. 'Looked at like that, it makes perfect sense for the killings to be so different. In which case, we're looking for a passionate, resourceful, practical, and utterly ruthless killer. Not a pleasant combination at all.'

'And if we think the same person is responsible for both, then it's definitely not Rosalie.'

'I should say it's definitely not. Unless someone is working with her.'

'But remember Occam's Bread Knife,' I said.

'Razor,' said Lady Hardcastle quickly. 'Oh, you minx. Well played.'

'Thank you. But the simpler solution is that it's someone else working alone.'

'It is, it is.'

'But who among them would do such a thing?' asked Lady Bickle.

'Who indeed?' said Lady Hardcastle. 'Alibis are going to be the key, I think, but that doesn't help us with this evening's murder – everyone backstage had ample opportunity to kill Davey.'

'Everyone except Hugo Bartlett,' I said. 'He was off dealing with his "urgent matters".'

'Unless Davey Browning was his urgent matter.'

It was a chilling thought, and we sat in quiet contemplation for a moment.

'Do help yourselves to sandwiches,' said Lady Bickle at length, breaking the spell. 'Heaven only knows what's keeping Ben.'

We tucked in and they turned out to be very pleasant sandwiches indeed, no matter how poorly presented. Sir Benjamin arrived a quarter of an hour later with a lengthy tale about a mouse, the cat who chased it across the kitchen, the tray of coffee cups that was dropped on the floor when he tripped over the cat, the dustpan and brush that swept up the pieces, and the fruitiness of the language that accompanied the whole adventure.

It was past one o'clock by the time we all retired.

Chapter Eight

Despite Rolls-Royce's much-vaunted levels of service, no one there was able to help us when Lady Hardcastle telephoned first thing on Tuesday morning. The person who had reluctantly answered told her that someone would contact her at home later in the day, but for now the Silver Ghost remained stranded outside the clink. Lady Hardcastle made another call, this time to the central police station, where she left a message for Inspector Sunderland, asking him to keep an eye on it for us. The person she spoke to was unsure if he would be in the office until later that day, if at all, but at least now there was a note in the desk sergeant's daybook that the vehicle hadn't been abandoned.

'A charming sergeant assures me it will be well looked after,' said Lady Hardcastle as she hung up the telephone. 'It's not like anyone's going to pinch it, mind you – it won't start.'

The Bickles very generously offered to have Stanley drive us home in their own Rolls, and by ten o'clock we were back at the house. Gwen was in the kitchen chattering away with Edna and Miss Jones when we arrived. They were relieved to see us.

'We thought sommat terrible 'ad 'appened,' said Edna.

'Oh, Edna,' chided Miss Jones. 'You does make a fuss. They's often out all hours.'

'And I often frets,' said Edna indignantly. 'I worries, that's all.'

'Well, I'm sorry that we've caused such distress,' said Lady Hardcastle. 'Things just got a little out of hand, that's all. The Rolls broke down, you see, and we had to impose on the hospitality of friends.'

'I didn't think they did that, Rolls-Royces. But all's well that ends well – you're home safely now.'

'We are, dear, yes, thank you. But don't let us interrupt – we shall leave you in peace.'

'You're not interrupting at all,' said Gwen. 'We were just trying to think of something for me to do today. The ladies have their work, of course, but I . . .'

'We shall have to find a way to entertain you, Gwenith dear. We have been negligent hosts again.'

'Yes, sorry, Gwen,' I said.

'Don't be daft,' said Gwen.

'Daft or not, we shall remedy the situation just as soon as I've had a bath and put on some day clothes,' said Lady Hardcastle. 'I'm long past the age where one appears exotic as one skulks home in last night's dress.'

'Coming in with the milkman, still clutching a half-empty bottle of champagne?' said Gwen.

'Ah, to be young and adventurous again,' said Lady Hardcastle with a sigh. 'Give me half an hour and we shall plan a day of excitement and wonder.'

Lady Hardcastle and I left Gwen and the servants to their conversation while we got ourselves into clean clothes.

◆　◆　◆

Shortly before twelve o'clock, Lady Hardcastle received a telephone call from the Rolls-Royce garage in Bristol.

'Hardcastle . . . Yes, that's right . . . No, it's the modified Silver Ghost Roadster with the electric starter motor . . . No, I know you don't – it was designed by a friend of mine, Lord Riddlethorpe . . . Yes, the racing-car designer . . . It's very convenient, yes, but its convenience has been somewhat undermined by the engine's refusal to start, no matter what we did . . . No, I don't have a chauffeur – my maid and I share the driving duties between us. We've had this conversation before, don't you remember? . . . Very modern, yes, but our modernity doesn't stretch to being able to effect mechanical repairs at the roadside in the middle of the night . . . I thought that might prompt you once more to suggest we employed one, yes, but I'm not sure what more a chauffeur might have done other than hail a taxi, and we were perfectly capable of doing that ourselves, for all the good it did us . . . Wouldn't take us all the way to Littleton Cotterell at that time of night . . . No, we were none too impressed, either . . . Yes, please, though your chap will have to fetch it from town and tow it to your garage. We were forced to abandon the vehicle on Bridewell Street, outside the central police station . . . A very safe place to leave it, yes – one imagines it would never be stolen from there . . . You do? Oh, how marvellous. We thought we would be without transport until ours was fixed . . . We shall be at home this afternoon, yes . . . Splendid, we shall see him then. Good day.'

She hung up the earpiece.

'They're going to lend us a motor car until Marley is mended,' she said.

'What sort?' I asked.

'I neglected to ask. As long as it has four wheels, an engine, and a roof to keep out the chill, I'm not sure I mind too much.'

'It's astonishing how quickly we've grown dependent on the car,' I said. 'Three years ago we were cadging lifts from our neighbours, or hoping the dog-cart man from the station was at the pub. And now look at us.'

'Thoroughly modern, mobile ladies. Though still, as Georgie would no doubt point out were she here, without the vote.'

'Votes for Women,' I said, shaking my fist.

'I wouldn't have the first idea who to vote for,' said Gwen, who had just arrived from the kitchen with a pot of tea on a tray. 'But it would be nice to have to think about it, I suppose.'

'Very nice indeed,' said Lady Hardcastle. 'I say, is that tea for us? Perfect timing. Drawing room?'

'It is. Edna thought you might like a pot.'

'Edna is so often right in these things.'

We withdrew to the withdrawing-room and sipped our tea.

Just after lunch, the doorbell rang. I answered it to find a uniformed chauffeur standing on the step.

'Good afternoon, madam,' he said. 'Is this the Hardcastle residence?'

'It is,' I said.

'I'm from the Rolls-Royce company, my lady. I've brought your replacement vehicle.'

He gestured towards the lane, where there stood not one but two Rolls-Royce Silver Ghosts. I raised my eyebrows in surprise.

'That was quick,' I said.

'We aim to please, my lady. The rearmost one is to be yours for the duration of the repairs, while the other is driven by my colleague, who will be taking me back to the garage.'

'I see,' I said, 'but I'm not—'

Lady Hardcastle had arrived behind me.

'Is that your new car, dear?' she said.

'A temporary replacement, madam,' said the driver, proudly.

'I say, it's absolutely divine. You must take me out for a drive as soon as this lovely man has gone.'

'I must,' I said, trying my very hardest not to tut. 'Is there paperwork to sign?'

'If you please, my lady,' said the driver, producing some folded documents from his coat pocket. 'Just sign here . . . and here.'

He handed me a pen and I signed Lady Hardcastle's name. I'd never been much of an artist, but I could replicate her signature with such accuracy that even she was often unsure which of us had written it. I returned the pen and the signed paperwork.

'This is your copy,' he said, handing back one sheet. 'Would you like me to show your chauffeur the vehicle, my lady?'

'I'm sure we'll manage, thank you, dear,' I said. I was enjoying being Lady Hardcastle.

'Right you are, my lady,' he said. 'You know how to reach us if there are any problems. Good day.'

With a tip of his peaked cap, he turned to leave.

'Good day to you, too, dear,' I said. 'Do drive carefully, won't you.'

He waved from the gate, and within a few moments he and his colleague were gone.

'You make a good me, dear,' said Lady Hardcastle as we watched the Rolls glide down the lane. 'But I don't think I say "dear" quite that often.'

I made no reply.

'Shall we investigate our replacement transport?' she said.

We traipsed down the garden path together and I immediately regretted not stopping to put on my overcoat. The gate screeched, and once more I made a mental note – one of many dozens still not acted upon – either to oil it again or get our gardener, Jed, to effect some more permanent fix.

The Silver Ghost, in grey and black, was something of an anti-climax when we finally reached it. The front was familiar, while the rear, with its passenger compartment still intact, lacked the jaunty racing lines of Lady Hardcastle's roadster. It was just another motor car. An expensive and luxurious one, to be sure, but just another like the many already thronging Britain's city streets.

Lady Hardcastle clambered inside at once and set about checking the controls, even though, I noticed, they were identical to our own car's. Nevertheless she energetically mimed driving it, and I suspected it was only a lingering vestige of maturity and self-respect that prevented her from shouting 'Poop! Poop!' as she did so.

'This will do admirably,' she said as she got out again, still grinning. 'And with the extra seats we can both show Gwenith the delights of Bristol while it's actually open.'

'That crossed my mind, too,' I said. 'It turns out to be surprisingly convenient that Marley broke down when he did.'

'Daisy will have something to say about it, I'm sure.'

'Will she?' I said. 'Why?'

'She believes in fate and all that sort of caper, doesn't she? She'll tell us everything happens for a reason.'

I laughed.

'I'm sure she will,' I said. 'And it will probably be all under the control of her late great-aunt Dolly, who watches over her and her friends.'

'Then we must buy Aunt Dolly a gift for providing us with such a useful motor car. Do ghosts like champagne, do you think?'

'I imagine they're rather more keen on spirits.'

Lady Hardcastle sighed, and shook her head sadly.

'That was rather more Harry's level, dear,' she said. 'I expected more of you.'

'I consider myself suitably chastised. But shall we get back indoors? I'm freezing.'

Gwen was in the drawing room with a cup of tea and the newspaper.

'Anything interesting?' I asked.

Gwen lowered the paper.

'Some woman turned up in Bristol with hardly any money and no means of identification, claiming to have lost her memory,' she said. 'Turned out she was from Swindon and was wanted by the police under a charge of "false pretences", whatever that means.'

'I'm not entirely sure what it means in a criminal sense,' said Lady Hardcastle. 'Though we'd all be locked up if it were applied too freely – I've been living under false pretences most of my life.'

'Amnesia seems like a desperate way to get out of it, though,' said Gwen. 'Do you think that ever works? Have you even met anyone with proper amnesia?'

'I'm afraid I can't remember, dear.'

Gwen and I just looked at each other.

'Oh, come on,' said Lady Hardcastle. 'That was much better than ghosts preferring spirits.'

'We've taken delivery of a replacement vehicle,' I said to Gwen, as though nothing had happened. 'How do you fancy another trip into town?'

'I'd love one,' she said. 'Now?'

'As soon as you like, dear,' said Lady Hardcastle. 'Actually, why don't we use this as an opportunity to drop in at the theatre and see if we can bump into Sarah Griffin again? We can try to enlist her help, and you can see for yourself what we've been talking about all this time.'

Gwen finished her tea with a mighty swig and stood up, folding the newspaper and putting it neatly on the small table.

'Just give me five minutes to titivate myself and put my hat on, and I'll be raring to go.'

Lady Hardcastle appointed herself tour guide and sat in the back with Gwen as I drove the Rolls down the Gloucester Road towards the city. She pointed out the sights as we passed them, though most of them seemed to involve some sort of mishap.

'That's where we frightened a coal man in Fishy's car,' she said. 'And here's where the engine blew up a few months later.'

'Blew up?' said Gwen.

'Yes, it was quite the spectacle. The hedge seems to have recovered somewhat, but you can still see a bit of a hole where we hit it. And here's the Bristol Aviation and Aeronautics Company, where we had adventures with aeroplanes and parachutes. I say, Flo, we never did buy a Dunnock, did we? We ought to look into that.'

'We never did,' I said from the front. 'It might be fun, though.'

'I take it a Dunnock is the aeroplane Flossie flew in,' said Gwen. 'She told me about it.'

'The very same,' said Lady Hardcastle. 'It's quite the prettiest aeroplane you ever saw.'

'It wouldn't be up against especially stiff competition – I've not seen many aeroplanes.'

'Well, the Dunnock is a particularly fine example and I still wonder about buying one.'

'You have to promise to take me up in it if you do.'

'Of course, dear – we'll pick you up on Woolwich Common and fly you over London.'

Before long we were in the city, and I parked on Frogmore Street outside the Duke's Theatre.

Haggarty was reading a battered copy of *The Comedy of Errors*. He looked up as we approached, and laughed when he saw Gwen and me.

'Well, I'll be . . .' he said. 'Look at you. I was just . . .' He held up his book.

'So you were, dear,' said Lady Hardcastle. She'd been out with Gwen and me a few times over the years but she still found people's reactions to us slightly baffling. 'We were wondering, is Miss Griffin in the theatre yet?'

He consulted his daybook.

'Yes, my lady. She came in at . . . two o'clock.'

'Do you think we might come in and see her?'

'I don't see why not. Mr Adlam said you was to have the run of the place, after all. You know your way to her dressing room?'

'We do, thank you, Mr Haggarty – she pointed it out to us the other night.'

'Then I shall leave you to it, my lady. Oh, but if I can just have your sister's name, Miss Goodheart . . . ?'

'Mrs Foster. Iris Foster,' said Gwen, remembering her pseudonym without hesitation.

'Mrs . . . Iris . . . Foster . . .' he said, writing it neatly in his ledger. 'Welcome to the Duke's.'

We made our way through the maze of corridors towards Sarah's dressing room. The paint was peeling from the walls in places and the ceilings were cracked, but the floors were swept and the fire buckets filled with clean sand. The theatre was shabby but well loved.

Lady Hardcastle rapped on Sarah Griffin's door.

'It's open,' came a voice from inside.

We entered.

Sarah was draped on a chaise longue, reading what I imagined was a script bound in a card cover.

'Ah,' she said, looking up. 'Some friendly faces at last. Jo . . . and a bunch of Violets. How enchanting to see you all.'

'Good afternoon, dear,' said Lady Hardcastle. 'I hope we're not interrupting.'

'Not at all, not at all. I was just trying to learn my lines for the next production, but the events of last night are playing on my mind so you're a most welcome distraction. Come in, do. Make yourselves comfortable.'

'You're very kind.'

We squashed together on an overstuffed sofa on the opposite side of the room. It was almost as untidy as Lady Hardcastle's studio, with discarded clothes on every surface and piles of unknown junk on the floor covered with yet more clothing. There were posters decorating the walls, and some brand-new electric lights illuminating a large mirror at the dressing table. The table itself was strewn with sticks of greasepaint and make-up, and a cracked cup half full of cold tea with a milky scum on top.

Sarah noticed my gaze.

'Sorry, darling,' she said, 'that's been there since last night. One can't get the staff, you know.' She gestured around the small room. 'It's not much to look at, but it's warmer than my digs so I like to come here to read and relax. But I can get a bit slatternly when it comes to cleaning away my teacups, I do apologize.'

I smiled but said nothing.

'But tell all,' she continued. 'How is it that we are blessed with mysteriously multiplying Violets?'

'I'm Iris,' said Gwen. She had moderated her accent once more and sounded even more like me than I did. It was rather disconcerting. 'Quite by chance I happened to be in Bristol at the same time as my sister. We met a few of the actors the other day and I expressed an interest in the theatre, so she invited me to come and see it for myself. I hope you don't mind.'

'It's utterly enchanting, darling. I'm delighted to make your acquaintance. Whom did you meet?'

'Nancy, Patrick and Harris,' I said. 'In Crane's.'

'How lovely. Look, I really must apologize for my reaction to you. I expect you're both terribly bored of people talking about you as though you were a circus curiosity, but I find twins absolutely fascinating.'

'Think nothing of it,' said Gwen. 'We're used to it.'

'That's a relief. But I promise not to go on about it too much. Instead I shall ask . . . what's your line? Are you interested in running a theatre, too?'

'No, that's Vi's passion. I don't have a "line", I'm afraid – I leave that to my husband. He's a military man.'

'Oh, I love an army officer. They're always so dashing.'

Dai wasn't an unattractive man, but at a stocky five foot five people were more likely to comment on his character than his looks, and he would be described as dependable rather than dashing. Gwen, though, was unfazed.

'You have no idea, darling,' she said. 'Turns heads wherever we go.'

'You lucky thing. But where are my manners? Would you all like some tea?'

'If it's not too much trouble,' said Lady Hardcastle.

'It's no trouble at all, and it gives me a chance to clean away that dirty cup. We can all pretend it was never there and my reputation shall be restored.'

She stood and busied herself at the small sink in the corner, filling a kettle and rinsing the offending teacup. She placed the kettle on a gas ring beside the sink and lit the gas with a match before turning her attention to the teapot. She chattered as she worked.

'You really must make sure your dressing rooms are equipped with as many modern conveniences as you can afford,' she said. 'It makes such a difference to the performers, you know. A few home comforts can help us concentrate on the job at hand rather than worrying about how cold, thirsty or uncomfortable we are.'

'Sound advice,' said Lady Hardcastle. 'I can imagine that mini-mizing distractions is rather important in your line of work. Which raises an interesting question, of course: how are you all dealing with the murders, and Rosalie's arrest? It can't be easy getting on with your jobs with all that going on around you.'

'It's not easy at all. We're all doing the English thing and not talking about it, but you can tell everyone is upset.'

'Am I remembering correctly? Did someone say at lunch last week that you and Mr Singleton were walking out together?'

'For a time, yes, but that ended quite a while ago. He and Rosalie were engaged to be married by the time . . . well, you know.'

'Yes, I do. That would explain the comment, though. Was it Nancy who said it? She said something about it being natural that you would think ill of Rosalie.'

'That was the conclusion most of them reached, yes. Paul jilted me for Rosalie, so obviously I must hate one or other of them – probably both. But it wasn't quite like that. Our relationship ended and theirs began. I didn't bear either of them any lasting grudges over it. These things happen – especially in our world. Emotions run high, people fall in and out of love all the time.'

'So you don't hate Rosalie?' I said.

'Good lord, no. I rather like her, to be honest.'

'So if we were to try to get her released, you'd be willing to help?'

'Released? From the clink? How?'

'We've been talking about it with Georgie Bickle,' said Lady Hardcastle. 'She's very concerned, and we had quite a chat the other evening. She knows someone in the police force – another inspector – and he's not impressed by Inspector Wyatt. They've convinced each other that Rosalie is almost certainly innocent, but there's nothing he can do about it without something to convince his colleague that she couldn't have done it. We said we were visiting again and we'd ask around and see if we could come up with anything.'

'How do you prove someone *didn't* do something?' asked Sarah as she filled the teapot from the boiling kettle.

'Well now, that's quite the philosophical question, and one we've been wrestling with. I suppose the best way would be to find some proof that she *couldn't* have killed Mr Singleton.'

'And how might we do that?'

'We were thinking that if we could establish exactly where everyone was at the time of the murder, that might show it was impossible for her to be involved.'

'I suppose you're right.' Sarah fussed with cups, pouring in milk from an old jug. 'All I remember is walking on stage and seeing him lying there with the knife in him. Rosie screamed. The curtain came down. That was it. None of us saw the murder, obviously.'

'Was Paul supposed to be with you as you entered?' I asked. I knew from having seen the second act the night before that he wasn't, but I was keen to get her to describe his routine to us.

'No, the second act opens with "Bertie" already on stage, sitting at the table. The three of us walk on and talk to him as though he's just missed some fun elsewhere at the party.'

'So it wasn't odd that you hadn't seen him.'

'Not at all. He was in the habit of going on as soon as the stagehands had set everything up, and then just sitting there, contemplating . . . whatever it was he contemplated.'

'When did he go on?'

'As I said, as soon as the stagehands had finished. Usually just a few minutes before curtain.'

'It was a very long interval,' said Lady Hardcastle. 'Was that unusual?'

'Not for this production. Quite a few of the crew are on the sick list so they're shorthanded. There's rather a lot to do to set the stage for Act Two, and it's been taking them a while. We just wait till we get the go-ahead.'

'So he was only alone for a few minutes,' I said. 'And that must be when he was stabbed.'

'In that case,' said Sarah, handing out the teas, 'it can't have been Rosalie. She and I met in the corridor a few moments before Patrick came to tell us everything was ready. She wasn't out of my sight until we went on.'

'Where had she come from when you met her?' asked Lady Hardcastle.

'From her dressing room,' said Sarah. 'I was walking past her door just as she popped out.'

'What did Patrick do next?'

'We don't have a page, so he was on his way round to the other dressing rooms to tell them we were ready.'

'And he'd come from the stage?' I asked.

'Yes, I suppose so . . . No, wait, he was coming from the opposite direction.'

'Did anyone else see you?' I asked. 'It might help if we can get someone to corroborate your version.'

'There was no one about,' said Sarah. 'Oh, but there was a chap in a dark suit and an old cloth cap ahead of us as we walked towards the stage, but he'd gone by the time we got there.'

'Did you recognize him?'

'No, sorry. Probably one of the stagehands. They've been hiring casuals some nights.'

'If Patrick had come from the other direction,' said Lady Hardcastle, 'how did he know the stage was ready?'

'One of the crew must have told him,' said Sarah. 'Communication isn't terribly efficient backstage. People just sort of rush around hoping to bump into the right person to tell. It's a little chaotic but it usually works. I presume one of the crew went and got him from his dressing room.'

'He was the stage manager, though,' I said. 'Why did he have a dressing room?'

'Stage manager and understudy, darling,' said Sarah. 'If there are enough rooms we all get one. And here at the Duke's they're awash with dressing rooms. They can mount quite large productions.'

'Fascinating,' said Lady Hardcastle. 'But the key information is that Rosalie was in her dressing room while the stage was being set, and didn't appear until after the crew had given the signal that all was ready. From then on she was with you. I think we can take that to Inspector Wyatt and secure the poor girl's release.'

'Oh, that would be wonderful,' said Sarah, finally reclining once more on her chaise longue.

'Just one thing,' said Gwen. She had been listening intently and I had thought she was going to leave everything to us. I hoped she wasn't about to say anything to undo our good work. 'If you knew she was with you when Mr Singleton was killed, you already knew she was innocent. Why have you not said anything before?'

Sarah smiled wickedly. 'I said I quite liked her and didn't bear her any lasting grudges, darling. I never said I wasn't a bit miffed by the whole thing. It amused me to see her locked up for a few nights. She stole my fella, after all. A girl has to have a tiny bit of revenge. I'd have piped up before it got out of hand.'

Lady Hardcastle frowned and pursed her lips.

'That's honest, at least,' she said after a moment. 'Would you be willing to speak to Inspector Wyatt about it?'

'Ready, willing and able, darling,' said Sarah. 'Make the arrangements and we'll set the dear girl free.'

◆　◆　◆

Inspector Dick Wyatt was not pleased to see us. To save the potential inconvenience of our fake identities being tumbled by some familiar officer at the Bridewell, Lady Hardcastle telephoned Wyatt from the office of Mr Adlam, the theatre manager. She later reported that there had been a tense moment when Adlam had seemed to recognize her, but it passed without further incident and she made her call.

Wyatt arrived about fifteen minutes later and knocked on the door just as Sarah was coming to the end of a particularly ribald anecdote.

'It's open,' she called, but returned immediately to her story. 'And so she said, "But that was why we wanted the saucepan in the first place." Ah, Inspector Wyatt. Do come in.'

A tall man in his mid-thirties, with a wispy moustache and a greasy stain on the lapel of his jacket, stood slightly hesitantly in the doorway, silhouetted by the harsh lights of the corridor. He seemed momentarily reluctant to enter. Then again, if I'd opened a door to find the room filled with four laughing women, one of them – dear Gwenith – guffawing like a drunk in the cheap seats at the music hall, I'd have been reluctant to enter, too. He looked about uncertainly.

'Good afternoon, Lady Webster-Green,' he said. 'I spoke to you last evening, didn't I?'

'You did, Inspector,' said Lady Hardcastle. 'After that poor man was killed in the workshop.'

'Indeed, my lady.'

'Have you caught the man responsible?'

'Not yet, madam, no.'

'But it certainly wasn't Rosalie Harding.'

'No, madam, she remains in custody. The officer who took your call said you have important information regarding the recent murder of Mr Paul Singleton.'

'That's right. Although it's Miss Griffin who has the actual information. We were talking earlier this afternoon and it seems Miss Rosalie Harding was not only incapable of murdering the stagehand, she might not even be Singleton's killer.'

'I'll be the judge of that, my lady,' said Wyatt, fishing in his coat pocket for his notebook and pencil. He smiled at Sarah and said, 'Now, Miss Griffin, what is this . . . information?'

I wondered if Lady Hardcastle might feel a little put out that he hadn't used this flirtatious tone of voice with her.

'Well, it's as I was telling the ladies,' said Sarah. 'Little Rosie can't have killed Paul, because she was with me when he died.'

Wyatt made a slow, laborious entry in his notebook.

'I see,' he said at last. 'And how do you know when that was?'

Sarah ran through the story again, complete with the timeline of events we had put together between us. When she was done, there was another lengthy pause while Wyatt painstakingly wrote it all down.

'I must say, it would have been more helpful if you could have mentioned all this when I spoke to you before, Miss Griffin,' he said when he was finally finished. 'But I can understand how distressed you must have been. Nevertheless, please bear in mind in future that wasting police time is a serious matter, most especially if it results in a wrongful arrest.'

'I really am most dreadfully sorry, Inspector darling,' said Sarah, fluttering her eyelashes. 'I honestly only put the whole thing together when I was talking to the ladies here. Since it's a wrongful arrest, do you think you'll be able to let poor Rosie go free now?'

'I didn't say that, miss, I was merely talking about the *possibility* of a wrongful arrest. I shall have to review the case in the light of this fresh information.'

'Do review it swiftly, though, won't you, darling. I couldn't bear the thought of that poor girl banged up for another night as a result of my stupidity.'

'Your stupidity, miss? Surely not.'

'Well, I should have thought it all through a little more carefully, shouldn't I? It was only because the ladies prompted me that I realized I'd been with her all the time.'

Wyatt treated her to his most winsome smile and consulted his notes.

'I may have to ask you to make a formal statement down at the station,' he said. 'But for now I shall consider what you've said and decide upon my next course of action.' He flicked back a few pages in the book. 'I was surprised last night to find you all still here. Will you be in Bristol for much longer? I thought you were moving on to Bath.'

'We were supposed to be, yes,' said Sarah. 'We were all due to be taking a couple of weeks off and then opening in Bath on the twenty-eighth, but our run has been extended by a fortnight and we'll be in Bristol until the Sunday. The twenty-sixth.'

More note-taking ensued. Wyatt looked around the room. He flicked back a few more pages in his notebook as he looked at Lady Hardcastle, and appeared to be checking that he'd written her name down. Then he noticed Gwen and me for the first time. His exaggeratedly surprised reaction was worthy of the hammiest music-hall-skit performer.

'And there are two of you. One of you I've met before, but . . .'

'You met me, Inspector,' I said. 'Miss Violet Goodheart. And this is my sister, Mrs Iris Foster.'

'Addresses, please.'

I wondered if he'd been given a wigging for not taking our addresses the night before. Violet, I decided, would be the sort to make mischief.

'You took them last night,' I said.

'I . . . er . . . well . . . I shall take them again to make sure . . . to make sure your accounts match.'

151

Oh, Dickie, you're not much of a fibber, I thought.

'Well,' I said, 'as we told you last night, Lady Webster-Green and I are staying at a guest house on Pembroke Road in Clifton. The Gorge View. Do you know it?'

'I do, miss, yes. It's famous in the area for having no views of Avon Gorge whatsoever.'

'As we discovered,' I said. 'It's charming enough, though.'

'So I understand, miss. How long will you be staying?'

'Another week or so. And then home to Bournemouth.'

'I'll need your address there,' he said. 'And yours, my lady.'

So much for mischief – now I was going to have to work for my fun. I thought quickly. I had no knowledge of any road names in Bournemouth, but I was confident that Wyatt had no idea, either.

'Twelve, Ladysmith Road,' I said – everywhere had streets commemorating the Boer War.

'Thank you,' he said. 'Lady Webster-Green?'

'Number 2, Hanover Crescent,' said Lady Hardcastle – everywhere had streets celebrating the royal families.

Wyatt wrote both these addresses down with excruciating slowness.

'And you, Mrs Foster?' he said.

'I'm at the Grand Hotel,' said Gwen. 'I don't know how long I shall be here, but when I leave I shall be returning to London. 6 Grenville Gardens, Mayfair.' She was good at this, too – former prime ministers are always a good bet for street names.

'Very well,' said Wyatt. 'Is there anything else you wish to tell me?'

'Not that I can think of, Inspector darling,' said Sarah. 'But we know where to find you if anything further occurs to us.'

I swear he almost swooned at being called 'darling'. I hadn't the heart to tell him she called everyone that.

'I shall bid you good day, then,' he said. 'I'm glad you've finally told the truth, but I shall be considering your negligence very carefully and I should warn you there may be consequences. We take this sort of thing very seriously.'

'I'm sure you do, darling, and I really am most dreadfully sorry. But you will be looking at releasing Rosie, won't you?'

'We shall see,' said Wyatt. He returned his notebook to his pocket and left without saying another word.

'Well, he seemed charming,' said Sarah once his footsteps had disappeared. 'I'm not so impressed by "there may be consequences", but otherwise . . .'

'As long as one of those consequences is the release of an innocent woman,' said Lady Hardcastle, 'I think we can cope with whatever else he throws our way, if and when it arrives.'

We chatted a little longer but time was getting on and Sarah needed to get ready for work. We thanked her for the tea, said our goodbyes, and went out of the theatre into the cold.

With no particular reason to head back to Littleton Cotterell, we decided to dine in town. Le Quai was full to bursting, and a very apologetic Jean-Pierre reluctantly sent us on our way. We tried the Grand but their dining room was full. We ended up at a small restaurant not far from the Duke's where we were able to secure a table for three and where we had wine and a slap-up three-course meal for the price of just one of the starters at Le Quai.

Full of hearty food and happy with our evening's work, Lady Hardcastle, Gwen and I left the little restaurant and walked back towards the Rolls. As we crossed the road we saw a policeman, bundled up in his greatcoat, walking towards us. It was Sergeant Massive Beard. I braced for confrontation.

'Good evening, Lady Hardcastle,' he said in a booming, cheery voice as we all paused beneath a street light. 'And Miss Armstrong.

Oh, and I see you've brought a spare Miss Armstrong with you.' He chuckled at his clever observation. 'Look after yourselves, won't you. It can be dangerous for ladies out on the streets at this time of night. You get yourselves home to Littleton Cotterell.'

We wished him good evening and he went on his way, crossing the street and almost careening into a young lady who had just passed us in the shadows on the other side of the road.

'I'm sorry, m'dear,' said the sergeant, and they fussed briefly, trying to decide who should go first before she stopped and let him walk ahead of her.

'That was odd,' I said, once they had both gone. 'Why can't he be like that all the time?'

'Work face, home face,' said Lady Hardcastle, sagely. 'He's clearly a different man away from the stresses of the front desk at the Bridewell.'

I agreed, and we continued on our way home.

Chapter Nine

We had no real plans for Wednesday morning. We updated the crime board with the new timeline and marked Rosalie as 'extremely unlikely' since she had a witness alibi for the first murder and was in gaol for the second. I added a note about the man in the dark suit and cloth cap but I wasn't convinced that would lead anywhere. After a few moments of fruitless contemplation, Gwen and I turned our attention to drinking tea and talking about our family.

We were the youngest, by some margin, of seven children, and I had completely lost touch with all of them except Gwen when I went to China with Sir Roderick and Lady Hardcastle in 1895. Our father died in an accident while I was away, and our mother fell ill and passed away soon after. Of our four brothers, the only thing even Gwen knew was that one of them had died in South Africa in 1900. Our sister, Bethan, was 'probably living in Carlisle', but neither of us had any more details. There were aunts, uncles and cousins in South Wales, and Gwen heard from some of them, but they were never particularly interested in us because we'd all moved away. They seemed to view it as some sort of betrayal. We knew nothing of our father's side of the family other than that they came from Northumberland. Or Cumbria. Probably.

'They say family's important,' said Gwen as she helped herself to one of the McVitie's Digestive biscuits Miss Jones had taken to buying. 'But I don't miss them. Not as much as I'd miss these biscuits, at any rate.'

'I've grown to like the biscuits,' I agreed. 'I was convinced for a while that Miss Jones only bought them for the tins – she does love a tin – but I can see some appeal in them now. I'd like to know what happened to them all, though.'

'The biscuits?'

'You're as bad as Herself. No, the Armstrong Clan, you idiot. We might be aunties.'

'I'd put money on it,' she said, experimentally dunking a digestive in her tea. 'Would you like that?'

'I think I would, actually, yes. Herself has a lovely little niece. Addie. Nine months old now and quite the little charmer. Why? You're not . . . ?'

'No,' she said, a little sadly. 'Not for want of trying, mind you.'

'If it's meant to happen, it'll happen,' I said. 'But please don't make me imagine you trying.'

'Fair dos, Floss. There's not many as wants to have to imagine Dai in the altogether, to be fair.'

Lady Hardcastle materialized at the drawing-room door and peered in.

'Why are we imagining Dafydd in the altogether?' she asked.

'We're trying not to,' said Gwen. 'I'm bound by the matrimonial contract to experience the delights, but no one else need ever feel obliged.'

'He's a lovely chap,' said Lady Hardcastle. 'I'm sure the delights would inspire songs and epic poetry.'

'Can we not?' I said. 'I have to eat with these people.'

'Of course, dear, of course. Is there any tea in that pot? I'm gasping. Edna brought a cup out to the orangery for me but . . .'

'It got cold?' suggested Gwen.

'I lost it,' said Lady Hardcastle, sheepishly.

'You lost it . . . ?'

'Gwenith Evans,' I said, 'meet Emily, Lady Hardcastle, the untidiest woman ever to wear a hat. You could lose an express locomotive and all its carriages in that orangery. Losing something as small as a cup of tea would never warrant an announcement in the parish notices. There must be an entire Wedgwood dinner service out there by now, hidden beneath bundles of paper, scraps of fabric, and piles of whatnots, doodahs and thingummies. It's a wonder she can get through the door, let alone find the table where she makes her magical films.'

'She's right, of course,' said Lady Hardcastle, 'and one does so regret the loss of the tea, but it can't be helped.'

'We can help,' said Gwen. 'I'm sure you could squeeze another cup out of our pot.'

'You're very kind, dear. Much kinder than your sister. She'd just have scolded me again for losing the first cup and told me to find it for myself. Do you want a job?'

'You'd miss me,' I said.

'I'd miss you terribly, dear,' said Lady Hardcastle. 'But not your nagging. I could live a long and happy life without ever experiencing that again.' She poured herself a cup of tea and sat down. 'Is there any news of Rosalie?'

'Nothing,' I said. 'Should we telephone . . . someone?'

'It might be worth telephoning Inspector Sunderland. Or Georgie, perhaps. Someone must know something. I'll call her now.'

She put down her tea and went out into the hall.

Earwigging on other people's telephone calls is never wholly satisfying with the other half of the conversation missing, but with the door closed we couldn't hear even Lady Hardcastle's half clearly. A little can be learned from the tone of voice, though, even when the words themselves are inaudible. It seemed to me that her voice retained its usual exuberance, and so I judged that at least she wasn't receiving bad news.

She returned a short while later, looking rather pleased with herself.

'Is all well at the House of Bickle?' I asked. 'That sounded like a happy call.'

'It was rather jolly, yes.'

'So Rosalie has been released?' suggested Gwen.

'Her liberty has been grudgingly restored. Wyatt, by all accounts, was ungracious and unapologetic, but she returned to the theatre last night in time for the final curtain, and there was much rejoicing. We are the heroines of the hour, and our presence is requested at our earliest convenience so that the freed woman can express her thanks in person. I said we'd take her to Crane's for a celebratory sandwich and a bun if you two agree.'

'I always agree to free buns,' I said. 'I'll get my hat.'

By the time we arrived at Crane's on Christmas Steps, Rosalie and her pal Nancy were already there, at the same table where we had met Hugo Bartlett the previous week. Nancy greeted us warmly.

'Hello, you three,' she said. 'Rosie, these are the three ladies responsible for your release. You've met Lady Webster-Green and Violet Goodheart, of course, that day on the steps outside when I was being so wet in my new boots. And this is Violet's sister, Iris Foster – I met her in here the other day. I do think Iris is such a pretty name. I knew an Iris at school. Although she was an absolute cow, now I come to think of it. Anyway, please sit down.'

Rosalie smiled at us politely as we shuffled into our seats, but there was something odd behind the friendly smile.

'Have you ordered anything?' I asked.

'Just a large pot of coffee,' said Nancy. 'We thought we ought to wait for you.'

Lady Hardcastle attracted the attention of our favourite waitress, and ordered far too many sandwiches and cakes before turning her attention back to the recently released Rosalie Harding.

'How are you, dear?' she asked. 'I do hope it wasn't too awful for you. What am I saying? Of course it was awful. But I do hope things are starting to improve now you've been released.'

'Thank you,' said Rosalie. 'It was . . . distressing. And rather frightening. So I really am most terribly grateful for everything you did to secure my release. You and Sarah.'

'We simply prompted Sarah to recall the sequence of events that evening, and persuaded Wyatt that you had to be innocent. He'd have got there on his own in the end.'

'I'm not so sure about that. He didn't seem all that interested in finding out what happened, just in getting an arrest and closing the case. He was most put out at having to let me go, and he blamed me for it. I set his investigation back days, he said.'

'What a cheek,' said Lady Hardcastle. 'Still, you're out now and free to rejoin your friends.'

'Yes,' said Rosalie. 'Thank you.'

I'd been watching her closely throughout this brief exchange, and there was still something not quite right. Her words were of relief and gratitude but her expression remained puzzled. Suspicious, even. It wasn't long before I found out why.

'I think I saw you three last night on my way to the theatre,' she said. 'You were walking down from that little café-restaurant place. Whistler's, is it called? You were under the street lamp and I thought I recognized you, Lady Webster-Green, but you'd gone before I could be certain.'

'We definitely ate at Whistler's,' said Lady Hardcastle. 'We had a lovely time.'

'The desk sergeant from the police station saw you. Miserable bloke. Hateful to everyone. And he greeted you like old pals. He knew you.'

'I certainly remember that . . .' said Lady Hardcastle. She, like me, could see where this was going.

'And he didn't call you Lady Webster-Green and Miss Goodheart. It was something like Hardacre and Anderson.'

Lady Hardcastle and I exchanged glances. This moment had always been a possibility. I shrugged.

'Yes, dear,' said Lady Hardcastle, 'that's right. He called us Lady Hardcastle and Miss Armstrong. Those are our real names.'

Nancy looked almost comically shocked.

'I've heard of you,' she said. 'You were in the newspapers. There was a murder in . . . Gloucestershire? Or was it more than one? You solved it, anyway. Or "them", perhaps I should say. If there was more than one.'

'We did,' said Lady Hardcastle. 'We live in Littleton Cotterell, a few miles out of town, and we're friends of Georgie Bickle. She asked us to keep an eye on the police investigation for her – she cares about you all. And then our friend Inspector Sunderland made the same request when he was taken off the case in favour of Inspector Wyatt. He wasn't certain Wyatt would do a good job.'

'So you lied to us,' said Nancy.

'We did, yes. Wyatt has never met us as "us", though we do have a reputation, and we surmised that he would be unhappy about our presence. And . . . well, not to put too fine a point on it, we think one of you is the murderer. We imagined you'd all be more candid if you thought us a couple of bumpkins from Bournemouth with more money than sense, than if you knew we were the women from the newspaper stories who keep solving crimes with the Bristol Constabulary.'

'And you did that by lying.' Nancy wasn't going to let this go.

160

'By lying, yes. We meant no harm, but someone in your company has murdered two people, and if it were left to Wyatt . . .'

'I'm grateful to you, whoever you are and why ever you misled everyone,' said Rosalie. 'But why is Paul and Davey's killer one of us? Why not one of the stagehands? Or a stranger from the audience?'

'We have considered that,' said Lady Hardcastle. 'We can't rule out theatre employees for the moment, though it's unlikely – it's usually someone known to the victim. It's true that the theatre staff all knew Davey Browning, but Paul Singleton was part of a touring company and we think it unlikely that anyone there would have borne him enough of a grudge to provoke that sort of public murder. But we are happy to rule out audience members, unless and until we're forced to consider them – you know yourselves that it's almost impossible to get backstage during a performance. Even more difficult to get back into the auditorium unnoticed after the event. It's someone from the cast or crew, and more likely the cast.'

'I'm going to have to tell the others,' said Nancy. 'They're not going to be happy to learn you've been deceiving us.'

'I shouldn't imagine they will be, dear. You must do as you see fit.'

'I'm not sure I can eat with you, either,' continued Nancy, gathering up her gloves and scarf. 'You stay if you want, Rosie, but I can't remain here.'

Within seconds she was out the door, leaving Rosalie shrugging with embarrassment.

'I'm so sorry,' she said. 'She's not usually like that. I'm sure you acted for the best. I really didn't intend to drop you in it. I thought I was being rather clever to have spotted you – I didn't think it was going to blow up like this. I . . .'

'It's quite all right,' said Lady Hardcastle. 'It was bound to come out in the end. We'll understand if you want to go with your friend. She's rather more upset than I imagined she would be.'

'Thank you,' said Rosalie, gathering up her own things. 'I'm so sorry.'

She hurried out in pursuit of Nancy, leaving the three of us to contemplate the enormous mound of sandwiches and cake that was already on its way to our table.

'Do you think they might put those in a box for us?' wondered Lady Hardcastle.

◆ ◆ ◆

After a brief conference on Christmas Steps, we returned to the Rolls and drove the short distance to Berkeley Crescent.

Lady Bickle was at home.

'Hello . . . ladies?' she said once we'd been shown into the drawing room.

'Hello, dear,' said Lady Hardcastle. 'I hope you don't mind us dropping in unannounced.' She noticed Lady Bickle's bemused expression. 'Oh, yes, sorry – you've not met. This is Flo's sister Gwenith.'

They both how-do-you-do'd.

'Make yourselves comfortable,' said Lady Bickle, 'and give me your news. You look like you've all lost a shilling and found a farthing.'

'You're as astute as ever, dear,' said Lady Hardcastle as we all settled ourselves. 'Although the actuality is even more disappointing than the adage. We have freed Rosalie Harding, as you know, but our ruse has been uncovered in the process. We took her and Nancy to lunch, and during the course of the conversation we were unmasked when Rosalie mentioned seeing us last night and hearing us being called by our real names. Young Nancy took immediately against us and flounced out of Crane's in high dudgeon.'

'She turned on a sixpence,' I said. 'One minute she was sweetness and charm and "these are the three ladies responsible for your release", the next she was repeatedly calling us liars and stomping out without eating her sandwiches. Poor Rosalie had to scurry off after her.'

'Oh dear,' said Lady Bickle. 'That doesn't sound like a fun luncheon. She's a bit like that, though, little Nancy. She's quite young and insecure. She seems perpetually afraid that people are mocking her. I imagine that discovering your deception was her worst nightmare come true. She would have thought you'd been laughing at her all along.'

'Ordinarily I find the insecurities of youth rather endearing,' said Lady Hardcastle, 'but this is most inconvenient. She will no doubt paint us in the worst possible light and we'll never get close to the Bartlett Players again. I'm so sorry, dear. We should probably have been honest from the start.'

'Nonsense. Your reasoning was sound and you've learned more as Jo and Violet than you ever would have as Emily and Flo. And the others know all too well what Nancy's like – they might not be so easily swayed as you suppose.'

'The killer will certainly back her,' I said. 'And if they're influential enough they'll convince the others to shut us out, even if the rest of them don't much mind one way or the other.'

'This is really too irritating,' said Lady Hardcastle. 'Inspector Sunderland is going to be so disappointed.'

'He'll just have to lump it,' said Lady Bickle. 'You don't work for him.'

'True, but one doesn't like to let one's friends down. Who knows what's going to happen now. Wyatt will ruin everything. The man hasn't got a clue, you know.'

'He's quite handsome, though,' said Gwen. 'That moustache can go, but the rest of him is pretty serviceable.'

'If only good looks were an indication of ability,' said Lady Hardcastle. 'I'm rather afraid the killer could go free. Worse still would be if the wrong person were hanged.'

'It won't come to that,' said Lady Bickle. 'Wiser heads will prevail. Ollie won't let it get out of hand – he'll intervene if needs be.'

'I suppose you're right. I'm just a little miffed, that's all. It'll pass.' Lady Hardcastle sighed and sat back in her chair. 'I say, would you like some sandwiches? We have boxes of them in the Rolls.'

◆ ◆ ◆

We stayed long enough Chez Bickle to enjoy the cup of coffee we'd missed at Crane's, then said our goodbyes. Lady Bickle politely declined our offer of sandwiches and cake – her cook had a formidable reputation as a pastry chef, after all, so there was really no need.

Gwen was keen to visit the WSPU shop, so we dropped in to see our old friend Lizzie Worrell before setting off for home.

'How lovely to see you both again at long last,' said Lizzie as we trooped in to the cramped little shop. 'You've not been to any meetings lately, so I was worried you might have forgotten us.'

'You're always in our thoughts, dear,' said Lady Hardcastle. 'But we've been rather busy of late, I'm afraid.'

'And I've not forgotten about the self-defence classes,' I said. 'But, as she says, it's all been a bit hectic over the past few months.'

'Oh, don't worry about that. The ladies are practising what you've already taught them – that'll keep them out of trouble for a while.'

'I'll be free soon,' I said. 'I'll teach them some new tricks.'

'There's no rush. I saw the newspaper stories about that business with the Cider Wardens up your way in the summer, and that business at the aeroplane factory, so I know you've been up to your ears in it. Dinah Caudle talks about little else.'

'She still tries to tell us about the Cider Warden shenanigans,' I said. 'And we were there.'

Lizzie laughed politely.

'Hello,' said Gwen, holding out her hand. 'I'm Flossie's sister, Gwen. They're never going to introduce me.'

'It's a pleasure to meet you,' said Lizzie. 'Though I'd have guessed whose sister you were. Are you a member?' She gestured around the shop at the WSPU posters and merchandise.

'Let's say I'm a sympathizer,' said Gwen. 'My husband is in the Royal Artillery so it might not go down too well if his commanding officer learned I was a paid-up suffragette, but I've been on a few marches, attended a few meetings.'

'You're not local, I take it?'

'No, we live in Woolwich.'

'Ah, of course. The Royal Artillery. Well, Mrs P believes in "deeds not words", and I think that might extend to "participation not membership", don't you?'

'That's a nice way of thinking about it. Thank you.'

We exchanged news for a short while, and offered further promises to attend meetings and for me to arrange another course of self-defence lessons. We also bought a few items, with Gwen particularly amused by the WSPU bloomers.

Rather than head directly to Littleton Cotterell with our uneaten lunch still on board the Rolls, we took our boxed treats into the city to seek out one of the local churches providing food and shelter for the homeless and destitute. The offer of sandwiches and cake bemused the young curate, who was more used to vegetables and offcuts of meat from which his volunteers could make soup, but he seemed grateful nonetheless.

We drove home, where Lady Hardcastle returned to her moving picture studio in the orangery while Gwen and I amused ourselves with the new board game she had bought, Suffragetto. It might best be described as a more convoluted form of draughts, where two players represented either the police or the suffragettes, with the police trying to get into the Albert Hall and the suffragettes attempting to invade the police station. We alternated roles, and I won all three games before we decided we had exhausted its entertainment possibilities.

I was about to offer to make yet more tea when the doorbell rang.

It was Dinah Caudle.

It took some while to extricate Lady Hardcastle from her animation endeavours and to make the promised pot of tea. I left Miss Caudle and Gwen to get to know each other, and by the time we finally assembled in the drawing room they were getting along famously. As I brought the tea tray through, Miss Caudle was mid-anecdote.

'. . . from the top of the church tower,' she said.

'Oh my word,' said Gwen. 'And then what?'

'And then we solved the mystery and everyone lived happily ever after,' I said. 'Don't let her trick you into believing her exaggerated tales, Gwen. She's paid to make things sound more exciting than they really are.'

'I'm paid to report the truth,' said Miss Caudle with mock indignation.

'You're paid to sell newspapers, dear,' said Lady Hardcastle. 'Bare facts have never sold newspapers. Scandal and gossip, on the other hand . . .'

'You speak true,' said Miss Caudle. 'Unfortunately. And I have scandal and gossip to impart in a moment, but now I finally have you all together I have a new fact for you. One that I shall relay unembellished.'

She paused for far too long.

'Well?' said Lady Hardcastle. 'Spit it out, dear.'

'Hugo Bartlett has been arrested for the murders of Paul Singleton and Davey Browning.'

There was a moment's pause before we all said, 'What?'

'Wyatt arrested him at lunchtime,' said Miss Caudle. 'Marched in to the Duke's with a uniformed sergeant and clapped him in irons. He's languishing in the cells at the Bridewell even as we speak.'

'Oh, this will never do,' said Lady Hardcastle. 'Why has Wyatt done such a foolish thing?'

'It seems he's fixated on the knife. I was at the booby hutch talking to Simeon – you know, in case there were any juicy new cases for me to exaggerate for the newspaper – when in comes Ollie Sunderland in the gloomiest of gloomy moods. He's usually so optimistic, or at least . . . what's the word? Accepting? Resigned? Fatalistic? Stoical, that's it. Stoical. Awful things happen and he just gets on with it. But this case seems to be affecting him for some reason. I've never heard him say a negative word about any of his colleagues, but he's really taken against Dickie Wyatt. And it seems the man Wyatt has decided that possession of the murder weapon is the key to cracking the case, and so Bartlett – being the man who had the dagger brought from the prop store in the first place – absolutely must be the killer. And on the – actually quite understandable – basis that it's extraordinarily unlikely that there are two murderers operating in the theatre at the same time, he's added the murder of the stagehand to the charge sheet for good measure.'

'Well, of all the empty-headed nonsense,' said Lady Hardcastle.

'He was going to telephone you – Ollie, I mean – but I needed to be out this way to interview a farmer's widow for a piece I'm writing about modern women running businesses in the twentieth century. Only she wasn't very modern so it's not actually much of a story. The business is thriving, of course – people always need food – but she wasn't quite the illustration of twentieth-century womanhood I was hoping for. Anyway, I said since I was going to be in the area I'd deliver the news in person.'

'It's very kind of you, dear. Though we might no longer be so closely involved with the case ourselves.' Lady Hardcastle briefly related our encounter with Nancy and Rosalie. 'We're very much braced for a cooling of diplomatic relations.'

'Ah well,' said Miss Caudle. 'It's not the end of the world. Ollie will have to do his best to keep an eye on Wyatt, and Georgie will have to go without her updates.'

'Well, yes . . .' said Lady Hardcastle. 'But one does feel a little helpless now at not being able to help poor Hugo.'

'I know none of you like Wyatt,' said Gwen, 'but are we sure he's wrong this time? I mean, from everything I've heard it was obvious he was more than a little hasty in nabbing Rosie, but does that mean his every move must be a mistake?'

'You see why I need Armstrongs about me?' said Lady Hardcastle. 'The voices of reason. You're right, Gwenith, of course. We don't know Hugo's whereabouts at the time of Singleton's murder, and he was apparently absent from the theatre on the night Browning was killed, though he could have been anywhere. From what we know at the moment, he had the opportunity to commit both crimes but . . . well, yes, it's purely prejudice on my part to suppose that Wyatt is wrong. Prejudice and intuition, perhaps. He's not applying scientific reasoning, he's just going at it like a bull at a gate, and all my instincts tell me that he must be wrong. Or that, if he's right, it's by blind chance rather than skilled detective work. And right or wrong we need to get Hugo freed.'

'Why?' asked Gwen. 'If he's right, Hugo's locked up where he's supposed to be.'

'For the same reason I was so keen to get Rosalie released. Let's suppose for a moment that Hugo is the murderer and Wyatt gets him before the beak. His barrister says, "The prosecution has no evidence other than the availability of a prop dagger to which everyone in the theatre had access, Your Worship. I move to dismiss the charges." The magistrate consults his clerk. There is muttering. The magistrate looks up. "A very poor showing from the police," he agrees. "Off you go, Mr Bartlett." A killer walks free because Wyatt is a nincompoop.'

'That makes sense,' said Gwen.

'Hence my frustration, you see? If only we'd managed to stay on the inside, we might have been able to prod Wyatt in the same way we did to get Rosalie Beaufort freed.'

'No use crying over spilt doodahs,' said Miss Caudle. 'What's done is done and all that.'

'I suppose you're right,' said Lady Hardcastle, wearily. She paused a moment before brightening slightly. 'I shall adopt Inspector Sunderland's sanity-saving stoicism. There's no profit in fretting over things beyond one's control, after all. Things will work out and the truth shall prevail.'

'That's the spirit.'

'You said you had scandal and gossip,' I said. 'That's usually fun.'

'Oh my word, yes. I know a chap who knows a chap who drinks with Eddie Adlam, the manager of the Duke's Theatre.'

'A reliable and verifiable source, then,' I said. 'Not third-hand hearsay and tittle-tattle.'

Miss Caudle totted up on her fingers.

'I think it might be fourth-hand, actually,' she said. She ran the calculation again. 'No, you're right: third-hand. Anyway, I have it on good authority—'

'From a friend of a friend of a friend,' said Gwen.

'Do you want to hear this or not? I have other things to be getting on with, you know.'

'Ignore them, dear,' said Lady Hardcastle. 'They get a bit giddy when they're together.'

'As I was saying,' said Miss Caudle, 'I have heard one or two things about the good folk of the Bartlett Players that might be of interest. Did you know, for instance, that Rosalie Harding, affianced of the late Paul Singleton, had previously been engaged to Harris Bridges?'

'Yes,' intoned Lady Hardcastle, Gwen and I together in mock weariness.

'Oh. Well, did you know that Paul had been recently overheard making lewd advances to young Nancy Beaufort?'

'We didn't know that,' said Lady Hardcastle. 'Did your correspondent's correspondent's correspondent happen to overhear Miss Beaufort's response to this?'

'She was not best pleased, apparently. She called him some rather fruity names and slapped him forcefully about the chops.'

'Good for her,' said Gwen.

'Well, quite,' said Miss Caudle. 'More intriguingly still, Rosalie Harding got to know of it and was similarly irked. She has the fiery temper associated with her colouring—'

'There's no scientific basis for that,' interrupted Lady Hardcastle. 'It's just romantic nonsense made up by lazy writers.'

'Well, I'm the laziest of lazy writers,' said Miss Caudle, 'and I shall continue to assert that redheads are fiery. Anyway, her temper was ignited and she was heard to utter dire imprecations concerning the fate that might befall Singleton should his lascivious activities continue.'

'So she might have killed him after all,' said Gwen. 'Wyatt might have arrested the right person first time round.'

'Possibly,' said Lady Hardcastle. 'But it was still for entirely the wrong reason. That silly man is fixated on the dagger.'

'Ah, but wait,' said Miss Caudle. 'There's more. I also learned that Emrys Thornell – the director – owed Paul a substantial amount of money. No one knows what he needed it for, nor are they entirely certain how it was that a jobbing actor had money to lend, but it was an unrecorded private debt and now . . . well, now it is no more.'

'So it was Thornell,' said Gwen. 'He killed him to erase his debt.'

'You'll have to forgive my sister,' I said. 'She gets a little giddy every time she hears a new motive.'

'So I see,' said Miss Caudle with a smile.

I did some quick calculations of my own.

'That means,' I said, 'that everyone *except* Hugo Bartlett had a motive for killing Singleton. Wyatt really is an idiot, isn't he?'

'It appears that way,' said Lady Hardcastle. 'But it's out of our hands now. What say we turn our attention to problems we can actually solve? Who has ideas for how to catch the Dog and Duck Booze Burglar?'

'I have an idea,' said Gwen. 'It'll need some careful setting up but it makes use of our unique gifts. I'm sure it'll work, and it'll guarantee you two free drinks for life.'

We listened carefully as she outlined her plan.

Chapter Ten

At about five o'clock on Wednesday afternoon, our worst fears were confirmed by a telephone call from Lady Bickle, who informed us that she had been visited by Nancy Beaufort. The young actress had brought news that the Bartlett Players were hurt and offended by our lies and wished to have nothing further to do with us. She herself was to be tolerated only because of her friendship with Hugo Bartlett's sister.

In an attempt to offset the disappointment, we made a quick visit to the Dog and Duck, where we outlined Gwen's plan to catch the thief. Joe and Daisy listened patiently, and were impressed and intrigued in equal measure. They agreed it was a fine plan. If the thief stuck to their usual timetable they were due the following evening, so we made plans to arrive in plenty of time to make everything ready.

Back at home, Lady Hardcastle treated Gwen and me to a demonstration of her studio in the orangery. I'd seen her at work before, of course, and I was in absolute awe of her talent and skill, though I usually thought it would be better for her if I didn't make too much fuss about it. She didn't lack self-esteem as it was, and I felt that further boosting her ego would be reckless and potentially hazardous.

Gwen, though, had no such qualms, and gawped in wonder and admiration as Lady Hardcastle explained her craft. She ooh-ed and ahh-ed at the appropriate times, and bombarded Herself with surprisingly perspicuous questions. By the time we'd finished, Lady Hardcastle was beaming, Gwen was thoroughly impressed by her talents, and I was quietly proud of them both.

They ignored my suggestion that we should tidy up a bit, and we retired to the house, where I made a supper from the ingredients prepared for me by Miss Jones earlier in the day.

As we sat down to eat, the telephone rang and I hurried to the hall to answer it.

'Chipping Bevington two-three,' I said. 'Hardcastle residence.'

'Flo, dear? Is that you?'

'It is, Lady Bickle. How lovely to hear from you again so soon. Would you like to speak to Lady Hardcastle?'

'Heavens no. I mean to say, I should love to speak to her – she's one of my dearest friends. But so are you, and this news is for you both. Would you be able to come to Berkeley Crescent tomorrow morning at around eleven?'

'I can't see any particular reason why not,' I said. 'The only plans I know of for certain involve our being back at home to pre-pare for a trip to the Dog and Duck between four and five.'

'A riotous afternoon of heavy drinking with the locals?'

'Would that it were. But unless Herself has made plans she's not told me about, I think we could make it to Clifton in the morning. Can I tell her what it's about?'

'I'd rather not. I feel it would be better if you arrived unpre-pared and free of prejudice.'

'I can't imagine that answer being well received here,' I said. 'I shall say that, in my foolish haste to return to the dinner table with your invitation, I neglected to ask you.'

'Oh, my dear, have I interrupted your meal? Hurry back to it at once. I shall see you tomorrow. Bring your sister if she wants to come – she was charming.'

We said our goodbyes and I rejoined Gwen and Lady Hardcastle.

'Who was that, dear?' asked Lady Hardcastle as I sat down.

'Lady Bickle,' I said. 'She wants us to call on her tomorrow morning at about eleven o'clock.'

'How lovely. Did she say why?'

'She didn't.'

'Didn't you think to ask?'

'I did not,' I said. 'Sufficient unto the day, and all that.'

'Quite right, too, dear. Would you cut me another slice of bread, please – I can't reach it from here.'

With dinner finished and everything tidied away, we spent the rest of the evening playing cards.

◆ ◆ ◆

There was chaos on Park Row the next morning. A brewer's dray delivering beer to the White Harte had collided with a carpenter's wagon on its way to the nearby Prince's Theatre. Their horses had panicked and both loads had been spilled, leaving beer barrels, crates full of bottles, and a tangle of timber all across the road.

Men who had no real idea what they were doing, but who were nevertheless possessed of an unshakable belief that they knew everything there was to be known about the management of horses, were attempting to mollify the distressed draught animals. Shifty-looking chancers were helping themselves to bottles from the crates, and one had managed to find a bucket that he was using to collect beer as it jetted from a split barrel. Two young boys made off with a bundle of planks of wood tucked under their tiny arms.

'Do you think there's anything we can do to help?' asked Lady Hardcastle from the driving seat.

'Jed could do with some timber for one of his garden projects if you want to half-inch some,' I said, 'but we'd be facing stiff competition from the local urchins.'

'I meant help them, not help ourselves.'

'Then I think it's all under control. The chap in the brown suit can be kicked by that horse just as painfully whether we're here or not.'

'I shall attempt to extricate us, then,' she said. 'Give me a moment, ladies.'

She managed to turn the Rolls around with only minor complaints from the gathering crowd of bystanders as she mounted the pavement, forcing them to leap out of her way. The other stranded road users, encouraged by her efforts, also began to attempt to turn their vehicles round. Reverse gear on the Rolls made it easier for Lady Hardcastle than for those driving carts and wagons – horses are notoriously unenthusiastic about reversing – but she had shown that it was possible and had cleared a path for them, so the congestion began to clear by the time we turned left towards Tyndall's Park and the University College.

We went up the hill and back down again, emerging on Queens Road after our brief diversion opposite Berkeley Crescent, our destination.

These shenanigans had cost us dear, and by the time Williams had taken our coats and shown us into the drawing room it was already a quarter past eleven. We were, it seemed, the last to arrive.

Lady Hardcastle was surprised to see who else had been invited.

'Good morning,' she said as Lady Bickle invited us to sit down on the last remaining chairs in the now-crowded room. 'I see we have quite a gathering this morning.'

The other guests – a deputation from the Bartlett Players – nodded their greetings. From the way the others looked to her for the first comment, our friend Sarah Griffin seemed to be their leader on this occasion. She had been joined by Rosalie Harding, Harris Bridges and, to my immense surprise, Nancy Beaufort – after her performance at Crane's the day before, I had been fully convinced that she would never speak to us again.

From the look on his face it was clearly a source of some discomfort and frustration for Bridges that Sarah had been nominated to speak for them, but he sat silent nonetheless.

Sarah waited until we were comfortable and had been handed our cups of tea.

'Thank you for coming,' she said. 'We asked Georgie not to tell you we would be here, in case it put you off.'

'I'm not sure it would have,' said Lady Hardcastle with a smile. 'But after we upset Nancy yesterday we didn't expect any further invitations.'

'You really did upset me—' began Nancy, but Rosalie put her hand on her arm and she subsided.

'We realized you were just trying to help,' said Sarah. 'You certainly demonstrated that by the way you spoke to Inspector Wyatt to get Rosie released. And now we're here to ask you to continue to help. As yourselves. As Lady Hardcastle and Florence Armstrong and . . . ?'

'Oh, Gwen Evans,' said Gwen. 'But I really am Flossie's sister. It would be a bit odd looking the way I do if I weren't, eh?'

'It would be most intriguing, certainly,' said Sarah. 'Something Hugo might want to write a play about when he's free again, perhaps. And would you all help us? You seem to have a way of getting Wyatt to do the right thing, and we need to get poor Hugo released.'

'I, for one, am not at all averse to helping,' said Lady Hardcastle, 'but I fear Wyatt might react even more angrily to our deception than did Miss Beaufort. We gave him false addresses as well as false names. In my experience the police never look kindly upon that sort of thing.'

'They don't have to know,' said Bridges. Clearly, remaining silent had become too much of a strain. 'You can be Lady Webster-Green and Miss Goodheart till the end of your days as far as he's concerned.'

'That had occurred to me,' said Lady Hardcastle, 'but our ruse was tumbled in the first instance when we were recognized by someone who works at the police station. It would only be a matter of time before someone else there let the cat out of the bag, blew the gaff, and otherwise exposed our mendacity to Inspector Wyatt. Better, I think, to come clean and hope to sway him with evidence. We have friends there, so we should be able to sidestep him if needs be.'

'So you'll help?' said Sarah. 'Hugo seems to be so self-confident, but being in gaol will destroy him. He's nowhere near as strong as he appears.'

Lady Hardcastle looked to me and I nodded my agreement.

'We'll help if we can,' she said. 'But how certain are you that Hugo is innocent?'

'It can't possibly be him,' said Nancy. 'Not Hugo. He's altogether too . . . too . . . too lovely. He's an absolute lamb.'

'I'm afraid being "an absolute lamb" isn't a defence in English law,' said Lady Hardcastle with a little laugh. 'We shall need something more robust than his being too lovely to have murdered anyone, if we're to persuade Wyatt of his innocence.'

'What proof did you have for Rosie?' asked Bridges. 'How do you even prove that someone didn't do something?'

'We showed that she *couldn't* have done it,' said Lady Hardcastle. 'You're right that it's rather difficult to prove that something isn't true, but it can be somewhat easier to prove that it's impossible for it to be true. We provided Wyatt with a witness – Sarah – who was able to say that Rosalie was nowhere near the stage when Mr Singleton was killed. Which, incidentally, also clears Sarah immediately if Wyatt goes after her next.'

'But Paul was killed during the interval,' persisted Bridges. 'And it was a jolly long one – the theatre is short of stagehands, you know – so how do we prove that Hugo was elsewhere for the entire time? As for the stage chappie—'

'Davey Browning,' said Sarah, irritably. 'The man died a horrible death in a theatre where you were working, the very least you can do is remember his name.'

'Yes, well,' huffed Bridges. 'No one knows where Hugo was when Davey Browning was killed.'

'We'll address Mr Browning's murder separately, I think,' said Lady Hardcastle. 'We're working on the assumption that one person was responsible for both deaths, so if we can rule Hugo out for one, we're comfortable with the idea that he would not have had a hand in the other. So . . . Because Mr Singleton was stabbed on stage, we know he wasn't murdered until the short-handed stagehands had finished their work. We have only a tiny amount of time to account for. Five minutes? Ten at the very most. If someone was with Hugo during that time and will swear to it, he's a free man.'

'Well, I was alone in my dressing room by then,' said Bridges, somewhat dejectedly. Perhaps he'd been hoping to be Hugo's saviour.

'And I was with Sarah, as you know,' said Rosalie, speaking up for the first time.

'Don't look at me,' said Nancy when everyone did exactly that. 'I wasn't even in the theatre by the time of the murder.'

'Where were you, dear?' asked Lady Hardcastle.

'I was . . . outside.'

'Outside?' said Bridges. 'Just before Act Two. What on earth . . . ?'

'I was just the understudy that night. I wasn't needed.'

'That's precisely why you should have been backstage with the rest of us. What if Sarah or Rosie had been taken ill?'

'Halfway through the show? "And tonight the role of Peggy will be played by Sarah Griffin in the first act and Nancy Beaufort in the second because that won't be in any way confusing." No one needed me so I was . . . outside.'

'Yes, but what were you doing "outside"?' Bridges wasn't going to let this go.

'Oh, do use your imagination, Harris darling,' said Sarah, wearily. 'She was with a chap.'

'What? Who is this "chap"?'

'I'm really not convinced that's any of our business. Leave the poor girl alone.'

'Well, I mean, really—'

'You're not her father, darling. You're not even her boss. Do shut up, there's a love.'

Bridges harrumphed but desisted.

'If none of you was with Mr Bartlett at the time of the murder,' I said, 'then we'll have to speak to the others. Someone at the theatre must have seen him. And if they didn't, well . . .'

'If they didn't then he might be guilty after all?' said Nancy. 'Is that what you're saying?'

'I wouldn't go that far,' I said. 'But it would definitely make it harder to persuade Inspector Wyatt to release him.'

'Then we'd better get you to the theatre to speak to the others,' said Sarah.

'Are you sure they'll be willing to?' asked Lady Hardcastle. 'Have they all accepted our deception in the same pragmatic way you have?'

'We'll persuade them,' said Sarah. 'For Hugo.'

179

Mindful of our need to return to Littleton Cotterell by no later than five o'clock, we had concluded our business at Lady Bickle's as swiftly as possible, and the actors had hastened back to the theatre on foot while we said our goodbyes. We promised to keep Lady Bickle informed of our progress and allowed Williams to help us into our coats. Gwen and I attempted to amuse Williams by pretending to be each other and claiming the wrong coats, but it wasn't our finest comedy-twins routine. He and Lady Bickle laughed politely. Lady Hardcastle sighed. We returned to the Rolls.

I took the wheel and chose to avoid the potential chaos on Park Row by approaching Frogmore Street from the opposite direction. I went round Brandon Hill via Berkeley Place and Woodwell Lane, and eventually sneaked up on it from behind by passing underneath the Park Street Viaduct.

'Was that Bristol Cathedral I saw a little while ago?' asked Gwen. 'We missed that on our tour, Floss.'

Lady Hardcastle was sitting with her in the back of the Silver Ghost.

'It was, dear,' she said. 'It's a striking building with a fascinating history. We can visit if you like.'

'That's kind,' said Gwen, 'but cathedrals give me the creeps. I'm happy with a glimpse in the distance from the back of a fancy motor car.'

'As you wish, dear. But the offer remains should you change your mind.'

I parked directly outside the Duke's Theatre, and we hurried round to the stage door in time to see the actors disappearing inside.

'It seems it's becoming quicker to walk in our cities these days,' said Lady Hardcastle. 'Heaven only knows what it will be like when everyone has a motor car.'

'Everyone?' said Gwen. 'The likes of me won't ever have a motor car.'

'The likes of you, dear Gwenith, will most definitely be owning cars. You'll be driving hither, thither, and occasionally yon before you know it. Or you'll be trying to, at least. The roads will be so full of other eager motorists that in actual fact none of you will be going anywhere.'

'I look forward to it,' said Gwen, cheerfully. 'Wotcher, Haggerty. All right if we go in?'

'Of course, miss,' said Haggarty. 'You're always welcome here.'

'Ta, love.'

'"Wotcher"?' I said. '"Ta, love"? You've been living in London too long, Gwenith Armstrong.'

'When in Rome and all that,' said Gwen.

We had managed to lose sight of the actors, so we made our way to the green room. It seemed as good a place as any to wait. About ten minutes later we were joined by Sarah Griffin.

'Ah, there you all are,' she said. 'You were right behind us coming in, and then suddenly you weren't. I've been looking everywhere.'

'We thought we could wander the labyrinth for aeons and still never find you, so we waited in here,' said Lady Hardcastle. 'Have you found us a witness?'

'I think we might have. You remember our director, Emrys Thornell, don't you?'

'Spectacles. Beard,' I said. 'Wore a velvet jacket at lunch. Isn't impressed by Harris Bridges.'

'The very same. We've had a word and he might be able to provide Hugo with the alibi he needs.'

'What did he say?' I asked.

'Come and talk to him yourself,' said Sarah. 'He's in his office.'

'He has an office?' said Lady Hardcastle.

'Well, he calls it that. It's just a spare dressing room, but he has no need to "dress" so he calls it his office. Makes him feel more important. Come on, I'll show you.'

◆ ◆ ◆

Thornell's dressing-room-cum-office was very similar to Sarah's, though a good deal tidier. The dressing table was piled high with bound scripts, bundles of paper tied together with ribbon, note-books, pens, bottles of ink, and a silver-topped walking cane.

There was a large, battered chesterfield sofa where Sarah's room had a chaise longue, and a rickety card table and a single chair in place of her small guest sofa. Thornell was sitting at the table writing, but he stopped work and stood as we entered.

'Good afternoon, ladies,' he said. 'I gather you might be able to get poor Hugo released. Is that true?'

'Good afternoon, Mr Thornell,' said Lady Hardcastle. 'It's certainly true that persuading the police that he has a sound alibi should secure his release, yes. But we are not possessed of magical powers. It's something any of you could do if you were able to say for certain where Hugo Bartlett was at the time of the murder.'

'Alas, experience has shown that the police are less than keen to take our word for anything. It needs someone with a little more respectability than we mere strolling players can claim.'

'But you're able to vouch for Mr Bartlett's whereabouts during the interval on the night Mr Singleton was murdered?'

'I am indeed. He was with me.'

'Where?'

'In here. We were going through some ideas for a new piece he's working on.'

'When was that?'

'He came in shortly after curtain-up, and was here until Patrick came to tell us what had happened on stage.'

'And would you be prepared to make a statement to the police to that effect?'

'Of course.'

Gwen looked puzzled.

'Why did you not say something before?' she asked.

'I don't know what you mean.'

'Well, you knew Rosalie had been released because Sarah stepped up and said that they'd both been together, why did you not just do the same thing?'

'I . . . well . . . I . . .'

Gwen seemed keen to press him further, but I put my hand on her arm to stop her.

'Not to worry,' I said. 'We know now.'

'Indeed,' said Lady Hardcastle. 'Would you be prepared to come with us to the Bridewell to speak to Inspector Wyatt?'

'Absolutely. Yes. Anything for poor Hugo.'

Sergeant Massive Beard was not pleased to see us. On the one hand it was comforting to see normality restored, and for the desk sergeant to be as curmudgeonly and unhelpful as ever after his disconcertingly cheery greeting on the street near the theatre. On the other hand, his manner really was tremendously wearing. Perhaps he could be encouraged to adopt some sort of middle ground between the two.

For now, though, we needed only to persuade him to let us see Inspector Wyatt.

'He's a very—' he began.

'—busy man,' I said. 'We know. But we have information pertinent to one of his cases, and he really will want to see us.'

He really didn't want to see us.

Obviously the sergeant had used our real names when he used the internal telephone system to alert the detective to our presence, which had resulted in a harshly worded refusal of our offer of help and a colourful suggestion of what we might do instead. He had never met us – or so he thought – but he had heard of our 'interference' in police cases and had no desire to muddy the waters of his own very smooth investigation of the Duke's Theatre Murders, as some of the newspapers were calling them. The sergeant declined to repeat the inspector's words verbatim, but the voice in the telephone receiver was sufficiently loud that he didn't need to. Wyatt was not a genteel man.

'Tell him . . .' began Lady Hardcastle. 'Tell him we're here on behalf of Lady Webster-Green and Miss Goodheart.'

The sergeant conveyed the message.

There was another fusillade of colourful invective from the telephone earpiece, but it ended with a grudging invitation to 'send them up'.

'You knows the way,' said the sergeant, dismissively, as he returned to his daybook. 'Two doors down from Inspector Sunderland on the right.'

We thanked him and led Gwen and Thornell up the stairs to the detectives' offices on the first floor. We passed Inspector Sunderland's room and found Wyatt's office next door but one, exactly as advertised. I knocked.

At his invitation, we trooped inside and stood together near the open door.

He looked at Lady Hardcastle. He looked at me. He looked at Gwen. He ignored Thornell. He looked back at Lady Hardcastle.

Inspector Dick Wyatt was not pleased to see us.

'I thought that Hardcastle woman and her lady's maid were coming up,' he said. 'What are you three doing here?'

'We *are* that Lady Hardcastle woman and her lady's maid,' said Lady Hardcastle in her most infuriatingly cheery voice. 'And this is Miss Armstrong's sister, Gwenith. Emrys Thornell you know.'

'You'll need to explain yourselves,' said Wyatt, with what he presumably hoped was an air of menace.

We explained ourselves.

He was unimpressed.

'Giving a false name and address to a police officer is a very serious offence,' he said when we were done.

'Is it, though?' said Lady Hardcastle. 'Is it really? You might choose to argue that we have obstructed your inquiries or wasted police time, but we have done neither of those things. We have *furthered* your inquiries and *saved* police time. Let's hear no more of your silly threats. We bring fresh evidence in the case. We have a witness, in the person of Mr Emrys Thornell, who can attest to the whereabouts of Mr Hugo Bartlett at the time of Paul Singleton's murder. And if he wasn't responsible for that, the odds are strongly against him having killed Davey Browning.'

Wyatt took a deep breath and seemed as though he was about to tell Lady Hardcastle what she could do with her fresh evidence, when there was a knock on the door-jamb.

'Sorry to barge in, Wyatt,' said Inspector Sunderland, 'but I thought I heard a familiar voice. Couldn't let a visit from Lady Hardcastle pass me by.'

'Good afternoon, Inspector,' said Lady Hardcastle. 'How lovely to see you. We were just bringing some fresh evidence to Inspector Wyatt on the Paul Singleton and Davey Browning cases.'

'Were you? Were you indeed? Excellent. How's the investigation going, Wyatt?'

'Quite well, thank you, Sunderland,' said Wyatt.

'Glad to hear it. Well done. I see from the arrests ledger that you have a suspect in custody.'

'I do. Mr Hugo Bartlett was the man responsible for asking for the murder weapon to be brought from the props store at the theatre.'

'I see. That's rather telling. What was his motive?'

'I'm not entirely certain yet – not for the Singleton murder, anyway. But the second was obviously committed in order to silence a potential witness to the first.'

'Well, I'm sure you'll find it. I presume he had ample opportunity to commit the murder? There's no one to vouch for him? No witnesses to say where he was?'

Wyatt sighed.

'That, apparently, is why Lady Hardcastle and her coterie have chosen to visit me this afternoon,' he said with weary resignation. He knew Inspector Sunderland had heard more than just Lady Hardcastle's dulcet tones, and that it would look bad for him to be dismissing this fresh evidence simply out of spite.

'That should clear things up for you,' said Inspector Sunderland, brightly. 'We're lucky to have such alert, concerned citizens helping us out.'

'We are, yes.'

'Well, I shan't keep you. Lady Hardcastle, Miss Armstrong, Mrs Evans – do drop in before you leave if you have time. There's always a pot of tea ready for you in my office.'

'You're very kind, Inspector,' said Lady Hardcastle. 'Though I fear we shall have to politely decline on this occasion – we have important business to attend to in the village. Some other time, I hope.'

'I hope so, too, my lady. Good day to you all.'

He walked back to his office, whistling.

Wyatt rummaged in his desk drawer for a statement form, which he handed to Thornell with a pen.

'If you would be kind enough to give me full details of your movements on the night of the murder, including any meetings you might have had with Mr Bartlett, I should be most obliged.'

'Certainly, Inspector,' said Thornell. 'May I . . . ?' He indicated the visitor's chair in front of Wyatt's desk.

Making no effort to appear polite or hospitable about it, Wyatt cleared as small a space as possible on the desk for Thornell to write his statement, and gestured for him to sit.

'Don't let me keep you, my lady,' said Wyatt once Thornell had begun writing. 'You told Sunderland you were busy.'

'That's correct,' said Lady Hardcastle. 'We are. Will you be all right, Mr Thornell? Is there anything else we can do?'

'Quite all right, thank you,' said Thornell. 'You've been an enormous help.'

'Then we shall bid you good day, Inspector. Thank you for agreeing to see us.'

Wyatt dismissed us with something approaching a growl.

We waved to Inspector Sunderland as we passed his office and made our way back out of the police station to the Rolls.

Chapter Eleven

We were home by about half past two, and I warmed some of Miss Jones's soup for lunch while Gwen went upstairs to rummage through my wardrobe. Lady Hardcastle joined me in the kitchen and sliced some bread.

'Do you think this plan will work?' she said as she sawed neatly through the loaf. 'I say, that's an almost perfect slice. We could send that to the Institute of Bread and Buns as an example of the bread slicer's art. Well done, me.'

'Well done you, indeed,' I said. 'And the plan is a sound one. It's a variation on the sort of tricks we played all the time as children. It still might not work, but it won't be the plan's fault.'

'There'll be many variables at play, yes,' she said, thoughtfully. 'But it's worth a try. It's not as though we can do a worse job than Joe and Daisy already have. It's not dangerous and it's not costing anyone anything—'

'Except perhaps another bottle of booze.'

'Except that, yes. But it's a price they'll have to be prepared to pay.'

We carried the soup and bread through to the dining room and were just setting out bowls and cutlery when Gwen arrived carrying two of my uniform dresses.

'You've some lovely clothes,' she said. 'I wish I could afford dresses like that – I might have to borrow some. But these are the only things I could find that match.' She held up the identical dresses. 'You've only got one of everything else. Oh, except some Chinese pyjama things. You've got loads of those.'

'I use them for my exercises,' I said.

'I've seen you doing them. Tai Chi, you said. But I can't imagine you go to the pub dressed like that, so prim and proper lady's maid will have to do.'

'They've definitely seen me dressed like that.'

'Not so much lately, though,' said Gwen. 'You've not worn a uniform at all since I got here.'

'That's true,' I said. 'I sort of got out of the habit. We've been working more and more lately, and there's not been much call for it.' I looked at Lady Hardcastle. 'You've never said anything. Do you mind?'

'Good heavens no,' she said. 'You are my right hand. My help in ages past. Without you, as I have observed many times, I would be dead in a ditch, my throat cut, my duties unfulfilled. It matters not a jot what you're wearing – although that blue dress you wear in the evenings sometimes is very fetching. We know who we are, we know what we have to do. The costume is just that.'

'Well, it explains why these two are in such good condition, at least,' said Gwen. 'I couldn't find two identical hats, though. I've got these, but they're not quite the same.' She produced two dark hats from among the folds of the dresses.

'They're as near as dammit,' said Lady Hardcastle. 'I'm going to put money on our thief being a man, and I've yet to meet a man who was not engaged in the clothing trade who could tell one lady's hat from another. They'll do splendidly.'

'You don't have two matching coats, either,' said Gwen.

'We'll work something out,' I said. 'It'll be fine.'

Gwen hung the dresses over the back of one of the dining chairs and laid the hats on the seat.

'That soup smells delicious,' she said.

We ate lunch.

'What do you think about the murders now?' asked Gwen as she buttered one of Lady Hardcastle's perfectly cut slices of bread.

'How do you mean, dear?' asked Lady Hardcastle.

'Well, you've got Rosalie off. And you've almost certainly got Hugo off. That's two down.'

'Four if we definitely believe Sarah and Thornell,' I said.

'Are they all really crossed off the list, though?' said Lady Hardcastle. 'We only have their own testimonies to go on, especially Thornell and Bartlett – the two men could be in cahoots. They're obviously good pals if they spend so much time together. What if that story about Thornell owing Singleton a large sum of money is true? What if he persuaded his good friend Hugo Bartlett to kill Singleton for him? Or what if he persuaded Bartlett to provide him with an alibi so that he could commit the murder himself? And no one has been able to tell us where Bartlett was the night Davey Browning was killed. We saw him before the show and then . . . nothing. "Urgent matters" was all we heard.'

'No one mentioned his absence, either,' I said. 'Do you think they know where he was that night?'

'No, and it might be suggestive if Thornell's story turns out to be false but, as with Rosalie, my objection to Bartlett's arrest was based on Wyatt's reason for it, not my doubts about his guilt. I'm convinced the dagger and the availability thereof is not the key to it all, but Wyatt can't seem to see past it.'

'You're right, of course,' I said, 'but we only have Bridges's word for it that he was in his dressing room at the time of the murder. No one seems to be able to confirm that Nancy really was outside with her chap. And no one's even mentioned Cowlin.'

'True, true,' said Lady Hardcastle. 'Though Cowlin doesn't seem to have a motive. The other two were tangled up in Singleton's amorous roguery in one way or another, but where does Cowlin fit in?'

'It's like we said before,' said Gwen.

'About him being the understudy?' I said.

'Exactly: professional jealousy. Cowlin was fed up with Singleton always getting the plum roles while he had to keep the props table tidy and learn everyone else's lines just in case. It's Cowlin, I bet you.'

'It's possible,' said Lady Hardcastle.

'So they all had motives if we look hard enough,' I said. 'And they all had access to the murder weapon. Wyatt needs to start asking questions about their movements.'

'He really ought,' agreed Lady Hardcastle. 'But one wonders if he will. Pass the pepper, would you?'

We ate on, and conversation returned to the evening's plans.

Having helped me to tidy away, Gwen disappeared upstairs once more.

She returned ten minutes later . . . as me. In one of my uniform dresses and with her hair up in one of the nearly matching hats, I wondered if even my best friends would be able to tell the difference. We'd know soon enough, though – Daisy was an important part of the plan.

Just before four o'clock we sent her on her way. She'd have to wait a while on her own, but it was her idea so I knew she didn't mind. Didn't mind or hadn't thought it through – either way we'd make it up to her if her plan worked. Or even if it didn't. She'd be fine.

Lady Hardcastle and I, meanwhile, had a little time to kill. We sat together in the drawing room, staring at the crime board.

'There's only a tiny window of time for anyone to have killed Singleton,' said Lady Hardcastle as she made notes on her timeline. 'Ten minutes at the very most. Surely we can establish what everyone was doing during those ten minutes.'

'We already know what four of them were up to,' I said. 'It should be easy enough to find out what the other three were doing.'

'It should, shouldn't it? We should take another look at the motives, too. I mean, it usually helps to work out why people might have wanted the victim dead. So far we have the love triangle between Sarah, Singleton and Rosalie, and the two women are each other's alibis anyway.'

'Sarah seems altogether too sanguine about the ending of their relationship for it to be a strong motive. She's a decent actress, of course, so it could all be for show, but I don't think she's overly upset by it. And Rosalie doesn't seem to have a motive – she was in love with the man, after all.'

'Not that we've discovered yet, at least,' I said.

'Well, quite. We have Nancy – whose big fear seems to be mockery – being propositioned by the glib Lothario, Singleton. Outraged by his suggestion and terrified of being a laughing stock, might she have done him in?'

'She might,' I conceded.

'Thornell owed Singleton money. Cowlin resented him for getting the plum parts. Harris is an oaf.'

'I'm not sure being an oaf is motive for murder.'

'It ought to be reason for locking him up, though,' she said. 'And then there's Hugo. I can't think of a motive for Hugo. But that's still a fair few motives. There's a lot going on between the members of that tightly knit group. We ought to do a little more digging.'

'You're right. We've allowed ourselves to be distracted. We've been so caught up in trying to sort out Wyatt's sideshow antics that we've done far too little actual investigating. To be fair, though,' I said, 'we weren't really given free rein to investigate – we had to do it on the q.t. We were asked to keep an eye on Wyatt, though.'

'And what a good job we did. But I think we've established by now that he's not going to solve the case on his own. It strikes me that he's simply intending to arrest each of them in turn until someone gets so bored of all his shenanigans that they confess.'

'It's not a terrible plan.'

'Oh, but it's an absolutely dreadful plan. We must call down to the engine room for full steam ahead on our own investigation, before something awful happens. He really could end up trying to get the wrong person hanged.'

'We need a systematic approach, then,' I said. 'Isn't that how you used to conduct your experiments? We shall corner each of the Bartlett Players in turn – alone if we can – and find out what makes them tick.'

'Systematic, yes, I like that. I should like to start with Harris Bridges.'

'Any particular reason?'

'I can't bear the man. I should love it to be him.'

I laughed and made a note on the board.

We discussed our plan of attack until it was time for me to get changed into my uniform.

We arrived at the Dog and Duck shortly before six o'clock. It was already beginning to fill up and the atmosphere was pleasingly lively. We approached the busy bar, where Daisy and Joe were waiting eagerly for us.

'Thank you for doin' this for us, m'dears,' said Old Joe, earnestly. 'It's drivin' I mad, losin' all this booze.'

'It's the least we can do to help our friends,' said Lady Hardcastle.

I nodded my agreement.

'It's lovely to see you at work at last,' said Daisy. 'It's excitin'.'

'It's mostly a matter of sitting about,' I said.

'I still thinks it's excitin'. Do you want a little somethin' to take with you to keep the cold out? It's nippy down in that cellar.'

'No, I'll be fine – got to keep my wits about me.'

'What about a bit of cordial? Don't want you gettin' thirsty.'

'I don't want to have to keep coming out to go to the ladies, either,' I said.

'Oh, go on. Just a small one.'

I sighed.

'All right, Dais,' I said. 'A small cordial. Thank you.'

'How about you, m'lady?' said Daisy. 'On the house.'

'Oh, that's very kind,' said Lady Hardcastle. 'I'll have a brandy. Thank you.'

'Large one?'

'Do you know, it's never occurred to me that there might be any other size. Do people ask for small ones?'

'Not many, no,' said Daisy with a laugh.

Daisy fussed about with our drinks while Joe excitedly told a couple of the regulars sitting at the bar that we were going to catch the thief once and for all.

Finally armed with a large glass of cordial, I made my way towards the rear of the pub and the door to the cellar. Looking around to check whether I was being observed, I opened the door and let myself into the darkness. There was a lantern and a box of matches on a small shelf just inside the door, but I ignored them and instead gave myself a few seconds to become accustomed to the gloom before cautiously descending the stairs.

By the time I reached the bottom, what little light had been coming under the door had been eaten by the darkness of the cellar and I could see nothing at all. I could hear something, though. A shuffling and creaking. Soft breathing.

'Is that you, Flossie?' said Gwen's voice from the blackness.

'Let's hope so, or you've just blown the gaff,' I said.

'The thief uses the lantern. Daisy told me it's always warm after they've been robbed.'

'She's cleverer than she likes people to know, that Daisy,' I said. 'Is there anywhere for me to sit?'

'There's a chair next to mine,' she said, tapping it with her fingernails so I might be able to locate it.

'How did you manage to sort chairs out for us?'

'I've got a lantern of my own.' It clanked and scraped on the stone floor as she gently knocked it with her boot. 'I'm cleverer than I like people to know, too.'

I fumbled towards her with my arms outstretched, and suddenly felt the familiar fabric of my uniform dress with the unusual sensation of someone else inside it.

'Steady on, Floss,' said Gwen with a chuckle. 'At least take me out for dinner and a show first.'

'If you'd just light the stupid lantern I wouldn't be groping about like this.'

'Where would be the fun in that?'

I poked her, and then gently lowered myself on to the chair.

'This is cosy,' I said. 'It's been years since we sat together in the dark.'

'Long nights in the circus wagon,' she agreed.

'Or sitting out under the stars waiting for dawn to rise on a new town.'

'That was dazzlingly bright by comparison. How did it go upstairs?'

'Daisy and Joe are either excellent actors—'

'Or they completely forgot what the plan was and just said what came naturally?'

'Exactly. Either way, there's not a man in the public bar who doesn't know that Herself and I have come to catch the booze thief and that I'm down here on my own waiting for them. Did anyone see you come in?'

'There wasn't a soul about. I didn't meet anyone between your house and the pub, and this place was deserted – just Daisy and Joe behind the bar talking about Joe's wife. What's she like?'

'Never met her,' I said. 'I sometimes wonder if she actually exists.'

'Well, he's very fond of her, whether she's real or not,' said Gwen. 'It was quite touching. How long do we give it?'

'A good half an hour, I'd say. Maybe a little longer. Daisy did remember to give me a drink so I'd have an excuse to get up and go to the WC, but we want to make it look reasonable.'

'Oh, lovely. Hand it over – I'm gasping.'

'Sorry, I spilt most of it on the stairs in the dark. It was only lime cordial.'

We sat together in the darkness for almost an hour, leaning against each other and reminiscing about childhood adventures.

After what we considered an appropriate length of time, Gwen and I swapped coats and hats in the dark. She gave me what was supposed to be a good-luck peck on the cheek but which caught my ear instead. We giggled and she stole cautiously up the stairs, leaving me alone in the dark.

I didn't have to wait long.

I estimated that about five minutes had passed before I heard the door open at the top of the stairs. I used the sounds of shuffling and lantern-lighting coming from above to cover my own stealthy move to a position of concealment. We had identified a handy nook next to the spirits shelf on our reconnaissance trip earlier in the week. I had imagined it would be easy enough to find, even in the pitch-blackness, but I had become anxious during the long wait that I'd give myself away in my fumbling about, or that I'd trip noisily on something. As it turned out, though, even the tiny amount of light coming downstairs from the lantern was enough to guide my way after so long in the dark.

I waited in silence as the footsteps clonked down the wooden stairs.

The light grew brighter.

The footsteps were heavy, laboured, slightly uneven.

Finally their owner reached the bottom of the stairs and scuffed towards the prize booze and my hiding place. I held my breath.

I waited until I heard the scrape of a bottle being dragged from the rack and then stepped out.

'Good evening—' In the lantern light I was slightly surprised to find myself looking at a plump little woman in a man's jacket '—Mrs . . . ?'

'Oo-er,' she said with a cheery smile. 'You give me quite a shock.'

'I'm sure I did. You're Mrs Grove's friend, aren't you?'

'That's right, m'dear. Agnes Bingle.'

'Well, Agnes Bingle, the jig is up.'

'What do you mean, dear?'

'You're the one who's been stealing Joe's spirits.'

She looked at the bottle in her hand as though surprised to see it.

'This? This is just . . .' she began.

'That's just a bottle of' – I glanced at the label – 'of Dewar's White Label. A bottle of scotch that you've just stolen from your friend Joe Arnold.'

She looked at the bottle again.

'I suppose it is when you put it like that.'

'How else would I put it?'

'Well, he makes a decent livin', doesn't he? Old Joe, I mean. I didn't think he'd miss the odd bottle now and again.'

'You've been taking at least one a week for a couple of months.'

'I i'n't doin' no harm.'

'You're stealing from one of your friends.'

'Oh, I'm sure he don't mind or he'd have made more of an effort to stop me.'

'He *has* been trying.'

'Not hard.'

This wasn't at all the confrontation I'd been expecting. Mrs Bingle seemed entirely unconcerned at having been caught in the act, and just smiled guilelessly as though somehow I was the one in the wrong.

'What on earth made you think it was all right to help yourself?' I asked.

'I noticed he never locks the cellar door,' she said, still smiling. 'I thought, "That's a bit careless. Anyone could nip down there and take somethin'." And then one day I just decided to come down and see what there was. I put on one of our Jack's old jackets so I could slip out the back without anyone thinkin' it odd there was a woman goin' out to the you-know-where, and came down here instead. He's got dozens of bottles on these shelves. I didn't think he'd miss one so I took it home for our Jack. And when he didn't miss one, I thought perhaps he might not miss two. And then it became a bit of a game. Like I said, I knew Joe wasn't really bothered or he'd have made more of an effort to stop me. He was just goin' through the motions, like.'

'But he and Daisy *were* making an effort. They tried all sorts of things to find out who was stealing the booze.'

'No, m'dear, they was always lookin' the other way. I knew they didn't mind. They kept their eyes on the farmhands, see? They was actin' like they was tryin' to catch one of the young lads so they never paid no attention to me.'

'But you're stealing. From your friend.'

'That's how I knows he don't mind. He don't mind givin' a few bottles of the good stuff to an old pal.'

'But he's not giving them to you . . .' I began. But somehow I knew I wasn't going to get through. 'Come on, you'd better come with me. We'll go and see Joe to see what he has to say.'

'Righto, m'dear.'

She started to lead the way.

'Aren't you forgetting something?' I said.

'What's that?'

'The scotch.'

'What about it?'

'Put it back.'

She looked at it in puzzlement.

'But . . .' she said. 'I's takin' it home for Jack.'

'Just put it back.'

She reluctantly did so and I followed her up the stairs. Part way up she stopped and turned to look at me, holding her lantern to my face.

'How did you get back down here, though?' she said. 'That's what I want to know. I watched you leave with Lady Hardcastle. You had a long conversation about how it wasn't no good and the thief wasn't goin' to turn up and how you might as well go home. That's when I knew it was safe to come down.'

'It's a mystery, that's for sure,' I said. 'Come on, I'm sure Joe will want a good long chat.'

At the top of the stairs she carefully extinguished the lantern and put it back on its shelf before letting herself out into the pub. I followed and pointed her in the direction of the public bar.

'I have someone to see you,' I said to Joe as we approached. 'I'm . . . well, I'm not entirely sure what to make of it, if I'm honest. I'm going to leave her with you and you can make up your own mind.'

Joe looked as confused as I was, but it suddenly didn't feel like it was any of my business so I left him to sort it out. If it had been one of the young lads I'd have been all for hauling him over to Sergeant Dobson and Constable Hancock at the village police station and inviting them to lock him in their cell for the night. But this? This was altogether too peculiar, and I thought it was something best sorted out between Joe and Mrs Bingle.

I found Daisy and quickly explained what had happened. She was as bewildered as I was and was keen for us to join Joe to find out more. But my heart wasn't in it, so I made my excuses and went out into the chilly November night.

I walked home, slightly disappointed.

Back at the house, Gwen and Lady Hardcastle had made themselves comfortable in the drawing room. There was a cheeseboard and some biscuits on one of the small tables, and one of them had ferreted out the brandy and port decanters.

'Evening, loafers,' I said once I'd take off my hat and coat and settled down to join them. 'What have I missed?'

'Not a great deal,' said Lady Hardcastle. 'I was asking Gwenith about the current state of the Royal Artillery.'

'Are you an expert on military preparedness, Gwen?' I asked.

'I keep my ears open,' said Gwen. 'It's surprising how much you can pick up if you pay attention.'

'That's the basis of my entire career,' I said. 'Servant of the gentry and servant of the Crown – it mostly just involves listening more than you speak.'

'When did you work for the gentry?' asked Lady Hardcastle.

'You're the gentry, you ninny.'

'Am I? How delightful. But what happened at the pub? Did you catch the mysterious grog-grabber of the Dog and Duck?'

'I did,' I said. 'But it was oddly disappointing.'

'How so?' asked Gwen.

'It was Agnes Bingle.'

They looked blankly at me.

'Mrs Grove's friend,' I said. 'We saw her the other night in the snug.'

'Cheerful, chubby lady?' said Gwen. 'She looked like she was more likely to bake you a wholesome pie than steal from you. Are you sure?'

'Caught her red-handed. But she was . . . she was a little odd. She didn't seem to realize she was doing anything wrong. It was quite distressing, actually. I don't think she's well. I should probably have stayed to help, but it upset me a little so I left them to it. Cowardly, I know, but I didn't have the will for it any more. I'll talk to Daisy tomorrow and see if there's anything we can do to help.'

'Did you say Bingle?' said Lady Hardcastle.

'Agnes Bingle, yes.'

'Any relation to Jack Bingle?'

'He's her husband from what I could make out,' I said. 'Yes.'

'Her late husband, if I'm not thinking of the wrong man. Don't you remember? Gertie told us about a horrible accident on one of the farms during the harvest. I remember thinking what an unfortunately amusing name Bingle was.'

'I'm not sure I was with you. I don't remember that at all.'

'Perhaps you weren't. Perhaps she was gossiping during one of those committee meetings I ended up not being able to wriggle out of. But I'd wager it's the same man – I can't believe the area is overburdened with Bingles.'

'Oh. Well, now I feel terrible. She was wearing Jack's jacket and talking about taking the whisky for him. Do you need me? I'm going back to the pub. That poor woman needs comfort and friendship, not accusations and trouble.'

Without waiting for a reply, I got up and went out into the hall to put my hat and coat back on.

Chapter Twelve

Friday morning was chilly and grey, but I rose early with a feeling of warm relief that something was being done to help Mrs Bingle.

I had found her still deep in conversation with Joe and Daisy when I returned to the pub the previous evening, and was pleased to see they were looking after her. Of course they knew her story – it seemed I was the only one who didn't – and they had tried to treat her kindly. Luckily her friend Mrs Grove came in for her nightly glass of sherry, and as soon as she found out what had been going on she hurried home to ask Reverend Bland if there was anything he could do.

Within the hour, the vicar's wife, Jagruti, had arrived with an offer of a room and a hot meal at the vicarage. The missing booze would be sorted out later – for now Agnes was everyone's priority. I liked living in the village.

While I pottered in the kitchen putting Lady Hardcastle's starter breakfast together, I told Edna and Miss Jones about my encounter with Agnes in the cellar the previous evening. They, too, knew what had happened to Jack Bingle and, though they were shocked that Agnes was the pub thief, they were pleased the vicar's wife had taken charge of things.

'She's a good woman, that Jagruti Bland,' said Edna with an emphatic nod. 'We's lucky to have her. The last vicar's wife was wetter than an otter's pocket. Never knew such a drip in all my born days.'

'She has a demented dog, though,' I said.

'Hamlet? He's no bother – he just wants to play. He's a little lamb, really.'

Hamlet was a Great Dane and stood only a few inches shorter than I did. He was neither little nor lamb-like, but I took her point. Most of the chaos that followed him about was caused by his exuberant joy at having found some new game to play.

'I suppose so,' I said. 'But he's still barmy.'

'Mad as a March hare,' agreed Edna. 'But I still love him. Is that toast for Lady H?'

'It was, but now I come to look at the clock it's a bit early to take it up to her. Would you like it instead? I'll make her some fresh in a minute or two.'

We chatted a little longer about Agnes Bingle and what else we might be able to do for her over the coming months, but eventually it was time to awaken the sleeping Hardcastle.

◆　◆　◆

I managed to get Lady Hardcastle upright and presentable before nine, which I considered a minor triumph in itself. We ate breakfast in the morning room with Gwen.

'What are you two planning for today?' asked Gwen as she tucked into a heaped plate of sausage, eggs, bacon, mushrooms and toast.

'We're heading into town to talk to the actors,' said Lady Hardcastle. 'It's about time we stopped just trying to rescue them from Wyatt's ineptitude and started trying to properly figure it out for ourselves.'

'You don't need me, do you?'

'Need you, dear? No, not "need". It's lovely to have you with us if you want to come, though. Why? Do you have plans of your own?'

'Sort of. After what Flossie told us last night about Mrs Bingle, I wanted to try to help. I've seen war widows going through the same thing, you see. When Dai's company was in South Africa – when you two were still on your way back from China – they lost a few fine men, and their wives and sweethearts back home had to cope as best they could. The War Office didn't care much once they'd sent their letters and authorized their pensions, so it was left to the rest of us to rally round and take care of them. I know what she's going through and I just thought . . .'

'That sounds like a splendid idea, Gwenith,' said Lady Hardcastle. 'Thank you. Jagruti will be pleased to have some experienced help, I'm sure. The world is a much better place with you Armstrong girls in it, you know.'

'I don't know about that,' said Gwen. 'Flossie's a nightmare. And she smells funny.'

'That's the smell of soap,' I said, poking my tongue out. 'You should try it for yourself one day.'

'Would you like an introduction at the vicarage?' asked Lady Hardcastle.

Gwen pointed to her own, smiling face.

'I think this is all the introduction I'll need,' she said. 'It's quite the icebreaker. "Oh," people say, "don't you look like Florence Armstrong?" It's not hard to explain who I am from there.'

'As you wish, dear. The vicar and his wife are perfectly delightful, anyway, so you shouldn't have any difficulties there, but the offer stands if you want it.'

'I shall be fine, but thank you.'

We were interrupted by a ring at the doorbell.

It was Inspector Sunderland.

'Good morning, Inspector,' I said.

He looked carefully at my left ear.

'Good morning, Miss Armstrong,' he said. 'I do hope I'm not interrupting breakfast.'

'Of course you are. But come and join us – there's always too much.'

'You're too kind. Are you sure Lady Hardcastle won't mind?'

'Have you ever known her to mind having you eat our food?'

'You make a good point.'

I took his hat and coat and accompanied him to the morning room.

'We have an unexpected guest for breakfast,' I said. 'I'll get you a plate.'

I left him to settle and went to fetch another place setting.

'I'll do that,' said Edna as I started getting the requisite crockery from the kitchen dresser. 'You get back to the mornin' room. Important man, that Inspector Sunderland. You don't want him sittin' there waitin' for you. Go on. Shoo.'

I rejoined the others to find that the inspector actually had been waiting for me to return before imparting his news.

'Here she is,' said Lady Hardcastle. 'Sans plate, I notice, but in person nonetheless. You can tease us no longer, Inspector. Tell us your news.'

'The plate's on its way,' I said as I sat down.

'Thank you,' said Inspector Sunderland. 'But I'm not teasing you, my lady – my news isn't nearly exciting enough to have to tell it twice, so I wanted to wait until we were all together. As you must surely have expected, Hugo Bartlett was released from custody late yesterday afternoon. Wyatt was disgruntled and disagreeable, but he bowed to pressure from the chief superintendent and reluctantly let the playwright go. So, well done, all of you.'

'We did little other than ask a simple question of Emrys Thornell,' said Lady Hardcastle. 'It was scarcely magic.'

'A simple question that Dick Wyatt should have asked days ago. Which brings me to my next titbit of news: I shall be taking charge of the investigation in a few days' time.'

'Oh, I say. That *is* good news.'

'Unbeknown to me, Wyatt was being given one last chance to prove himself. I thought he was the blue-eyed boy, destined for greatness, but it turns out his ambition and self-confidence have far outstripped his abilities and he's on his final, final chance. The chief super thought a straightforward murder case would be Wyatt's opportunity to show once and for all that he was as good as he told everyone he was. But it turns out he was as lazy and inept as everyone else said he was. His latest bonnet bee is a mysterious stranger in a hat who he claims someone saw prowling about backstage, but no one has been able to provide any more information and we're beginning to think he invented it to make it look as though he was on top of things. Anyway, he's being quietly shuffled into an admin job where he can do less damage. They'll make it look like a step up to save the lad's embarrassment, but the sooner he's in charge of the stores or organizing the canteen rota or whatever it is they have him doing, the safer the city will be.'

'What's happening in the meantime?' I asked as Edna arrived with a tray.

She quickly set out a plate, cutlery, teacup and a napkin for the inspector, and slid out again without saying a word.

'Until I'm able to take charge of the case, you mean?' said the inspector as he tucked eagerly into the lavish breakfast. 'That's the main reason for my visit, actually. I was hoping you might do what you do best and continue to poke your noses in for me. See what you can find out before I swoop in and take all the glory.'

'You can have all the glory you crave, Inspector dear,' said Lady Hardcastle. 'And we were planning to engage in some concerted and systematic nose-pokery this very day. We have been far too passive. "Keeping a watching brief", as my dear brother has it – honestly, I don't know where he gets all his dim-witted jargon—'

'It's a legal term,' I said. 'It's when you instruct counsel to keep an eye on a case.'

'Is it?' she said, suddenly interested. 'Is it really? Well I never. But anyway, I find his "watching briefs" entirely tedious. He has access to the thugs of Special Branch to carry out that sort of mundane donkey-work. If there's sitting about and "keeping a weather-eye on things", he can leave it to them. We are skilled operatives. Valuable assets. We do not do "watching briefs".'

The inspector looked slightly crestfallen.

'Oh, don't look so hurt,' said Lady Hardcastle. 'I didn't mind keeping an eye on the case for you and dear Georgie, but I was champing at the bit to get properly stuck in. This is all the excuse we need.'

'I don't mind quietly watching, actually,' I said. 'People try to kill me far less often when I'm just lurking in the background keeping my eyes and ears open. Things get ugly very quickly once we start trying to become active participants in the fun and games.'

'Be fair, Flo dear, they mostly try to kill me.'

'Of course they do – it's a perfectly understandable impulse – but who has to stop them?'

'It adds a bit of spice to life. Don't try to pretend you don't enjoy it.'

I tutted and made a moue, but she was right.

'I don't imagine anyone will try to kill you over this,' said the inspector. 'Experience suggests that this will all turn out to be petty jealousy over some slight or other. He'll have been chasing one of the girls, or stepping on someone's lines. I once arrested a chap who'd stabbed his friend because he kept moving the pegs on the cribbage board when he thought no one was looking.'

'Whatever it turns out to be, we shall labour night and day to uncover the truth,' said Lady Hardcastle.

The inspector chuckled.

'Just get the ball rolling,' he said. 'Ask the questions Wyatt should already have asked.'

'Right you are, dear. We shall be heading into town as soon as we've finished here, I think.'

'So soon? I thought actors didn't turn up to work until late afternoon.'

'Ordinarily that seems to be the case, but there's often someone lurking about the theatre after lunch. I think many of them find it warmer and homelier there than at their digs. And we shall spend the time until lunch doing other extremely important things – I have an appointment with my dressmaker.'

'I shall leave you to it, then. I have some loose ends to tidy up on my current case – that's why I'm in your neck of the woods, as a matter of fact. Do you know North Nibley at all? My main suspect lives there.'

'We've never had cause to visit,' said Lady Hardcastle. 'But the name amuses me. Isn't there a pointy tower there? A monument to . . .'

'William Tyndale,' I said. 'He translated the New Testament into English in the sixteenth century.'

'I knew that,' whispered Lady Hardcastle. 'I just wanted to give her the chance to show off.'

'Well, I shall report back on the magnificence of the monument once I've interviewed my man,' said the inspector. 'I'm hopeful it will put an end to the case, and then I shall be free to arrest whichever of the cast of *The Hedonists* it was who ruined your birthday evening.'

'We shall do our utmost to make that easy for you. Would you like some more toast, dear?'

Conversation moved on to other things, and we waved the inspector off at about half past ten. After that it was time for hats, coats, and a drive into Bristol. We gave Gwen directions to the vicarage and set off.

◆ ◆ ◆

Visits to Lady Hardcastle's dressmaker were always hilarious. Imagine, if you will, the world's most outspokenly self-assured person meeting the world's biggest ego (I leave it to you to decide which was which), add generous helpings of champagne, the latest fashions from Paris, and an assistant who is not allowed to say the word 'no', then sit back and watch the show.

We left shortly before one o'clock with half a dozen dresses ordered – three of which were for me, although I would send one to Gwen in Woolwich when it was made – along with a selection of undergarments and accessories. The fireworks as strong opinions clashed and collided in the small 'consulting room' hadn't disappointed, and I looked forward to our return visit.

Having spent the morning being so genteel and refined (if occasionally a little forthright), Lady Hardcastle declared herself in the mood for something altogether more down-to-earth for lunch, so we stopped at the chip shop at the bottom of Christmas Steps for hake and chips liberally doused with salt and vinegar.

We ate our lunch as we strolled back towards the Tramways Centre, and were able to discard our newspaper wrappers in a handy litter bin before heading up to Frogmore Street and the Duke's Theatre.

Haggarty waved us in with barely a second glance, and we wandered into the labyrinth of passageways that made up the vast backstage area of the theatre. It belatedly occurred to us that we had no idea where we were going. We returned to the stage door and asked Haggarty for directions to Harris Bridges's dressing room.

We found it after missing only one turning, and Lady Hardcastle knocked on the door.

'Come,' called Bridges in a strong baritone, trained over many years to be able to project all the way to the cheap seats in the gods.

We entered.

'Aha,' said Bridges with a smile, rising from an armchair and putting down a script on the dressing table. 'Lady Hardcastle and Miss Armstrong. Come in, do. Make yourselves at home.'

He gestured to a sofa opposite the chair where he had been sitting, and we settled ourselves.

'Are we interrupting?' asked Lady Hardcastle.

'Not at all, my dear lady.' He gestured to the script. 'I was just trying to learn my part for the next production. I find the passage of time is not my friend. Every year that passes seems to add another day to the time it takes me to learn a script. If that carries on I'll soon find myself trying to learn my role for the play we did two months earlier. I'm glad to take a break, honestly. Tea?'

'Thank you, that would be most welcome. We ate our lunch on the hoof and didn't have the opportunity to have a drink with it.'

I nodded my own agreement and he set about fussing with the kettle and the gas ring. Lady Hardcastle took a notebook and pencil from her bag and began making notes.

'To what do I owe the pleasure of this most welcome interruption?' said Bridges.

'Inspector Sunderland has asked us to help him out with some preliminary inquiries here at the theatre. To try to put together a picture of the events on the night Paul Singleton was murdered.'

'Sunderland? I thought Wyatt was in charge.'

'He was.'

Bridges stopped spooning tea leaves into the pot and turned round.

'"Was"?' he said.

'There's been a change of assignments. Inspector Sunderland has taken over.'

'And he works differently?'

'He does.'

'So why did Wyatt not put together a picture of events on that terrible night?'

'That's not for us to say,' said Lady Hardcastle.

Bridges frowned as he turned back to his tea-making.

'Nuff said,' he replied. 'But I think you already know most people's movements that evening.'

'Perhaps,' said Lady Hardcastle. 'But would you indulge us anyway? What did you do during the interval?'

'I had a brief meeting with Patrick and Nancy in Patrick's dressing room, and then I came back here.'

'On your own?' I asked.

He splashed some milk into three mismatched cups.

'On, as you say, my own,' he said. He turned to lean against the dressing table while he waited for the tea to steep. 'It was not always thus, I must say. Once upon a time I was engaged to be married to Rosie, and we would retire to one or other of our dressing rooms to bill and coo. Sweet nothings were whispered. Eternal love was pledged. You know the sort of thing. But these days, alone is very much how I spend my time.'

'You and Rosalie were engaged?' said Lady Hardcastle, with rather more surprise in her voice than she usually allowed when she was questioning someone.

'There's no need to sound like that,' he said, defensively. 'We were very much in love.'

'When was this? I mean, when did it end?'

'A few months ago. Paul and Sarah broke up, then Rosie decided she was in love not with me, but with the newly available Paul.'

'It all happened in that order?' I said.

'That's what I choose to believe,' he said. 'Otherwise I'd have to think she was carrying on with Paul while she was still engaged to me.'

'And while he was still engaged to Sarah,' I said.

'Well, quite. And I'd prefer not to think of it like that. That way madness lies.'

'But you all got on well?' asked Lady Hardcastle.

'Like the proverbial house on fire, my lady. Actors fall in and out of love all the time. It's a very intimate business.'

'So we've been told. What was the meeting about?'

'I beg your pardon?'

'You said you met Patrick and Nancy before returning here. What was on the agenda?'

'Is that any of your business?'

'Of course not. But the more we know, the more we can tell Inspector Sunderland. And the more he knows, the quicker he'll apprehend Paul's killer.'

'We are thinking of forming our own theatre company,' he said with a resigned sigh.

'Is that also why you were together at Crane's the other day?' I asked.

'It was, yes.'

'You're going to leave the Bartlett Players?' continued Lady Hardcastle. 'But why? I was under the impression that you all got along splendidly.'

'And so we do. But we're rather tied to performing dear Hugo's romantic romps. They're fun and the audiences lap it up, but . . . I played Hamlet, you know. The reviews said I could rival Henry Irving. I want to be able to show my range before I'm too old to play anything but wise old grandfathers. Patrick and Nancy feel the same way. Not about getting too old, of course – neither of them is thirty yet – but, like me, they feel constrained by the light comedy. We want to spread our wings a little.'

'Do the others know?' I asked.

'We had to be a little cagey about it,' said Bridges. 'We . . . well, we didn't want everyone to join us, d'you see? Some chaps just aren't of the calibre we wanted.'

'So Paul Singleton wasn't one of your chosen few?' said Lady Hardcastle.

'He . . . was not. He was splendid company and always stood his round at the bar, but . . . well . . . no, he wasn't up to it.'

'Did he know what you were planning?' I asked.

'Well, now, there's the rub. He found out somehow and was threatening to blow the gaff.'

'Tell Hugo, you mean? Why would he do that?' asked Lady Hardcastle.

'And the others,' he said. 'But I've no idea. Spite? I can't think what he would have gained from it other than spoiling it for us.'

'Would he have spoiled it, though? The others might be aggrieved that you hadn't invited them, but they'd have been upset as soon as you left, anyway. The same goes for Hugo Bartlett. He couldn't stop you going your own way, so what would it matter that he knew before you were ready to strike out on your own?'

'That's just it, you see. We weren't ready to strike out on our own. We still had much to arrange and it could all have gone very wrong. Which would mean we were stuck here working with Bartlett and the others, with them knowing we didn't want to be – that would mean we'd be overlooked for the plum roles. Or worse, they might ask us to leave. And then where would we be?'

'Surely there's plenty of work for talented actors.'

'One would hope so but, alas, times are hard and there are always more actors than roles. The other potential problem, of course, is that if word got out before our plans were complete, there would be time for disgruntled parties to speak ill of us, tarnish our reputations, and generally queer our pitch. Any new venture we subsequently managed to launch would be fighting an uphill battle against naysayers in the business from the very beginning. That, dear lady, is why we were so pleased to see you when we thought you were Lady Webster-Green, would-be impresario. You might have been the answer to our prayers.'

I wanted to distract him before he realized he'd just given himself a very plausible motive for killing Paul Singleton and began to try to change his story or offer water-muddying equivocations. I needed to change the subject.

'Did you see Mr Singleton at all during the interval?' I asked.

Bridges poured the tea and handed us our cups as he considered this.

'Do you know, I think I might have,' he said. 'Yes, yes, now you come to ask me, I believe I did see him.'

'You're sure?' said Lady Hardcastle. 'It's rather important. Thus far our ideas concerning Singleton's whereabouts have been based entirely upon surmise and supposition. If you can confirm a definite sighting, that would be most helpful.'

'I'm reasonably sure, yes. He was always swanning about in a peacock-blue smoking jacket, d'you see. He bought it in Manchester. He was inordinately proud of the wretched thing. I thought it made him look like the worst sort of fop, but he loved it so. He always put it on in the interval but he'd been complaining that someone had pinched it during our first week here. He must have found it, though, because I'm sure I saw him wearing it, going in to his dressing room as we were coming back from our meeting.'

'Which dressing room was his?'

'Number six. He had a thing about the number six. Brought him luck or some such rot.'

'When did you see him?' I asked.

'During the interval,' he said with a puzzled frown.

'Yes, I know. But near the beginning? Near the end? How long had you spent in your meeting? There are clocks everywhere.' I pointed to the rather new-looking clock on the wall above the dressing table.

'Those blasted things. They installed them here earlier this year. Haggarty has a master clock in his little cubby and all these are enslaved to it. They all tell the same time. It's hellish. There's something comforting about an old-fashioned clock, don't you think? Like the one with the cracked wooden case my mother had on the mantelpiece. It lost about fifteen minutes a day and she had to set it right by the chimes of the church clock every morning and evening. But its sonorous tick . . . tock . . . tick . . . tock marked the passage of time in a way that was unique to our house. These have no soul. No ideas of their own. They just repeat what the master clock tells them.'

'And what time did it say it was when you returned here?' asked Lady Hardcastle.

'I've no idea. I never look at the wretched thing. I rely on bells and calls to tell me when to go on.'

'I see,' said Lady Hardcastle. 'Did you see anyone else on your way back here?'

'Not a soul. Everyone was in their dressing rooms by then. And at least one of them wasn't alone, if you know what I mean.' He winked.

'Oh?' I said. 'Who?'

'Emrys Thornell had a woman in his room.'

'Did he? Are you sure?'

'Madam, I think I know what a woman sounds like.'

'What were they talking about?' asked Lady Hardcastle.

Bridges gave an unpleasantly lascivious chuckle.

'My dear, they weren't *talking* at all,' he said.

With a shake of her head, Lady Hardcastle closed her notebook. 'Well, thank you for sparing us so much of your time, Mr Bridges—'

'Harris, please.'

'And thank you for your candour. We have a little extra to add to our picture now, thanks to you.'

'It's entirely my pleasure,' he said. 'If there's anything else I can do, you need only ask.'

'We shall. Thank you. For now, though, we shall leave you to your preparations.'

We both stood to leave. I took Lady Hardcastle's half-drunk cup of tea and put it on the dressing table with my own.

We said our goodbyes and went out into the corridor, shutting the door behind us.

It was still only early afternoon. We agreed that we'd prefer not to leave Gwen on her own for the evening again, but that still left us a decent amount of time to explore the theatre a little.

'So far on this floor,' said Lady Hardcastle, 'we've seen only the workshop where we found poor Mr Browning, the green room, and the dressing rooms.'

'I can't imagine there's anything else here.'

'Nor I. So are we presuming the fabled props store is downstairs somewhere?'

'I should imagine so. They'll have furnaces down there for heating, too, I should think. And . . . well, who knows what else?'

'There's one frightfully good way to find out. We just need to remember where we were when Sarah showed us the door.'

We hunted round the corridors for a while, narrating our search to each other as we went. Eventually we came upon a grey door marked *Authorized Staff Only*.

'This is it,' said Lady Hardcastle. 'I distinctly remember mentally congratulating them on not giving in to the French spelling.'

'Which we've been using for hundreds of years,' I said.

'But it still seems wrong. The word goes *zzz*, not *sss*. Heigh ho. Do you have your picklocks?'

'I do,' I said, turning the knob and opening the door, 'but I find it can save time simply to check whether a door is open before I scrabble about on my knees picking the lock.'

'Clever clogs.'

We entered and Lady Hardcastle flicked the electric light switch. The yellow light from the bare bulb illuminated a short, bare passageway leading to a flight of stone steps.

We descended.

At the bottom of the stairs was another dimly lit passage. There were two doors labelled, as we had predicted, *Furnace Room* and *Props Store*. There were two more without signs which I supposed to be general storage, but it was the third that caught my attention.

'That looks exciting,' said Lady Hardcastle as she saw it, too.

Danger – Trap Room – Keep Out

'I always want to know what's on the other side of a door that says *Keep Out*,' she said. 'Do that magic thing you do.'

'Try the handle, you mean? Of course, my lady.'

I twisted the doorknob, but this time the door was locked. I was fishing in my bag for my picklocks when we heard footsteps behind us.

'Can I help you, ladies?' said an unfamiliar man's voice.

We turned to see the stagehands' foreman looking at us, head cocked. He was holding a rolled-up rug under his arm.

'We're exploring,' said Lady Hardcastle. 'You don't mind, do you, Mr . . . ?'

'Stone's the name,' he said. 'Ned Stone. No, I gots no objection to you goin' wherever you likes. Mr Adlam said you had the run of the place. But some places i'n't safe so I'd be happiest if you'd get yourselves back upstairs while there's no one to look after you. I's responsible for safety, see? I can't be keepin' an eye on visitors as well as all me other jobs.'

'Quite right, too. We don't want to be a nuisance. Satisfy our curiosity, though, what's through that door?'

'Some old stage machinery, that's all. It don't get used much and it's all heavy, dangerous stuff in the wrong hands, so we locks it all up.'

'It's locked all the time?'

'Ar. Last time we went in there would have been two Christmases ago, when the pantomime was on. The Prince's usually gets the pantos so we don't have much cause to play with our toys.'

'I see. Well, thank you, Mr Stone. We shan't keep you from your work.'

He pressed himself against the wall so that we could pass, and we made our way back upstairs.

'What now?' I said once we were back on the ground floor.

Lady Hardcastle looked at her wristwatch.

'It's half past two,' she said. 'It'll take us well over an hour to get home, and it'll start getting gloomy at around . . . what is it now . . . four?'

I nodded.

'So if we tarry any longer, we'll arrive home once it's started to get properly dark, and I do so hate that. I suggest we call it a day and head back to our rustic sanctuary. We can take a proper run at interviewing this lot tomorrow.'

We slipped back out into the chill.

Chapter Thirteen

We didn't see Gwen when we got home, and so we spent the evening on our own, reading or playing the piano according to our preference.

On Saturday morning I was pottering in the kitchen with Edna and Miss Jones when a bleary-eyed Gwen appeared at the kitchen door in her nightdress.

'*Bore da, annwyl*,' I said. 'What time did you get in?'

'About midnight,' she said with a yawn. 'I was at the vicarage.'

'They throw a wild party at the vicarage,' I said. 'That James Bland is quite the carouser.'

'Jag, Minnie and I were talking to Agnes. We played a few games of cards and just chatted over endless cups of tea.'

'It's Minnie now, is it?' I said.

'Their housekeeper. Miranda "Minnie" Grove.'

'I know, but I always call her Mrs Grove. Or sometimes Miss Grove. I've never known which.'

'She's Mrs, but her husband died at the Battle of Laing's Nek in '81. He was a BSM, just like Dai. He was only twenty-seven.'

'Ah,' I said. 'Thank you. I've never had a chance to talk to her properly. So, how's Agnes Bingle?'

'I think she's turned a corner. She spent most of the evening crying, but by the time we tucked her up in bed she seemed as though she was coming back to reality. She's a lovely old girl, and she's got some good friends. It'll take her a while, but she'll get there.'

'You're a good woman, Mrs Evans,' said Edna. 'There i'n't many as would give up their own time to help a stranger like that.'

'Thank you, Edna,' said Gwen. 'But I was just doing what anyone would do.'

'You and your sister would. And Lady Hardcastle, o' course. But there's people round here who wouldn't cross the road to help no one.'

Gwen just smiled.

'Do you want a cup of tea, then?' I said.

'Don't you usually have coffee in the morning? I don't like the idea of you having to make tea just for me.'

'We has tea, m'dear,' said Edna, indicating Miss Jones as she spoke. 'There's always a pot on the go.'

'Then tea, please. Thank you, Edna. I can't get used to coffee. What did you two get up to yesterday, Floss?'

'Herself's dressmaker and then the theatre,' I said.

'Did you learn anything?'

'We did, as a matter of fact. Not much, but the victim was seen going in to his dressing room early in the interval, so we're starting to get a clearer idea of the sequence of events.'

'You'll have it solved in no time. What time do you take up her . . . what is it you call it? Her starter breakfast?'

I looked at the kitchen clock.

'Any time now,' I said. 'I just need to butter some toast.'

'What's she like first thing? Is she generally *compos mentis*?'

I could tell from the twinkle in her eye that Gwen had mischief in mind.

'Don't you dare,' I said. '*I'll* take the coffee and toast and *you* can get yourself dressed for breakfast. We'll have no teasing of my friends, thank you.'

'Spoilsport,' she said, and helped herself to a cup of tea from the pot on the kitchen table.

◆ ◆ ◆

Over breakfast, Lady Hardcastle expressed her weariness with our endless visits to the theatre and I wasn't able to disagree with her.

'Why don't you just call on the actors in their digs?' asked Gwen. 'You don't actually need to see them at work.'

'You make a good point,' said Lady Hardcastle. 'To be honest, I think it's just old-fashioned etiquette that makes me reluctant. I don't mind smashing down the door of a wrong 'un at any time of the day or night, but one doesn't just drop in unannounced on acquaintances.'

'You're forever dropping in unannounced at Georgie's gaff.'

'She's a pal, dear. One can get away with unannounced calls on pals. But these actor types are mere acquaintances.'

'Then announce it.'

'That's not a terrible idea, young Gwenith. We could cable them, couldn't we? Georgie might have addresses, or a means of acquiring them. Would you pass the marmalade, please.'

She telephoned Lady Bickle after breakfast, and only a quarter of an hour later received a return call with the address in Cotham of Mrs Rippon's boarding house, the temporary address of Nancy Beaufort and Rosalie Harding.

We set off straight after breakfast, with only a brief stop at the post office so I could send the telegram. By the time we arrived in Cotham they would at least be expecting us, even if they had no opportunity to respond to tell us to go hang.

'Do you remember the last time we were in Cotham?' said Lady Hardcastle as we turned on to the Gloucester Road heading south.

'I do,' I said. 'That was quite the experience.'

'We were offered jobs, Gwenith,' said Lady Hardcastle over her shoulder.

'Something dangerous and exciting?' asked Gwen.

'Potentially exciting, I suppose, depending upon your tastes. We had to visit a house run by one Madam Jemima to interview a witness in the Lizzie Worrel case.'

Gwen laughed delightedly.

'You two? Working in a brothel? I'd pay to see that.'

'That's rather the point,' I said. 'You'd have to.'

She laughed again.

'Well, it's something to fall back on if the spying work dries up,' she said.

'It's good to have a contingency plan,' agreed Lady Hardcastle.

Three-quarters of an hour later we passed the house owned and run by Madam Jemima in Cotham, and were delighted to find that Mrs Rippon's boarding house was only a few doors away.

'Do you think your girls' landlady knows what's going on just down the road?' asked Gwen as we pulled up outside the boarding house.

'I've often wondered about that sort of thing,' said Lady Hardcastle. 'Surely the neighbours know exactly what's happening.'

'Perhaps they just pretend they don't and get on with life as though everything is normal,' I said. 'People are very good at ignoring what's going on right under their noses.'

We got out and went through the wrought-iron gate into a well-kept front garden. At the other end of the path there were three stone steps leading to Mrs Rippon's blue-painted front door. Lady Hardcastle mounted them and tugged on the bell pull while

Gwen and I arranged ourselves symmetrically behind her on the next step down, making us look even smaller than we were.

After a few moments, a rather attractive woman in her fifties opened the door. She was plainly, but neatly, dressed.

She smiled as she said, 'I'm sorry, I've no vacancies. There's a sign in the window.' She pointed to her left, where, sure enough, a printed sign in the bay window did indeed say that there were no vacancies. She began to close the door but Lady Hardcastle put out her hand to stop her.

'It's quite all right, we're not seeking accommodation, we—'

'I'm afraid I don't donate to charities at the doorstep,' said Mrs Rippon, her smile now gone.

'No, that's quite all right, we—'

'And I'm quite happy with my choice of church, thank you.'

'Of course, of course. What we—'

'And my choice of laundry soap.'

Lady Hardcastle pulled a silver case from her coat pocket and deftly produced a calling card, which she handed over.

'I am Lady Hardcastle,' she said. 'And these are my associates Miss Armstrong and Mrs Evans.'

Mrs Rippon looked at the card, then looked up again. She seemed to notice Gwen and me for the first time.

'How do you know which is which?' she said with the smile of someone who is rather too pleased with their own joke.

'They have their names tattooed on the backs of their knees. We're here to see two of your boarders: Miss Harding and Miss Beaufort. We sent a telegram.'

Mrs Rippon had clearly thought her observation a terribly witty one and seemed disconcerted to have Lady Hardcastle top it with an absurdity. But she was on safe ground with visitors to her boarders – she knew how to deal with them.

'I don't allow my girls to have more than two visitors at a time,' she said, nodding at each of us in turn to emphasize that there were three of us.

'That shouldn't be a problem,' said Lady Hardcastle. 'You can count Mrs Evans and me as Miss Harding's visitors, while Miss Armstrong can visit Miss Beaufort. How about that?'

The smile had gone again and Mrs Rippon was obviously irked at having lost control of the conversation. I imagined she wasn't used to having anyone calmly stand up to her. A blazing row she could cope with – I'd wager she could get the best of anyone in a straight fight – but cheerful cheekiness left her angry and confused. She opted to take back control with some good old-fashioned nastiness.

'How about you sling your hook before I wallop you one, you cheeky mare. I've wasted far too much time on you already.'

She moved to close the door again but Lady Hardcastle already had an elegant boot in the way. Even though the topmost step was lower than the door, she still stood taller than the diminutive landlady and must have looked an intimidating sight from Mrs Rippon's perspective. She shoved at the door but Lady Hardcastle's boots were made of strong stuff and it refused to close those final few inches.

'If you would just tell the ladies we've called,' said Lady Hardcastle, 'perhaps they might choose to see us outside. I noticed a nice tea room as we drove here.'

'I'm not doing you any favours. Get your foot out of my door.'

'But you'd not be doing me a favour, dear, you'd be doing it for your paying guests. Surely you wish to look after them – you must rely on repeat custom for your income.'

With a huffed 'Very well', Mrs Rippon turned back towards the hall and disappeared. Lady Hardcastle removed her foot and inspected her boot for damage.

'I must commend my bootmaker on a splendid job. These are a great deal more robust than they appear.'

She held out her foot for us to admire. There was some minor scuffing, but nothing that wouldn't buff out.

'I can see to that,' said Gwen. 'Dai taught me how to polish boots. Oh, unless . . .' She looked at me.

'Help yourself,' I said. 'I could live a long and happy life without ever cleaning another shoe.'

'I wouldn't want to step on your toes,' she said.

'Especially not after you'd put such a lovely shine on my boots.'

We waited in the cold for a few more minutes before Mrs Rippon reappeared at the door.

'They'll meet you in the St Michael's Tea Rooms in fifteen minutes,' she said, and slammed the door.

'Come along then, ladies,' said Lady Hardcastle. 'Best highly polished feet forwards.'

We secured a table big enough for five at the pleasant little tea room, and ordered tea and a selection of buns. While we waited, Gwen and I entertained Lady Hardcastle with more tales of twinly mischief from our youth. By the time the actresses arrived, Lady Hardcastle had a pleasingly large grin on her face and I was certain that my reputation as the Sensible One had been tarnished for ever.

'Good morning, ladies,' said Lady Hardcastle. 'Do sit down, won't you? And help yourselves to cakes. We seem to have ordered far too many, as usual.'

'Thank you,' said Nancy.

'Yes, thank you,' said Rosalie. 'And we're sorry about Mrs Rippon.'

'It's kind of you to be concerned, dear, but she's not your responsibility.'

'No, but it's still embarrassing when people come to call.'

'Nonsense. We have an after-dinner anecdote now.'

'One that doesn't end with either of you killing someone,' said Gwen.

'What?' said Nancy. 'None of your stories end with you killing people, surely?'

'Not all of them,' said Lady Hardcastle. 'But Mrs Rippon interests me, strangely. She seems so lovely, so charming. Such a welcoming smile. And then . . .'

'And then you said something to challenge her and she flew off the handle?' said Rosalie.

'Exactly that, dear. Exactly that. Ah well. It takes all sorts, I suppose.'

'You've killed people?' said Nancy, who wasn't letting this one go.

'Only the ones who tried to kill us, dear,' said Lady Hardcastle.

'I don't believe you.'

'Quite right, too. I wouldn't believe me, either. But have one of these delicious rum babas.'

The two women poured themselves cups of tea and dug hungrily into the pile of cakes and buns. After an entertaining round of 'mmm's, 'ahh's and 'thank you so much's, Rosalie wiped her mouth on a napkin and looked across the table at us.

'So,' she said, 'to what do we owe the pleasure of this visit? Harris droned on about how he was now at the centre of a major investigation by two famous and formidable private detectives, but I stopped listening after a while – he does go on. But I'm assuming that you are the famous detectives and that you're . . . what? Working with the police? Working instead of the police?'

'We're not famous, I hope, and we're certainly not formidable—'

'Except when you kill people,' interrupted Nancy.

'Will you give it a rest, Nance,' said Rosalie. 'You sound like a child sometimes.'

Nancy flushed scarlet and began a close examination of the half-eaten cream horn on her plate.

Lady Hardcastle chose to ignore the interruption.

'But we are working with our good friend Inspector Sunderland,' she said. 'He needs a day or two to get some other matters sorted out and he has asked us to see if we can get a picture of the events of that horrible first evening for him. The second evening, too, if we can.'

'And you just do that, do you? Question people on behalf of the police?'

'Sometimes, dear, yes. In this instance he thought that since we'd been at the theatre on both nights, and since we were already acquainted with the Bartlett Players, we might be well placed to speak to you all informally and try, as I say, to form that all-import-ant picture of events. Who was where, and when, and what they saw while they were there – that sort of thing.'

'It sounds perfectly reasonable when you put it like that. So what do you want to know?'

'Thank you, dear,' said Lady Hardcastle. She fished in her bag for her notebook and mechanical pencil.

'You don't mind if I make a few notes as we speak, do you?' she said.

'Not at all,' said Rosalie.

Nancy shook her head.

'Thank you,' said Lady Hardcastle. 'Now, we know Mr Singleton—'

'Please call him Paul,' said Rosalie. 'He was my Paul, not Mr Singleton.'

'Of course, dear. My apologies. We know Paul was killed during the interval, so let's start with the end of Act One. You were on stage with Paul, Harris and Sarah. You got your big laugh before the curtain came down . . . and then what?'

'Paul and I had a sneaky canoodle in the wings and then went our separate ways. That was the last time I saw him.' Rosalie stopped for a moment, her eyes glistening with tears. 'And then I went to my dressing room. I came out when I heard movement in the corridor – that's a sure sign we're about to get the call for the second act – and I met Sarah. We gossiped for a moment and then made our way to the stage.'

'What did you gossip about?'

Rosalie glanced quickly at Nancy.

'I can't remember,' she said. 'Nothing important, I shouldn't think.'

'You're on remarkably good terms with Sarah,' I said. 'Considering . . .'

'Her previous relationship with Paul? That just sort of ended. She never said why. Nor did he. But she doesn't bear me a grudge or anything.'

'Do you recall seeing anyone else?' asked Lady Hardcastle.

'When?'

'At any time. Did you meet anyone on your way to your dressing room, for instance?'

'No, I don't think so. Oh, I saw you, Nance. You were talking to Adlam.'

'I was,' said Nancy. 'Just a quick word before . . .'

'It's all right, dear,' said Lady Hardcastle, 'we've heard where you were before your assignation outside. Would you rather discuss it in private?'

'No, it's quite all right – Rosie knows what's happening.'

'I do,' said Rosalie. 'They invited me to join their conspiracy but I regretfully declined.'

'Why?' I asked. 'Setting up a new theatre company seems like an exciting idea.'

'A very exciting idea indeed,' said Rosalie. 'But it would mean working with Harris Bridges. He and I don't get along.'

'You were engaged to be married, were you not?' said Lady Hardcastle.

'We were. And then we were not. And therein lies the cause of our continuing animosity.'

'I'm just being nosy,' said Gwen, 'and I'm sure it's not at all relevant to the case, but why did you break up?'

'Dear Harris and I had a difference of opinion over whether it was acceptable for him to share his affections with as many women as possible while we were engaged. He insisted it was absolutely fine. I disagreed.'

'Ah, yes, I can see how that might be a problem.'

'Also, it turns out that once you get to know him – to really, truly know him – you find that under that arrogant, overbearing, patronizing exterior there beats the heart of an arrogant, overbearing, patronizing man. You really should think twice about working with him, Nance. At the moment he has Emrys and Hugo to keep him in check, but without them . . .'

'Patrick is part of the group,' said Nancy, defensively.

Rosalie just made a face at this.

Lady Hardcastle was keen to get things back on track.

'So,' she said, 'you spoke briefly to the theatre manager, Mr Adlam, and then went to your meeting with Harris Bridges and Patrick Cowlin. Where was that held?'

'In Patrick's dressing room,' said Nancy.

'How long did the meeting last?'

'About fifteen minutes, I'd say.'

'And when it was over?'

'I walked along the corridor with Harris as far as his dressing room, then I . . . well, I slipped outside. As you heard before.'

'Of course,' said Lady Hardcastle. 'And when *that* meeting was over?'

'I heard all the commotion inside and came in to find out what was going on.'

'Did you see anyone as you walked towards Harris's dressing room?' I asked, remembering something Bridges had said.

'I don't think so . . . No, wait, I saw Paul going into his dressing room.'

'Did you say anything to him?'

'No, he was at the other end of the corridor, but I distinctly remember seeing him.'

'I saw someone, I think,' said Rosalie.

'Oh?' I said. 'A man in a dark suit and cloth cap?'

'No. A woman in an expensive dress.'

'A woman?' said Lady Hardcastle. 'Backstage?'

'Yes. I thought she must have been visiting one of the boys. We often see ladies backstage. She was on her way back from the you-know-where.'

I looked at Lady Hardcastle, hoping she might remember Harris Bridges having mentioned that Thornell had a woman in his room. She nodded to indicate that she knew exactly what I was thinking, but then returned to her note-taking. After a moment, she finished and looked up.

'Well, ladies, thank you very much,' she said. 'You've been most helpful.'

'Is there nothing else?' said Rosalie.

'Not for the moment, no. As I said, we're merely trying to get an idea of the sequence of events for the inspector. You've given us quite enough to be getting on with.'

'You know where we are if you need anything further.'

'We do. Thank you.'

'It's a shame you're not really thinking of opening a theatre,' said Nancy. 'We could bring our new acting company to work with you.'

'Now wouldn't that be simply marvellous,' said Lady Hardcastle.

'I confess I thought seriously about it myself while we were talking to you all,' I agreed. 'Perhaps when we retire again.'

'Retire from what?' asked Rosalie. 'What is it you actually do?'

'We are merely civil servants, I'm afraid,' said Lady Hardcastle. 'Nothing terribly thrilling.'

'Civil servants who occasionally kill people,' said Nancy.

'Only occasionally, dear. And only when they really deserve it.'

'Oh, one more thing,' I said. 'Have either of you been victims of the recent thefts?'

'What thefts?' said Rosalie.

'Hugo told us there'd been a . . . a spate of thefts backstage,' I said, ignoring Gwen's grin at my use, once again, of the word 'spate'.

'Oh, that. No. I've heard people grumbling, but nothing of mine's gone missing. Nance?'

'No, nor mine.'

'That's fine,' I said. 'Thank you.'

Nancy looked at the clock on the tea-room wall and raised her eyebrows at Rosalie, who turned to glance at it herself.

'I'm sorry, ladies,' said Rosalie, 'but we ought to be getting to the theatre. We have a read-through for the next production. We're taking advantage of not having a matinée performance and we're making use of the stage.'

'They've got us working tomorrow afternoon, as well,' added Nancy, clearly unimpressed by this intrusion into her Sunday plans. 'I've never had to be at the theatre by one o'clock on a Sunday. It didn't ought to be allowed.'

'Oh, that's no fun,' said Lady Hardcastle. 'But of course you must go. Thank you so much for sparing the time to see us – you've been of enormous help.'

With more smiles, nods, and 'thank-you's, the two actresses extricated themselves from the table and retrieved their coats from the hatstand by the door. They left with a final wave and we returned to the serious business of cream cakes.

'Was that useful?' asked Gwen as she tucked in to yet another rum baba. 'It didn't sound it.'

'It was,' I said. 'The curtain came down on Act One at about half past eight, and Paul Singleton was definitely alive then because we saw him leaving the stage. He and Rosalie "canoodled" for a few minutes in the wings. We don't know what he did next, but Nancy has confirmed something Bridges said to us yesterday about seeing him going into his dressing room at what we're now assuming is somewhere after a quarter to nine, but probably before ten to. We're narrowing down the time of death.'

'We also know,' added Lady Hardcastle, 'that Bridges and Rosalie did not part on good terms and that the story of their break-up is more complicated than Bridges said it was. He heavily implied that Paul and Rosalie had been carrying on before they broke off the engagement, but her version is that it was he who was doing all the carrying on.'

'It could be a little of both,' suggested Gwen.

'Indeed it could. And it probably is.'

'Bridges gave himself a pretty hefty motive for wanting Paul dead yesterday,' I said. 'If Singleton was threatening to tell everyone about their plans for a new company, he might have wanted him out of the way.'

'Quite so,' said Lady Hardcastle. 'And by confirming that the break-up was acrimonious, Rosalie has rather confirmed another possible motive – he might still have blamed Singleton for it.'

'So it's Bridges,' said Gwen, emphatically.

Lady Hardcastle laughed.

'Well, it's certainly not *not* Bridges,' she said. 'At least not yet.'

'But is it Rosie or Nancy?'

'That seems less likely. Rosalie has an alibi for our supposed time of death – helpfully provided by Sarah. But Nancy . . . well, I suppose if we're saying that Bridges might have killed Paul after seeing him go into his room, then she might have done it just as easily. We only have her word for it that she was outside with this unknown "chap".'

'Or they're working together,' said Gwen. 'They're both covering for each other and they killed him over the breakaway theatre troupe thing. He wanted Paul dead anyway and she's easily led so . . .'

'There's that, of course. But I'm not convinced yet. What say you, Flo?'

'I can't see it being Nancy,' I said. 'She doesn't have a proper motive of her own. And for all that it was me who thought I was on to something when I heard Bridges talking about the new troupe, it's not quite the motive I thought it was now I've had time to think about it. But, like Gwen says, if he wanted Paul dead for other reasons it might have pushed him over the edge. I must say, their romantic merry-go-round seems like exactly the sort of thing that could end in violence.'

'And Rosalie?'

'Why would she kill her lover?' I said. 'That doesn't make sense to me at all. And you said yourself that she has an alibi for the time of the murder. The mystery man in the cloth cap seems to have turned into a mystery woman in an expensive dress, though. That's odd.'

'I rather assumed the woman was Thornell's companion,' said Lady Hardcastle. 'The one Bridges was pruriently chuckling over.

It might be worth our while finding out who she was and how she got there.'

'It might,' I agreed. 'Oh, do you think she was the one we saw on the night of Browning's murder?'

'While we were on the stage? She could be, certainly.'

'It would be just our luck to spend all this time investigating the theatre company only to find out that it was a visiting stranger after all.'

'It would. We shall have to ask around about her.' She flicked through her notes and appeared, if not exactly satisfied, at least as though progress was being made.

'It's not much,' she said, closing her notebook, 'but it will save Inspector Sunderland some time, at least. Do either of you want that last custard slice?'

Chapter Fourteen

Full of cake and with no desire for lunch, we decided to head for the theatre after all. The chance to watch the rehearsal had some appeal, and it seemed that that's where all the actors would be anyway, so if we wanted to speak to them, that's where we'd have to go.

Haggarty looked up from his book and said, 'Afternoon, Lady Hardcastle,' and waved us through.

'Our little untruth didn't bother him, it seems,' I said as we navigated the corridors towards the stage.

'He's used to people pretending to be someone else,' said Lady Hardcastle.

We arrived at the short flight of steps without making even one wrong turn, and shushed each other as I opened the door to the stage – we didn't want to interrupt the rehearsal.

There was no one there.

'Well, that's disappointing,' said Lady Hardcastle to the empty auditorium. 'At the very least I was hoping to observe the creative process at close quarters, even if we learned nothing new about the murder.'

'What now?' asked Gwen.

'We could loiter here until they all arrive, I suppose.'

'Or we could go and tap on a few doors,' I said. 'Talk to some people. Get some answers. Learn the truth about all this. Waiting is for chumps.'

'She's very forthright, your sister, isn't she?' said Lady Hardcastle. 'She thinks we're chumps.'

'With respect,' said Gwen, 'I think she was saying that you're a chump. I wasn't mentioned.'

'Neither of you is a chump,' I said with a sigh. 'I'm just trying to galvanize us to action.'

'It's all right, dear,' said Lady Hardcastle to Gwen with a wink. 'We're being galvanized. We should have known.'

'You should,' I said. 'Now come along, the pair of you, before I have to start slapping people.'

I led the way off stage and they followed me. I could have sworn I heard them giggling.

I wandered for a while and eventually found myself in a corridor we'd not explored before. I knocked on the next door I came to. There was no reply. I looked at my companions. Lady Hardcastle motioned for me to try the door handle.

It opened.

My first view was of a card table, atop which sat a gleaming Royal Standard typewriter. There was a pile of paper beside it. This must be Hugo Bartlett's dressing room.

There was a scrabbling sound from where I presumed the dressing table would be.

'Just a minute,' said Hugo.

There was more scrabbling.

Without my intending it to, the door swung open further to reveal Hugo Bartlett sitting on the chair in front of the dressing table. In the mirror I was able to see his face. His beard was half on, half off, and the beardless half didn't look at all like the handsome man I'd been expecting. Bartlett wasn't a man at all.

'Shut the bloody door,' she said.

'What's going on?' asked Lady Hardcastle as she jostled for a better view. 'Oh, hello dear. You must be Helena. It's a pleasure to meet you properly at last.'

Lady Hardcastle ushered me into the room and followed, with Gwen close behind. Gwen closed the door.

Helena turned to face us, the neat Edward VII beard still hanging half off her face.

'You knew?' she said.

'I suspected, at least,' said Lady Hardcastle.

'What gave me away?'

'Oh, one notices things. The soft voice and the precision and consistency of the beard were clues, I think. But what really gave you away was your behaviour at that first meeting at Crane's.'

'My behaviour? But I tried to be the perfect gentleman.'

'And so you were, dear. But you made one fatal error.'

'Which was?'

'You listened to us. Two women came to you with the frankly absurd idea of opening a theatre in a seaside town and you sat and listened to us. You didn't put us down, you didn't patronizingly correct our misapprehensions, you just listened. You were enthusiastic. You were helpful. You were everything the majority of men we run into in our daily lives are not.'

Helena Bartlett laughed.

'I must work on that,' she said.

'Oh, and having a noisy rendezvous with your lover Emrys Thornell in his dressing room was a bit of a giveaway, too.'

Helena laughed again.

'How did you find out about that?' she asked.

'Bridges overheard you. He was certain Thornell had a woman in there but we knew that couldn't be true – Thornell provided your alibi and said you were with him during the interval. So unless he was lying, the woman was you.'

'I told him it was risky,' said Helena.

'You're the mystery woman Rosalie saw backstage on the night of Paul's murder,' I said. 'And the one we saw in the auditorium on Monday when Browning was killed.'

'Guilty on both counts. I don't like seeing Emrys when I'm dressed as Hugo – it's quite unsettling for us both – so sometimes I take a chance and go as myself. That first time I was absolutely desperate for the loo, and we'd lost track of the time. I didn't realize it was the interval until I was on my way back. I thought I'd got away with it, but apparently not. And that night when you were on the stage . . . Well. I was terrified, I can tell you. I had to meet someone in town and I couldn't leave through the stage door as me, so I thought I could get out through the foyer. I didn't expect you'd still be there – I thought you'd be wandering about the theatre by then.'

'It was a puzzle for a while,' said Lady Hardcastle. 'But it makes sense now. Can the person you were going to see confirm your whereabouts on Monday?'

'She can. Priscilla Cooper. She's an actress I knew when I was starting out – the one who suggested I do all this.' She indicated her Hugo costume. 'I like to have dinner with her when we're in town. We dined at Le Quai, actually – I gather they know you there.'

'They do indeed. Thank you.'

'None of the others know who you really are?' I asked.

'None of them. They just think I'm a slightly timid man.'

'How did Thornell work it out?' I said.

'I told him. I'd rather fallen for him by then, so things might have become quite uncomfortable for the poor chap if I'd carried on the charade.'

'But why pretend to be a man in the first place?' asked Gwen.

We all turned to look at her, our mouths open.

'I mean,' she said, slightly taken aback by our response, 'it's not like there aren't plenty of women writers. There's Jane Austen for one. And Mary Shelley. And—'

'The list is a long one,' said Helena, 'as is the list of female playwrights. But we're outnumbered hundreds to one by the men, and you can count the number of respected female theatre company directors on the fingers of one foot. Imagine how much easier it has been for me to get my work taken seriously by actors and theatre owners as Hugo than it would have been as Helena. I'd been struggling to get anyone even to look at my work until Priscilla suggested I invent Hugo and taught me all the make-up and costume tricks. And if I have to do a bit of strategic binding, and wear a maddeningly uncomfortable false beard, it's a small price to pay to pursue my passion.'

'Talking of binding,' I said, 'how do you manage to hide . . . you know . . . ?'

She opened the front of her shirt at the belly to reveal thick padding.

'It's a combination of squashing what God gave me up top, and building up the belly with padding below so they don't show so much anyway. It's not an attractive look – I resemble some sort of barrel like this – but it hides the bumps where the bumps shouldn't be.'

'Ingenious,' said Lady Hardcastle. 'We should make a note of that one in case we ever need to dress you up as a chap, Flo.'

'Dress yourself up as a chap,' I said. 'I put up with enough as it is.'

'It's certainly not fun,' agreed Helena. 'But it offers enormous advantages in life. I wish I'd known about it at school, actually. My performance as Romeo was panned because of my unboyish figure.'

'So we heard,' said Lady Hardcastle.

Helena laughed.

'Georgie's still telling that story, is she?' she said.

'With great fondness.'

'That's rather lovely. But I know all the tricks now, and if I want to be free of it all but still keep an eye on things, I sometimes visit the theatre dressed to the nines and sit in the audience.'

'You ought to sort out that beard before someone else comes along,' said Lady Hardcastle. 'I shouldn't want us to be the cause of your ruse unravelling. We know what that's like and we didn't have an entire career hanging on our deception.'

'Thank you,' said Helena. 'Was there anything I can do for you? I rather feel I owe you a debt for springing me from chokey.'

'No, dear. We're just trying to build a picture of the events of the evenings of the murders, but we already know where you were. And presumably you didn't see anyone.'

'Only Emrys and Priscilla,' said Helena as she deftly applied gum to her jawline and reaffixed Hugo's neat beard. 'How do I look?'

'Like a well-respected playwright,' said Lady Hardcastle.

Hugo looked at us, earnestly. The timid playwright was back.

'Obviously I have no power to compel you to silence on this,' he said, 'but I beg you, for the sake of my place in this precarious business, to keep it to yourselves.'

We nodded our assent.

'Of course,' I said.

'Absolutely,' said Gwen.

'You have my word,' said Lady Hardcastle. 'Although, if it should turn out that you had anything to do with either death, then it will come out anyway.'

'Then I'm safe,' said Hugo. 'I was at Le Quai on Monday, and last week I really was with Emrys. We didn't leave his dressing room until we heard all the kerfuffle in the corridor as everyone started running about at the beginning of Act Two. I had to change before I could come out to see what was going on.'

'In that case, you have nothing to worry about. But . . .'

'But what?'

'Dear Georgie ought to know.'

Hugo looked melancholy for a moment.

'She ought, but I have no idea how to tell her now. We were such good friends when we were young, and I so desperately wanted to see her every time we came to Bristol, but I couldn't risk it. It would have been like one of my less sophisticated farces to be going up to Clifton as Helena, then meeting her at the theatre as Hugo, with her wondering why she never saw us both together. After a while, though, the Hugo disguise was so much a part of me that I decided just to drop in on her like this. She accepted me entirely at face value and I've been selfishly able to rekindle an old friendship without risking exposure.'

'You must work something out,' said Lady Hardcastle. 'She's as keen to see Helena as you were to see her. Don't let your selfishness deprive her of that.'

'You're right, of course. I shall give it some thought.'

'Thank you. She deserves better. But for now, we ought to leave you to dandify yourself before you lead your rehearsal. Our silence will mean nothing if your make-up isn't up to snuff.'

'You aware of our rehearsal as well?' said Hugo. 'Is there nothing you don't know?'

'It takes all the books in all the libraries in all the world to hold even a fraction of the things I don't know, dear, but I try to keep my eyes and ears open. Good luck.'

'We don't say that in the theatre,' said Hugo. 'Frightfully bad luck. The phrase is "break a leg".'

'Good heavens. Why?'

'No one knows.'

'Well, break a leg, then, dear. We shall leave you in peace.'

Gwen opened the door and we trooped out into the corridor once more, leaving Bartlett to prepare.

◆ ◆ ◆

'Now what?' said Gwen as we prowled backstage once more.

'Now we wonder if we were too quick to dismiss Hugo Bartlett as a suspect,' said Lady Hardcastle.

'How's that?'

'Suppose Paul Singleton knew his secret,' I said. 'You heard what he said – his whole career would end overnight if word got out. We've known people prepared to kill for a lot less than protecting their life's work.'

'But he was with Thornell when Singleton died,' persisted Gwen. 'And with her pal Priscilla when Browning was killed.'

'So she says.'

'We can easily track down this Priscilla character. And Bridges heard her with Thornell.'

'Actually, Flo dear,' said Lady Hardcastle, 'she's got us there. Perhaps we're free to dismiss them both, after all.'

'Who next, then?' asked Gwen.

'She's very eager, isn't she?' said Lady Hardcastle.

'You do this sort of thing all the time,' said Gwen. 'I've got to go home soon – this might be my only chance to catch a killer. What about old whatshisface? The stage-manager-understudy fella. Cowlick.'

'Cowslip,' said Lady Hardcastle.

'I'm not rising to it,' I said. 'You both know full well what his name is.'

'Cow Parsley,' said Gwen.

'Cow-Catcher,' said Lady Hardcastle.

'What's a cow-catcher?'

'It's a large metal grille they put on the front of railway loco-motives in America to scoop cows off the tracks.' She mimed a ploughing action with her hands. 'Though in reality it's more of a cow disintegrator.'

'Yuck,' said Gwen.

'Cowlin,' I said, exasperatedly. 'You win. He's called Patrick Cowlin and you're a couple of idiots.'

'I prefer to think of myself as impish,' said Lady Hardcastle.

'Or playfully waggish,' said Gwen.

'You do both remember that I can kill you, don't you? With a flick of my dainty wrist. They'll never find the bodies.'

'We'll be good,' said Gwen.

We found ourselves back at the stage, where some of the actors had already begun to gather. Bridges was on stage with Sarah, Rosalie and Nancy leading some sort of loud vocal warm-up. Patrick Cowlin was fussing with champagne bottles on the props table.

'There's one missing,' he said when he noticed us. 'They're empty bottles. Who would pinch an empty bottle? I despair sometimes.'

'People do the strangest things,' said Lady Hardcastle. 'Aside from trying to fathom what might have happened to your missing props, are you busy?'

'I have to be part of the read-through in a moment, but that's it. What can I do for you?'

'You might have heard that Inspector Wyatt has been taken off Paul's case and has been replaced by Inspector Sunderland.'

'Is he the chap who came backstage to speak to us on the night of the first murder?'

'He is, yes. He has a few things to attend to before he can get properly stuck in, and he's asked us to save him some time by getting an idea of where everyone was during the interval on the Tuesday night.'

'Why you? And why not both nights?'

'We help him out from time to time. It's an informal arrangement but it seems to work. And we rather think that if we catch Paul's killer, we'll have Davey Browning's killer at the same time. The odds are very much in favour of it being the same person.'

'I see. Well, you can tell him Harris and Nancy came to talk to me in my dressing room shortly after the curtain came down. We spoke for about ten or fifteen minutes, then they left. I stayed there and drank a cup of tea, then went to the stage after the foreman came to tell me it was ready for Act Two.'

'You were there alone?'

'Just me and my tea.'

'And when you got to the stage, did you see anything untoward?'

'Like Paul's dead body, you mean? No. Look: the leg's in the way.' He indicated the black curtain I had stood behind when we first examined the stage. 'I glanced on-stage to make sure everything was where it was supposed to be. I checked the props table over here . . . then waited till we got the signal from front of house that everything was ready. When Sarah, Harris and Rosie arrived, I opened the tabs and sent them on.' He pointed to a winch that seemed to be connected to the main curtains.

'Wasn't Paul supposed to be on the stage?' asked Gwen. 'Didn't you check he was there before you went ahead?'

Cowlin looked sheepish.

'Ah, well,' he said. 'Actually . . . Look, I knew he wasn't there, all right? I can see the chair where he's supposed to be from my place in the wings, and I thought . . . well, I thought I could catch him out. It really bothered me that he got that part. I would have been perfect for it. I *am* perfect for it. I get much bigger laughs than he ever did. I was just waiting for the cocky little blighter to be late so

I could show him up. "I need to be on stage alone so I can prepare," he said. "Make sure no one disturbs me." Night after night he went on and scowled at me if I so much as looked at him. And then my chance came. He wasn't in his chair when everyone else was ready, so up went the curtains.'

'You weren't concerned about ruining the play?' I asked.

'It's not Shakespeare,' he said. 'It's not a sacred text. The others would have improvised something until he turned up, and then they'd have all got themselves back on track. Once the curtain came down, that's when the trouble would have started. That's when I'd have made my case for replacing him. But . . . well, he wasn't late, was he? He was . . .'

'We know, yes. We were in the audience. Did you see anything else, though? No one acting furtively? No one where they shouldn't have been?'

'No one at all. It's not a technical show. We need some stage-hands to reset everything between acts, but once they're done they all slope off to their room next to the workshop for tea and cards. There's never anyone about.'

'I see. Well, thank you very much, dear. We'll leave you to your read-through.'

With a nod, Cowlin joined his colleagues, stage centre.

'While everyone's busy,' said Lady Hardcastle, 'I should like to take a look at Paul Singleton's dressing room.'

'What will that tell us?' asked Gwen.

'Almost certainly nothing. But it feels as though it's the sort of thing we ought to do. I'd wager Inspector Sunderland will want to know what's in there.'

'It's number six,' I said.

'Oh, well remembered. I knew I'd asked Bridges, but I wrote it down so I couldn't remember what he'd said.'

Gwen gave her a puzzled frown.

'I can remember things,' said Lady Hardcastle, 'or I can write them down and remember where I wrote them. I find that doing both is a waste of energy. I was taking notes while we spoke to Bridges and I have a general recollection of the conversation, but I haven't troubled to commit any of the details to memory because I know they're all in my notebook.'

'And she knows she can rely on me to remember them anyway,' I said.

'There's that, too,' said Lady Hardcastle. 'Why keep a dog and bark oneself?'

'Woof,' I said with a weary shrug. 'I do wish you'd think twice before you compare me to dogs. We went through a phase of you calling me a bloodhound or some such. I don't enjoy it.'

'I'm sorry, dear. Where's room six, though?'

'It's this way.'

'Who's a good girl?' she said. 'Are you a good girl? Yes you are. Yes, you're a good girl.'

'With a flick of my dainty wrist,' I said as I set off towards Paul Singleton's dressing room.

We arrived at the door and I tried the handle, but this time it was locked. I rummaged in my bag for my picklocks.

'You should watch closely,' said Lady Hardcastle to Gwen. 'She's an absolute wiz at this.'

'Gwen can do it, too,' I said as I knelt down to examine the lock. 'We learned together. Marvellous Marius Marcu, Romania's foremost escapologist, taught us how to open anything from a padlock to a bank vault.'

'It's true,' said Gwen. 'Though he was really Morris Middleton from Mexborough. Nice man. His wife used to make us parkin.'

'Oh, and bonfire toffee on Guy Fawkes night,' I said. 'There you are – one picked lock.'

I stood and opened the door.

It was another dressing room, much like all the others, but this one hadn't been opened for a week. It smelled musty and neglected. Paul Singleton's Act One costume lay in a crumpled mess across the back of an armchair. There was a shaving kit beside the small sink in the corner. Greasepaint sticks cluttered the dressing table beside a cup of what would once have been tea but which was now home to a species of green mould that would have kept the scientists at the university busy for weeks.

There were scripts on the threadbare sofa, along with a peacock-blue smoking jacket.

'He wasn't a tidy chap,' I said, indicating the mess.

'Oh, I don't know,' said Lady Hardcastle. 'It looks perfectly neat to me.'

I made a face but said nothing further.

'And there's the jacket Bridges mentioned,' said Gwen. 'Peacock blue. It looks quite garish, doesn't it?'

'Not badly made, though,' I said, picking it up. 'Nice bit of satin.'

Out of habit, I ran my hands over it, feeling the lining and the seams for hidden . . . Actually, I didn't know what might be hidden there. In our other job it was secret documents or concealed weapons, but I honestly had no reason to think an actor would have anything worth hiding.

I was right. Nothing. I checked the pockets and found a bag of humbugs and a scrunched-up piece of paper. I smoothed it out and read it aloud.

'*I must see you – I can wait no longer. Meet me in the trap room in the interval. N.*'

'Well, now,' said Lady Hardcastle. 'There's a thing.'

Our first thought was to try to get back to the trap room, but there was something going on down in the basement. There were stage-hands and maintenance men going up and down the stairs, and we knew from our previous attempt that they'd politely but firmly tell us to get lost if we tried to explore.

Instead we returned to the side of the stage and watched in silence as the company worked their way through another of Hugo Bartlett's light comedies.

There were some genuinely hilarious lines and the story seemed quite clever from the little we saw. It really would be a shame if 'Hugo' Bartlett had to stop writing for any reason – the world would be just a tiny bit less jolly.

Gwen and I were used to standing quietly and watching per-formers rehearsing, but Lady Hardcastle was all over the shop. She was fidgeting, umm-ing, ahh-ing, looking this way and that.

'Is everything all right?' I whispered, hoping to distract her enough to make her stand still.

'Quite all right, dear, thank you,' she whispered back. 'I just need to get a better look at the stage. I really don't know why I didn't think of this before.'

There was an impatient 'Shh!' from the stage, and Lady Hardcastle held up a hand in apology. She gestured for Gwen and me to follow her back to the corridor.

'We have to get downstairs as soon as we can,' she said once the door was shut behind us. 'I've been a fool.'

'What's down there?' I asked.

'An answer.'

Chapter Fifteen

We went to the door at the top of the basement stairs to find it propped open with a fire bucket. The sounds of banging, clanking, and colourful Bristolian swearing came from below.

The foreman, Ned Stone, clumped up the stairs in heavy boots and walked towards us.

'Evenin', ladies,' he said. 'Still explorin'?'

'Exploring, and imbibing the atmosphere of this wonderful theatre, Mr Stone,' said Lady Hardcastle. 'What goes on in your subterranean labyrinth?'

Stone was unfazed by her peculiar phrasing – he dealt with flowery-tongued actors all the time. He sucked on his pipe and let out a cloud of sweet smoke.

'Furnace is actin' up,' he said. 'Gots to get it fixed afore th'audience turns up and starts complainin' about the cold.'

Now he mentioned it, I had been feeling slightly chillier than usual. It hadn't occurred to me that the heating might be on the blink – I'd thought it was just me.

'Then we shall keep out of your way,' said Lady Hardcastle. 'Unless there's anything we can do? Would your men like some tea?'

Stone smiled.

'Never say no to tea, ma'am,' he said. 'Much obliged to you. There's five of us.'

He clomped off on his way towards the workshop and Lady Hardcastle looked hopefully at Gwen and me.

'That was a little reckless of me,' she said. 'I have no idea where anything is. Do you think . . . ?'

'Come on, Gwen,' I said. 'Let's see if we can organize tea for five.'

◆ ◆ ◆

Gwen and I managed to find a huge teapot and a mismatched assortment of cups and saucers in the green room. We took the tea down to the furnace room, where it was gratefully pounced upon by four men wearing overalls and puzzled frowns. We gathered from the conversation that they had no real idea what they were doing but were confident that the correct application of heavy wrenches and a few light taps with a hammer should see the ageing heating system brought back to life.

We left them to it.

Lady Hardcastle, meanwhile, had buttonholed Mr Adlam, the theatre manager. We found them talking in the corridor.

'. . . and so, you see, it's fallen to us to ask a few questions on his behalf and . . . Oh, hello, ladies. I was just explaining our assignment to Mr Adlam here. Mr Adlam, this is my associate Miss Armstrong and her sister Mrs Evans.'

'How do you do?' said Mr Adlam. 'I must say I'm a little confused. I remember telling Hugo Bartlett that a Lady Webster-Green and a Miss Goodheart could have the run of the place as his guests – I'm always happy to help a fellow impresario. As long as they're based a long way away and can't take any business from me, mind you.' He gave a gleefully self-satisfied chuckle. 'But now it turns out that they didn't exist and that you're working on behalf of the police inspector I first spoke to on the night of the murder, who isn't the one who's investigating the case. Except that he now is, because the one who was has been reassigned. It really is most baffling.'

'I'm so sorry. We really should have introduced ourselves. It must be a terrible time for you, with a police investigation hanging over you.'

'Oh, my dear, it's marvellous. Business has never been better. We could do with having a murder every week, to tell you the truth.' He looked even more pleased with himself at this.

'Well, that's something, at least,' said Lady Hardcastle. 'So you still have no objections to us poking about?'

'My dear lady, poke away. And if you uncover the killer, do please make as much fuss as you possibly can. Shout it from the rooftops that the Duke's is home to a notorious murderer. We'll be full every night.'

And with that, he turned and strutted away, muttering delightedly to himself about having a murder every week.

'He did it,' said Gwen, emphatically. 'He's worried about his declining box-office receipts and he hoped a murder would bring in the gawpers.'

I tutted and shook my head.

'We've supplied the horny-handed sons of toil with tea,' I said. 'We nicked a tin of biscuits from the green room for them as well. They don't know when they'll be finished but they're cracking on as fast as they can.'

'Although it looks like a toss-up between them getting the furnace fixed and blowing the place up,' added Gwen. 'They're very much of the brute-force school of engineering: if you can't fix it with a hammer, you're just not hitting it hard enough.'

'Perhaps we should retire to that café we found near here the other night and fortify ourselves for our evening's labours,' said Lady Hardcastle.

'Will we need fortifying?' I asked. 'We still don't know what we're doing.'

'Oh, I always need fortifying, dear – I thought you'd know that about me after all these years. You know how irritable and irrational I become when I'm hungry.'

'How am I supposed to tell the difference? You're irritable and irrational all the time.'

'Quiet, you. Now are you going to accompany me to Whistler's or am I to dine alone?'

We accompanied her to Whistler's.

By the time we returned to the Duke's, the second act of *The Hedonists* was well underway, the furnace was working, and the stagehands had retired to their lair. We checked that there was no one about, then made our way once more through the *Authorized Staff Only* door and down to the rumbling bowels of the theatre.

The furnace-room door was ajar – that was the source of the rumbling – but there was no one about. We found the *Trap Room – Keep Out* door and I offered Gwen my picklocks.

'Can you still do it?' I asked.

'Quicker than you, I bet,' she said, and set to work.

I'm not certain she was quicker than I would have been, but once again I was proud as my 'big sister' showed off her skills and earned an 'I say, well done you' from Lady Hardcastle.

There was a light switch just inside the door and I flicked it on.

We were in a tall space beneath the stage. Heavy wooden pillars and joists supported the stage floor above us, much as I had expected, but there was a good deal more than that going on down there. Wooden steps led up to several platforms set a few feet below the boards of the stage, and closer inspection revealed that they corresponded to cut sections of the floorboards. Trapdoors. So that's what a trap room was.

There were two grave traps upstage, a cauldron trap centre stage, a star trap stage right, and two stage lifts, left and right, each beneath a drop-and-slide trapdoor. Obviously I didn't know all the names at the time – I've looked them up since.

It was an impressive place and, for the most part, it showed strong evidence of having been unused for many months. There were cobwebs everywhere, and I caught a glimpse out of the corner of my eye of one of the resident spiders scuttling for cover in the unaccustomed light. There was a louder scuttling from the far corner as the larger inhabitants sought shelter, too. As so often before, I wondered what the rats found to eat in places like this, but they sounded as though they were heavy and moving fast so they were clearly finding something.

There was a thick layer of dust on the stone floor, most of which had clearly lain undisturbed for quite some time. There were signs, though, that someone had been in there recently. The dust was disturbed between the door and the stage-left lift. It had been roughly brushed or swept, so it wasn't possible to discern any footprints, but it was apparent that at least one person had been down here within the past few days.

I pointed this out to Lady Hardcastle and she inclined her head in acknowledgement.

We could hear the actors walking about above our heads and, even though we couldn't hear their words, the sound of the footsteps made us feel as though they were very close. I tiptoed to the lift itself and examined the deck. There was a small bloodstain – or what looked very much like one – towards one end, and I wordlessly indicated it to the other two, who both nodded.

Gwen found the mechanism. It was a complex arrangement of pulleys, gears and counterweights, but it looked as though the whole thing could be easily operated by one person – a couple of levers and a windlass seemed to be all it needed. From my own cursory examination it appeared he would simply pull down on the first lever to release the safety brake, then let the lever up at the appropriate moment to set the device in motion. The trap would open, the lift would rise, and the lift platform would fill the hole left by the trapdoor. The windlass would winch the counter-weights back into position and then the other lever would reverse the process.

I had an idea and looked down at the floor. It had been swept but there was still quite a bit of sand scattered about, and a few threads of hessian. I pointed them out to Lady Hardcastle and she nodded again.

There wasn't much else to see, and it was obvious from the undisturbed dust everywhere else that our visitor, or visitors, hadn't ventured further than the lift. I motioned for the other two to follow me and crossed back to the door.

We shut and locked the door behind us before anyone spoke.

'We've got the timeline wrong,' said Lady Hardcastle and I together.

Gwen laughed.

'Do you do that a lot? It sounds like you do.'

Lady Hardcastle and I looked at each other and shrugged.

'No,' we said together.

'That's definitely the first time,' I said.

'It was rather fun, though,' said Lady Hardcastle. 'Perhaps we should rehearse it for the future. Imagine the look on people's faces when we make our announcements in unison.'

'Why is the timeline wrong?' asked Gwen. 'What did all that show?'

We walked towards the stairs.

'We've been working on the assumption that Paul was killed at the end of the interval,' I said, 'because there were people on the stage until about ten minutes before the curtain went up for Act Two.'

'But we've just seen that he could have been killed at any time after the curtain came down on Act One,' said Lady Hardcastle.

'In the trap room?' said Gwen.

'In the trap room,' I said.

'But the killer would have to wait there to operate the lift. It doesn't change the time at all.'

'Sandbag,' I said.

We emerged into the corridor on the ground floor.

'No,' said Gwen, 'still not with you.'

'I should imagine those trapdoor levers don't need a great deal of force to hold them down,' said Lady Hardcastle. 'Probably a good bit less than the weight of one or two of the sandbags that seem to be used to weigh everything down around here.'

'Keep going,' said Gwen, 'I've nearly got you.'

'Tie a bag or two to the lever,' I said, 'and then pull it down to release the ratchet. Cut a small hole in one – or both – of the bags and scarper. I'm not sure how many bags it would take or how big the hole would need to be, but it wouldn't take much experimentation to find out. Then, when you're safely back in your dressing room, or hanging about somewhere with your pals, the sand has leaked out and the bags are too light to hold the lever down any more. Up it goes, and the dead body is lifted on to the stage so that everyone assumes that's where he was killed. I heard a noise just before the curtain went up. I thought it was some furniture being moved at the last minute, but I'd bet it was the lift slotting itself into place. The plan nearly didn't work – it was almost too late.'

'But people would notice it was the lift, not the stage floor,' said Gwen.

'That was a gamble, certainly,' said Lady Hardcastle, 'but a fairly safe one. Anyone who got close enough to Singleton to see it would have been looking at him, not the floor he was lying on. All the killer had to do was go back to the trap room at some later time, bring the lift back down, sweep up the sand, return the sandbags to wherever they came from, and lock up. No one, as we found out ourselves, ever goes in there. By the time the Duke's staged some complex production that required the use of any of those trapdoors in another couple of years' time, the murder would be forgotten and no one would even notice that someone had been in there.'

'So who's the killer?' said Gwen. 'Nancy? She signed the note. Oh, but she has an alibi for the new time of the murder.'

'She does,' I said, 'but she shares it with Bridges and Cowlin, and they all three have a fair reason to want Singleton dead.'

'As do Bartlett and Thornell,' said Lady Hardcastle. 'And they're vouching for each other, too.'

'There's one more problem,' I said. 'Singleton was seen alive at about a quarter to nine.'

'You've already solved that one yourself, silly,' said Lady Hardcastle. 'At the pub. Come on, I need to think this through. Somewhere away from prying ears.'

'Do ears pry?' I said.

'They do now. I feel an uninvited late-evening trip to Georgie's coming on.'

'Poor Lady Bickle.'

'Oh, she loves it,' said Lady Hardcastle, blithely. 'We add a welcome air of glamour and excitement to her humdrum life.'

◆ ◆ ◆

By the time we were trying to leave the theatre, the play had ended and the actors were coming off stage. All, it seemed, was not well.

'. . . bloody unprofessional,' said Harris Bridges to Patrick Cowlin as they passed us in the corridor. 'Oh, good evening, ladies. I hope you didn't see that.'

'Sorry, dear,' said Lady Hardcastle. 'We were otherwise engaged.'

'Lucky for you,' he said, and they carried on back to their dressing rooms, leaving us shrugging our shoulders.

'What was all that about?' said Gwen.

It wasn't long before we found out.

Moments later, Sarah Griffin and Rosalie Harding staggered into the corridor, holding each other up.

'What ho, you chaps,' said Sarah, far too loudly.

Rosalie giggled and saluted us with the champagne bottle she was holding by its neck.

'Good evening, ladies,' said Lady Hardcastle. 'You seem in fine spirits.'

Sarah put her finger to her lips.

'Shh,' she said. 'Don't tell the boys, but we smuggled some real champagne on to the stage.'

Rosalie waved the bottle at us and giggled again.

'We just saw them,' I said. 'I don't think they noticed.'

Sarah swayed gently and pointed at Gwen and me with an unsteady finger.

'You're twins,' she said. 'I always wanted to be a twin.'

'Did you?' I said. 'Why?'

'I lost my sister. She was older than me and left me all alone. I wanted a twin.'

'I'm so sorry to hear that,' I said. 'I hope it's not been too distressing having us about the place all the time.'

'No, no, no, no,' she said. 'It's been delightful. She was murdered, you know. My sister. She was seventeen. Just seventeen.' The mock pout changed to genuine sadness and her eyes glistened.

'Strangled in Six Oaks Wood. It's in Suffolk, you know. Do you know Suffolk? I'm from Suffolk. They never caught him. I knew who he was, but I was just fifteen so they didn't take my word for it.'

Rosalie's giggles had gone, and she looked alarmed at this dark turn in the conversation.

Lady Hardcastle noticed.

'I think you ought to take her back to her digs,' she said to Rosalie. 'Look after her.'

Rosalie nodded.

'Come on, you,' she said. 'Let's get you tucked up in a nice warm bed.'

'Don't want to go to bed,' said Sarah. 'Want to talk to the twins. I love twins. I wanted to be a twin, you know.'

'I know, darling,' said Rosalie. 'We'll get you home now, though.'

'That would be nice. Night night, Lady Webster-Green-Hardcastle. Night night, twins.'

Rosalie led her away.

'It's enough to make one sign the pledge,' said Lady Hardcastle.

'If you sign the pledge,' I said, 'I'll donate all the money you owe me from our card games to the charity of your choice.'

'You're pledging my own money to charity? That doesn't sound like much of an offer. What's in it for me?'

'A lifetime of sobriety. A longer lifetime, at that. Your liver will thank you.'

'It probably would. I shall consider your offer. But for now, shall we go to Georgie's? I need a drink and she keeps a marvellous cellar.'

◆　◆　◆

It was around half past ten by the time we arrived at Berkeley Crescent, and I was more than a little uncomfortable. There were rules for this sort of thing, conventions, protocols. Repeatedly turning up at someone's house unannounced at half past ten at night just wasn't the done thing. I tried to melt into the background as Lady Hardcastle rang the doorbell.

Once again, Sir Benjamin answered his own door.

'Hah!' he said with a cheerful smile. 'I bet Georgie ten bob it would be you lot. Come on in. She's in the drawing room. She'll be pleased to see you, I bet – I've got some pals over from the hospital.'

We followed him in. He gallantly helped us with our coats and then waved us into the drawing room.

'You know the way,' he said as he headed towards the dining room. 'We'll try to keep the noise down.'

A roar of laughter wrapped in a great fog of cigar smoke billowed into the hall as he opened the door. He waved a cheery farewell and closed the door behind him.

We let ourselves into the drawing room.

'Emily,' said Lady Bickle, delightedly. 'Flo. Gwenith. Oh, how absolutely lovely to see you. I was just thinking how wonderful it would be to have some company.'

'And, as if in answer to your prayers, here we are,' said Lady Hardcastle.

'Just so. Sit yourselves down. Can I get you anything? The servants have gone to bed, I'm afraid. But you know that – this is your usual visiting hour. Still, I know my way round my own kitchen. Some sandwiches again, perhaps?'

'We ate a hearty meal at Whistler's, thank you, dear.'

'Some cheese, then? I quite fancy some cheese. Give me a moment.' She put down her book and stood. 'Help yourselves to drinks, won't you?'

She left the room, and I poured a brandy for Lady Hardcastle and a port for Gwen. There was a jug of water and I filled a glass for myself. I was going to be driving home.

There were some WSPU leaflets on the low coffee table and we chatted about the suffragettes while we waited. Lady Bickle returned a little while later with a tray laden with cheese and biscuits. There were grapes, too, and a small pot of quince cheese.

'Here we are,' she said. 'Dig in. I'm just in the mood for a bit of Double Gloucester.'

'A drink for you, my lady?' I said.

'Oh, don't call me that, dear. Not after all this time. And yes, please. Another port while you're up.' She held out her empty glass. 'So, what news have you? How goes the murder investigation?'

Quickly and succinctly, Lady Hardcastle outlined almost everything we'd discovered since we'd last spoken to her. We decided not to reveal Hugo's real identity – that was something Helena would have to explain to her old friend. Even without that, the web of motives, the flimsy alibis, the ingenious use of the stage lift was rather impressive when it was all laid out in one go.

Lady Bickle seemed impressed, certainly.

'I say, well done you,' she said. 'Although . . .'

'Yes?' said Lady Hardcastle.

'Well, you haven't actually found out who did it yet, have you?'

'Oh, I'm fairly certain I know. The trouble is, I can't prove it. We need to find a way to make them reveal themselves to us.'

'And how do you propose to do that?'

'Ah. Well. Now that's where you have me, I'm afraid. I've no idea at the moment, and that's rather why we've come to call on you. Two heads are better than one, and four are better than three. I wondered if we might put them together and come up with some manner of plan. A scheme. A stratagem. A wheeze of such delightful efficacy that songs will be written about us. Or just something that flushes them out. Honestly, it needn't be all that clever as long as it works.'

'We shall come up with something. Will you stay the night? It's a long way back to Littleton Cotterell if you don't have to go.'

'That would be most welcome, dear, thank you.'

'Excellent,' said Lady Bickle, standing. 'Another round of drinks, then. You too, Flo. I saw you drinking water in case you had to drive them home. What'll you have?'

'Brandy, please,' I said.

We set about making a plan.

Chapter Sixteen

We were up bright and early on Sunday morning. That is to say, *I* was up bright and early on Sunday morning because I couldn't stop myself. I had quite a few things to do, though, so I had no real objections to being up and dressed long before the others stirred. I tried not to get in the way of the Bickles' household servants as the housemaid lit fires and swept floors, and the cook prepared breakfast.

I prevailed upon Miss Gossman – Lady Bickle's lady's maid – to allow me the use of her sewing box as I made a few cosmetic alterations to my and Gwen's dresses. It was impossible to make them identical at short notice, but they might fool an inattentive observer as long as we didn't linger too long in their field of view.

Gwen arrived next, and I made sure she was comfortable with tea and toast while I arranged a starter breakfast for Lady Hardcastle. I needn't have worried about Gwen, though, who had a pleasing knack for making people comfortable. She was a hit with the staff as soon as she breezed in and started chattering to them about their work, their families and their favourite things to do on their afternoons off.

Lady Hardcastle, remembering that we had a potentially interesting day ahead, managed to suppress her instinct to complain about being woken. There was a modicum of grumbling, of course, but she was quickly persuaded that it was all for the best.

By the time Lady Hardcastle was fit for company, Lady Bickle was in the morning room with Gwen, and the two new best friends were already helping themselves to breakfast.

'Good morning, darlings,' said Lady Bickle as we entered. 'Come and tuck in. I didn't think I'd be hungry this morning, what with all the excitement, but I'm famished for some reason.'

'Thank you,' said Lady Hardcastle. 'Will Ben be joining us?'

'Dear, sweet Ben is still in bed, moaning and groaning. I've sent his man up with tinctures, nostrums and elixirs in an attempt to alleviate the symptoms of his hangover, but like most doctors he's a terrible patient. I don't expect he'll surface much before noon.'

'They were up very late. What time did his friends leave?'

'About three, I think, and they weren't quiet about it. The uncharitable side of me thinks a hangover is the very least they all deserve.'

'I hope he recovers soon, nevertheless,' said Lady Hardcastle with a smile. 'Are we all raring to go?'

We murmured our assent. It sounded less enthusiastically convincing than perhaps Lady Hardcastle had hoped for, but we were British – what did she expect?'

'Splendid,' she said. 'And everyone knows what to do?'

Once again we mumbled and murmured our confirmation through mouthfuls of eggs and sausage.

Despite these assurances of both our eagerness and our preparedness, Lady Hardcastle insisted on running through the plan once more as we ate.

◆ ◆ ◆

As soon as breakfast was over, Lady Bickle made a telephone call to the Bridewell and spoke to Inspector Sunderland. It seemed as though things were properly underway now, but actually there was little else for us to do until closer to lunchtime. We wished to see the actors together before their rehearsal, and we knew from our conversation with Nancy and Rosalie at the tea room in Cotham the day before that they weren't due to rehearse until one o'clock. We spent the morning reading, gossiping, and playing word games at which Gwen excelled and Lady Bickle proved to be surprisingly inept.

Sir Benjamin put in a sheepish appearance just after twelve, and made a valiant attempt to be jovially sociable, but in the end he stayed only long enough to acquire a pot of coffee and several rounds of toast before sloping back to his bedroom.

By half past we decided it was time to go, so we donned hats, coats and gloves and made ready to set off. We had been in the habit of driving to the theatre from Berkeley Crescent, but it was a pleasant morning so we decided to walk.

As we approached the theatre, Gwen and I hung back to allow Ladies Hardcastle and Bickle to enter the theatre without us. That means that from here onwards I've had to rely on accounts provided to me by both those ladies, and later by Gwen, as to what happened when they got there. Their stories tallied for the most part so I'm confident that what follows is a reasonably accurate account of events.

Lady Hardcastle and Lady Bickle entered the theatre together and went straight to Hugo Bartlett's dressing room. Lady Hardcastle rat-a-tatted on the door.

'Yes?' came the voice from inside.

'It's Emily and Georgie, dear,' said Lady Hardcastle. 'May we come in?'

'Just a minute.'

After a few moments of rustling and clonking, the door opened and Helena Bartlett's face peeped out.

'Come in, quickly,' she said.

Lady Bickle merely gawped.

'No, really, Georgie,' said Helena, 'get in here now.'

The two ladies entered and Lady Hardcastle closed the door behind them.

'Oh, Nell,' said Lady Bickle. 'How lovely to see you. When did you get here? Why didn't you call on us? Where's Hugo? Why . . .' She looked again at Helena's clothes. 'Oh. But . . .'

'It's a long story, Georgie old thing,' said Helena. 'Short version: it's easier to be a man in the theatre business than a woman. I wanted to tell you, but it was all so complicated so I just sort of . . . didn't.'

'I see,' said Lady Bickle, slightly more coldly than Lady Hardcastle had been expecting. 'Well, now I know. Why have you chosen to appear beardless now? You didn't come to the theatre like that, I presume.'

'I took it off when I heard it was you at the door. Emily tried to persuade me yesterday that I should tell you but I couldn't think of a way. And then you were here and—'

Lady Bickle rounded on Lady Hardcastle.

'You knew?' she said. 'You knew my oldest friend was here in town masquerading as her own brother and you didn't say anything?'

'I was sworn to secrecy, dear,' said Lady Hardcastle. 'Surely if you know anything about me at all it's that I take secrecy very seriously. I've made a career of it.'

'Yes. Well.' Lady Bickle was not to be mollified. 'Do you even have a brother?' she said to Helena.

'Two sisters,' she said. 'You met them in London shortly after we left school. Do you remember?'

'I do. Amelia and Sophia. Charming girls. No wonder none of you mentioned Hugo. He doesn't exist.'

'Except that he does,' said Helena, sitting down to reaffix Hugo's beard. 'He's a very successful playwright with a theatre company and a string of hit plays to his name.'

'And yet—' began Lady Bickle, but Lady Hardcastle wasn't in the mood for any of this.

'You must sort this out between you at a later date,' she said.

'And with you,' said Lady Bickle.

'And with me if you like, yes. But for now we have something more important to be getting on with. Hugo, we need your help in gathering the company together. Will you all be on stage for your rehearsal?'

'We shall,' said Bartlett.

'Can we briefly take advantage of you all being in the same place at the same time to make an announcement, please?'

'About what?'

'About the murders of Paul Singleton and Davey Browning.'

'You have news? What is it? Have you uncovered the culprit?'

'It will be easier to explain it to you all at once,' said Lady Hardcastle. 'Will that be possible?'

'I don't see why not,' said Bartlett. 'I'm sure they all want to know what's been going on.'

'Thank you, dear. When are you due to begin?'

'One o'clock sharp.'

'We shall leave you to your preparations and see you on the stage at one, then.'

◆ ◆ ◆

Ladies Hardcastle and Bickle arrived at the stage at the stroke of one to find the actors already assembled. As a courtesy they had also invited Mr Adlam to join them. He, by all accounts, was excited at the prospect of further scandal and notoriety to boost attendances and increase his profits.

Lady Hardcastle strode to the centre of the stage, her boot heels tapping loudly on the boards. The group fell silent.

'Good afternoon, everyone,' she said. 'Thank you for allowing me to interrupt your work. I shan't keep you long but I thought you might wish to know about developments in the investigation into the murders of your friend Paul Singleton and of the stagehand Davey Browning.'

'Have you caught the blighter?' asked Sarah – though there is some dispute between the two accounts as to the actual word used in place of 'blighter'.

'Not yet, dear,' said Lady Hardcastle. 'But the net is closing. What we do have is some vital evidence in the form of a note inviting Mr Singleton—'

'Paul, please,' said Rosalie. 'I asked you to call him Paul.'

'My apologies. A note inviting Paul to meet his murderer. Inspector Sunderland will be coming to the theatre in due course to collect this note so that it might be examined by handwriting experts in London to determine its author. For now, though, my associate, Miss Armstrong, has the note in her possession and is keeping it safe. She's also guarding the scene of the first murder in order to preserve certain other physical clues left behind by Paul's killer that we hope will lead to the arrest of the perpetrator of these most loathsome murders.'

As one, the actors looked downstage left to the spot where Singleton's body had been found. They appeared more than a little puzzled to find that I wasn't there.

'What other physical clues?' asked Nancy.

'And why isn't she there?' asked Sarah, pointing at the stage.

'All will become clear in the fullness of time,' said Lady Hardcastle. 'For now I just wanted you to know that the agony of not knowing will soon be over, and to reassure you that the culprit will be brought to justice.'

'Some good news at last,' said Sarah. 'I think I speak for us all when I say that we're anxious for this to be over and done with. We've put a brave face on it, but this has been a terrible, terrible time for us. We'll never forget it, but it will be a relief to be able to put it all behind us.'

'I'm confident that you'll be able to do that soon,' said Lady Hardcastle. 'We shall leave you to your important work, but don't be alarmed if you see police officers in the building later.'

Urgent conversations broke out immediately. Lady Hardcastle and Lady Bickle discreetly slipped off to the wings and left the stage.

◆　◆　◆

While all this was going on, Gwen and I had made our way to the trap room. Obviously we had. If a ruse works, there's no real need to expend effort in coming up with a new one just to sate the world's appetite for novelty, so we sat together in the trap room, quietly gossiping.

We were able to have the lights on – everyone was supposed to know I was there – and we sat together on the stage lift, reminiscing about the past, analysing the present and speculating about the future. We heard Lady Hardcastle's distinctive footsteps on the floor above our heads as she went on to the stage, then again as she left. In the parlance of our current location, that was our cue. We were on.

We waited.

After what seemed like for ever we were still far from running out of things to talk about, but we were very much ruing the fact that neither of us owned a watch. Eventually, the change in the pattern of the footsteps on the stage gave us our clue that the actors were taking a break. This was our next cue.

We gave them a few minutes to get clear and to start wandering the corridors in search of tea or toilets, then Gwen put on her coat and left the room. I had gone to great lengths to make our clothes look reasonably similar, as we had at the pub, but in the end it hadn't made much difference. The circumstances here were entirely different – no one had seen us come down to the basement, for one – but it still felt like it was something worth doing. From here I have to rely on Gwen's account of events.

Gwen mounted the stairs and made her way out into the corridor, being sure not to be too quiet. With a cheery wave to Haggarty on the door, she left the theatre and walked down the alley that led out on to Frogmore Street. As she passed the galvanized dustbins near the alley's mouth, there was a sinister metallic click behind her.

'That's far enough, Mrs Evans,' said a familiar woman's voice.

Gwen turned to see Sarah Griffin silhouetted in the alleyway, pointing a small nickel-plated revolver at her midriff.

'You thought I'd go straight down to the trap room, didn't you? "Oh, look, Armstrong's gone for a sly walk while she thinks no one's looking. Now's my chance to get down there and clean up the evidence." Though I'm not sure what evidence I left behind – I thought I'd cleaned up pretty thoroughly. Anyway, I'm not falling for that old trick. I used to dream of being a twin, too, remember. I used to imagine all the fun we could have, pretending to be one another. You think you're the only ones who ever thought of it? Idiots.'

'If you'd figured it out,' said Gwen, 'then why not just go down there with your shiny gun and confront Flo?'

'Because, unlike you, I'm *not* an idiot. I know all about little Florence Armstrong and her party tricks. I've read the newspaper stories about how she disarmed people and subdued them with nothing more than a flick of the wrist. I'm not going to take her on directly, now, am I? I need a bargaining chip. I need, my dear Mrs Evans, a hostage.'

'So if Flo lets you clean up, you'll let me go?'

'I shall frame it slightly differently, but yes, essentially. If Flo gives me the note and lets me clean up, I won't shoot you both.'

'You'll hang in the end.'

'Only if they catch me. Now kneel down facing the wall and put your hands behind your head.'

Gwen did as she was told, and Sarah walked past her so that she would be behind Gwen as they walked back to the stage door.

'Ups-a-daisy,' said Sarah. 'Walk nice and slowly back to the trap room. If anyone says anything, be polite and calm. If you make a fuss I'll just shoot you and work it out from there.'

'That sounds rational.'

'Or I could just shoot you now and take my chances with your sister. Don't push your luck, there's a good girl.'

Gwen led the way back in through the stage door, offering Haggarty a cheery wave as she entered. She walked calmly along the corridor to the *Authorized Staff Only* door and down the stairs. She paused outside the trap-room door.

'Don't keep me waiting,' said Sarah. 'I've got a train to catch.'

Gwen opened the door and stepped inside. Sarah followed close behind.

The room was empty.

'So where's the famous Florence Armstrong?' said Sarah, irritably.

With a speed that took Sarah entirely by surprise, Gwen spun on her heel and lashed out with her left hand, grabbing Sarah's wrist. Still turning, she pulled Sarah over her hip, flipping her on to her back and wrenching the pistol from her hand.

'*I'm* the famous Florence Armstrong,' I said, pointing the pistol at her. 'Idiot. I thought you said you knew all about pretending to be one another.'

'But you're wearing Gwen's boots. She always wears those boots. It's how I've been telling you apart.'

'Oddly, we have the same size feet, so we're able to swap boots.'

I do feel slightly guilty at having been misleading in my account, but our intention had been to mislead, after all. Sarah was exceedingly irritated by the deception and she lay and glowered at me, still winded from the fall.

I detest guns, so I put the pretty little pistol in my coat pocket, reasoning that I could keep her under control without it. Sarah watched me intently and then, with a suddenness and accuracy I hadn't expected, she lashed out with her right leg, catching me painfully on the knee. I staggered backwards and bumped into part of the machinery for one of the grave traps, falling inelegantly on to my rear. I heard the skirt of my dress rip as I fell.

This was most dismaying and, as it turned out, not a little dangerous. Sarah was already on her feet and charging at me with wild fury in her beautiful eyes.

I was still off balance from my fall, and her first frenzied blows made painful contact. There was no plan, and she seemed to have no goal other than to hurt me as much as she could. For a few seconds she did a reasonably good job of it but I managed to move my arms from propping me up to being able to do something about the wild and uncoordinated blows raining down on my head.

Slightly too late, I realized that there was a plan after all. As I raised my arms to protect myself, her right hand shot with uncanny speed into my coat pocket to retrieve her pistol. With her left hand still flailing at my face, I was too slow to stop her, and before I knew it she'd rolled clear and was levelling the stupid gun at me again.

She stood slowly, making sure to maintain a safe distance between us.

'Let's try again, shall we?' she said. 'What evidence do you think you've found? I thought I'd made a very thorough job of cleaning up.'

'Killers always make a mistake.'

For the first time she seemed to doubt herself. She looked quickly around.

'Well?' she said. 'Where's this evidence?'

'There's the note, for one,' I said, wiping blood from my lip, where she'd caught me with her ring.

'The note I wrote to entice Paul to come down here? The note he thought was from Nancy? No, that's my insurance. It's signed "N", don't forget. You were supposed to find that. It was supposed to lead you to Nancy.'

'You enticed Paul down here?' I asked. 'Why?'

Sarah sighed.

'Do you want me to say it?' she said, wearily. 'You know my confession would count for nothing, don't you? Even if I get caught my barrister will just say, "Hearsay, m'lud," and your "evidence" will be thrown out.'

'Indulge me,' I said. 'I'm curious to know if we worked it all out correctly.'

'Very well, then,' she said with another sigh. 'I enticed him down here so I could kill him. I was going to use the kitchen knife from the green room, but that dagger was sitting on the table in the corridor as I walked past and I thought that would make it even easier to pin the murder on Nancy or even the behatted stranger. Although no one ever really bought that one. Heigh ho.'

'There was no stranger in a dark suit and cloth cap?'

'Of course there wasn't.'

'Maybe you should have made more of the strange woman who's been walking about the theatre.'

'What woman?'

'If you don't know about her it doesn't matter, but she would have been a much better red herring.'

'Perhaps she would, but it seems irrelevant now – we've moved on a step or two.' She gestured with the gun. 'Ups-a-daisy, little Flo. Let's have a look at the stage lift and see what I missed, shall we?'

I stood slowly and carefully, trying not to glance at the door.

We edged over to the stage lift and she inspected it closely.

'Nothing here,' she said. 'I missed a tiny bit of blood, but that doesn't prove anything.'

She bent forwards slightly to inspect the floor. She was still clumsily pointing the gun at me, but her attention was on the entirely evidence-free floor. Now it was my turn to strike unexpectedly.

I grabbed the gun-wielding hand first, pushing it up and away so that even if she reflexively pulled the trigger she would shoot something that wasn't me. I continued the motion, closing fast, though this time I decided that circumstances required something more emphatic than simply flipping her on to her back. I drove my open palm into her face, knocking her backwards on to the stage lift. I took the pistol again and was about to call on my companions when I saw her struggling upright once more.

I leapt on to the lift platform and tried to subdue her, but she still wasn't done. She began struggling again.

'Why won't you just stay down?' I asked in exasperation. 'I've had less trouble from highly trained thugs.'

'Stage-fighting, darling, didn't they tell you?' she snarled. 'Never fight an actor – we know all the best moves.'

She swung her legs off the platform and was trying to get purchase on something to lever herself up. The something she found, though, was the lever that released the mechanism.

There was a clonk and a rumble as the lift started to raise us towards the stage. She was momentarily confused as to what she'd done, and I took the opportunity to strike her once more. She fell backwards, knocking her head on the platform. She was out cold. Finally.

I was planning just to enjoy the ride and our triumphant arrival on stage when I noticed that her legs were still hanging over the edge of the lift. If I didn't move her quickly she'd lose them.

I struggled for a few panicked seconds, trying to haul her further on to the platform as the trap above us opened. Closer and closer we came, but she just wouldn't budge. I risked a glance over the edge as the opening drew perilously near.

Her boot was caught on the lever.

With a mighty heave, I wrenched it free and we emerged on to the stage.

I was panting from the exertion and Sarah was still unconscious. I lay beside her for a few moments until I heard footsteps on the stage.

'Are you all right, dear?' said Lady Hardcastle.

'Right as rain,' I said, sitting up. 'Did you hear all that? Will it do as a confession?'

Lady Hardcastle knelt beside me, checking me over, with Inspector Sunderland at her shoulder. The burly sergeant we'd seen in the auditorium on the night of the murder stood behind him, with Gwenith and Lady Bickle at the rear, trying their best to see.

'That will do nicely, Miss Armstrong,' said the inspector. 'Thank you.'

There was a groan from beside me as Sarah started to come to.

'Miss Sarah Griffin,' said Inspector Sunderland, 'I am arresting you for the wilful murder of Paul Singleton on Tuesday, the seventh of November, 1911, and for the wilful murder of Mr David Browning on Monday, the thirteenth of November, 1911. Do you wish to say anything? You are not obliged to say anything unless you wish to do so, but whatever you say will be taken down in writing and may be given in evidence against you.'

'Trousers,' said Sarah with a woozy giggle.

'Funnily enough, you're the first person ever to say that to me,' said the inspector wearily. 'Cuffs, please, Sergeant.'

We moved aside to allow the sergeant access, and Sarah was cuffed and hauled to her feet. She was led away, still giggling about trousers.

Inspector Sunderland turned to us before following them.

'Thank you so very much,' he said. 'I'll need full statements from you all as usual, but for now I need to get her locked up. I'll be back later.'

With a wave, he walked off the stage, his heels clicking loudly on the floor.

'It doesn't even make sense,' said Gwen as she and the other ladies clustered around me and helped me to my feet.

'What doesn't?' I asked.

'He said, ". . . taken down in writing". It only works if he'd said, ". . . will be taken down".'

'Is that what you're taking from this?' I said. 'All that and you're irritated that her joke didn't work?'

'Details are important, Floss,' she said. 'Come here, *fach,* let's have a look at you.' She fussed at my face with her handkerchief, and I let her. 'She caught you a proper one on the lip. That'll look nasty tomorrow.'

'At least then I'll be able to tell you apart,' said Lady Bickle. 'I've tried not to make a fuss, but I've been really struggling.'

Gwen and I tutted in unison.

Chapter Seventeen

Thanks to some information we had received from Inspector Sunderland before we left the Bickle residence, we had been reasonably sure Sarah was the killer. Not absolutely certain, but enough that when I suggested a variation on the Dog and Duck ruse, they had all agreed that it seemed like a sensible idea.

The original plan had been for me to remain in the trap room as before, with Ladies Bickle and Hardcastle in the furnace room, ready to back me up if needs be. If Inspector Sunderland arrived in time for the fun, then so much the better – he could wait with them.

But Sarah was right: Gwen and I hadn't invented the pretending-to-be-each-other trick. We had even seen a stage magician use a variation of it in his magic-cabinet act, so I knew there was a chance that anyone who worked in the theatre would guess what we were up to. If she decided to play rough, that would leave Gwen exposed as she left the theatre alone, so I suggested we swap places. That way, if things got ugly in the alley, it would be me facing a murderer, not my sister.

Once we'd settled on that, Lady Hardcastle suggested that Gwen should leave the trap room as well and join them in the furnace room. I pointed out that this entirely negated the twin trick, but I was overruled. If Sarah didn't tumble the deception, or if it was someone else entirely who wouldn't have guessed anyway, there'd be no problem in having the room empty when they got there. In that event, Lady Hardcastle could simply appear at the door with her trusty pistol and still have her 'aha' moment.

And so that's what we had done.

Falling over and being slapped repeatedly about the face hadn't been part of the plan, but if you're going to get yourself into fights with enraged murderers these things are bound to happen from time to time. My lip would heal, after all.

The only moment of confusion had come when they realized that we were on our way up to the stage. The 'aha' moment was briefly postponed while they all turned and ran back up the stairs, and then abandoned completely when they found Sarah spark out on the stage-left trapdoor with me puffing and panting beside her.

Still, all's well that ends well, and all that.

'I think we ought to get out of the way,' said Lady Hardcastle. 'The others will be back for their rehearsal in a moment.'

'Shall we tell them what's happened?' asked Lady Bickle. 'They'll want to know.'

'All in good time,' said Lady Hardcastle. 'Let them have their rehearsal and we'll tell them when Inspector Sunderland gets back from the Bridewell – he'll want to hear the details, too.'

'Very well,' said Lady Bickle. 'Tea at Crane's until he gets back? My treat.'

We told Haggarty where we would be, and when Inspector Sunderland returned to the theatre, Haggarty dispatched a messenger boy to Crane's to fetch us.

We found the inspector asking Haggarty about the performers he had met during his long service as the Duke's stage-door manager. He smiled as we arrived.

'Ah, ladies, there you are. I'm sorry to interrupt your afternoon tea.'

'Think nothing of it, Inspector dear,' said Lady Hardcastle. 'We were merely keen not to get in the actors' way while they were working, and Crane's has the finest coffee in town.'

'As well as the nicest cakes,' said Gwen. 'I wish we had a Crane's in Woolwich.'

'They certainly do a nice cream bun,' said the inspector.

I handed him a small box.

'We got you one,' I said. I handed Haggarty a similar box. 'And one for you, too, Mr Haggarty.'

'Thank you very much,' they said in unison.

'We haven't kept you waiting?' said Lady Hardcastle.

'I've had a most enjoyable time – I've been talking to Mr Haggarty. Did you know he once met Sir Henry Irving?'

'Did you?' said Lady Bickle. 'How marvellous. What was he like?'

'Lovely bloke,' said Haggarty. 'Always had time for theatre staff. Said we was as important as his actors.'

'Quite right, too,' said Lady Bickle.

'Talking of the actors,' said Lady Hardcastle, 'I presume . . .'

'All present and correct, m'lady,' said Haggarty. 'No one's been out since you left.'

'Splendid. Thank you, Mr Haggarty. Shall we go through, then? I'm sure everyone's dying to hear our explanations.'

'Lead the way, my lady,' said the inspector.

◆ ◆ ◆

We arrived on stage to find the actors perched on the various items of furniture used in the first act of *The Hedonists*. They had their scripts for the new play in their hands, and one or two were scribbling on them in pencil as Hugo Bartlett ran through his notes.

'. . . and now I've heard it out loud, I think it would be better if Henrietta says "with a banana" on page twenty-three rather than "with a pineapple". I'd still like to make some amendments to the third scene in Act Two, where Alice and William are arguing about the halibut, so don't trouble to learn that, please. And finally—' He noticed our arrival. 'Ah, we have visitors. Welcome. Do the police have your evidence now? Can we finally learn who killed Paul? And I don't suppose you have any idea what's happened to Sarah? We've not seen her since we took our break.'

'That's rather why we're here, actually,' said Lady Hardcastle. 'Is now a bad time to interrupt?'

'Not at all,' said Hugo. 'I just need to mention that we need everyone in the theatre tomorrow at noon so that Emrys can block *Too Many T(ea)s*. We'll have to work round the *Hedonists* set but we're meeting our set designer on Tuesday, so we need a firm idea of the space requirements by then. Thank you. Lady Hardcastle, we are all yours.'

Hugo bowed and went to perch on the arm of the chair where Emrys Thornell was sitting, sucking on a meerschaum pipe carved with a miniature bust of William Shakespeare.

'Thank you,' said Lady Hardcastle. 'As you all now know, Miss Armstrong and I were asked to intrude upon your lives last week following the murder of your friend, Paul Singleton. Over the past ten days or so we've learned a little about you all, and we slowly came to understand exactly how and why the events of that Tuesday evening unfolded.'

The actors were paying close attention now. They clearly wanted to know why their lives had been turned upside down.

'We started here on the stage,' continued Lady Hardcastle. 'We found that although Paul's body was lying in full view of anyone on the stage – or in the audience once the curtains were open – he could not easily be seen from the wings. There's a little curtain in the way, you see?' She pointed.

'It's a leg,' said Patrick. 'We call them legs. And the "curtains" are tabs.'

'Thank you, dear,' said Lady Hardcastle. 'But that meant that he must have been murdered after the stagehands had set the stage for Act Two, but before any of you arrived to make your entrances. The interval began at around half past eight and lasted for half an hour until almost nine o'clock. It took the stagehands between fifteen and twenty minutes to set the stage and the Act Two beginners were in the wings only a minute or two before curtain-up. We estimated the time of the murder to be between ten minutes to nine and nine o'clock.'

She looked around. They were still with her.

'We made the assumption that one of you was the murderer.'

There were exclamations of protest at this, but she held up her hands for silence.

'It was the simplest explanation,' she continued. 'It might conceivably have been a stagehand or some other complete stranger, but the majority of murders are committed by someone known to the victim.'

This pacified them a little.

'We established that, at the time of the murder, Sarah and Rosalie were in the corridors on their way to the stage. Emrys and Hugo were in Emrys's dressing room planning future projects. Nancy was outside, and Harris was in his dressing room, having both paid Patrick a social call at the start of the interval. Everyone seemed to be accounted for. And we knew Paul was still alive because he had been seen going into his dressing room in his distinctive peacock-blue smoking jacket at around a quarter to nine. So who could have killed him? None of you, certainly. There was mention of a dark-suited man in a cloth cap—'

'I never heard anything about that,' said Harris Bridges.

'No, and we forgot all about it for the most part. Luckily, as it turned out – it was a lie.' She had clearly decided not to mention the mysterious lady who had been seen wandering the corridors. Hugo Bartlett didn't need questions to be asked about her.

'Who would lie?' said Bridges.

'We shall come to that in due course,' said Lady Hardcastle. 'Having established that everyone had an alibi for the time of the murder, we were temporarily stumped, so we turned our attention to motive. You all had a motive for wanting Paul dead—'

This time the outrage was expressed more forcefully, and she had to let the storm blow itself out before she could continue.

'It would be a betrayal of confidence to discuss your motives now,' she said when the hubbub had died down, 'but you each revealed something that would give you a reason for killing him. Some were stronger than others, but you all had a motive so that was little help to us. And you all, as Inspector Wyatt repeatedly noted, had easy access to the murder weapon. Something was clearly wrong with our reasoning. There was a gap in our knowledge. And we began to fill that gap when we explored the theatre and discovered the trap room.'

'We never use trap doors,' said Emrys. 'I can't stand them.'

'Which is very much something the killer was relying on. In the trap room, we found a small bloodstain on the downstage-left stage lift' – she pointed to the spot where Paul's body had been discovered – 'and evidence that the mechanism had been rigged to operate on its own. This changed our ideas about the time of the murder. If Paul had been lured to the trap room and stabbed there, and then had been placed on the stage by the self-operating machinery towards the end of the interval, suddenly everyone's alibis had to be re-examined. We still had the problem that Paul had been seen alive halfway through the interval, but it was an incident at our local pub late last week that provided the answer to that one. Someone had been pretending to be someone else by wearing their jacket, you see. And here at the theatre, witnesses were happy to swear they'd seen Paul alive, but what they'd actually noticed was just his jacket.'

'So you're saying he was killed in the trap room in the basement,' said Rosalie, 'and the killer put on his jacket and walked into his dressing room, making us think he was still alive?'

'And giving themselves an alibi into the bargain,' said Lady Hardcastle. 'By shifting the apparent time of the murder, they'd fooled us into asking entirely the wrong questions. It didn't help a great deal, but it was another step along the road to understanding.'

'This is all well and good,' said Bridges, 'but it doesn't tell us who did it. Who murdered Paul? Was it someone here? Or Sarah? Was it Sarah?'

There was another round of murmured speculation. Lady Hardcastle held up her hands again.

'We came closer to understanding what had happened this morning, when we asked Inspector Sunderland here to make some enquiries of his counterparts in Suffolk. Once we had the answers, we began to close in on the killer. In the summer of 1896, a murder shocked the county. A young girl, just seventeen years old, was strangled to death in Six Oaks Wood. Ida Oxborrow was her name. They never caught the killer, thought it was believed locally that it was a boy of about the same age – Harvey Bird – who was known to be sweet on the girl and had been spending time with her and her younger sister, Audrey. Time passed. Audrey and her parents moved away from Suffolk and Audrey became an actress. She adopted the stage name of Sarah Griffin. In a peculiar twist, Harvey, too, entered the acting profession, under the name Paul Singleton. No one knows why they both chose to change their names, and no one can possibly say how they came to be working in the same theatre company fifteen years later. But they did. We assume Paul didn't recognize Sarah, but somehow she recognized him. Perhaps it was something he said when they were engaged, some casual remark while they walked hand in hand in the woods one day? We may never know, but whatever it was, that unguarded revelation sealed his fate. She broke off the engagement and set about planning his murder. She lured him to the trap room by sending him a note seemingly signed by Nancy, and there she stabbed him with the prop-store dagger. She put on his smoking jacket—'

'Wait a moment,' said Patrick. 'Paul lost that jacket the first week we were here. He never stopped complaining about it.'

'Exactly,' said Lady Hardcastle. 'Sarah stole it from his dressing room. She made sure to steal other things from around the theatre, too, to make sure no one thought too hard about the jacket being missing – we might well find them in the mess in her dressing room if she didn't dispose of them. But she entered Paul's dressing room, making sure someone saw her – Harris and Nancy, as it turned out – then left the jacket there with the incriminating note still in the pocket, in case no one believed her lie about seeing a mysterious stranger in a cloth cap wandering the corridors. We'll find out more when Inspector Sunderland questions her later, but I suspect she intended to disappear at the end of the run. The jacket and the note would be found, muddying the waters still further by implicating Nancy, and if anyone ever managed to work out what had happened she'd be long gone, living in another town under another name. She hadn't reckoned on the run being extended. Nor had she reckoned on having been seen at the time of the murder. Again we shall have to wait for the inspector's interrogation to be certain, but I think it reasonable to assume that Davey Browning caught sight of her, or perhaps Paul, going to the trap room on that fateful night. Perhaps he merely asked her about it, perhaps he tried to blackmail her over it. Either way, she decided he had to die.'

'How certain are you that it was Sarah?' asked Nancy.

'She confessed to Miss Armstrong while we were listening outside the trap room a short while ago,' said Lady Hardcastle. 'We're as certain as we can be.'

There were a few moments of absolute silence as the Bartlett Players digested everything they'd just heard.

The silence was eventually broken by Inspector Sunderland.

'In view of the information gathered by Lady Hardcastle, Miss Armstrong and Mrs Evans,' he said, 'I shall be charging Sarah Griffin with murder later today. We already have statements from you all, but I think you'll agree that they're incomplete, so I shall be asking you to review them and add any pertinent information you can remember. Please make yourselves available to my officers over the next few days.'

'I think that's everything,' said Lady Hardcastle. 'Unless anyone has any further questions?'

Heads were shaken, but no one spoke.

'Then we shall leave you to your Sunday evening,' said Lady Hardcastle. To us she said, 'Shall we?'

She indicated the door and we exited, stage left.

We said our goodbyes to the inspector on Frogmore Street, and waved him on his way back to the Bridewell with assurances that we, too, would be available to give statements whenever he needed us to.

Lady Hardcastle, Lady Bickle, Gwen and I walked up the treacherously steep Lodge Street to Park Row, and then onwards to Queens Road and Berkeley Crescent.

'How is it,' I asked as we puffed and panted our way up Lodge Street, 'that every journey in Bristol is uphill? I'm sure we walked uphill to get to the theatre this morning.'

'We didn't,' laughed Lady Bickle, 'but I know what you mean. I've noticed it many times as I've walked about Clifton and Redland visiting friends. I walk uphill on the way there and think, "Well, at least it will be downhill on the way home." Sure enough, though, I have to walk uphill on the way home. I honestly can't fathom how it works.'

'Witchcraft,' said Lady Hardcastle. 'Either that or you forget how far downhill you walked on the way there and only remember the irksome uphill part of the journey. One of the two. I leave it to you to decide which it is.'

'You've no romance in your soul, Emily Hardcastle,' said Lady Bickle. 'I choose to believe there is something magical and mystical about my adopted city.'

'Quite right, too. I'm too dreary by three-quarters.'

The rest of the journey was ever-so-slightly uphill and I was forced to concede that I had been wrong, though it had been encouraging to have my perception at least partially confirmed by Lady Bickle, even if Lady Hardcastle's explanation had taken the shine off it a bit.

Williams took our coats when we arrived and made appropriately amazed noises when Lady Bickle told him that, once again, a murderer had been apprehended thanks to Lady Hardcastle. Sir Benjamin was finally up and about and was similarly impressed.

'I'm going to have to make sure you're away on one of your jaunts when I decide to bump someone off,' he said. 'You'll have me locked up before I can say "bistoury".'

'We'll make sure Georgie is allowed to visit you, dear,' said Lady Hardcastle.

'Whom are you planning to kill, Ben darling?' asked Lady Bickle.

'The list is long, my sweet,' he said. 'There are at least half a dozen on the board at the hospital who would never be missed, for a start.'

'Well, as long as you get old Sir Whatshisface de-Thingummy I shall overlook any others. He definitely has to go.'

'He's at the very top of the list, don't you worry.'

We were invited to stay for dinner, and Sir Benjamin cajoled us into telling him the entire story – with frequent interruptions for clarification – from the beginning. Lady Bickle made a half-hearted attempt to tell him to leave us in peace and talk about something else, but it was plain to see that she was as keen to hear all the details as he was.

At the description of the fight he recommended an orthopaedic surgeon to check my knee for damage, but I assured him it was fine. He did peer closely at the bruises on my face, though, earning him a rebuke from his wife, who reminded him that he was a brain surgeon and had no business poking people's faces.

'It's very near the brain, darling,' he said. 'It's on the front of the container.'

'Just leave the poor woman alone,' said Lady Bickle. 'She'll heal just as well without your inexpert interference.'

Dinner was delicious as it always was at the Bickles', and the company was friendly and entertaining. We talked for quite a while over brandies and coffee, and it was nearly midnight by the time we gathered ourselves to leave.

I had steered clear of the wine, brandy and port all evening, so I was able to drive us home to Littleton Cotterell, where we collapsed into bed to sleep a well-earned sleep.

Chapter Eighteen

On Monday Gwen received a telegram from Dai. He had been called back to barracks early on some urgent battery business. There was nothing to worry about, though, and he was safely back in their home in Woolwich.

'I'd better be getting back,' she said. 'He'd never ask me to, but I don't like the thought of what damage he might do to my kitchen while he's cooking up his famous stew on his own. He's not exactly helpless in the kitchen, but he's so messy.'

I looked reproachfully at Lady Hardcastle, who merely grinned in reply.

'You're welcome to stay as long as you like, dear,' said Lady Hardcastle. 'You know that. But we shall run you to the station whenever you're ready to leave if that's what you prefer. The choice is entirely yours.'

'Thank you,' said Gwen.

She consulted *Bradshaw's* and found that there was a service to London at eleven o'clock the next morning which would suit her admirably. I looked at the book.

'You'll have changed twice before you even get to Swindon,' I said. 'And you'll have to change there as well. Look here, though. If you take the 11.23 from Bristol Temple Meads you can get straight to Paddington in half the time. Hop across town on the tube to

Charing Cross and you can be in Woolwich before Dai has even started trying to burn the house down. We'll take you to Temple Meads in the morning.'

'I shan't say no,' said Gwen. 'I do like being chauffeured about in your Rolls-Royce.'

'That's settled, then,' said Lady Hardcastle. 'What would you like to do for the rest of the day?'

'I wouldn't mind a local tour if you both have time. I've been here over a week and I've seen more of Bristol than where you actually live.'

And so we drove over to Chipping Bevington, where we introduced her to the delights of the book shop, the dress shop, the haberdasher's and, most importantly of all, Pomphrey's Bric-a-Brac Emporium, where, to my delight – and Lady Hardcastle's dismay – she, too, was enchanted by my favourite piece: the hookah-smoking stuffed moose-head wearing the tropical topi.

We lunched at the Grey Goose and returned home for a few games of Suffragetto before a light dinner and a trip to the Dog and Duck.

Daisy was thrilled to see us.

'Evenin', you lot,' she said. 'Two brandies and a port, is it?'

'Yes, dear, thank you,' said Lady Hardcastle, fishing in her handbag for her purse.

'Put that away, m'lady,' said Joe, who had noticed us as we entered and had left his game of dominoes to come and talk to us. 'You're money i'n't no good here. You saved I a fortune in stolen liquor.'

'Not to mention savin' Agnes Bingle from 'erself,' said Daisy. 'You's local heroes.'

'I did nothing,' said Lady Hardcastle. 'It was all down to the Armstrong girls.'

'Nevertheless,' said Joe toothlessly, 'you've all done us a great service and your drinks is on the house.'

'Thank you, Joe,' said Lady Hardcastle. 'You're very kind.'

With an 'Ar' and a tap of his finger to his forehead in salute, Joe returned to his game, leaving Daisy to pour our drinks.

'Jagruti Bland was askin' after you yesterday after Evensong, Gwen,' she said. 'They'd been over to Agnes's house and got all the booze back. All the bottles were in her kitchen, unopened. Anyway, I said we 'adn't seen you for a couple of days. Agnes is doin' all right, though. She's stayin' with them for a few weeks while she comes to herself again.'

'I'm glad,' said Gwen. 'I'd have been over to the vicarage myself but we've been a bit busy these last few days.'

'Anythin' excitin'?'

And for the next half an hour we told Daisy the story of the murder at the theatre. Before long, we had quite an audience. Gwen hugely exaggerated the thrillingness of my scrap with Sarah Griffin, and an argument broke out between three of the farmers' wives in the crowd as to the best treatment for bruises. By the time we were done there were enough brandies and glasses of port lined up for us on the bar to see Dai's entire regiment taken out of the line with alcohol poisoning. We had to offer them back to the regulars, who toasted our generosity again, having apparently forgotten that they'd bought the drinks in the first place.

We left at ten and shivered our way home along the frosty lane. Lady Hardcastle wanted to stay up and play cards, but Gwen was obviously shattered and I persuaded her to let us all get to bed instead.

On Tuesday morning we ran Gwen to Temple Meads station and waved her off on the Paddington express.

As we drove back through the city we passed the Prince's Theatre on Park Row.

'What shall we do this evening?' asked Lady Hardcastle. 'Do you fancy seeing a play?'

Author's Note

The Duke's Theatre is fictional. As far as I've been able to tell, there has never been a theatre on Frogmore Street in Bristol, though it is presently the site of the entertainment venue the O2 Academy (formerly a nightclub called The Studio). At the time of the story the two main theatres in the heart of the city were the Prince's Theatre on Park Row and the Theatre Royal (now known as the Bristol Old Vic) on Great King Street (now known as King Street). The Prince's is long gone, but the Bristol Old Vic continues to thrive and holds the record as the oldest continually operating theatre in the English-speaking world. Which is quite a thing when you think about it.

For the purposes of the story I needed to have complete control of the layout of the theatre. I knew that fans of the Old Vic would be irked if I played fast and loose with the design of this much-loved venue so I created a fictional theatre a short distance away. It was also helpful to have the freedom to invent the theatre management and their business arrangements without causing further distress to theatre historians.

Obviously *The Hedonists* is made up, too. In case you're interested, at the time of Lady Hardcastle's birthday in 1911, the Theatre Royal was showing a melodrama entitled *The Bad Girl of the Family* by Fred Melville. Seats were priced at 2 shillings, 1s 6d,

1s, 8d, and 4d. The following week: *Through the Divorce Court. The Worst Woman in London* is a real play, also by Fred Melville, but Mr Adolphus Bedlington and his highly acclaimed melodrama, *The Disappointing Wife*, are an invention.

Restaurants come and go with dismaying frequency, and for all I know there may once have been a restaurant in the middle of town called Le Quai. If there was, it's not the one in the story.

To save you wondering, you haven't missed the story where Emily and Flo have a set-to in the alley behind the Duke's Theatre – it's another of their untold adventures.

The newspaper stories Georgie Bickle mentions really are from the *Daily Telegraph* (then known as the *Daily Telegraph and Courier*) of Wednesday, 8 November 1911.

The Lord Chamberlain is a member of the United Kingdom's royal household and sits on the Privy Council. Between 1737 and 1968, the Lord Chamberlain was also given official responsibility for censorship in British theatres (having been effectively in control of London's theatres since the sixteenth century). The Lord Chamberlain had the power to prevent the performance of any play for any reason, and while risqué jokes about trousers might have passed scrutiny, theatres were understandably cautious.

While looking for old slang words for drunks and drunkenness I learned that 'artilleryman' was Victorian slang for a drunkard. It was not, as I first presumed, because the men of the Royal Artillery were noted imbibers, but because a drunk was notable for 'the explosiveness of his talk and actions'.

Gwen's story about the Swindon woman who lost her memory is taken from the Monday, 13 November 1911 edition of the *Bristol Times and Mirror*.

Suffragetto is a board game from 1907 or 1908. It was published by the WSPU with the straplines 'The Very Latest Craze!' and 'An Original and Interesting Game of Skill between Suffragettes and Policemen, for Two Players'. Gameplay is much as described by Flo in the story.

If you're looking on a map for Woodwell Lane in Bristol, you might imagine I made it up. It's still there, but it's now known as Jacob's Wells Road. The route down the hill to sneak up on Frogmore Street from behind by scooting underneath Park Street is essentially the same.

The origin of the phrase 'break a leg' is, as Bartlett says, unknown. Acting superstitions are many and varied and their origins poorly recorded. There is a German phrase, *Hals- und Beinbruch!* which translates literally as 'May you break your neck and your leg' and is used in a similar context, but there's no direct evidence of a link. One of the more fanciful explanations is that it comes from the fact that the curtains at the side of a proscenium stage shielding actors from view as they wait in the wings are known as the legs. Acting is a precarious business and it is good luck to win a part and appear on stage. In order to appear on stage one has to 'break a leg', or appear from behind one of these shielding curtains. There is absolutely no recorded evidence of this being the origin of the phrase, but it does make a wonderfully entertaining story. It's more likely that since the superstition has it that wishing someone luck means that they might not have any, then wishing some calamity on them is preferable – when that wish inevitably doesn't come true, all is well.

As far as I know, there is no Six Oaks Wood anywhere, even in Suffolk.

Acknowledgements

As always, I am indebted to the amazing team at Thomas & Mercer who look after me so skilfully and carefully. My editor, Victoria Pepe, always offers the best advice and indulges my witterings about badgers and foxes with kind patience. Laura Gerrard was the source of more editorial advice, and managed to help me turn my witless ramblings into a book we were all proud of.

Nicole Wagner, my 'Author Relations Manager', never seems to get a mention, but she's an invaluable source of practical help and another ear I can bend about badgers and foxes.

I entered a set of signed Lady Hardcastle books as a lot in the 2021 signed book auction, Children In Read, held to support the BBC Children In Need appeal. To add a little spice, I also offered the winner the chance to have a character named after them in a forthcoming Lady Hardcastle book. The winner of the lot was Joanna (Jo) Webster-Green, owner of a wonderful toy shop in Bristol called Little Treasures. Her generous bid added to the magnificent total raised by the auction, and meant that Lady Hardcastle herself was able to use her name as her *nom de guerre*.

About the Author

Photo © 2018 Clifton Photographic Company

T E Kinsey grew up in London and read history at Bristol University. *An Act of Foul Play* is the ninth story in the Lady Hardcastle Mystery series, and he is also the author of the Dizzy Heights Mystery series. His website is at tekinsey.uk and you can follow him on Twitter @tekinsey, as well as on Facebook—www.facebook.com/tekinsey—and Instagram @tekinseymysteries.